GONE TOMORROW

GONE TOMORROW

Lee Child

WINDSOR
PARAGON

First published 2009
by Transworld Publishers
This Large Print edition published 2009
by BBC Audiobooks Ltd
by arrangement with
Transworld Publishers Ltd

Hardcover ISBN: 978 1 408 42933 4
Softcover ISBN: 978 1 408 42934 1

This book is a work of fiction and, except in the case of historical fact, any resemblance to actual persons, living or dead, is purely coincidental

British Library Cataloguing in Publication Data available

Printed and bound in Great Britain by
CPI Antony Rowe, Chippenham and Eastbourne

For my sisters-in-law Leslie and Sally,
two women of rare charm and quality.

ONE

Suicide bombers are easy to spot. they give out all kinds of tell-tale signs. Mostly because they're nervous. By definition they're all first-timers.

Israeli counterintelligence wrote the defensive playbook. They told us what to look for. They used pragmatic observation and psychological insight and came up with a list of behavioural indicators. I learned the list from an Israeli army captain twenty years ago. He swore by it. Therefore I swore by it too, because at the time I was on three weeks' detached duty mostly about a yard from his shoulder, in Israel itself, in Jerusalem, on the West Bank, in the Lebanon, sometimes in Syria, sometimes in Jordan, on buses, in stores, on crowded sidewalks. I kept my eyes moving and my mind running free down the bullet points.

Twenty years later I still know the list. And my eyes still move. Pure habit. From another bunch of guys I learned another mantra: Look, don't see, listen, don't hear. The more you engage, the longer you survive.

The list is twelve points long if you're looking at a male suspect. Eleven, if you're looking at a woman. The difference is a fresh shave. Male bombers take off their beards. It helps them blend in. Makes them less suspicious. The result is paler skin on the lower half of the face. No recent exposure to the sun.

But I wasn't interested in shaves.

I was working on the eleven-point list.

I was looking at a woman.

I was riding the subway, in New York City. The 6 train, the Lexington Avenue local, heading uptown, two o'clock in the morning. I had gotten on at Bleecker Street from the south end of the platform into a car that was empty except for five people. Subway cars feel small and intimate when they're full. When they're empty they feel vast and cavernous and lonely. At night their lights feel hotter and brighter, even though they're the same lights they use in the day. They're all the lights there are. I was sprawled on a two-person bench north of the end doors on the track side of the car. The other five passengers were all south of me on the long bench seats, in profile, side on, far from each other, staring blankly across the width of the car, three on the left and two on the right.

The car's number was 7622. I once rode eight stops on the 6 train next to a crazy person who talked about the car we were in with the same kind of enthusiasm that most men reserve for sports or women. Therefore I knew that car number 7622 was an R142A model, the newest on the New York system, built by Kawasaki in Kobe, Japan, shipped over, trucked to the 207th Street yards, craned on to the tracks, towed down to 180th Street and tested. I knew it could run two hundred thousand miles without major attention. I knew its automated announcement system gave instructions in a man's voice and information in a woman's, which was claimed to be a coincidence but was really because the transportation chiefs believed such a division of labour was psychologically compelling. I knew the voices came from Bloomberg TV, but years before Mike became mayor. I knew there were six hundred R142As on the tracks and that each one was a fraction over fifty-one feet long and a little more than eight feet wide. I knew that the no-cab unit like we had been in then and I was in now had been designed to carry a maximum of forty people seated and up to 148 standing. The crazy person had been clear on all that data. I could see for myself that the car's seats were blue plastic, the same shade as a late summer sky or a British air force uniform. I could see that its wall panels were moulded from graffiti-resistant fibreglass. I could see its twin strips of advertisements running away from me where the wall panels met the roof. I could see small cheerful posters touting television shows and language instruction and easy college degrees and major earning opportunities.

I could see a police notice advising me: If you see something, say something.

The nearest passenger to me was a Hispanic woman. She was across the car from me, on my left, forward of the first set of doors, all alone on a bench built for eight, well off centre. She was small, somewhere between thirty and fifty, and she looked very hot and very tired. She had a well-worn supermarket bag looped over her wrist and she was staring across at the empty place opposite with eyes too weary to be seeing much.

Next up was a man on the other side, maybe four feet farther down the car. He was all alone on his own eight-person bench. He could have been from the Balkans, or the Black Sea. Dark hair, lined skin. He was sinewy, worn down by work and weather. He had his feet planted and he was leaning forward with his elbows on his knees. Not asleep, but close to it. Suspended animation, marking time, rocking with the movements of the train. He was about fifty, dressed in clothes far too young for him. Baggy jeans that reached only his calves, and an oversized NBA shirt with a player's name on it that I didn't recognize.

Third up was a woman who might have been West African. She was on the left, south of the centre doors. Tired, inert, her black skin made dusty and grey by fatigue and the lights. She was wearing a colourful batik dress with a matching square of cloth tied over her hair. Her eyes were closed. I know New York reasonably well. I call myself a citizen of the world and New York the capital of the world, so I can make sense of the city the same way a Brit knows London or a Frenchman knows Paris. I'm familiar but not intimate with its habits. But it was an easy guess that any three people like these already seated on a late-night northbound 6 train south of Bleecker were office cleaners heading home from evening shifts around City Hall, or restaurant service workers from Chinatown or Little Italy. They were probably set for Hunts Point in the Bronx, or maybe all the way up to Pelham Bay, ready for short fitful sleeps before more long days.

The fourth and the fifth passengers were different.

The fifth was a man. He was maybe my age, wedged at forty-five degrees on the two-person bench diagonally opposite me, all the way across and down the length of the car. He was dressed casually but not cheaply. Chinos, and a golf shirt. He was awake. His eyes were fixed somewhere in front of him. Their focus changed and narrowed constantly, like he was alert and speculating. They reminded me of a ballplayer's eyes. They had a certain canny, calculating shrewdness in them.

But it was passenger number four that I was looking at.

If you see something, say something.

She was seated on the right side of the car, all alone on the farther eight-person bench, across from and about halfway between the exhausted West African woman and the guy with the ballplayer's eyes. She was white and probably in her forties. She was plain. She had black hair, neatly but unstylishly cut and too uniformly dark to be natural. She was dressed all in black. I could see her fairly well. The guy nearest to me on the right was still sitting forward and the V-shaped void between his bent back and the wall of the car made my line of sight uninterrupted except for a forest of stainless steel grab bars.

Not a perfect view, but good enough to ring every bell on the eleven-point list. The bullet headings lit up like cherries on a Vegas machine.

According to Israeli counterintelligence I was looking at a suicide bomber.

TWO

I dismissed the thought immediately. Not because of racial profiling. White women are as capable of craziness as anyone else. I dismissed the thought because of tactical implausibility. The timing was wrong. The New York subway would make a fine target for a suicide bombing. The 6 train would be as good as any other and better than most. It stops under Grand Central Terminal. Eight in the morning, six at night, a crowded car, forty seated, 148 standing, wait until the doors open on packed platforms, push the button. A hundred dead, a couple of hundred grievously injured, panic, infrastructure damage, possibly fire, a major transportation hub shut down for days or weeks and maybe never really trusted again. A significant score, for people whose heads work in ways we can't quite understand.

But not at two o'clock in the morning.

Not in a car holding just six people. Not when Grand Central's subway platforms would hold only drifting trash and empty cups and a couple of old homeless guys on benches.

The train stopped at Astor Place. The doors hissed open. No one got on. No one got off. The doors thumped shut again and the motors whined and the train moved on.

The bullet points stayed lit up.

The first was the obvious no-brainer: inappropriate clothing. By now explosive belts are as evolved as baseball gloves. Take a three-foot by two-foot sheet of heavy canvas, fold once longitudinally, and you have a continuous pocket a foot deep. Wrap the pocket around the bomber, and sew it together in back. Zippers or snaps can lead to second thoughts. Insert a stockade of dynamite sticks into the pocket all the way around, wire them up, pack nails or ball bearings into the voids, sew the top seam shut, add crude shoulder straps to take the weight. Altogether effective, but altogether bulky. The only practical concealment, an oversized garment like a padded winter parka. Never appropriate in the Middle East, and plausible in New York maybe three months in twelve.

But this was September, and it was as hot as summer, and ten degrees hotter underground. I was wearing a T-shirt. Passenger number four was wearing a North Face down jacket, black, puffy, shiny, a little too large and zipped to her chin.

If you see something, say something.

I took a pass on the second of the eleven points. Not immediately applicable. The second point is: a robotic walk. Significant at a checkpoint or in a crowded marketplace or outside a church or a mosque, but not relevant with a seated suspect on public transportation. Bombers walk robotically not because they're overcome with ecstasy at the thought of imminent martyrdom, but because they're carrying forty extra pounds of unaccustomed weight, which is biting into their shoulders through crude suspender straps, and because they're drugged. Martyrdom's appeal goes only so far. Most bombers are browbeaten simpletons with a slug of raw opium paste held between gum and cheek. We know this because dynamite belts explode with a characteristic doughnut-shaped pressure wave that rolls up the torso in a fraction of a nanosecond and lifts the head clean off the shoulders. The human head isn't bolted on. It just rests there by gravity, somewhat tied down by skin and muscles and tendons and ligaments, but those insubstantial biological anchors don't do much against the force of a violent chemical explosion. My Israeli mentor told me the easiest way to determine that an open-air attack was caused by a suicide bomber rather than by a car bomb or a package bomb is to search on an eighty- or ninety-foot radius and look for a severed human head, which is likely to be strangely intact and undamaged, even down to the opium plug in the cheek.

The train stopped at Union Square. No one got on. No one got off. Hot air billowed in from the platform and fought the interior air conditioning. Then the doors closed again and the train moved on.

Points three through six are variations on a subjective theme: irritability, sweating, tics, and nervous behaviour. Although in my opinion sweating is as likely to be caused by physical overheating as by nerves. The inappropriate clothing, and the dynamite. Dynamite is wood pulp soaked with nitroglycerine and moulded into baton-sized sticks. Wood pulp is a good thermal insulator. So sweating comes with the territory. But the irritability and the tics and the nervous behaviour are valuable indicators. These people are in the last weird moments of their lives, anxious, scared of pain, woozy with narcotics. They are irrational by definition. Believing or half believing or not really believing at all in paradise and rivers of milk and honey and lush pastures and virgins, driven by ideological pressures or by the expectations of their peers and their families, suddenly in too deep and unable to back out. Brave talk in clandestine meetings is one thing. Action is another. Hence suppressed panic, with all its visible signs.

Passenger number four was showing them all. She looked exactly like a woman heading for the end of her life, as surely and certainly as the train was heading for the end of the line.

Therefore point seven: breathing.

She was panting, low and controlled. In, out, in, out. Like a technique to conquer the pain of childbirth, or like the result of a ghastly shock, or like a last desperate barrier against screaming with dread and fear and terror.

In, out, in, out.

Point eight: suicide bombers about to go into action stare rigidly ahead. No one knows why, but video evidence and surviving eyewitnesses have been entirely consistent in their reports. Bombers stare straight ahead. Perhaps they have screwed their commitment up to the sticking point and fear intervention. Perhaps like dogs and children they feel that if they're not seeing anyone, then no one is seeing them. Perhaps a last shred of conscience means they can't look at the people they're about to destroy. No one knows why, but they all do it.

Passenger number four was doing it. That was for sure. She was staring across at the blank window opposite so hard she was almost burning a hole in the glass.

Points one through eight, check. I shifted my weight forward in my seat.

Then I stopped. The idea was tactically absurd. The time was wrong.

Then I looked again. And moved again. Because points nine, ten, and eleven were all present and correct too, and they were the most important points of all.

THREE

Point nine: mumbled prayers. To date all known attacks have been inspired, or motivated, or validated, or invigilated by religion, almost exclusively the Islamic religion, and Islamic people are accustomed to praying in public. Surviving eyewitnesses report long formulaic incantations run through and repeated endlessly and more or less inaudibly, but with visibly moving lips. Passenger number four was really going at it. Her lips were moving below her fixed stare, in a long, panting, ritualistic recitation that seemed to repeat itself every twenty seconds or so. Maybe she was already introducing herself to whatever deity she expected to meet on the other side of the line. Maybe she was trying to convince herself that there really was a deity, and a line.

The train stopped at 23rd Street. The doors opened. No one got off. No one got on. I saw the red exit signs above the platform: 22nd and Park, northeast corner, or 23rd and Park, southeast corner. Unremarkable lengths of Manhattan sidewalk, but suddenly attractive.

I stayed in my seat. The doors closed. The train moved on.

Point ten: a large bag.

Dynamite is a stable explosive, as long as it's fresh. It doesn't go off by accident. It needs to be triggered by blasting caps. Blasting caps are wired with detonator cord to an electricity supply and a switch. The big plungers in old western movies were both things together. The first part of the handle's travel spun up a dynamo, like a field telephone, and then a switch was tripped. Not practical for portable use. For portable use you need a battery, and for a linear yard of explosive you need some volts and amps. Tiny AA cells put out a weak volt and a half. Not enough, according to prevailing rules of thumb. A nine-volt battery is better, and for a decent kick you want one of the big square soup-can size cells sold for serious flashlights. Too big and too heavy for a pocket, hence the bag. The battery nestles in the bottom of the bag, wires come off it to the switch, then they head on out through an unobtrusive slit in the back of the bag, and then they loop up under the hem of the inappropriate garment.

Passenger number four was wearing a black canvas messenger bag, urban style, looped in front of one shoulder and behind the other, and hauled around into her lap. The way the stiff fabric bulged and sagged made it look empty apart from a single heavy item.

The train stopped at 28th Street. The doors opened. No one got on. No one got off. The doors closed and the train moved on.

Point eleven: hands in the bag.

Twenty years ago point eleven was a recent addition. Previously the list had ended at point ten. But things evolve. Action, and then reaction. Israeli security forces and some brave members of the public had adopted a new tactic. If your suspicions were aroused, you didn't run. No point, really. You can't run faster than shrapnel. What you did instead was grab the suspect in a desperate bear hug. You pinned their arms to their sides. You stopped them reaching the button. Several attacks were prevented that way. Many lives were saved. But the bombers learned. Now they are taught to keep their thumbs on the button at all times, to make the bear hug irrelevant. The button is in the bag, next to the battery. Hence, hands in the bag.

Passenger number four had her hands in her bag. The flap was bunched and creased between her wrists.

The train stopped at 33rd Street. The doors opened. No one got off. A lone passenger on the platform hesitated and then stepped to her right and entered the next car. I turned and looked through the little window behind my head and saw her take a seat close to me. Two stainless bulkheads, and the coupler space. I wanted to wave her away. She might survive at the other end of her car. But I didn't wave. We had no eye contact and she would have ignored me anyway. I know New York. Crazy gestures on late night trains carry no credibility.

The doors stayed open a beat longer than normal. For a mad second I thought of trying to shepherd everyone out. But I didn't. It would have been a comedy. Surprise, incomprehension, maybe language barriers. I wasn't sure that I knew the Spanish word for bomb. *Bomba*, maybe. Or was that light bulb? A crazy guy ranting about light bulbs wasn't going to help anyone.

No, light bulb was *bombilla*, I thought.

Maybe.

Possibly.

But certainly I didn't know any Balkan languages. And I didn't know any West African dialects. Although maybe the woman in the dress spoke French. Some of West Africa is francophone. And I speak French. *Une bombe. La femme là-bas a une bombe sous son manteau. The woman over there has a bomb under her coat.* The woman in the dress might understand. Or she might get the message some other way and simply follow us out.

If she woke up in time. If she opened her eyes.

In the end I just stayed in my seat.

The doors closed.

The train moved on.

I stared at passenger number four. Pictured her slim pale thumb on the hidden button. The button probably came from Radio Shack. An innocent component, for a hobby. Probably cost a buck and a half. I pictured a tangle of wires, red and black, taped and crimped and clamped. A thick detonator cord, exiting the bag, tucked under her coat, connecting twelve or twenty blasting caps in a long lethal parallel ladder. Electricity moves close to the speed of light. Dynamite is unbelievably powerful. In a closed environment like a subway car the pressure wave alone would crush us all to paste. The nails and the ball bearings would be entirely gratuitous. Like bullets against ice cream. Very little of us would survive. Bone fragments, maybe, the size of grape pits. Possibly the stirrup and the anvil from the inner ear might survive intact. They are the smallest bones in the human body and therefore statistically the most likely to be missed by the shrapnel cloud.

I stared at the woman. No way of approaching her. I was thirty feet away. Her thumb was already on the button. Cheap brass contacts were maybe an eighth of an inch apart, that tiny gap perhaps narrowing and widening fractionally and rhythmically as her heart beat and her arm trembled.

She was good to go, and I wasn't.

The train rocked onward, with its characteristic symphony of sounds. The howl of rushing air in the tunnel, the thump and clatter of the expansion joints under the iron rims, the scrape of the current collector against the live rail, the whine of the motors, the sequential squeals as the cars lurched one after the other through curves and the wheel flanges bit down.

Where was she going? What did the 6 train pass under? Could a building be brought down by a human bomb? I thought not. So what big crowds were still assembled after two o'clock in the morning? Not many. Nightclubs, maybe, but we had already left most of them behind, and she wouldn't get past a velvet rope anyway.

I stared on at her.

Too hard.

She felt it.

She turned her head, slowly, smoothly, like a preprogrammed movement.

She stared right back at me.

Our eyes met.

Her face changed.

She knew I knew.

FOUR

We looked straight at each other for the best part of ten seconds. Then I got to my feet. Braced against the motion and took a step. I would be killed thirty feet away, no question. I couldn't get any deader by being any closer. I passed the Hispanic woman on my left. Passed the guy in the NBA shirt on my right. Passed the West African woman on my left. Her eyes were still closed. I handed myself from one grab bar to the next, left and right, swaying. Passenger number four stared at me all the way, frightened, panting, muttering. Her hands stayed in her bag.

I stopped six feet from her.

I said, 'I really want to be wrong about this.'

She didn't reply. Her lips moved. Her hands moved under the thick black canvas. The large object in her bag shifted slightly.

I said, 'I need to see your hands.'

She didn't reply.

'I'm a cop,' I lied. 'I can help you.'

She didn't reply.

I said, 'We can talk.'

She didn't reply.

I let go of the grab bars and dropped my hands to my sides. It made me smaller. Less threatening. Just a guy. I stood as still as the moving train would let me. I did nothing. I had no option. She would need a split second. I would need more than that. Except that there was absolutely nothing I could do. I could have grabbed her bag and tried to tear it away from her. But it was looped around her body and its strap was a wide band of tightly woven cotton. The same knit as a fire hose. It was pre-washed and pre-aged and pre-distressed like new stuff is now but it would still be very strong. I would have ended up jerking her up off her seat and dumping her down on the floor.

Except that I wouldn't have gotten anywhere near her. She would have hit the button before my hand was halfway there.

I could have tried to jerk the bag upward and swipe behind it with my other hand to rip the detonator cord out of its terminals. Except that for the sake of her easy movement there would be enough spare length in the cord that I would have needed to haul it through a giant two-foot arc before I met any resistance. By which time she would have hit the button, if only in involuntary shock.

I could have grabbed at her jacket and tried to tear some other wires loose. But there were fat pockets of goose feathers between me and the wires. A slippery nylon shell. No touch, no feel.

No hope.

I could have tried to incapacitate her. Hit her hard in the head, knock her out, one punch, instantaneous. But as fast as I still am, a decent swing from six feet away would have taken most of half a second. She had to move the ball of her thumb an eighth of an inch.

She would have gotten there first.

I asked, 'Can I sit down? Next to you?'

She said, 'No, stay away from me.'

A neutral, toneless voice. No obvious accent. American, but she could have been from anywhere. Up close she didn't look really wild or deranged. Just resigned, and grave, and scared, and tired. She was staring up at me with the same intensity she had been using on the opposite window. She looked completely alert and aware. I felt completely scrutinized. I couldn't move. I couldn't do anything.

'It's late,' I said. 'You should wait for rush hour.'

She didn't reply.

'Six more hours,' I said. 'It will work much better then.'

Her hands moved, inside her bag.

I said, 'Not now.'

She said nothing.

'Just one,' I said. 'Show me one hand. You don't need both of them in there.'

The train slowed hard. I staggered backward and stepped forward again and reached up to the grab bar close to the roof. My hands were damp. The steel felt hot. Grand Central, I thought. But it wasn't. I glanced out the window expecting lights and white tiles and saw the glow of a dim blue lamp instead. We were stopping in the tunnel. Maintenance, or signalling.

I turned back.

'Show me one hand,' I said again.

The woman didn't answer. She was staring at my waist. With my hands high my T-shirt had ridden up and the scar low on my stomach was visible above the waistband of my pants. Raised white skin, hard and lumpy. Big crude stitches, like a cartoon. Shrapnel, from a truck bomb in Beirut, a long time ago. I had been a hundred yards from the explosion.

I was ninety-eight yards closer to the woman on the bench.

She stared on. Most people ask how I had gotten the scar. I didn't want her to. I didn't want to talk about bombs. Not with her.

I said, 'Show me one hand.'

She asked, 'Why?'

'You don't need two in there.'

'Then what good can it do you?'

'I don't know,' I said. I had no real idea what I was doing. I'm not a hostage negotiator. I was just talking for the sake of it. Which is uncharacteristic. Mostly I'm a very silent person. It would be statistically very unlikely for me to die halfway through a sentence.

Maybe that's why I was talking.

The woman moved her hands. I saw her take a solo grip inside her bag with her right and she brought her left out slowly. Small, pale, faintly ridged with veins and tendons. Middle-aged skin. Plain nails, trimmed short. No rings. Not married, not engaged to be. She turned her hand over, to show me the other side. Empty palm, red because she was hot.

'Thank you,' I said.

She laid her hand palm-down on the seat next to her and left it there, like it was nothing to do with the rest of her. Which it wasn't, at that point. The train stopped in the darkness. I lowered my hands. The hem of my shirt fell back into place.

I said, 'Now show me what's in the bag.'

'Why?'

'I just want to see it. Whatever it is.'

She didn't reply.

She didn't move.

I said, 'I won't try to take it away from you. I promise. I just want to see it. I'm sure you can understand that.'

The train moved on again. Slow acceleration, no jerk, low speed. A gentle cruise into the station. A slow roll. Maybe two hundred yards, I thought.

I said, 'I think I'm entitled to at least see it. Wouldn't you agree?'

She made a face, like she didn't understand.

She said, 'I don't see why you're entitled to see it.'

'You don't?'

'No.'

'Because I'm involved here. And maybe I can check it's fixed right. For later. Because you need to do this later. Not now.'

'You said you were a cop.'

'We can work this out,' I said. 'I can help you.' I glanced over my shoulder. The train was creeping along. White light up ahead. I turned back. The woman's right hand was moving. She was juggling it into a firmer grip and slowly shaking it free of the bag, all at once.

I watched. The bag snagged on her wrist and she used her left hand to free it up. Her right hand came out.

Not a battery. No wires. No switch, no button, no plunger.

Something else entirely.

FIVE

The woman had a gun in her hand. She was pointing it straight at me. Low down, dead centre, on a line between my groin and my navel. All kinds of necessary stuff in that region. Organs, spine, intestines, various arteries and veins. The gun was a Ruger Speed-Six. A big old .357 Magnum revolver with a short four-inch barrel, capable of blowing a hole in me big enough to see daylight through.

But overall I was a lot more cheerful than I had been a second before. Many reasons. Bombs kill people all at once, guns kill one at a time. Bombs don't need aiming, and guns do. The Speed-Six weighs north of two pounds fully loaded. A lot of mass for a slender wrist to control. And Magnum rounds produce searing muzzle flash and punishing recoil. If she had used the gun before, she would know that. She would have what shooters call Magnum flinch. A split second before pulling the trigger her arm would clench and her eyes would close and her head would turn away. She had a decent chance of missing, even from six feet. Most handguns miss. Maybe not on the range, with ear defenders and eye protection and time and calm and nothing at stake. But in the real world, with panic and stress and the shakes and a thumping heart, handguns are all about luck, good or bad. Mine and hers.

If she missed, she wouldn't get a second shot.

I said, 'Take it easy.' Just to be making sounds. Her finger was bone-white on the trigger, but she hadn't moved it yet. The Speed-Six is a double-action revolver, which means that the first half of the trigger's pull moves the hammer back and rotates the cylinder. The second half drops the hammer and fires the gun. Complex mechanics, which take time. Not much, but some. I stared at her finger. Sensed the guy with the ballplayer's eyes, watching. I guessed my back was blocking the view from farther up the car.

I said, 'You've got no beef with me, lady. You don't even know me. Put the gun down and talk.'

She didn't reply. Maybe something passed across her face, but I wasn't watching her face. I was watching her finger. It was the only part of her that interested me. And I was concentrating on the vibrations coming up through the floor. Waiting for the car to stop. My crazy fellow passenger had told me that the R142As weigh thirty-five tons each. They can do sixty-two miles an hour. Therefore their brakes are very powerful. Too powerful for finesse at low speeds. No feathering is possible. They clamp and jerk and grind. Trains often skid the last yard on locked wheels. Hence the characteristic yelp as they stop.

I figured the same would apply even after our slow crawl. Maybe more so, relatively speaking. The gun was essentially a weight on the end of a pendulum. A long thin arm, two pounds of steel. When the brakes bit down, momentum would carry the gun onward. Uptown. Newton's Law of Motion. I was ready to fight my own momentum and push off the bars the other way and jump downtown. If the gun jerked just five inches north and I jerked just five inches south I would be in the clear.

Maybe four inches would do it.

Or four and a half, for safety's sake.

The woman asked, 'Where did you get your scar?'

I didn't answer.

'Were you gut shot?'

'Bomb,' I said.

She moved the muzzle, to her left and my right. She aimed at where the scar was hidden by the hem of my shirt.

The train rolled on. Into the station. Infinitely slow. Barely walking pace. Grand Central's platforms are long. The lead car was heading all the way to the end. I waited for the brakes to bite. I figured there would be a nice little lurch.

We never got there.

The gun barrel moved back to my centre mass. Then it moved vertical. For a split second I thought the woman was surrendering. But the barrel kept on moving. The woman raised her chin high, like a proud, obstinate gesture. She tucked the muzzle into the soft flesh beneath it. Squeezed the trigger halfway. The cylinder turned and the hammer scraped back across the nylon of her coat.

Then she pulled the trigger the rest of the way and blew her own head off.

SIX

The doors didn't open for a long time. Maybe someone had used the emergency intercom or maybe the conductor had heard the shot. But whatever, the system went into full-on lockdown mode. It was undoubtedly something they rehearsed. And the procedure made a lot of sense. Better that a crazed gunman was contained in a single car, rather than being allowed to run around all over town.

But the waiting wasn't pleasant. The .357 Magnum round was invented in 1935. Magnum is

Latin for big. Heavier bullet, and a lot more propellant charge. Technically the propellant charge does not explode. It deflagrates, which is a chemical process halfway between burning and exploding. The idea is to create a huge bubble of hot gas that accelerates the bullet down the barrel, like a pent-up spring. Normally the gas follows the bullet out of the muzzle and sets fire to the oxygen in the air close by. Hence muzzle flash. But with a hard contact shot to the head like passenger number four had chosen, the bullet makes a hole in the skin and the gas pumps itself straight in after it. It expands violently under the skin and either rips itself a huge star-shaped exit wound, or it blows all the flesh and skin right off the bone and unwraps the skull completely, like peeling a banana upside down.

That was what had happened in this case. The woman's face was reduced to rags and tatters of bloody flesh hanging off shattered bone. The bullet had travelled vertically through her mouth and had dumped its massive kinetic energy in her brain pan, and the sudden huge pressure had sought relief and found it where the plates of her skull had sealed themselves way back in childhood. They had burst open again and the pressure had pasted three or four large fragments of bone all over the wall above and behind her. One way or the other her head was basically gone. But the graffiti-resistant fibreglass was doing its job. White bone and dark blood and grey tissue were running down the slick surface, not sticking, leaving thin snail trails behind. The woman's body had collapsed into a slumped position on the bench. Her right index finger was still hooked through the trigger guard. The gun had bounced off her thigh and was resting on the seat next to her.

The sound of the shot was still ringing in my ears. Behind me I could hear muted sounds. I could smell the woman's blood. I ducked forward and checked her bag. Empty. I unzipped her jacket and opened it up. Nothing there. Just a white cotton blouse and the stink of voided bowel and bladder.

I found the emergency panel and called through to the conductor myself. I said, 'Suicide by gunshot. Last but one car. It's all over now. We're secure. No further threat.' I didn't want to wait until the NYPD assembled SWAT teams and body armour and rifles and came in all stealthy. That could take a long time.

I didn't get a reply from the conductor. But a minute later his voice came through the train PA. He said, 'Passengers are advised that the doors will remain closed for a few minutes due to an evolving incident.' He spoke slowly. He was probably reading from a card. His voice was shaky. Not at all like the smooth tones of the Bloomberg anchors.

I took a last look around the car and sat down three feet from the headless corpse and waited.

* * *

Whole episodes of TV cop shows could have run before the real-life cops even arrived. DNA could have been extracted and analysed, matches could have been made, perpetrators could have been hunted and caught and tried and sentenced. But eventually six officers came down the stairs. They were in caps and vests and they had drawn their weapons. NYPD patrolmen on the night shift, probably out of the 14th Precinct on West 35th Street, the famous Midtown South. They ran along the platform and started checking the train from the front. I got up again and watched through the windows above the couplers, down the whole length of the train, like peering into a long lit-up stainless steel tunnel. The view got murky farther down, due to dirt and green impurities in the layers of glass. But I could see the cops opening doors car by car, checking, clearing, turning the passengers out and hustling them upstairs to the street. It was a lightly loaded night train and it didn't take long for them to reach us. They checked through the windows and saw the body and the gun and tensed up. The doors hissed open and they swarmed on board, two through each set of doors. We all raised our hands, like a reflex.

One cop blocked each of the doorways and the other three moved straight towards the dead woman. They stopped and stood off about six feet. Didn't check for a pulse or any other sign of life. Didn't hold a mirror under her nose, to check for breathing. Partly because it was obvious she wasn't breathing, and partly because she didn't have a nose. The cartilage had torn away, leaving jagged splinters of bone between where the internal pressure had popped her eyeballs out.

A big cop with sergeant's stripes turned around. He had gone a little pale but was otherwise well into a pretty good impersonation of just another night's work. He asked, 'Who saw what happened here?'

There was silence at the front of the car. The

Hispanic woman, the man in the NBA shirt, and the African lady. They were all sitting tight and saying nothing. Point eight: a rigid stare ahead. They were all doing it. *If I can't see you, you can't see me*. The guy in the golf shirt said nothing. So I said, 'She took the gun out of her bag and shot herself.'

'Just like that?'

'More or less.'

'Why?'

'How would I know?'

'Where and when?'

'On the run-in to the station. Whenever that was.'

The guy processed the information. Suicide by gunshot. The subway was the NYPD's responsibility. The deceleration zone between 41st and 42nd was the 14th Precinct's turf. His case. No question. He nodded. Said, 'OK, please all of you exit the car and wait on the platform. We'll need names and addresses and statements from you.'

Then he keyed his collar microphone and was answered by a loud blast of static. He answered that in turn with a long stream of codes and numbers. I guessed he was calling for paramedics and an ambulance. After that it would be up to the transportation people to get the car unhooked and cleaned and the schedule back on track. Not difficult, I thought. There was plenty of time before the morning rush hour.

We got out into a gathering crowd on the platform. Transport cops, more regular cops arriving, subway workers clustering all around, Grand Central personnel showing up. Five minutes later an FDNY paramedic crew clattered down the stairs with a gurney. They came through the barrier and stepped on the train and the first-response cops stepped off. I didn't see what happened after that because the cops started moving through the crowd, looking around, making ready to find a passenger each and walk them away for further inquiries. The big sergeant came for me. I had answered his questions on the train. Therefore he made me first in line. He led me deep into the station and put me in a hot stale white-tiled room that could have been part of the transport police facility. He sat me down alone in a wooden chair and asked me for my name.

'Jack Reacher,' I said.

He wrote it down and didn't speak again. Just hung around in the doorway and watched me. And waited. For a detective to show up, I guessed.

SEVEN

The detective who showed up was a woman and she came alone. She was wearing pants and a grey short-sleeved shirt. Maybe silk, maybe man-made. Shiny, anyway. It was untucked and I guessed the tails were hiding her gun and her cuffs and whatever else she was carrying. Inside the shirt she was small and slim. Above the shirt she had dark hair tied back and a small oval face. No jewellery. Not even a wedding band. She was somewhere in her late thirties. Maybe forty. An attractive woman. I liked her immediately. She looked relaxed and friendly. She showed me her gold shield and handed me her business card. It had numbers on it for her office and her cell. It had an NYPD e-mail address. She said the name on it out loud for me. The name was Theresa Lee, with the T and the h pronounced together, like *theme* or *therapy*. *Theresa*. She wasn't Asian. Maybe the Lee came from an old marriage or was an Ellis Island version of Leigh, or some other longer and more complicated name. Or maybe she was descended from Robert E.

She said, 'Can you tell me exactly what happened?'

She spoke softly, with raised eyebrows and in a breathy voice brimming with care and consideration, like her primary concern was my own post-traumatic stress. *Can you tell me? Can you?* Like, *can you bear to relive it?* I smiled, briefly. Midtown South was down to low single-digit homicides per year, and even if she had dealt with all of them by herself since the first day she came on the job, I had still seen more corpses than she had. By a big multiple. The woman on the train hadn't been the most pleasant of them, but she had been a very long way from the worst.

So I told her exactly what had happened, all the way up from Bleecker Street, all the way through the eleven-point list, my tentative approach, the fractured conversation, the gun, the suicide.

Theresa Lee wanted to talk about the list.

'We have a copy,' she said. 'It's supposed to be confidential.'

'It's been out in the world for twenty years,' I said. 'Everyone has a copy. It's hardly confidential.'

'Where did you see it?'

'In Israel,' I said. 'Just after it was written.'

'How?'

So I ran through my résumé for her. The abridged version. The U.S. Army, thirteen years a military policeman, the elite 110th investigative unit, service all over the world, plus detached duty here and there, as and when ordered. Then the Soviet collapse, the peace dividend, the smaller defence budget, suddenly getting cut loose.

'Officer or enlisted man?' she asked.

'Final rank of major,' I said.

'And now?'

'I'm retired.'

'You're young to be retired.'

'I figured I should enjoy it while I can.'

'And are you?'

'Never better.'

'What were you doing tonight? Down there in the Village?'

'Music,' I said. 'Those blues clubs on Bleecker.'

'And where were you headed on the 6 train?'

'I was going to get a room somewhere or head over to the Port Authority to get a bus.'

'To where?'

'Wherever.'

'Short visit?'

'The best kind.'

'Where do you live?'

'Nowhere. My year is one short visit after another.'

'Where's your luggage?'

'I don't have any.'

Most people ask follow-up questions after that, but Theresa Lee didn't. Instead her eyes changed focus again and she said, 'I'm not happy that the list was wrong. I thought it was supposed to be definitive.' She spoke inclusively, cop to cop, as if my old job made a difference to her.

'It was only half wrong,' I said. 'The suicide part was right.'

'I suppose so,' she said. 'The signs would be the same, I guess. But it was still a false positive.'

'Better than a false negative.'

'I suppose so,' she said again.

I asked, 'Do we know who she was?'

'Not yet. But we'll find out. They tell me they found keys and a wallet at the scene. They'll probably be definitive. But what was up with the winter jacket?'

I said, 'I have no idea.'

She went quiet, like she was profoundly disappointed. I said, 'These things are always works in progress. Personally I think we should add a twelfth point to the women's list, too. If a woman bomber takes off her headscarf, there's going to be a suntan clue, the same as the men.'

'Good point,' she said.

'And I read a book that figured the part about the virgins is a mistranslation. The word is ambiguous. It comes in a passage full of food imagery. Milk and honey. It probably means raisins. Plump, and possibly candied or sugared.'

'They kill themselves for raisins?'

'I'd love to see their faces.'

'Are you a linguist?'

'I speak English,' I said. 'And French. And why would a woman bomber want virgins anyway? A lot of sacred texts are mistranslated. Especially where virgins are concerned. Even the New Testament, probably. Some people say Mary was a first-time mother, that's all. From the Hebrew word. Not a virgin. The original writers would laugh, seeing what we made of it all.'

Theresa Lee didn't comment on that. Instead she asked, 'Are you OK?'

I took it to be an inquiry as to whether I was shaken up. As to whether I should be offered counselling. Maybe because she took me for a taciturn man who was talking too much. But I was wrong. I said, 'I'm fine,' and she looked a little surprised and said, 'I would be regretting the approach, myself. On the train. I think you tipped her over the edge. Another couple of stops and she might have gotten over whatever was upsetting her.'

* * *

We sat in silence for a minute after that and then the big sergeant stuck his head in and nodded Lee out to the corridor. I heard a short whispered conversation and then Lee came back in and asked me to head over to West 35th Street with her. To the precinct house.

I asked, 'Why?'

She hesitated.

'Formality,' she said. 'To get your statement typed up, to close the file.'

'Do I get a choice in the matter?'

'Don't go there,' she said. 'The Israeli list is involved. We could call this whole thing a matter of national security. You're a material witness, we could keep you until you grew old and died. Better just to play ball like a good citizen.'

So I shrugged and followed her out of the Grand Central labyrinth to Vanderbilt Avenue, where her car was parked. It was an unmarked Ford Crown Victoria, battered and grimy, but it worked OK. It got us over to West 35th just fine. We went in through the grand old portal and she led me upstairs to an interview room. She stepped back and waited in the corridor and let me go in ahead of her. Then she stayed in the corridor and closed the door behind me and locked it from the outside.

EIGHT

Theresa Lee came back twenty minutes later with the beginnings of an official file and another guy. She put the file on the table and introduced the other guy as her partner. She said his name was Docherty. She said he had come up with a bunch of questions that maybe should have been asked and answered at the outset.

'What questions?' I asked.

First she offered me coffee and the bathroom. I said yes to both. Docherty escorted me down the corridor and when we got back there were three foam cups on the table, next to the file. Two coffees, one tea. I took a coffee and tried it. It was OK. Lee took the tea. Docherty took the second coffee and said, 'Run through it all again.'

So I did, concisely, bare bones, and Docherty fussed a bit about how the Israeli list had produced a false positive, the same way that Lee had. I answered him the same way I had answered her, that a false positive was better than a false negative, and that looking at it from the dead woman's point of view, whether she was heading for a solo exit or planning to take a crowd with her might not alter the personal symptoms she would be displaying. For five minutes we had a collegiate atmosphere going, three reasonable people discussing an interesting phenomenon.

Then the tone changed.

Docherty asked, 'How did you feel?'

I asked, 'About what?'

'While she was killing herself.'

'Glad that she wasn't killing me.'

Docherty said, 'We're homicide detectives. We have to look at all violent deaths. You understand that, right? Just in case.'

I said, 'Just in case of what?'

'Just in case there's more than meets the eye.'

'There isn't. She shot herself.'

'Says you.'

'No one can say different. Because that's what happened.'

Docherty said, 'There are always alternative scenarios.'

'You think?'

'Maybe *you* shot her.'

Theresa Lee gave me a sympathetic look.

I said, 'I didn't.'

Docherty said, 'Maybe it was your gun.'

I said, 'It wasn't. It was a two-pound piece. I don't have a bag.'

'You're a big guy. Big pants. Big pockets.'

Theresa Lee gave me another sympathetic look. Like she was saying, *I'm sorry*.

I said, 'What is this? Good cop, dumb cop?'

Docherty said, 'You think I'm dumb?'

'You just proved it. If I shot her with a .357

Magnum, I'd have residue on me up to my elbow. But you just stood outside the men's room while I washed my hands. You're full of shit. You haven't fingerprinted me and you haven't Mirandized me. You're blowing smoke.'

'We're obliged to make certain.'

'What does the medical examiner say?'

'We don't know yet.'

'There were witnesses.'

Lee shook her head. 'No use. They didn't see anything.'

'They must have.'

'Their view was blocked by your back. Plus they weren't looking, plus they were half asleep, and plus they don't speak much English. They had nothing to offer. Basically I think they wanted to get going before we started checking green cards.'

'What about the other guy? He was in front of me. He was wide awake. And he looked like a citizen and an English speaker.'

'What other guy?'

'The fifth passenger. Chinos and a golf shirt.'

Lee opened the file. Shook her head. 'There were only four passengers, plus the woman.'

NINE

Lee took a sheet of paper out of the file and reversed it and slid it halfway across the table. It was a handwritten list of witnesses. Four names. Mine, plus a Rodriguez, a Frlujlov, and an Mbele.

'Four passengers,' she said again.

I said, 'I was on the train. I can count. I know

how many passengers there were.' Then I re-ran the scene in my head. Stepping off the train, waiting among the small milling crowd. The arrival of the paramedic crew. The cops, stepping off the train in turn, moving through the throng, taking an elbow each, leading the witnesses away to separate rooms. I had gotten grabbed first, by the big sergeant. Impossible to say whether four cops had followed behind us, or only three.

I said, 'He must have slipped away.'

Docherty asked, 'Who was he?'

'Just a guy. Alert, but nothing special about him. My age, not poor.'

'Did he interact in any way with the woman?'

'Not that I saw.'

'Did he shoot her?'

'She shot herself.'

Docherty shrugged. 'So he's just a reluctant witness. Doesn't want paperwork showing he was out and about at two in the morning. Probably cheating on his wife. Happens all the time.'

'He ran. But you're giving him a free pass and looking at me instead?'

'You just testified that he wasn't involved.'

'I wasn't involved either.'

'Says you.'

'You believe me about the other guy but not about myself?'

'Why would you lie about the other guy?'

I said, 'This is a waste of time.' And it was. It was such an extreme, clumsy waste of time that I suddenly realized it wasn't for real. It was stage managed. I realized that in fact, in their own peculiar way, Lee and Docherty were doing me a small favour.

There's more than meets the eye.

I said, 'Who was she?'

Docherty said, 'Why should she be someone?'

'Because you made the ID and the computers lit up like Christmas trees. Someone called you and told you to hold on to me until they get here. You didn't want to put an arrest on my record so you're stalling me with all this bullshit.'

'We didn't particularly care about your record. We just didn't want to do the paperwork.'

'So who was she?'

'Apparently she worked for the government. A federal agency is on its way to question you. We're not allowed to say which one.'

* * *

They left me locked in the room. It was an OK space. Grimy, hot, battered, no windows, out-of-date crime prevention posters on the walls and the smell of sweat and anxiety and burnt coffee in the air. The table, and three chairs. Two for the detectives, one for the suspect. Back in the day maybe the suspect got smacked around and tumbled out of the chair. Maybe he still did. It's hard to say exactly what happens, in a room with no windows.

I timed the delay in my head. The clock had already been running about an hour, since Theresa Lee's whispered talk in the Grand Central corridor. So I knew it wasn't the FBI coming for me. Their New York field office is the largest in the nation, based down in Federal Plaza, near City Hall. Ten minutes to react, ten minutes to assemble a team, ten minutes to drive uptown with lights and sirens. The FBI would have arrived long ago. But that left a whole bunch of other three-letter agencies. I made a bet with myself that whoever was heading my way would have IA as the last two letters on their badges. CIA, DIA. Central Intelligence Agency, Defense Intelligence Agency. Maybe others recently invented and hitherto unpublicized. Middle-of-the-night panics were very much their style.

After a second hour tacked on to the first I figured they must be coming all the way from D.C., which implied a small specialist outfit. Anyone else would have a field office closer to hand. I gave up speculating and tipped my chair back and put my feet on the table and went to sleep.

* * *

I didn't find out exactly who they were. Not then. They wouldn't tell me. At five in the morning three men in suits came in and woke me up. They were polite and businesslike. Their suits were mid-priced and clean and pressed. Their shoes were polished. Their eyes were bright. Their haircuts were fresh and short. Their faces were pink and ruddy. Their bodies were stocky but toned. They looked like they could run half-marathons without much trouble, but without much enjoyment, either. My first impression was recent ex-military. Gung-ho staff officers, head-hunted into some limestone building inside the Beltway. True believers, doing important work. I asked to see ID and badges and credentials, but they quoted the Patriot Act at me and said they weren't obliged to identify themselves. Probably true, and they certainly enjoyed saying so. I considered clamming up in retaliation, but they saw me considering, and quoted some more of the Act at me, which left me in no doubt at all that a world of trouble lay at the end of that particular road. I am afraid of very little, but hassle with today's security apparatus is always best avoided. Franz Kafka and George Orwell would have given me the same advice. So I shrugged and told them to go ahead and ask their questions.

They started out by saying that they were aware of my military service and very respectful of it, which was either a bullshit boilerplate platitude, or meant that they had been recruited out of the MPs themselves. Nobody respects an MP except another MP. Then they said that they would be observing me very closely and would know whether I was telling the truth or lying. Which was total bullshit, because only the best of us can do that, and these guys weren't the best of us, otherwise they would have been in very senior positions, meaning that right then they would have been home and asleep in a Virginia suburb, rather than running up and down I-95 in the middle of the night.

But I didn't have anything to hide, so I told them again to go ahead.

They had three areas of concern. The first: Did I know the woman who had killed herself on the train? Had I ever seen her before?

I said, 'No.' Short and sweet, quiet but firm.

They didn't follow up with supplementaries. Which told me roughly who they were and exactly what they were doing. They were somebody's B team, sent north to dead-end an open investigation. They were walling it off, burying it, drawing a line under something somebody had been only half suspicious about to begin with. They wanted a negative answer to every question, so that the file could be closed and the matter put to bed. They wanted a positive absence of loose ends, and they didn't want to draw attention to the issue by making it a big drama. They wanted to get back on the road with the whole thing forgotten.

The second question was: Did I know a woman called Lila Hoth?

I said, 'No,' because I didn't. Not then.

The third question was more of a sustained dialogue. The lead agent opened it. The main man. He was a little older and a little smaller than the other two. Maybe a little smarter, too. He said, 'You approached the woman on the train.'

I didn't reply. I was there to answer questions, not to comment on statements.

The guy asked, 'How close did you get?'

'Six feet,' I said. 'Give or take.'

'Close enough to touch her?'

'No.'

'If you had extended your arm, and she had extended hers, could you have touched hands?'

'Maybe,' I said.

'Is that a yes or a no?'

'It's a maybe. I know how long my arms are. I don't know how long hers were.'

'Did she pass anything to you?'

'No.'

'Did you accept anything from her?'

'No.'

'Did you take anything from her after she was dead?'

'No.'

'Did anyone else?'

'Not that I saw.'

'Did you see anything fall from her hand, or her bag, or her clothing?'

'No.'

'Did she tell you anything?'

'Nothing of substance.'

'Did she speak to anyone else?'

'No.'

The guy asked, 'Would you mind turning out your pockets?'

I shrugged. I had nothing to hide. I went through each pocket in turn and dumped the contents on the battered table. A folded wad of cash money, and a few coins. My old passport. My ATM card. My clip-together toothbrush. The Metrocard that had gotten me into the subway in the first place. And Theresa Lee's business card.

The guy stirred through my stuff with a single extended finger and nodded to one of his underlings, who stepped up close to pat me down. He did a semi-expert job and found nothing more and shook his head.

The main guy said, 'Thank you, Mr Reacher.'

And then they left, all three of them, as quickly as they had come in. I was a little surprised, but happy enough. I put my stuff back in my pockets and waited for them to clear the corridor and then I wandered out. The place was quiet. I saw Theresa Lee doing nothing at a desk and her partner Docherty walking a guy across the squad room to a cubicle at the back. The guy was a worn-out mid-sized forty-something. He had on a creased grey T-shirt and a pair of red sweat pants.

He had left home without combing his hair. That was clear. It was grey and sticking up all over the place. Theresa Lee saw me looking and said, 'Family member.'

'The woman's?'

Lee nodded. 'She had contact details in her wallet. That's her brother. He's a cop himself. Small town in New Jersey. He drove straight over.'

'Poor guy.'

'I know. We didn't ask him to make the formal ID. She's too messed up. We told him that a closed casket is the way to go. He got the message.'

'So are you sure it's her?'

Lee nodded again. 'Fingerprints.'

'Who was she?'

'I'm not allowed to say.'

'Am I done here?'

'The feds finished with you?'

'Apparently.'

'Then beat it. You're done.'

I made it to the top of the stairs and she called after me. She said, 'I didn't mean it about tipping her over the edge.'

'Yes, you did,' I said. 'And you might have been right.'

* * *

I stepped out to the dawn cool and turned left on 35th Street and headed east. *You're done*. But I wasn't. Right there on the corner were four more guys waiting to talk to me. Similar types as before, but not federal agents. Their suits were too expensive.

TEN

The world is the same jungle all over, but New York is its purest distillation. What is useful elsewhere is vital in the big city. You see four guys bunched on a corner waiting for you, you either run like hell in the opposite direction without hesitation, or you keep on walking without slowing down or speeding up or breaking stride. You look ahead with studied neutrality, you check their faces, you look away, like you're saying *is that all you got*?

Truth is, it's smarter to run. The best fight is the one you don't have. But I have never claimed to be smart. Just obstinate, and occasionally bad-tempered. Some guys kick cats. I keep walking.

The suits were all midnight blue and looked like they came from the kind of store that has a foreign person's name above the door. The men inside the suits looked capable. Like NCOs. Wise to the ways of the world, proud of their ability to get the job done. They were certainly ex-military, or ex-law enforcement, or ex-both. They were the kind of guys who had taken a step up in salary and a step away from rules and regulations, and regarded both moves as equally valuable.

They separated into two pairs when I was still four paces away. Left me room to pass if I wanted to, but the front guy on the left raised both palms a little and patted the air, in a kind of dual-purpose *please stop* and *we're no threat* gesture. I spent the next step deciding. You can't let yourself get caught in the middle of four guys. Either you stop early or you barge on through. At that point my options were still open. Easy to stop, easy to keep going. If they closed ranks while I was still moving, they would go down like ninepins. I weigh 250 and was moving at four miles an hour. They didn't, and weren't.

Two steps out, the lead guy said, 'Can we talk?'

I stopped walking. Said, 'About what?'

'You're the witness, right?'

'But who are you?'

The guy answered by peeling back the flap of his suit coat, slow and unthreatening, showing me nothing except a red satin lining and a shirt. No gun, no holster, no belt. He put his right fingers into his left inside pocket and came out with a business card. Leaned forward and handed it to me. It was a cheap product. The first line said: *Sure and Certain, Inc*. The second line said: *Protection, Investigation, Intervention*. The third line had a telephone number, with a 212 area code. Manhattan.

'Kinko's is a wonderful place,' I said. 'Isn't it? Maybe I'll get some cards that say John Smith, King of the World.'

'The card is legit,' the guy said. 'And we're legit.'

'Who are you working for?'

'We can't say.'

'Then I can't help you.'

'Better that you talk to us than our principal. We can keep things civilized.'

'Now I'm really scared.'

'Just a couple of questions. That's all. Help us out. We're just working stiffs, trying to get paid. Like you.'

'I'm not a working stiff. I'm a gentleman of

leisure.'

'Then look down on us from your lofty perch and take pity.'

'What questions?'

'Did she give anything to you?'

'Who?'

'You know who. Did you take anything from her?'

'And? What's the next question?'

'Did she say anything?'

'She said plenty. She was talking all the way from Bleecker to Grand Central.'

'Saying what?'

'I didn't hear very much of it.'

'Information?'

'I didn't hear.'

'Did she mention names?'

'She might have.'

'Did she say the name Lila Hoth?'

'Not that I heard.'

'Did she say John Sansom?'

I didn't answer. The guy asked, 'What?'

I said, 'I heard that name somewhere.'

'From her?'

'No.'

'Did she give you anything?'

'What kind of a thing?'

'Anything at all.'

'Tell me what difference it would make.'

'Our principal wants to know.'

'Tell him to come ask me himself.'

'Better to talk to us.'

I smiled and walked on, through the alley they had created. But one of the guys on the right sidestepped and tried to push me back. I caught him shoulder-to-chest and spun him out of my way. He came after me again and I stopped and started and feinted left and right and slid in behind him and shoved him hard in the back so that he stumbled on ahead of me. His jacket had a single centre vent. French tailoring. British suits favour twin side vents and Italian suits favour none at all. I leaned down and caught a coat tail in each hand and heaved and tore the seam all the way up the back. Then I shoved him again. He stumbled ahead and veered right. His coat was hanging off him by the collar. Unbuttoned at the front, open at the back, like a hospital gown.

Then I ran three steps and stopped and turned around. It would have been much more stylish to just keep on walking slowly, but also much dumber. Insouciance is good, but being ready is better. The four of them were caught in a moment of real indecision. They wanted to come get me. That was for sure. But they were on West 35th Street at dawn. At that hour virtually all the traffic would be cops. So in the end they just gave me hard looks and moved away. They crossed 35th in single file and headed south at the corner.

You're done.

But I wasn't. I turned to move away and a guy came out of the precinct house and ran after me. Creased grey T-shirt, red sweat pants, grey hair sticking up all over the place. The family member. The brother. The small-town cop from Jersey. He caught up with me and grabbed my elbow in a wiry grip and told me he had seen me inside and had guessed I was the witness. Then he told me his sister hadn't committed suicide.

ELEVEN

I took the guy to a coffee shop on Eighth Avenue. A long time ago I was sent on a one-day MP seminar at Fort Rucker, to learn sensitivity around the recently bereaved. Sometimes MPs had to deliver bad news to relatives. We called them death messages. My skills were widely held to be deficient. I used to walk in and just tell them. I thought that was the nature of a message. But apparently I was wrong. So I was sent to Rucker. I learned good stuff there. I learned to take emotions seriously. Above all I learned that cafés and diners and coffee shops were good environments for bad news. The public atmosphere limits the likelihood of falling apart, and the process of ordering and waiting and sipping punctuates the flow of information in a way that makes it easier to absorb.

We took a booth next to a mirror. That helps, too. You can look at each other in the glass. Face to face, but not really. The place was about half full. Cops from the precinct, taxi drivers on their way to the West Side garages. We ordered coffee. I wanted food too, but I wasn't going to eat if he didn't. Not respectful. He said he wasn't hungry. I sat quiet and waited. Let them talk first, the Rucker psychologists had said.

He told me that his name was Jacob Mark. Originally Markakis in his grandfather's day, back when a Greek name was no good to anyone, except if you were in the deli business, which his grandfather wasn't. His grandfather was in the construction business. Hence the change. He said I could call him Jake. I said he could call me Reacher. He told me he was a cop. I told him I had been one once, in the military. He told me he wasn't married and lived alone. I said the same went for me. Establish common ground, the teachers at Rucker had said. Up close and looking past his physical disarray he was a squared-away guy. He had any cop's weary gloss, but under it lay a normal suburban man. With a different guidance counsellor he might have become a science teacher or a dentist or an auto parts manager. He was in his forties, already very grey, but his face was youthful and unlined. His eyes were dark and wide and staring, but that was temporary. Some hours ago, when he went to bed, he must have been a handsome man. I liked him on sight, and I felt sorry for his situation.

He took a breath and told me his sister's name was Susan Mark. At one time Susan Molina, but many years divorced and reverted. Now living alone. He talked about her in the present tense. He was a long way from acceptance.

He said, 'She can't have killed herself. It's just not possible.'

I said, 'Jake, I was there.'

The waitress brought our coffee and we sipped in silence for a moment. Passing time, letting reality sink in just a little more. The Rucker psychologists had been explicit: the suddenly bereaved have the IQ of Labradors. Indelicate, because they were army, but accurate, because they were psychologists.

Jake said, 'So tell me what happened.'

I asked him, 'Where are you from?'

He named a small town in northern New Jersey, well inside the New York metro area, full of commuters and soccer moms, prosperous, safe, contented. He said the police department was well funded, well equipped, and generally understretched. I asked him if his department had a copy of the Israeli list. He said that after the Twin Towers every police department in the country had been buried under paper, and every officer had been required to learn every point on every list.

I said, 'Your sister was behaving strangely, Jake. She rang every bell. She looked like a suicide bomber.'

'Bullshit,' he said, like a good brother should.

'Obviously she wasn't,' I said. 'But you would have thought the same thing. You would have had to, with your training.'

'So the list is more about suicide than bombing.'

'Apparently.'

'She wasn't an unhappy person.'

'She must have been.'

He didn't reply. We sipped a little more. People came and went. Checks were paid, tips were left. Traffic built up on Eighth.

I said, 'Tell me about her.'

He asked, 'What gun did she use?'

'An old Ruger Speed-Six.'

'Our dad's gun. She inherited it.'

'Where did she live? Here, in the city?'

He shook his head. 'Annandale, Virginia.'

'Did you know she was up here?'

He shook his head again.

'Why would she come?'

'I don't know.'

'Why would she be wearing a winter coat?'

'I don't know.'

I said, 'Some federal agents came and asked me questions. Then some private guys found me, just before you did. They were all talking about a woman called Lila Hoth. You ever hear that name from your sister?'

'No.'

'What about John Sansom?'

'He's a congressman from North Carolina. Wants to be a senator. Some kind of hard-ass.'

I nodded. I remembered, vaguely. Election season was gearing up. I had seen newspaper stories and television coverage. Sansom had been a late entrant to politics and was a rising star. He was seen as tough and uncompromising. And ambitious. He had done well in business for a spell and before that he had done well in the army. He hinted at a glamorous Special Forces career, without supplying details. Special Forces careers are good for that kind of thing. Most of what they do is secret, or can be claimed to be.

I asked, 'Did your sister ever mention Sansom?'

He said, 'I don't think so.'

'Did she know him?'

'I can't see how.'

I asked, 'What did she do for a living?'

He wouldn't tell me.

TWELVE

He didn't need to tell me. I already knew enough for a ballpark guess. Her fingerprints were on file and three shiny pink ex-staff officers had hustled up the highway but had left again within minutes. Which put Susan Mark somewhere in the defence business, but not in an elevated position. And she lived in Annandale, Virginia. Southwest of Arlington, as I recalled. Probably changed since I was last there. But probably still a decent place to live, and still an easy commute to the world's largest office building. Route 244, one end to the other.

'She worked at the Pentagon,' I said.

Jake said, 'She wasn't supposed to talk about her job.'

I shook my head. 'If it was really a secret, she would have told you she worked at Wal-Mart.'

He didn't answer. I said, 'I had an office in the Pentagon once. I'm familiar with the place. Try me.'

He paused a beat and then he shrugged and said, 'She was a civilian clerk. But she made it sound exciting. She worked for an outfit called CGUSAHRC. She never told me much about it. She made it sound like a hush-hush thing. People can't talk so much now, after the Twin Towers.'

'It's not an outfit,' I said. 'It's a guy. CGUSAHRC means Commanding General, United States Army, Human Resources Command. And it's not very exciting. It's a personnel department. Paperwork and records.'

Jake didn't reply. I thought I had offended him, by belittling his sister's career. Maybe the Rucker seminar hadn't taught me enough. Maybe I should have paid more attention. The silence went on a beat too long and grew awkward. I asked, 'Did she tell you anything about it at all?'

'Not really. Maybe there wasn't much to tell.' He said it with a hint of bitterness, as if his sister had been caught in a lie.

I said, 'People dress things up, Jake. It's human nature. And usually there's no harm in it. Maybe she just wanted to compete, with you being a cop.'

'We weren't close.'

'You were still family.'

'I guess.'

'Did she enjoy her job?'

'She seemed to. And it must have suited her. She had the right skills, for a records department. Great memory, meticulous, very organized. She was good with computers.'

The silence came back. I started to think about Annandale again. A pleasant but unremarkable community. A dormitory, basically. Under the present circumstances it had just one significant characteristic.

It was a very long way from New York City.

She wasn't an unhappy person.

Jake said, 'What?'

I said, 'Nothing. None of my business.'

'But what?'

'Just thinking.'

'About what?'

There's more than meets the eye.

I asked, 'How long have you been a cop?'

'Eighteen years.'

'All in the same place?'

'I trained with the State Troopers. Then I moved over. Like a farm system.'

'Have you seen many suicides in Jersey?'

'One or two a year, maybe.'

'Anyone see any of them coming?'

'Not really. They're usually a big surprise.'

'Like this one.'

'You got that right.'

'But behind each one of them there must have been a reason.'

'Always. Financial, sexual, some kind of shit about to hit the fan.'

'So your sister must have had a reason.'

'I don't know what.'

I went quiet again. Jake said, 'Just say it. Tell me.'

'Not my place.'

'You were a cop,' he said. 'You're seeing something.'

I nodded. Said, 'My guess is that out of the suicides you've seen, maybe seven out of ten happened at home, and three out of ten, they drove to some local lane and hitched up the hosepipe.'

'More or less.'

'But always somewhere familiar. Somewhere quiet and alone. Always at some kind of a destination. You get there, you compose yourself, you do it.'

'What are you saying?'

'I'm saying that I never heard of a suicide where the person travels hundreds of miles from home and does it while the journey is still in progress.'

'I told you.'

'You told me she didn't kill herself. But she did. I saw her do it. But I'm saying she did it in a very unconventional manner. In fact I don't think I ever heard of a suicide inside a subway car before. Under one, maybe, but not inside. Did you ever hear of a suicide on public transportation, during the ride?'

'So?'

'So nothing. I'm just asking, that's all.'

'Why?'

'Because. Think like a cop, Jake. Not like a brother. What do you do when something is way out of line?'

'You dig deeper.'

'So do it.'

'It won't bring her back.'

'But understanding a thing helps a lot.' Which was also a concept they taught at Fort Rucker. But not in the psychology class.

* * *

I got a refill of coffee and Jacob Mark picked up a packet of sugar and turned it over and over in his fingers so that the powder fell from one end of the paper rectangle to the other, repeatedly, like an hourglass. I could see his head working like a cop and his heart working like a brother. It was all right there in his face. *Dig deeper. It won't bring her back*.

He asked, 'What else?'

'There was a passenger who took off before the NYPD got to him.'

'Who?'

'Just a guy. The cops figured he didn't want his

name in the system. They figured he was maybe cheating on his wife.'

'Possible.'

'Yes,' I said. 'Possible.'

'And?'

'Both the feds and the private guys asked me if your sister had handed me anything.'

'What kind of anything?'

'They didn't specify. I'm guessing something small.'

'Who were the feds?'

'They wouldn't say.'

'Who were the private guys?'

I hitched up off the bench and took the business card out of my back pocket. Cheap stock, already creased, and already rubbed a little blue from my jeans. New pants, fresh dye. I put it on the table and reversed it and slid it across. Jake read it slowly, maybe twice. *Sure and Certain, Inc. Protection, Investigation, Intervention*. The telephone number. He took out a cell and dialled. I heard a delay and a chirpy little three-note ding-dong tone and a recorded message. Jake closed his phone and said, 'Not in service. Phony number.'

THIRTEEN

I took a second refill of coffee. Jake just stared at the waitress like he had never heard of the concept. Eventually she lost interest and moved away. Jake slid the business card back to me. I picked it up and put it in my pocket and he said, 'I don't like this.'

I said, 'I wouldn't like it, either.'

'We should go back and talk to the NYPD.'

'She killed herself, Jake. That's the bottom line. That's all they need to know. They don't care how or where or why.'

'They should.'

'Maybe so. But they don't. Would you?'

'Probably not,' he said. I saw his eyes go blank. Maybe he was re-running old cases in his head. Big houses, leafy roads, lawyers living the high life on their clients' escrow money, unable to make good, ducking out ahead of shame and scandal and disbarment. Or teachers, with pregnant students. Or family men, with boyfriends in Chelsea or the West Village. The local cops, full of tact and rough sympathy, large and intrusive in the neat quiet dwellings, checking the scenes, establishing the facts, typing reports, closing files, forgetting, moving on to the next thing, not caring how or where or why.

He said, 'You got a theory?'

I said, 'It's too early for a theory. All we got so far is facts.'

'What facts?'

'The Pentagon didn't entirely trust your sister.'

'That's a hell of a thing to say.'

'She was on a watch list, Jake. She must have been. As soon as her name hit the wires, those feds saddled up. Three of them. That was a procedure.'

'They didn't stay long.'

I nodded. 'Which means they weren't very suspicious. They were being cautious, that's all. Maybe they had some small thing on their minds, but they didn't really believe it. They came up here to rule it out.'

'What kind of thing?'

'Information,' I said. 'That's all the Human Resources Command has got.'

'They thought she was passing information?'

'They wanted to rule it out.'

'Which means at some point they must have ruled it in.'

I nodded again. 'Maybe she was seen in the wrong office, opening the wrong file cabinet. Maybe they figured there was an innocent explanation, but they wanted to be sure. Or maybe something went missing and they didn't know who to watch, so they were watching them all.'

'What kind of information?'

'I have no idea.'

'Like a copied file?'

'Smaller,' I said. 'A folded note, a computer memory. Something that could be passed from hand to hand in a subway car.'

'She was a patriot. She loved her country. She wouldn't do that.'

'And she didn't do that. She didn't pass anything to anyone.'

'So we've got nothing.'

'We've got your sister hundreds of miles from home with a loaded gun.'

'And afraid,' Jake said.

'Wearing a winter jacket in ninety-degree weather.'

'With two names floating around,' he said. 'John Sansom and Lila Hoth, whoever the hell she is. And Hoth sounds foreign.'

'So did Markakis, once upon a time.'

He went quiet again and I sipped coffee. Traffic was getting slower on Eighth. The morning rush was building. The sun was up, a little south of east. Its rays were not aligned with the street grid. They came in at a low angle and threw long diagonal shadows.

Jake said, 'Give me somewhere to start.'

I said, 'We don't know enough.'

'Speculate.'

'I can't. I could make up a story, but it would be full of holes. And it might be completely the wrong story to begin with.'

'Try it. Give me something. Like brainstorming.'

I shrugged. 'You ever met any ex-Special Forces guys?'

'Two or three. Maybe four or five, counting the Troopers I knew.'

'You probably didn't. Most Special Forces careers never happened. It's like people who claim to have been at Woodstock. Believe them all, the crowd must have been ten million strong. Or like New Yorkers who saw the planes hit the towers. They all did, to listen to them. No one was looking the wrong way at the time. People who say they were Special Forces are usually bullshitting. Most of them never made it out of the infantry. Some of them were never in the army at all. People dress things up.'

'Like my sister.'

'It's human nature.'

'What's your point?'

'I'm working with what we've got. We've got two random names, and election season starting up, and your sister in HRC.'

'You think John Sansom is lying about his past?'

'Probably not,' I said. 'But it's a common area of exaggeration. And politics is a dirty business. You can bet that right now someone is checking on the guy who did Sansom's dry-cleaning twenty years ago, wanting to know if he had a green card. So it's a no-brainer to assume that people are fact-checking his actual biography. It's a national sport.'

'So maybe Lila Hoth is a journalist. Or a researcher. Cable news, or something. Or talk radio.'

'Maybe she's Sansom's opponent.'

'Not with a name like that. Not in North Carolina.'

'OK, let's say she's a journalist or a researcher. Maybe she put the squeeze on an HRC clerk for Sansom's service record. Maybe she picked your sister.'

'Where was her leverage?'

I said, 'That's the first big hole in the story.' Which it was. Susan Mark had been desperate and terrified. It was hard to imagine a journalist finding that kind of leverage. Journalists can be manipulative and persuasive, but no one is particularly afraid of them.

'Was Susan political?' I asked.

'Why?'

'Maybe she didn't like Sansom. Didn't like what he stood for. Maybe she was cooperating. Or volunteering.'

'Then why would she be so scared?'

'Because she was breaking the law,' I said. 'Her heart would have been in her mouth.'

'And why was she carrying the gun?'

'Didn't she normally carry it?'

'Never. It was an heirloom. She kept it in her sock drawer, like people do.'

I shrugged. The gun was the second big hole in the story. People take their guns out of their sock drawers for a variety of reasons. Protection, aggression. But never just in case they feel a spur of the moment impulse to off themselves far from home.

Jake said, 'Susan wasn't very political.'

'OK.'

'Therefore there can't be a connection with Sansom.'

'Then why did his name come up?'

'I don't know.'

I said, 'Susan must have driven up. Can't take a gun on a plane. Her car is probably getting towed right now. She must have come through the Holland Tunnel and parked way downtown.'

Jake didn't reply. My coffee was cold. The waitress had given up on refills. We were an unprofitable table. The rest of the clientele had changed twice over. Working people, moving fast, fuelling up, getting ready for a busy day. I pictured Susan Mark twelve hours earlier, getting ready for a busy night. Dressing. Finding her father's gun, loading it, packing it into the black bag. Climbing into her car, taking 236 to the Beltway, going clockwise, maybe getting gas, hitting 95, heading north, eyes wide and desperate, drilling the darkness ahead.

Speculate, Jake had said. But suddenly I didn't want to. Because I could hear Theresa Lee in my head. The detective. *You tipped her over the edge*. Jake saw me thinking and asked, 'What?'

'Let's assume the leverage,' I said. 'Let's assume it was totally compelling. So let's assume Susan was on her way to deliver whatever information she was told to get. And let's assume these were bad people. She didn't trust them to release whatever hold they had over her. Probably she thought they were going to up the stakes and ask for more. She was in, and she didn't see a way of getting out. And above all, she was very afraid of them. So she was desperate. So she took the gun. Possibly she thought she could fight her way out, but she wasn't optimistic about her chances. All in all, she didn't think things were going to end well.'

'So?'

'She had business to attend to. She was almost there. She never intended to shoot herself.'

'But what about the list? The behaviours?'

'Same difference,' I said. 'She was on the way to where she expected someone else to end her life, maybe some other way, either literally or figuratively.'

FOURTEEN

Jacob Mark said, 'It doesn't explain the coat.' But I thought he was wrong. I thought it explained the coat pretty well. And it explained the fact that she parked downtown and rode up on the subway. I figured she was looking to come upon whoever she was meeting from an unexpected angle, out of a hole in the ground, armed, dressed all in black, ready for some conflict in the dark. Maybe the winter parka was the only black coat she owned.

And it explained everything else, too. The dread, the sense of doom. Maybe the mumbling had been her way of rehearsing pleas, or exculpations, or arguments, or maybe even threats. Maybe repeating them over and over again had made them more convincing to her. More plausible. More reassuring.

Jake said, 'She can't have been on her way to deliver something, because she didn't have anything with her.'

'She might have had something,' I said. 'In her head. You told me she had a great memory. Units, dates, time lines, whatever they needed.'

He paused, and tried to find a reason to disagree.

He failed.

'Classified information,' he said. 'Army secrets. Jesus, I can't believe it.'

'She was under pressure, Jake.'

'What kind of secrets does a personnel department have anyway, that are worth getting killed for?'

I didn't answer. Because I had no idea. In my day HRC had been called PERSCOM. Personnel Command, not Human Resources Command. I had served thirteen years without ever thinking about it. Not even once. Paperwork and records. All the interesting information had been somewhere else.

Jake moved in his seat. He ran his fingers through his unwashed hair and clamped his palms on his ears and moved his head through a complete oval, like he was easing stiffness in his neck, or acting out some kind of inner turmoil that was bringing him full circle, back to his most basic question.

He said, 'So why? Why did she just up and kill herself before she got where she was going?'

I paused a beat. Café noises went on all around us. The squeak of sneakers on linoleum, the clink and scrape of crockery, the sound of TV news from sets high on the walls, the ding of the short-order bell.

'She was breaking the law,' I said. 'She was in breach of all kinds of trusts and professional obligations. And she must have suspected some kind of surveillance. Maybe she had even been warned. So she was tense, right from the moment she got in her car. All the way up she was watching for red lights in her mirror. Every cop at every toll was a potential danger. Every guy she saw in a suit could have been a federal agent. And on the train, any one of us could have been getting ready to bust her.'

Jake didn't reply.

I said, 'And then I approached her.'

'And?'

'She flipped. She thought I was about to arrest her. Right then and there, the game was over. She was at the end of the road. She was damned if she did, and damned if she didn't. She couldn't go forward, couldn't go back. She was trapped. Whatever threats they were using against her were going to come to pass, and she was going to jail.'

'Why would she think you were going to arrest her?'

'She must have thought I was a cop.'

'Why would she think you were a cop?'

I'm a cop, I had said. *I can help you. We can talk.*

'She was paranoid,' I said. 'Understandably.'

'You don't look like a cop. You look like a bum. She would more likely have thought you were hustling her for spare change.'

'Maybe she thought I was undercover.'

'She was a records clerk, according to you. She wouldn't have known what undercover cops look like.'

'Jake, I'm sorry, but I told her I was a cop.'

'Why?'

'I thought she was a bomber. I was just trying to get through the next three seconds without her pushing the button. I was ready to say anything.'

He asked, 'What exactly did you say?' So I told him, and he said, 'Jesus, that even sounds like internal affairs bullshit.'

I think you tipped her over the edge.

'I'm sorry,' I said again.

* * *

For the next few minutes I was getting it from all sides. Jacob Mark was glaring at me because I had killed his sister. The waitress was angry because she could have sold about eight breakfasts in the time we had lingered over two cups of coffee. I took out a twenty dollar bill and trapped it under my saucer. She saw me do it. Eight breakfasts' worth of tips, right there. That solved the waitress problem. The Jacob Mark problem was tougher. He was still and silent and bristling. I saw him glance away, twice. Getting ready to disengage. Eventually he said, 'I got to go. I got things to do. I have to find a way to tell her family.'

I said, 'Family?'

'Molina, the ex-husband. And they have a son, Peter. My nephew.'

'Susan had a son?'

'What's it to you?'

The IQ of Labradors.

I said, 'Jake, we've been sitting here talking about leverage, and you didn't think to mention that Susan had a kid?'

He went blank for a second. Said, 'He's not a kid. He's twenty-two years old. He's a senior at USC. He plays football. He's bigger than you are. And he's not close with his mother. He lived with his father after the divorce.'

I said, 'Call him.'

'It's four o'clock in the morning in California.'

'Call him now.'

'I'll wake him up.'

'I sure hope you will.'

'He needs to be prepared for this.'

'First he needs to be answering his phone.'

So Jake took out his cell again and beeped through his address book and hit the green button against a name pretty low down on the list. Alphabetical order, I guessed. P for Peter. Jake held the phone against his ear and looked one kind of worried through the first five rings, and then another kind after the sixth. He kept the phone up a little while longer and then lowered it slowly and said, 'Voice mail.'

FIFTEEN

I said, 'Go to work. Call the LAPD or the USC campus cops and ask for some favours, blue to blue. Get someone to head over and check whether he's home.'

'They'll laugh at me. It's a college jock not

answering his phone at four in the morning.'

I said, 'Just do it.'

Jake said, 'Come with me.'

I shook my head. 'I'm staying here. I want to talk to those private guys again.'

'You'll never find them.'

'They'll find me. I never answered their question, about whether Susan gave me anything. I think they'll want to ask it again.'

* * *

We arranged to meet in five hours' time, in the same coffee shop. I watched him get back in his car and then I walked south on Eighth, slowly, like I had nowhere special to go, which I didn't. I was tired from not sleeping much but wired from all the coffee, so overall I figured it was a wash in terms of alertness and energy. And I figured the private guys would be in the same boat. We had all been up all night. Which fact got me thinking about time. Just as two in the morning was the wrong time for a suicide bombing, it was also a weird time for Susan Mark to be heading for a rendezvous and delivering information. So I stood for a spell at the newspaper rack outside a deli and leafed through the tabloids. I found what I was half expecting buried deep inside the *Daily News*. The New Jersey Turnpike had been closed northbound for four hours the previous evening. A tanker wreck, in fog. An acid spill. Multiple fatalities.

I pictured Susan Mark trapped on the road between exits. A four-hour jam. A four-hour delay. Disbelief. Mounting tension. No way forward, no way back. A rock and a hard place. Time, ticking away. A deadline, approaching. A deadline, missed. Threats and sanctions and penalties, now presumed live and operational. The 6 train had seemed fast to me. It must have felt awful slow to her. *You tipped her over the edge*. Maybe so, but she hadn't needed a whole lot of tipping.

I butted the newspapers back into saleable condition and set off strolling again. I figured the guy with the torn jacket would have gone home to change, but the other three would be close by. They would have watched me enter the coffee shop, and they would have picked me up when I came out. I couldn't see them on the street, but I wasn't really looking for them. No point in looking for something when you know for sure it's there.

Back in the day Eighth Avenue had been a dangerous thoroughfare. Broken streetlights, vacant lots, shuttered stores, crack, hookers, muggers. I had seen all kinds of things there. I had never been attacked personally. Which was no big surprise. To make me a potential victim, the world's population would have to be reduced all the way down to two. Me and a mugger, and I would have won. Now Eighth was as safe as anywhere else. It bustled with commercial activity and there were people all over the place. So I didn't care exactly where the three guys approached me. I made no attempt to channel them to a place of my choosing. I just walked. Their call. The day was on its way from warm to hot and sidewalk smells were rising up all around me, like a crude calendar: garbage stinks in the summer and doesn't in the winter.

* * *

They approached me a block south of Madison Square Garden and the big old post office. Construction on a corner lot shunted pedestrians along a narrow fenced-off lane in the gutter. I got a yard into it and one guy stepped ahead of me and one fell in behind and the leader came alongside me. Neat moves. The leader said, 'We're prepared to forget the thing with the coat.'

'That's good,' I said. 'Because I already did.'

'But we need to know if you have something that belongs to us.'

'To you?'

'To our principal.'

'Who are you guys?'

'I gave you our card.'

'And at first I was very impressed by it. It looked like a work of art, arithmetically. There are more than three million possible combinations for a seven-digit phone number. But you didn't choose randomly. You picked one you knew was disconnected. I imagined that's tough to do. So I was impressed. But then I figured in fact that's impossible to do, given Manhattan's population. Someone dies or moves away, their number gets recycled pretty fast. So then I guessed you had access to a list of numbers that never work. Phone companies keep a few, for when a number shows up in the movies or on TV. Can't use real numbers for that, because customers might get harassed. So then I guessed you know people in the movie and TV business. Probably because most of the week you rent out as sidewalk security when there's a show in town. Therefore the closest you get to action is fending off autograph hunters. Which must be a disappointment to guys like you. I'm sure you had something better in mind when you set up in business. And worse, it implies a certain erosion of abilities, through lack of practice. So now I'm even less worried about you than I was before. So all in all I'd say the card was a mistake, in terms of image management.'

The guy said, 'Can we buy you a cup of coffee?'

* * *

I never say no to a cup of coffee, but I was all done with sitting down, so I agreed to go-cups only. We could sip and talk as we walked. We stopped in at the next Starbucks we saw, which as in most cities was half a block away. I ignored the fancy brews and got a tall house blend, black, no room for cream. My standard order, at Starbucks. A fine bean, in my opinion. Not that I really care. It's all about the caffeine for me, not the taste.

We came out and carried on down Eighth. But four people made an awkward group for mobile conversation and the traffic was loud, so we ended up ten yards into the mouth of a cross street, static, with me in the shade, leaning on a railing, and the other three in the sun in front of me and leaning towards me like they had points to make. At our feet a burst garbage bag leaked cheerful sections of the Sunday newspaper on the sidewalk. The guy who did all the talking said, 'You're seriously underestimating us, not that we want to get into a pissing contest.'

'OK,' I said.

'You're ex-military, right?'

'Army,' I said.

'You've still got the look.'

'You too. Special Forces?'

'No. We didn't get that far.'

I smiled. An honest man.

The guy said, 'We got hired as the local end for a temporary operation. The dead woman was carrying an item of value. It's up to us to recover it.'

'What item? What value?'

'Information.'

I said, 'I can't help you.'

'Our principal was expecting digital data, on a computer chip, like a USB flash memory stick. We said no, that's too hard to get out of the Pentagon. We said it would be verbal. Like, read and memorized.'

I said nothing. Thought back to Susan Mark on the train. The mumbling. Maybe she wasn't rehearsing pleas or exculpations or threats or arguments. Maybe she was running through the details she was supposed to deliver, over and over again, so she wouldn't forget them or get them confused in her stress and her panic. Learning by rote. And saying to herself, *I'm obeying, I'm obeying, I'm obeying*. Reassuring herself. Hoping that it would all turn out right.

I asked, 'Who is your principal?'

'We can't say.'

'What was his leverage?'

'We don't know. We don't want to know.'

I sipped my coffee. Said nothing.

The guy said, 'The woman spoke to you on the train.'

'Yes,' I said. 'She did.'

'So now the operational assumption is that whatever she knew, you know.'

'Possible,' I said.

'Our principal is convinced of it. Which gives you a problem. Data on a computer chip, no big deal. We could hit you over the head and turn out your pockets. But something in your head would need to be extracted some other way.'

I said nothing.

The guy said, 'So you really need to tell us what you know.'

'So you'll look competent?'

The guy shook his head. 'So you'll stay whole.'

I took another sip of coffee and the guy said, 'I'm appealing to you, man to man. Soldier to soldier. This is not about us. We go back empty, sure, we'll get fired. But Monday morning we'll be working again, for someone else. But if we're out of the picture, you're exposed. Our principal brought a whole crew. Right now they're on a leash, because they don't fit in here. But if we're gone, they're off the leash. No alternative. And you really don't want them talking to you.'

'I don't want anyone talking to me. Not them, not you. I don't like talking.'

'This is not a joke.'

'You got that right. A woman died.'

'Suicide is not a crime.'

'But whatever drove her to it might be. The woman worked at the Pentagon. That's national security, right there. You need to get out in front of this. You should talk to the NYPD.'

The guy shook his head. 'I'd go to jail before I crossed these people. You hear what I'm saying?'

'I hear you,' I said. 'You've gotten comfortable

with your autograph hunters.'

'We're the kid gloves here. You should take advantage.'

'You're no kind of gloves at all.'

'What were you, in the service?'

'MPs,' I said.

'Then you're a dead man. You never saw anything like this.'

'Who is he?'

The guy just shook his head.

'How many?'

The guy shook his head again.

'Give me something.'

'You're not listening. If I won't talk to the NYPD, why the hell would I talk to you?'

I shrugged and drained my cup and pushed off the railing. Took three steps and tossed the cup into a trash basket. I said, 'Call your principal and tell him he was right and you were wrong. Tell him the woman's information was all on a memory stick, which is right now in my pocket. Then resign by phone and go home and stay the hell out of my way.'

I crossed the street between two moving cars and headed for Eighth. The leader called after me, loud. He said my name. I turned and saw him holding his cell phone at arm's length. It was pointing at me and he was staring at its screen. Then he lowered it and all three guys moved away and a white truck passed between us and they were out of sight before I realized I had been photographed.

SIXTEEN

Radio Shacks are about a tenth as common as Starbucks, but they're never more than a few blocks away. And they open early. I stopped in at the next one I saw and a guy from the Indian subcontinent stepped forward to help me. He seemed keen. Maybe I was the first customer of the day. I asked him about cell phones with cameras. He said practically all of them had cameras. Some of them even had video. I told him I wanted to see how good the still pictures came out. He picked up a random phone and I stood at the back of the store and he snapped me from the register. The resulting image was small and lacked definition. My features were indistinct. But my overall size and shape and posture were captured fairly well. Well enough to be a problem, anyway. Truth is, my face is plain and ordinary. Very forgettable. My guess is most people recognize me by my silhouette, which is not ordinary.

I told the guy I didn't want the phone. He tried to sell me a digital camera instead. It was full of megapixels. It would take a better picture. I said I didn't want a camera, either. But I bought a memory stick from him. A USB device, for computer data. Smallest capacity he had, lowest price. It was for window dressing only, and I didn't want to spend a fortune. It was a tiny thing, in a big package made of tough plastic. I had the guy open it up with scissors. You can ruin your teeth on stuff like that. The stick came with a choice of two soft neoprene sleeves, blue or pink. I used the pink. Susan Mark hadn't looked particularly like a pink type of woman, but people see what they want to see. A pink sleeve equals a woman's property. I put the stick in my pocket next to my toothbrush and thanked the guy for his help and left him to ditch the trash.

* * *

I walked two and a half blocks east on 28th Street. Plenty of people were behind me all the way, but I didn't know any of them, and none of them seemed to know me. I went down into the subway at Broadway and swiped my card. Then I missed the next nine downtown trains. I just sat in the heat on a wooden bench and let them all go. Partly to take a break, partly to kill time until the rest of the city's businesses opened up, and partly to check I hadn't been followed. Nine sets of passengers came and went, and nine times I was all alone on the platform for a second or two. No one showed the slightest interest in me. When I was done with watching for people I started watching for rats instead. I like rats. There are a lot of myths about them. Sightings are rarer than people think. Rats are shy. Visible rats are usually young or sick or starving. They don't bite sleeping babies' faces for the fun of it. They're tempted by traces of food, that's all. Wash your kid's mouth before you put it to bed and it'll be OK. And there are no giant rats as big as cats. All rats are the same size.

I saw no rats at all, and eventually I got restless. I stood up and turned my back on the track and looked at the posters on the wall. One of them was a map of the whole subway system. Two were advertisements for Broadway musicals. One was an official notice prohibiting something called subway surfing. There was a black and white illustration of a guy clamped like a starfish on the outside of a subway car's door. Apparently the older stock on the New York system had toe boards under the doors, designed to bridge part of the gap between the car and the platform, and small rain gutters above the doors, designed to stop dripping water getting in. I knew the new R142As had neither feature. My crazy co-rider had told me so. But with the older cars it was possible to wait on the platform until the doors closed, and then jam your toes on the toe board, and hook your fingertips in the rain gutter, and hug the car, and get carried through the tunnels on the outside. Subway surfing. A lot of fun for some, maybe, but now illegal.

I turned back to the track and got on the tenth train to pull in. It was an R train. It had toe boards and rain gutters. But I rode inside, two stops to the big station at Union Square.

* * *

I came up in the northwest corner of Union Square and headed for a huge bookstore I remembered on 17th Street. Campaigning politicians usually publish biographies ahead of election season, and news magazines are always full of coverage. I could have looked for an internet café instead, but I'm not proficient with the technology and anyway internet cafés are much rarer than they were. Now everyone carries small electronic devices named after fruits or trees.

Internet cafés are going the same way as phone booths, killed by new wireless inventions.

The bookstore had tables at the front of the ground floor. They were piled high with new titles. I found the non-fiction releases and came up empty. History, biography, economics, but no politics. I moved on and found what I wanted on the back side of the second table. Commentary and opinion from the left and the right, plus ghosted candidate autobiographies with shiny jackets and glossy airbrushed photographs. John Sansom's book was about a half-inch thick and was called *Always on a Mission*. I took it with me and rode up on the escalator to the third floor, where the store directory told me the magazines were. I picked out all the news weeklies and carried them with the book to the military history shelves. I spent a moment there with some non-fiction publications and confirmed what I had suspected, which was that the army's Human Resources Command didn't do anything that the Personnel Command hadn't done before it. It was a change of name only. A rebranding. No new functions. Paperwork and records, like always.

Then I sat on a window sill and settled in to read the stuff I had picked up. My back was hot from the sun coming in through the glass, and my front was cold from an air conditioning vent directly above me. I used to feel bad about reading stuff in stores, with no intention to buy. But the stores themselves seem happy enough about it. They even encourage it. Some of them provide armchairs for the purpose. A new business model, apparently. And everyone does it. The store was only just open, but already the whole place looked like a refugee centre. There were people everywhere, sitting or sprawled on the floor, surrounded by piles of merchandise much bigger than mine.

The news weeklies all had campaign reports, squeezed in between advertisements and stories about medical breakthroughs and technology updates. Most of the coverage was top-ticket stuff, but the House and Senate contests got a few lines each. We were four months ahead of the first primaries and fourteen months ahead of the elections themselves, and some candidates were already lame ducks, but Sansom was still solidly in his race. He was polling well throughout his state, he was raising lots of money, his blunt manner was seen as refreshing, and his military background was held to qualify him for just about everything. Although in my opinion that's like saying a sanitation worker could be mayor. Maybe so, maybe not. There's no logic in the assumption. But clearly most journalists liked the guy. And clearly they had him earmarked for bigger things. He was seen as a potential presidential candidate either four or eight years down the line. One writer even hinted he could be airlifted out of his Senate race to become his party's vice-presidential nominee this time around. He was already some kind of a celebrity.

His book cover was stylish. It was made up of his name and the title and two photographs. The larger was a blurred and grainy action picture blown up big enough to form a background to the whole thing. It showed a young man in worn and unbuttoned battledress and full camouflage face paint under a beanie hat. Laid over it was a newer studio portrait of the same guy, many years farther down the road, in a business suit. Sansom, obviously, then and now. His whole pitch, in a single visual.

The recent picture was well lit and perfectly focused and artfully posed and showed him to be a small lean guy, maybe five-nine and a hundred and fifty pounds. A whippet or a terrier rather than a pit bull, full of endurance and wiry stamina, like the best Special Forces soldiers always are. Although the older picture was probably from an earlier time in a regular unit. The Rangers, maybe. In my experience Delta guys of his vintage favoured beards and sunglasses and kaffiyeh scarves pulled down to their throats. Partly because of where they were likely to serve, and partly because they liked to appear disguised and anonymous, which in itself was part necessity and part dramatic fantasy. But probably his campaign manager had selected the photograph himself, accepting the junior unit in exchange for a picture that was recognizable, and recognizably American. Maybe people who looked like weird Palestinian hippies wouldn't go down well in North Carolina.

The stuff inside the cover flap featured his full name and military rank, written out with a degree of formality: Major John T. Sansom, U.S. Army, Retired. Then it said he was the winner of the Distinguished Service Cross, the Distinguished Service Medal, and two Silver Stars. Then it said he had been a successful CEO, of something called Sansom Consulting. Again, his whole pitch, right there. I wondered what the rest of the book was for.

I skimmed it and found it fell into five main

sections: his early life, his time in the service, his subsequent marriage and family, his time in business, and his political vision for the future. The early stuff was conventional for the genre. Hardscrabble local youth, no money, no frills, his mom a pillar of strength, his dad working two jobs to make ends meet. Almost certainly exaggerated. If you take political candidates as a population sample, then the United States is a Third World country. Everyone grows up poor, running water is a luxury, shoes are rare, a square meal is cause for jubilant celebration.

I skipped ahead to where he met his wife and found more of the same platitudes. She was wonderful, their kids were great. End of story. I didn't understand much of the business part. Sansom Consulting had been a bunch of consultants, which made sense, but I couldn't work out exactly what they had done. They had made suggestions, basically, and then bought into the corporations they were advising, and then sold their stakes and gotten rich. Sansom himself had made what he described as a fortune. I wasn't sure how much he meant. I feel pretty good with a couple hundred bucks in my pocket. I suspected Sansom came out with more than that, but he didn't specify how much more. Another four zeros? Five? Six?

I looked at the part about his political vision for the future and didn't find much I hadn't already gleaned from the news magazines. It boiled down to giving the voters everything they wanted. Low taxes, you got it. Public services, have at it. It made no sense to me. But all in all Sansom came across as a decent guy. I felt he would try to do the right thing, as much as any of them can. I felt he was in it for all the right reasons.

There were photographs in the middle of the book. All except one were bland snapshots tracing Sansom's life from the age of three months to the present day. They were the kind of things that I imagine most guys could dig out of a shoebox in the back of a closet. Parents, childhood, schooldays, his service years, his bride-to-be, their kids, business portraits. Normal stuff, probably interchangeable with the pictures in all the other candidate biographies.

But the photograph that was different was bizarre.

SEVENTEEN

The photograph that was different was a news picture I had seen before. It was of an American politician called Donald Rumsfeld, in Baghdad, shaking hands with Saddam Hussein, the Iraqi dictator, back in 1983. Donald Rumsfeld had twice been Secretary of Defense, but at the time of the picture had been a special presidential envoy for Ronald Reagan. He had gone to Baghdad to kiss Saddam's ass and pat him on the back and give him a pair of solid gold spurs as a gift and a symbol of America's everlasting gratitude. Eight years later we had been kicking Saddam's ass, not kissing it. Fifteen years after that, we killed him. Sansom had captioned the picture *Sometimes our friends become our enemies, and sometimes our enemies become our friends*. Political commentary,

I supposed. Or a business homily, although I could find no mention of the actual episode in the text itself.

I turned back to his service career, and prepared to read about it carefully. That was my area of expertise, after all. Sansom joined the army in 1975 and left in 1992. A seventeen-year window, four years longer than mine, by virtue of starting nine years earlier and quitting five years earlier. A good era, basically, compared to most. The Vietnam paroxysm was over, and the new professional all-volunteer army was well established and still well funded. It looked like Sansom had enjoyed it. His narrative was coherent. He described basic training accurately, described Officer Candidate School well, was entertaining about his early infantry service. He was open about being ambitious. He picked up every qualification available to him and moved to the Rangers and then the nascent Delta Force. As usual he dramatized Delta's induction process, the hell weeks, the attrition, the endurance, the exhaustion. As usual he didn't criticize its incompleteness. Delta is full of guys who can stay awake for a week and walk a hundred miles and shoot the balls off a tsetse fly, but it's relatively empty of guys who can do all that and then tell you the difference between a Shiite and a trip to the latrine.

But overall I felt Sansom was pretty honest. Truth is, most Delta missions are aborted before they even start, and most that do start fail. Some guys never see action. Sansom didn't dress it up. He was straightforward about the patchy excitement, and frank about the failures. Above all he didn't mention goatherds, not even once. Most Special Forces after-action reports blame mission failures on itinerant goat tenders. Guys are infiltrated into what they claim are inhospitable and virtually uninhabited regions, and are immediately discovered by local peasants with large herds of goats. Statistically unlikely. Nutritionally unlikely, given the barren terrain. Goats have to eat something. Maybe it was true one time, but since then it has become a code. Much more palliative to say *We were hunkered down and a goatherd stumbled over us* than to say *We screwed up*. But Sansom never mentioned either the ruminant animals or their attendant agricultural personnel, which was a big point in his favour.

In fact, he didn't mention much of anything. Certainly not a whole lot in the success column. There was what must have been fairly routine stuff in West Africa, plus Panama, plus some SCUD hunting in Iraq during the first Gulf War in 1991. Apart from that, nothing. Just a lot of training and standing by, which was always followed by standing down and then more training. His was maybe the first unexaggerated Special Forces memoir that I had ever seen. More than that, even. Not just unexaggerated. It was downplayed. Minimized, and de-emphasized. Dressed down, not up.

Which was interesting.

EIGHTEEN

I took a lot of care getting back to the coffee shop on Eighth. *Our principal brought a whole crew*. And by now they all knew roughly what I looked like. The Radio Shack guy had told me how pictures and video could be phoned through from one person to another. For my part I had no idea what the opposition looked like, but if their principal had been forced to hire guys in nice suits as local camouflage, then his own crew probably looked somewhat different themselves. Otherwise, no point. I saw lots of different-looking people. Maybe a couple hundred thousand. You always do, in New York City. But none of them showed any interest in me. None of them stayed with me. Not that I made it easy. I took the 4 train to Grand Central, walked two circuits through the crowds, took the shuttle to Times Square, walked a long and illogical loop from there to Ninth Avenue, and came on the diner from the west, straight past the 14th Precinct.

Jacob Mark was already inside.

He was in a back booth, cleaned up, hair brushed, wearing dark pants and a white shirt and a navy windbreaker. He could have had *off duty cop* tattooed across his forehead. He looked unhappy but not frightened. I slid in opposite him and sat sideways, so I could watch the street through the windows.

'Did you talk to Peter?' I asked him.

He shook his head.

'But?'

'I think he's OK.'

'You think or you know?'

He didn't answer, because the waitress came by. The same woman from the morning. I was too hungry to be sensitive about whether or not Jake was going to eat. I ordered a big platter, tuna salad with eggs and a bunch of other stuff. Plus coffee to drink. Jake followed my lead and got a grilled cheese sandwich and water.

I said, 'Tell me what happened.'

He said, 'The campus cops helped me out. They were happy to. Peter's a football star. He wasn't home. So they rousted his buddies and got the story. Turns out Peter is away somewhere with a woman.'

'Where?'

'We don't know.'

'What woman?'

'A girl from a bar. Peter and the guys were out four nights ago. The girl was in the place. Peter left with her.'

I said nothing.

Jake said, 'What?'

I asked, 'Who picked up who?'

He nodded. 'This is what makes me feel OK. He did all the work. His buddies said it was a four-hour project. He had to put everything into it. Like a championship game, the guys said. So it wasn't Mata Hari or anything.'

'Description?'

'A total babe. And these are jocks talking, so they mean it. A little older, but not much. Maybe twenty-five or six. You're a college senior, that's an irresistible challenge, right there.'

'Name?'

Jake shook his head. 'The others kept their distance. It's an etiquette thing.'

'Their regular place?'

'On their circuit.'

'Hooker? Decoy?'

'No way. These guys get around. They ain't dumb. They can tell. And Peter did all the work, anyway. Four hours, everything he had ever learned.'

'It would have been over in four minutes if she had wanted it to be.'

Jake nodded again. 'Believe me, I've been through it a hundred times. Any funny business, an hour would have been enough to make it look kosher. Two, tops. Nobody would stretch it to four. So it's OK. More than OK, from Peter's point of view. Four days with a total babe? What were you doing when you were twenty-two?'

'I hear you,' I said. When I was twenty-two I had the same kinds of priorities. Although a four-day relationship would have seemed long to me. Practically like engagement, or marriage.

Jake said, 'But?'

'Susan was delayed four hours on the Turnpike. I'm wondering what kind of a deadline could have passed, to make a mother feel like killing herself.'

'Peter's OK. Don't worry about it. He'll be home soon, weak at the knees but happy.'

I said nothing more. The waitress came by with the food. It looked pretty good, and there was a lot of it. Jake asked, 'Did the private guys find you?'

I nodded and told him the story between forkfuls of tuna.

He said, 'They knew your name? That's not good.'

'Not ideal, no. And they knew I talked to Susan on the train.'

'How?'

'They're ex-cops. They've still got friends on the job. No other explanation.'

'Lee and Docherty?'

'Maybe. Or maybe some day guy who came in and read the file.'

'And they took your picture? That's not good, either.'

'Not ideal,' I said again.

'Any sign of this other crew they were talking about?' he asked.

I checked the window and said, 'So far, nothing.'

'What else?'

'John Sansom isn't exaggerating about his career. He seems to have done nothing very special. And that kind of a claim isn't really worth refuting.'

'Dead end, then.'

'Maybe not,' I said. 'He was a major. That's one automatic promotion plus two on merit. He must have done something they liked. I was a major too. I know how it works.'

'What did you do that they liked?'

'Something they regretted later, probably.'

'Length of service,' Jake said. 'You stick around, you get promoted.'

I shook my head. 'That's not how it works. Plus this guy won three of the top four medals available to him, one of them twice. So he must have done something special. Four somethings, in fact.'

'Everybody gets medals.'

'Not those medals. I got a Silver Star myself, which is pocket change to this guy, and I know for a fact they don't fall out of the box with the breakfast cereal. And I got a Purple Heart, too, which Sansom apparently didn't. He doesn't mention one in his book. And no politician would forget about a wound in action. Not in a million years. But it's relatively unusual to win a gallantry medal without a wound. Normally the two things go hand in hand.'

'So maybe he's bullshitting about the medals.'

I shook my head again. 'Can't be done. Maybe with a combat pip on a Vietnam ribbon, something like that, but these are heavy-duty awards. This guy's got everything except the Medal of Honor.'

'So?'

'So I think he *is* bullshitting about his career, but in reverse. He's leaving stuff out, not putting stuff in.'

'Why would he?'

'Because he was on at least four secret missions, and he still can't talk about them. Which makes them very secret indeed, because the guy is in the middle of an election campaign, and the urge to talk must be huge.'

'What kind of secret missions?'

'Could be anything. Black ops, covert actions, against anybody.'

'So maybe Susan was asked for details.'

'Impossible,' I said. 'Delta's orders and operational logs and after-action reports aren't anywhere near HRC. They're either destroyed or locked up for sixty years at Fort Bragg. No disrespect, but your sister couldn't have gotten within a million miles of them.'

'So how does this help us?'

'It eliminates Sansom's combat career, that's

how. If Sansom is involved at all, it's in some other capacity.'

'Is he involved?'

'Why else would his name have been mentioned?'

'What capacity?'

I put my fork down and drained my cup and said, 'I don't want to stay in here. It's ground zero for this other crew. It's the first place they'll check.'

I left a tip on the table and headed for the register. This time the waitress was pleased. We were in and out in record time.

* * *

Manhattan is both the best and the worst place in the world to be hunted. The best, because it is teeming with people, and every square yard of it has literally hundreds of witnesses all around. The worst, because it is teeming with people, and you have to check each and every one of them, just in case, which is tiring, and frustrating, and fatiguing, and eventually drives you crazy, or makes you lazy. So for the sake of convenience we went back to West 35th and walked the shady side of the street, up and down opposite the row of parked cop cars, which seemed like the safest stretch of sidewalk in the city.

'What capacity?' Jake asked again.

'What did you tell me were the reasons behind the suicides you saw in Jersey?'

'Financial or sexual.'

'And Sansom didn't make his money in the army.'

'You think he was having an affair with Susan?'

'Possible,' I said. 'He could have met her at work. He's the kind of guy who is always in and out of the place. Photo opportunities, stuff like that.'

'He's married.'

'Exactly. And it's election season.'

'I don't see it. Susan wasn't like that. So suppose he wasn't having an affair with her.'

'Then maybe he was having one with another HRC staffer, and Susan was a witness.'

'I still don't see it.'

'Me either,' I said. 'Because I don't see how information would be involved. Information is a big word. An affair is a yes-no answer.'

'Maybe Susan was working with Sansom. Not against him. Maybe Sansom wanted dirt on someone else.'

'Then why would Susan come to New York, instead of D.C. or North Carolina?'

Jake said, 'I don't know.'

'And why would Sansom ask Susan for anything, anyway? He's got a hundred better sources than an HRC clerk he didn't know.'

'So where's the connection?'

'Maybe Sansom had an affair long ago, with someone else, when he was still in the army.'

'He wasn't married then.'

'But there were rules. Maybe he was banging a subordinate. That resonates now, in politics.'

'Did that happen?'

'All the time,' I said.

'To you?'

'As often as possible. Both ways around. Sometimes I was the subordinate.'

'Did you get in trouble?'

'Not then. But there would be questions now, if I was running for office.'

'So you think there are rumours about Sansom, and Susan was asked to confirm them?'

'She couldn't confirm the behaviour. That kind of stuff is in a different set of files. But maybe she could confirm that person A and person B served in the same place at the same time. That's exactly what HRC is good for.'

'So maybe Lila Hoth was in the army with him. Maybe someone is trying to link the two names, for a big scandal.'

'I don't know,' I said. 'It all sounds pretty good. But I've got a local tough guy too scared to talk to the NYPD, and I've got all kinds of dire threats, and I've got a story about some barbarian crew ready to slip the leash. Politics is a dirty business, but is it that bad?'

Jake didn't answer.

I said, 'And we don't know where Peter is.'

'Don't worry about Peter. He's a grown-up. He's a defensive tackle. He's going to the NFL. He's three hundred pounds of muscle. He can take care of himself. Remember the name. Peter Molina. One day you're going to read about him in the paper.'

'But not soon, I hope.'

'Relax.'

I said, 'So what do you want to do now?'

Jake shrugged and stumped around, up and down on the sidewalk, an inarticulate man further stymied by the complexity of his emotions. He stopped, and leaned on a wall, directly across the street from the 14th Precinct's door. He looked at all the parked vehicles, left to right, the Impalas and the Crown Vics, marked and unmarked, and the strange little traffic carts.

'She's dead,' he said. 'Nothing is going to bring her back.'

I didn't speak.

'So I'm going to call the funeral director,' he said.

'And then?'

'Nothing. She shot herself. Knowing the reason won't help. Most of the time you never really know the reason, anyway. Even when you think you do.'

I said, 'I want to know the reason.'

'Why? She was my sister, not yours.'

'You didn't see it happen.'

He said nothing. Just gazed at the parked cars opposite. I saw the vehicle that Theresa Lee had used. It was fourth from the left. One of the unmarked Crown Vics farther along the row was newer than the others. Shinier. It winked in the sun. It was black, with two short thin antennas on the trunk lid, like needles. Federal, I thought. Some big-budget agency with the pick of the litter when it came to transportation choices. And communications devices.

Jake said, 'I'm going to tell her family, and we're going to bury her, and we're going to move on. Life's a bitch and then you die. Maybe there's a reason we don't care how or where or why. Better not to know. No good can come of it. Just more pain. Just something bad about to hit the fan.'

'Your choice,' I said.

He nodded and said nothing more. Just shook my hand and moved away. I saw him walk into a garage on the block west of Ninth, and four minutes later I saw a small green Toyota SUV drive out. It went west with the traffic. I guessed he was heading for the Lincoln Tunnel, and home. I wondered when I would see him again. Between three days and a week, I thought.

I was wrong.

NINETEEN

I was still directly across the street from the 14th Precinct's door when Theresa Lee came out with two guys in blue suits and white button-down shirts. She looked tired. She had caught the call at two in the morning, which put her on the night watch, so she should have quit around seven and been home in bed by eight. She was six hours into overtime. Good for her bank balance, not so good for anything else. She stood in the sunlight and blinked and stretched and then she saw me on the far sidewalk and did a classic double take. She smacked the guy next to her on the elbow and said something and pointed straight at me. I was too far away to hear her words, but her body language screamed *Hey, that's him right there*, with a big exclamation point in the vehemence of her physical gesture.

The guys in the suits automatically checked left for traffic, which told me they were based in town. Odd-numbered streets run east to west, even numbers run west to east. They knew that, in their bones. Therefore they were local. But they were more used to driving than walking, because they didn't check for bicycle messengers coming the wrong way. They just hustled across the street, dodging cars, scrambling, splitting up and coming at me from the left and the right simultaneously, which told me they were field-trained to some degree, and in a hurry. I guessed the Crown Vic with the needle antennas was theirs. I stood in the shade and waited for them. They had black shoes and blue ties and their undershirts showed through at the neck, white under white. The left sides of their suit coats bulged more than the right. Right-handed agents with shoulder holsters. They were late thirties, early forties. In their prime. Not rookies, not out to pasture.

They saw that I wasn't going anywhere, so they slowed up a little and approached me at a fast walk. FBI, I thought, closer to cops than paramilitaries. They didn't show me ID. They just assumed I knew what they were.

'We need to talk to you,' the left-hand guy said.

'I know,' I said.

'How?'

'Because you just ran through traffic to get here.'

'Do you know why?'

'No idea. Unless it's to offer me counselling because of my traumatic experience.'

The guy's mouth set in an impatient scowl, like he was ready to bawl me out for my sarcasm. Then his expression changed a little to a wry smile, and he said, 'OK, here's my counsel. Answer some questions and then forget you were ever on that train.'

'What train?'

The guy started to reply, and then stopped, late to catch on that I was yanking his chain, and embarrassed about looking slow.

I said, 'What questions?'

He asked, 'What's your phone number?'

I said, 'I don't have a phone number.'

'Not even a cell?'

'Especially not even,' I said.

'Really?'

'I'm that guy,' I said. 'Congratulations. You found me.'

'What guy?'

'The only guy in the world who doesn't have a cell phone.'

'Are you Canadian?'

'Why would I be Canadian?'

'The detective told us you speak French.'

'Lots of people speak French. There's a whole country in Europe.'

'Are you French?'

'My mother was.'

'When were you last in Canada?'

'I don't recall. Years ago, probably.'

'You sure?'

'Pretty much.'

'You got any Canadian friends or associates?'

'No.'

The guy went quiet. Theresa Lee was still on the sidewalk outside the 14th Precinct's door. She was standing in the sun and watching us from across the street. The other guy said, 'It was just a suicide on a train. Upsetting, but no big deal. Shit happens. Are we clear?'

I said, 'Are we done?'

'Did she give you anything?'

'No.'

'Are you sure?'

'Completely. Are we done?'

The guy asked, ‘You got plans?’

‘I’m leaving town.’

‘Heading where?’

‘Someplace else.’

The guy nodded. ‘OK, we’re done. Now beat it.’

I stayed where I was. I let them walk away, back to their car. They got in and waited for a gap in the traffic and eased out and drove away. I guessed they would take the West Side Highway all the way downtown, back to their desks.

Theresa Lee was still on the sidewalk.

I crossed the street and threaded between two parked blue and white prowl cars and stepped up on the kerb and stood near her, far enough away to be respectful, close enough to be heard, facing the building so I wouldn’t have the sun in my eyes. I asked, ‘What was that all about?’

She said, ‘They found Susan Mark’s car. It was parked way down in SoHo. It was towed this morning.’

‘And?’

‘They searched it, obviously.’

‘Why obviously? They’re making a lot of fuss about something they claim is no big deal.’

‘They don’t explain their thinking. Not to us, anyway.’

‘What did they find?’

‘A piece of paper, with what they think is a phone number on it. Like a scribbled note. Screwed up, like trash.’

‘What was the number?’

‘It had a 600 area code, which they say is a Canadian cellular service. Some special network. Then a number, then the letter D, like an initial.’

‘Means nothing to me,’ I said.

'Me either. Except I don't think it's a phone number at all. There's no exchange number and then it has one too many digits.'

'If it's a special network maybe it doesn't need an exchange number.'

'It doesn't look right.'

'So what was it?'

She answered me by reaching behind her and pulling a small notebook out of her back pocket. Not official police issue. It had a stiff black board cover and an elastic strap that held it closed. The whole book was slightly curled, like it spent a lot of time in her pocket. She slipped the strap and opened it up and showed me a fawn-coloured page with *600-82219-D* written on it in neat handwriting. Her handwriting, I guessed. Information only, not a facsimile. Not an exact reproduction of a scribbled note.

600-82219-D.

'See anything?' she asked.

I said, 'Maybe Canadian cell phones have more numbers.' I knew that phone companies the world over were worried about running out. Adding an extra digit would increase an area code's capacity by a factor of ten. Thirty million, not three. Although Canada had a small population. A big land mass, but most of it was empty. About thirty-three million people, I thought. Smaller than California. And California got by with regular phone numbers.

Lee said, 'It's not a phone number. It's something else. Like a code or a serial number. Or a file number. Those guys are wasting their time.'

'Maybe it's not connected. Trash in a car, it could be anything.'

'Not my problem.'

I asked, 'Was there luggage in the car?'

'No. Nothing except the usual kind of crap that piles up in a car.'

'So it was supposed to be a quick trip. In and out.'

Lee didn't answer. She yawned and said nothing. She was tired.

I asked, 'Did those guys talk to Susan's brother?'

'I don't know.'

'He seems to want to sweep it all under the rug.'

'Understandable,' Lee said. 'There's always a reason, and it's never very attractive. That's been my experience, anyway.'

'Are you closing the file?'

'It's already closed.'

'You happy with that?'

'Why shouldn't I be?'

'Statistics,' I said. 'Eighty per cent of suicides are men. Suicide is much rarer in the East than the West. And where she did it was weird.'

'But she did it. You saw her. There's no doubt about it. There's no dispute. It wasn't a homicide, cleverly disguised.'

'Maybe she was driven to it. Maybe it was a homicide by proxy.'

'Then all suicides are.'

She glanced up and down the street, wanting to go, too polite to say so. I said, 'Well, it was a pleasure meeting you.'

'You leaving town?'

I nodded. 'I'm going to Washington D.C.'

TWENTY

I took the train from Penn Station. More public transportation. Getting there was tense. Just a three-block walk through the crowds, but I was watching for people checking faces against their cell phone screens, and it seemed like the entire world had some kind of an electronic device out and open. But I arrived intact and bought a ticket with cash.

The train itself was full and very different from the subway. All the passengers faced forward, and they were all hidden behind high-backed chairs. The only people I could see were alongside me. A woman in the seat next to me, and two guys across the aisle. I figured all three of them for lawyers. Not major leaguers. Double- or Triple-A players, probably, senior associates with busy lives. Not suicide bombers, anyway. The two men had fresh shaves and all three of them were irritable, but apart from that nothing rang a bell. Not that the D.C. Amtrak would attract suicide bombers anyway. It was tailor-made for a suitcase bomb instead. At Penn the track is announced at the last minute. The crowd mills around on the concourse and then rushes down and piles on. No security. Identical black roll-ons are stacked on the luggage racks. Easy enough for a guy to get off in Philadelphia and leave his bag behind, and then explode it a little later, by cell phone, as the train pulls into Union Station without him, right in the heart of the capital.

* * *

But we got there OK and I made it out to Delaware Avenue unharmed. D.C. was as hot as New York had been, and damper. The sidewalks ahead of me were dotted with knots of tourists. Family groups, mostly, from far and wide. Dutiful parents, sullen children, all dressed in gaudy shorts and T-shirts, maps in their hands, cameras at the ready. Not that I was either well dressed or a frequent visitor. I had worked in the area from time to time, but always on the left of the river. But I knew where I was going. My destination was unmistakable and right there in front of me. The U.S. Capitol. It had been built to impress. Foreign diplomats were supposed to visit during the fledgling days of the Republic and come away convinced that the new nation was a player. The design had succeeded. Beyond it across Independence Avenue were the House offices. At one time I had a rudimentary grasp of congressional politics. Investigations had sometimes led all the way to committees. I knew that the Rayburn Building was full of bloated old hacks who had been in Washington for ever. I figured a relatively new guy like Sansom would have been given space in the Cannon Building instead. Prestigious, but not top drawer.

The Cannon Building was on Independence and First, crouching opposite the far corner of the Capitol like it was paying homage or mounting a threat. It had all kinds of security at the door. I asked a guy in a uniform if Mr Sansom of North Carolina was inside. The guy checked a list and said yes, he was. I asked if I could messenger a note to his office. The guy said yes, I could. He supplied a pencil and special House notepaper and an envelope. I addressed the envelope to *Major John T. Sansom, U.S. Army, Retired*, and added the date and the time. On the paper I wrote: *Early this morning I saw a woman die with your name on her lips*. Not true, but close enough. I added: *Library of Congress steps in one hour*. I signed it *Major Jack-none-Reacher, U.S. Army, Retired*. There was a box to tick at the bottom. It asked: *Are you my constituent?* I ticked the box. Not strictly true. I didn't live in Sansom's district, but no more so than I didn't live in any of the other 434 districts. And I had served in North Carolina, three separate times. So I felt I was entitled. I sealed the envelope and handed it in and went back outside to wait.

TWENTY-ONE

I walked in the heat on Independence as far as the Air and Space Museum and then about-turned and headed for the library. I sat down on the steps fifty minutes into the hour. The stone was warm. There were men in uniform behind the doors above me, but none of them came out. Threat assessment exercises must have placed the library low on the list.

I waited.

I didn't expect Sansom himself to show. I figured I would get staffers instead. Maybe campaign workers. How old and how many, I couldn't guess. Between one and four, maybe, between post-grad and professional. I was interested to find out. One youngster would show that Sansom wasn't taking my note very seriously. Four senior people would suggest he had sensitivity on the issue. And maybe something to hide.

The sixty minute deadline came and went and I got no staffers and no campaign workers, neither young nor old. Instead I got Sansom's wife, and his head of security. Ten minutes after the hour was up I saw a mismatched couple climb out of a Town Car and pause at the foot of the steps and look around. I recognized the woman from the pictures in Sansom's book. In person she looked exactly like a millionaire's wife should. She had expensive salon hair and good bones and a lot of tone and was probably two inches taller than her husband. Four, in heels. The guy with her looked like a Delta veteran in a suit. He was small, but hard and wiry and tough. The same physical type as Sansom himself, but rougher than Sansom had looked in his photographs. His suit was conservatively tailored out of good material, but he had it all bunched and creased like well-worn battledress.

The two of them stood together and glanced around at the people in the vicinity and eliminated one possibility after another. When I was all that was left I raised a hand in greeting. I didn't stand. I figured they would walk up and stop below me, so if I stood I would be looking about three feet over their heads. Less threatening to stay seated. More conducive to conversation. And more practical, in terms of energy expenditure. I was tired.

They came up towards me, Mrs Sansom in good shoes, taking precise delicate steps, and the Delta guy pacing himself alongside her. They stopped two levels below me and introduced themselves. Mrs Sansom called herself Elspeth, and the guy called himself Browning, and said it was spelled like the automatic rifle, which I guessed was supposed to put it in some kind of a menacing context. He was news to me. He wasn't in Sansom's book. He went on to list his whole pedigree, which started out with military service at Sansom's side, and went on to include civilian service as head of security during Sansom's business years, and then head of security during Sansom's House terms, and was projected to include the same kind of duty during Sansom's Senate terms and beyond. The whole presentation was about loyalty. The wife, and the faithful retainer. I guessed I was supposed to be in no doubt at all about where their interests lay. Overkill, possibly. Although I felt that sending the wife from the get-go was a smart move, politically. Most scandals go sour when a guy is dealing with something his wife doesn't know about. Putting her in the loop from the start was a statement.

She said, 'We've won plenty of elections so far and we're going to win plenty more. People have tried what you're trying a dozen times. They didn't succeed and you won't, either.'

I said, 'I'm not trying anything. And I don't care about who wins elections. A woman died, that's all, and I want to know why.'

'What woman?'

'A Pentagon clerk. She shot herself in the head, last night, on the New York subway.'

Elspeth Sansom glanced at Browning and Browning nodded and said, 'I saw it on line. The

New York Times and the *Washington Post*. It happened too late for the printed papers.'

'A little after two o'clock in the morning,' I said.

Elspeth Sansom looked back at me and asked, 'What was your involvement?'

'Witness,' I said.

'And she mentioned my husband's name?'

'That's something I'll need to discuss with him. Or with the *New York Times* or the *Washington Post*.'

'Is that a threat?' Browning asked.

'I guess it is,' I said. 'What are you going to do about it?'

'Always remember,' he said. 'You don't do what John Sansom has done in his life if you're soft. And I'm not soft either. And neither is Mrs Sansom.'

'Terrific,' I said. 'We've established that none of us is soft. In fact we're all as hard as rocks. Now let's move on. When do I get to see your boss?'

'What were you in the service?'

'The kind of guy even you should have been scared of. Although you probably weren't. Not that it matters. I'm not looking to hurt anyone. Unless someone needs to get hurt, that is.'

Elspeth Sansom said, 'Seven o'clock, this evening.' She named what I guessed was a restaurant, on Dupont Circle. 'My husband will give you five minutes.' Then she looked at me again and said, 'Don't come dressed like that, or you won't get in.'

* * *

They got back in the Town Car and drove away. I

had three hours to kill. I caught a cab to the corner of 18th Street and Mass Avenue and found a store and bought a pair of plain blue pants and a blue checked shirt with a collar. Then I walked on down to a hotel I saw two blocks south on 18th. It was a big place, and quite grand, but big grand places are usually the best for a little off-the-books convenience. I nodded my way past the lobby staff and took an elevator up to a random floor and walked the corridor until I found a maid servicing an empty room. It was past four o'clock in the afternoon. Check-in time was two. Therefore the room was going to stay empty that night. Maybe the next night, too. Big hotels are rarely a hundred per cent full. And big hotels never treat their maids very well. Therefore the woman was happy to take thirty bucks in cash and a thirty-minute break. I guessed she would move on to the next room on her list and come back later.

She hadn't gotten to the bathroom yet, but there were two clean towels still on the rack. Nobody could possibly use all the towels that a big hotel provides. There was a cake of soap still wrapped next to the sink and half a bottle of shampoo in the stall. I brushed my teeth and took a long shower. I dried off and put on my new pants and shirt. I swapped my pocket contents over and left my old garments in the bathroom trash. Thirty bucks for the room. Cheaper than a spa. And faster. I was back on the street inside twenty-eight minutes.

* * *

I walked up to Dupont and spied out the restaurant. Afghan cuisine, outside tables in a front courtyard, inside tables behind a wooden door. It looked like the kind of place that would fill up with power players willing to drop twenty bucks for an appetizer worth twenty cents on the streets of Kabul. I was OK with the food but not with the prices. I figured I would talk to Sansom and then go eat somewhere else.

I walked on P Street west to Rock Creek Park, and clambered down close to the water. I sat on a broad flat stone and listened to the stream below me and the traffic above. Over time the traffic got louder and the water got quieter. When the clock in my head hit five to seven I scrambled back up and headed for the restaurant.

TWENTY-TWO

At seven in the evening D.C. was going dark and all the Dupont establishments had their lights on. The Afghan place had paper lanterns strung out all over the courtyard. The kerb was clogged with limousines. Most of the courtyard tables were already full. But not with Sansom and his party. All I saw were young men in suits and young women in skirts. They were gathered in pairs and trios and quartets, talking, making calls from their cells, reading e-mails on hand-held devices, taking papers from briefcases and stuffing them back. I guessed Sansom was inside, behind the wooden door.

There was a hostess podium close to the sidewalk but before I got to it Browning pushed through a knot of people and stepped in front of me. He nodded towards a black Town Car twenty yards away and said, 'Let's go.'

I said, 'Where? I thought Sansom was here.'

'Think again. He wouldn't eat in a place like this. And we wouldn't let him even if he wanted to. Wrong demographic, too insecure.'

'Then why bring me here?'

'We had to bring you somewhere.' He stood there like it meant absolutely nothing to him whether I went along or walked away. I said, 'So where is he?'

'Close by. He's got a meeting. He can give you five minutes before it starts.'

'OK,' I said. 'Let's go.'

There was a driver sitting in the Town Car. The engine was already running. Browning and I climbed in the back and the driver pulled out and drove most of the way around the circle and then peeled off south and west down New Hampshire Avenue. We passed the Historical Society. As I recalled New Hampshire Avenue there wasn't much ahead of us except for a string of hotels and then George Washington University.

We didn't stop at any of the hotels. We didn't stop at George Washington University. Instead we swept a fast right on to Virginia Avenue and drove a couple hundred yards and pulled into the Watergate. The famous old complex. The scene of the crime. Hotel rooms, apartments, offices, the Potomac dark and slow beyond them. The driver stopped outside an office building. Browning stayed in his seat. He said, 'These are the ground rules. I'll take you up. You'll go in alone. But I'll be right outside the door. Are we clear?'

I nodded. We were clear. We got out. There was

a security guy in a uniform at a desk inside the door, but he paid us no attention. We got in the elevator. Browning hit four. We rode up in silence. We got out of the elevator and walked twenty feet across grey carpet to a door marked *Universal Research*. A bland title and an unremarkable slab of wood. Browning opened it and ushered me inside. I saw a waiting room, medium budget. An unoccupied reception desk, four low leather chairs, inner offices to the left and the right. Browning pointed me left and said, 'Knock and enter. I'll wait for you here.'

I stepped over to the left hand door and knocked and entered.

There were three men waiting for me in the inner office.

None of them was Sansom.

TWENTY-THREE

The room was a plain spare space mostly empty of furniture. The three guys were the three federal agents who had made the trip up to the 14th Precinct in New York City. They didn't seem pleased to see me again. They didn't speak at first. Instead their leader took a small silver object out of his pocket. A voice recorder. Digital. Office equipment, made by Olympus. He pressed a button and there was a short pause and then I heard his voice ask, 'Did she tell you anything?' The words were fuzzy with distortion and clouded by echo, but I recognized them. From the interview, at five o'clock that morning, me in the chair, sleepy, them alert and standing, the smell of sweat and anxiety and burnt coffee in the air.

I heard myself reply, 'Nothing of substance.'

The guy clicked another button and the recorded sound died away. He put the device back in his pocket and pulled a folded sheet of paper from another. I recognized it. It was the House notepaper the Capitol guard had given me at the door of the Cannon Building. The guy unfolded it and read out loud, 'Early this morning I saw a woman die with your name on her lips.' He held the paper out towards me so that I could see my own handwriting.

He said, 'She told you something of substance. You lied to federal investigators. People go to prison for that.'

'But not me,' I said.

'You think? What makes you special?'

'Nothing makes me special. But what makes you federal investigators?'

The guy didn't answer.

I said, 'You can't have it both ways around. You want to play all cloak and dagger and refuse to show ID, then how should I know who you are? Maybe you were NYPD file clerks, showing up early for work, looking to pass the time. And there's no law about lying to civilians. Or your bosses would all be in jail.'

'We told you who we were.'

'People claim all kinds of things.'

'Do we look like file clerks?'

'Pretty much. And maybe I didn't lie to you, anyway. Maybe I lied to Sansom.'

'So which was it?'

'That's my business. I still haven't seen ID.'

'What exactly are you doing here in Washington? With Sansom?'

'That's my business too.'

'You want to ask him questions?'

'You got a law against asking people questions?'

'You were a witness. Now you're investigating?'

'Free country,' I said.

'Sansom can't afford to tell you anything.'

'Maybe so,' I said. 'Maybe not.'

The guy paused a beat and said, 'You like tennis?'

I said, 'No.'

'You heard of Jimmy Connors? Bjorn Borg? John McEnroe?'

I said, 'Tennis players, from way back.'

'What would happen if they played the U.S. Open next year?'

'I have no idea.'

'They would get their asses kicked all over the court. They would get their heads handed to them on a plate. Even the women would beat them. Great champions in their day, but they're old men now and they come from a whole different era. Time moves on. The game changes. You understand what I'm telling you?'

I said, 'No.'

'We've seen your record. You were hot shit back in prehistory. But this is a new world now. You're out of your depth.'

I turned and glanced at the door. 'Is Browning still out there? Or did he dump me?'

'Who is Browning?'

'The guy who delivered me here. Sansom's guy.'

'He's gone. And his name isn't Browning. You're a babe in the woods.'

I said nothing. Just heard the word *babe* and thought about Jacob Mark, and his nephew Peter. *A girl from a bar. A total babe. Peter left with her.*

One of the other two guys in the room said, 'We need you to forget all about being an investigator, OK? We need you to stick to being a witness. We need to know how Sansom's name is linked with the dead woman. You're not going to leave this room until we find out.'

I said, 'I'll leave this room exactly when I decide to. It will take more than three file clerks to keep me somewhere I don't want to be.'

'Big talk.'

I said, 'Sansom's name is already way out there, anyway. I heard it from four private investigators in New York City.'

'Who were they?'

'Four guys in suits with a phony business card.'

'Is that the best you can do? That's a pretty thin story. I think you heard it from Susan Mark herself.'

'Why do you even care? What could an HRC clerk know that would hurt a guy like Sansom?'

Nobody spoke, but the silence was very strange. It seemed to carry in it an unstated answer that spiralled and ballooned crazily upward and outward, like: *It's not just Sansom we're worried about, it's the army, it's the military, it's the past, it's the future, it's the government, it's the country, it's the whole wide world, it's the entire damn universe.*

I asked, 'Who are you guys?'

No answer.

I said, 'What the hell did Sansom do back then?'

'Back when?'

'During his seventeen years.'

'What do you think he did?'

'Four secret missions.'

The room went quiet.

The lead agent asked, 'How do you know about Sansom's missions?'

I said, 'I read his book.'

'They're not in his book.'

'But his promotions and his medals are. With no clear explanation of where else they came from.'

Nobody spoke.

I said, 'Susan Mark didn't know anything. She can't have. It's just not possible. She could have turned HRC upside down for a year without finding the slightest mention.'

'But someone asked her.'

'So what? No harm, no foul.'

'We want to know who it was, that's all. We like to keep track of things like that.'

'I don't know who it was.'

'But clearly you want to know. Otherwise why would you be here?'

'I saw her shoot herself. It wasn't pretty.'

'It never is. But that's no reason to get sentimental. Or in trouble.'

'You worried about me?'

No one answered.

'Or are you worried I'll find something out?'

The third guy said, 'What makes you think the two worries are different? Maybe they're the same thing. You find something out, you'll be locked up for life. Or caught in the crossfire.'

I said nothing. The room went quiet again.

The lead agent said, 'Last chance. Stick to being a witness. Did the woman mention Sansom's name or not?'

'No,' I said. 'She didn't.'

'But his name is out there anyway.'

'Yes,' I said. 'It is.'

'And you don't know who's asking.'

'No,' I said. 'I don't.'

'OK,' the guy said. 'Now forget all about us and move on. We have no desire to complicate your life.'

'But?'

'We will if we have to. Remember the trouble you could make for people, back in the 110th? It's much worse now. A hundred times worse. So do the smart thing. If you want to play, stick to the senior circuit. Stay away from this. The game has changed.'

* * *

They let me go. I went down in the elevator and walked past the guy at the door and stood on a broad paved area and looked at the river flowing slowly by. Reflected lights moved with the current. I thought about Elspeth Sansom. She impressed me. *Don't come dressed like that, or you won't get in*. Perfect misdirection. She had suckered me completely. I had bought a shirt I didn't need or want.

Not soft.

That was for damn sure.

The night was warm. The air was heavy and full of waterborne smells. I headed back towards Dupont Circle. A mile and a quarter, I figured. Twenty minutes on foot, maybe less.

TWENTY-FOUR

Restaurant meals in D.C. rarely run shorter than an hour or longer than two. That had been my experience. So I expected to find Sansom finishing up his entrée or ordering his dessert. Maybe already drinking coffee and thinking about a cigar.

Back at the restaurant about half the courtyard tables had turned over their clientele. There were new boys in suits, and new girls in skirts. More pairs now than threesomes or quartets, and more romance than work. More bright chatter designed to impress, and less scanning of electronic devices. I walked past the hostess station and the woman there called after me and I said, 'I'm with the Congressman.' I pushed through the wooden door and scanned the inside room. It was a low rectangular space full of dim light and spicy smells and loud conversation and occasional laughter.

Sansom wasn't in it.

No sign of him, no sign of his wife, no sign of the guy who had called himself Browning, no pack of eager staffers or campaign volunteers.

I backed out again and the woman at the hostess station looked at me quizzically and asked, 'Who were you joining?'

I said, 'John Sansom.'

'He isn't here.'

'Evidently.'

A kid at a table next to my elbow said, 'North Carolina Fourteenth? He left town. He's got a fundraiser breakfast tomorrow in Greensboro. Banking and insurance, no tobacco. I heard him tell my guy all about it.' His last sentence was directed at the girl opposite him, not at me. Maybe the whole speech was. *My guy*. Clearly the kid was a hell of an important player, or wanted to be.

I stepped back to the sidewalk and stood still for a second and then set out for Greensboro, North Carolina.

* * *

I got there on a late bus that was scheduled to stop first in Richmond, Virginia, and then in Raleigh, and then in Durham, and then in Burlington. I didn't notice the itinerary. I slept all the way. We arrived in Greensboro close to four o'clock in the morning. I walked past bail bond offices and shuttered pawn shops and ignored a couple of greasy spoon eateries until I found the kind of diner I wanted. I wasn't choosing on the basis of food. All diner food tastes the same to me. I was looking for phone books and racks of free local newspapers and it took a long walk to find them. The place I picked was just opening for business. A guy in an undershirt was greasing a griddle. Coffee was dripping into a flask. I hauled the Yellow Pages to a booth and checked H for hotels. Greensboro had plenty. It was a decent-sized place. Maybe a quarter-million people.

I figured a fundraising breakfast would take place in a fairly upscale location. Donors are rich, and they don't go to the Red Roof Inn for five hundred dollars a plate. Not if they work in banking and insurance. I guessed the Hyatt or the Sheraton. Greensboro had both. Fifty-fifty. I closed the Yellow Pages and started leafing through the free papers, looking for confirmation. Free papers carry all kinds of local coverage.

I found a story about the breakfast in the second paper I opened. But I was wrong about the hotels. Not the Hyatt, not the Sheraton. Instead Sansom was fixed up at a place called the O. Henry Hotel, which I guessed was named for the famous North Carolina writer. There was an address given. The event was planned to start at seven in the morning. I tore out the story and folded it small and put it in my pocket. The guy behind the counter finished his preparations and brought me a mug of coffee without asking. I took a sip. Nothing better than a fresh brew in the first minute of its life. Then I ordered the biggest combo on the menu and sat back and watched the guy cook it.

* * *

I took a cab to the O. Henry Hotel. I could have walked, and it took longer to find the cab than to make the drive, but I wanted to arrive in style. I got there at a quarter after six. The hotel was a modern facsimile of a stylish old place. It looked like an independent establishment, but probably wasn't. Few hotels are. The lobby was rich and dim and full of clubby leather armchairs. I walked past them to the reception desk with as much panache and confidence as was possible for a guy in a creased nineteen-dollar shirt. There was a young woman on duty behind the counter. She looked tentative, as if she had just come in and wasn't settled yet. She looked up at me and I said, 'I'm here for the Sansom breakfast.'

The young woman didn't reply. She struggled to

find a reaction, like I was embarrassing her with too much information. I said, 'They were supposed to leave my ticket here.'

'Your ticket?'

'My invitation.'

'Who was?'

'Elspeth,' I said. 'Mrs Sansom, I mean. Or their guy.'

'Which guy?'

'Their security person.'

'Mr Springfield?'

I smiled to myself. Springfield was a manufacturer of autoloader rifles, the same as Browning was. The guy liked word games, which was fun, but dumb. False names work better if they're completely unconnected with reality.

I asked, 'Have you seen them yet this morning?' It was an attempt at finesse. I was guessing Greensboro wasn't in Sansom's own congressional district. A Senate campaign needed state-wide funding and exposure. I figured Sansom's own patch was already sewn up tight, and that by now he would be trawling farther afield. Therefore he had probably stayed in the hotel overnight, to be ready for the early start. But I couldn't be sure. To ask if he had come down from his room yet would make me look like an idiot if he lived five minutes away. To ask if he had arrived yet would make me look just as bad if he lived two hundred miles away. So I aimed for neutrality.

The woman said, 'They're still upstairs, as far as I know.'

I said, 'Thanks,' and walked back into the lobby, away from the elevators, so she wouldn't have anything to worry about. I waited until her phone rang and she started tapping on her keyboard and concentrating on her computer screen, and then I drifted around the edge of the room and hit the up button.

*   *   *

I figured that Sansom would be in a big suite, and that the big suites would all be on the top floor, so I hit the highest number the elevator had to offer. A long moment later I stepped out in a hushed carpeted corridor and saw a uniformed cop standing easy outside a double mahogany door. A patrolman, from the Greensboro PD. Not young. A veteran, with first dibs on some effortless overtime. A token presence. I walked towards him with a rueful smile on my face, like *Hey, you're working, I'm working, what's a guy to do?* I figured he must have processed a few visitors already. Room service coffee, staffers with legitimate reasons to be there, maybe journalists. I nodded to him and said, 'Jack Reacher for Mr Sansom,' and leaned beyond him and knocked on the door. He didn't react. Didn't complain. Just stood there, like the window dressing he was. Whatever Sansom was going to be next, right then he was still only a congressman from the sticks, and he was a long way from getting serious protection.

There was a short delay, and then the suite door opened. Sansom's wife stood there with her hand on the inside handle. She was dressed, coiffed, made up, and ready for the day.

'Hello, Elspeth,' I said. 'Can I come in?'

TWENTY-FIVE

I saw a fast, expert, politician's-wife calculation run behind Elspeth Sansom's eyes. First instinct: throw the bum out. But: there was a cop in the corridor, and probably media in the building, and almost certainly hotel staff within earshot. And local people talk. So she swallowed once and said, 'Major Reacher, how nice to see you again,' and stood back to give me room to pass.

The suite was large and dark because of draped windows and full of heavy furniture in rich and muted colours. There was a living room with a breakfast bar and an open door that must have led to a bedroom. Elspeth Sansom walked me to the middle of the space and stopped, like she didn't know what to do with me next. Then John Sansom stepped out of the bedroom to see what the fuss was all about.

He was in pants and a shirt and a tie and socks. No shoes. He looked small, like a miniature man. Wiry build, narrow through the shoulders. His head was a little large compared to the rest of his body. His hair was cut short and neatly brushed. His skin was tanned, but in a creased, active, outdoors kind of a way. Rugged. No sun lamps for this guy. He glowed with wealth, and power, and energy, and charisma. It was easy to see how he had won plenty of elections. Easy to see why the news weeklies were in love with him. He looked at me and then looked at his wife and asked, 'Where's Springfield?'

Elspeth said, 'He went downstairs to check on

things. They must have passed in the elevators.'

Sansom nodded, not much more than a fast up-and-down with his eyelids. A practised decision maker, and a pragmatic man, not much given to crying over spilled milk. He glanced at me and said, 'You don't give up.'

I said, 'I never have.'

'Didn't you listen to those federal boys in Washington?'

'Who were they, exactly?'

'Those guys? You know how it is. I could tell you, but then I'd have to kill you. But whatever, they were supposed to warn you off.'

'Didn't resonate.'

'They copied me on your record. I told them they'd fail.'

'They talked to me like I was a moron. And they called me too old. Which makes you way too old.'

'I am way too old. For most of this shit, anyway.'

'You got ten minutes?'

'I can give you five.'

'You got coffee?'

'You're wasting time.'

'We've got plenty of time. More than five minutes, anyway. More than ten, even. You need to lace your shoes and put a jacket on. How long can that take?'

Sansom shrugged and stepped over to the breakfast bar and poured me a cup of coffee. He carried it back and gave it to me and said, 'Now cut to the chase. I know who you are and why you're here.'

'Did you know Susan Mark?' I asked him.

He shook his head. 'Never met her, never even heard of her before last night.'

I was watching his eyes, and I believed him. I asked, 'Why would an HRC clerk be coerced into checking you out?'

'Is that what was happening?'

'Best guess.'

'Then I have no idea. HRC is the new PERSCOM, right? What did you ever get from PERSCOM? What did anyone? What have they got there? Dates and units, that's all. And my life is public record anyway. I've been on CNN a hundred times. I joined the army, I went to OCS, I was commissioned, I was promoted three times, and I left. No secrets there.'

'Your Delta missions were secrets.'

The room went a little quieter. Sansom asked, 'How do you know that?'

'You got four good medals. You don't explain why.'

Sansom nodded.

'That damn book,' he said. 'The medals are a matter of record, too. I couldn't disown them. It wouldn't have been respectful. Politics is a minefield. Damned if you do, damned if you don't. Either way around, they can always get to you.'

I said nothing. He looked at me and asked, 'How many people are going to make the connection? Besides you, I mean?'

'About three million,' I said. 'Maybe more. Everyone in the army, and all the vets with enough eyesight left to read. They know how things work.'

He shook his head. 'Not that many. Most people don't have inquiring minds. And even if they do, most people respect secrecy in matters like that. I don't think there's a problem.'

'There's a problem somewhere. Otherwise why

was Susan Mark being asked questions?'

'Did she actually mention my name?'

I shook my head. 'That was to get your attention. I heard your name from a bunch of guys I'm assuming were employed by the person asking the questions.'

'And what's in this for you?'

'Nothing. But she looked like a nice person, caught between a rock and a hard place.'

'And you care?'

'You do, too, if only a little bit. You're not in politics just for what you can get out of it for yourself. At least I sincerely hope you're not.'

'Are you actually my constituent?'

'Not until they elect you President.'

Sansom was quiet for a beat and then he said, 'The FBI briefed me, too. I'm in a position where I can do favours for them, so they make a point of keeping me in the loop. They say the NYPD feels you're reacting to this whole thing with a measure of guilt. Like you pushed too hard on the train. And guilt is never a sound basis for good decisions.'

I said, 'That's just one woman's opinion.'

'Was she wrong?'

I said nothing.

Sansom said, 'I'm not going to tell you a damn thing about the missions.'

I said, 'I don't expect you to.'

'But?'

'How much could come back and bite you in the ass?'

'Nothing in this life is entirely black and white. You know that. But no crimes were committed. And no one could get to the truth through an HRC clerk, anyway. This is a fishing expedition. This is half-baked amateur muck-raking journalism at its worst.'

'I don't think it is,' I said. 'Susan Mark was terrified and her son is missing.'

Sansom glanced at his wife. Back at me. He said, 'We didn't know that.'

'It hasn't been reported. He's a jock at USC. He left a bar with a girl five days ago. Hasn't been seen since. He's presumed AWOL, having the time of his life.'

'And you know this how?'

'Through Susan Mark's brother. The boy's uncle.'

'And you don't buy the story?'

'Too coincidental.'

'Not necessarily. Boys leave bars with girls all the time.'

'You're a parent,' I said. 'What would make you shoot yourself, and what would make you not?'

The room went quieter still. Elspeth Sansom said, 'Shit.' John Sansom got the kind of faraway look in his eyes that I had seen before from good field officers reacting to a tactical setback. Rethink, redeploy, reorganize, all in a fast second or two. I saw him scanning back through history and coming to a firm conclusion. He said, 'I'm sorry about the Mark family's situation. I really am. And I would help if I could, but I can't. There's nothing in my Delta career that could be accessed through HRC. Nothing at all. Either this is about something else entirely, or someone is looking in the wrong place.'

'Where else would they look?'

'You know where. And you know they wouldn't

even get close. And someone who knew enough to want Delta records would know where to look for them, and where not to, surely. So this is not about Special Forces. Can't be.'

'So what else could it be about?'

'Nothing. I'm spotless.'

'Really?'

'Completely. One hundred per cent. I'm not an idiot. I wouldn't have gotten into politics if I had the tiniest thing to hide. Not the way things are now. I never even had a parking ticket.'

'OK,' I said.

'I'm sorry about the woman on the subway.'

'OK,' I said again.

'But now we really have to go. We have some serious begging to do.'

I asked, 'You ever heard the name Lila Hoth?'

'Lila Hoth?' Sansom said. 'No, I never heard that name.'

I was watching his eyes, and I felt he was telling the absolute truth. And lying through his teeth. Both at the same time.

TWENTY-SIX

I passed Springfield on my return trip through the hotel lobby. I was heading for the street door, he was coming out of a dining room. Beyond him I saw round tables with snowy white tablecloths and large floral decorations in their centres. Springfield looked at me with no surprise in his face. It was as if he was judging my performance, and finding it satisfactory. As if I had gotten to his principals in about the span of time he had expected. Not fast, not slow, but right there in the middle of the window he had allowed. He gave me a look of professional appraisal and moved on without a word.

* * *

I went back to New York the same way I had left it, but in reverse. Cab to the Greensboro depot, bus to D.C., and then the train. The trip took all day and some of the evening. The bus schedule and the train schedule were not well integrated, and the first two trains from D.C. were sold out. I spent the travel time thinking, firstly about what Sansom had said, and what he hadn't. *Nothing in this life is entirely black and white. But no crimes were committed. And no one could get to the truth through an HRC clerk, anyway*. No denial of questionable activity. Almost the opposite. Practically a confession. But he felt he hadn't strayed outside the envelope. *No crimes*. And he had absolute confidence that the details were locked away for ever. Altogether a common position, among sharp-end ex-military. *Questionable* was a big word for all of us. Twelve letters, and a textbook's worth of implications. Certainly my own career would not withstand extended scrutiny. I don't lose sleep over it. But in general I'm happy that the details stay locked away. And so was Sansom, clearly. I know my details. But what were his? Something damaging to him, obviously. Either personally, or to his election bid. Or both, inevitably. The feds had made that perfectly clear. *Sansom can't afford to tell you anything.* But damaging in a wider context too, or why else would the feds be involved in the first place?

And who the hell was Lila Hoth?

I asked myself these questions all the way through the jolting bus ride, and all the way through the long layover at Union Station, and then I gave them up when the train I made rolled north through Baltimore. I had gotten nowhere with them, and by then I was thinking about something else, anyway. I was thinking about where exactly in New York City Susan Mark had been headed. She had driven in from the south and had planned to ditch her car and arrive at her destination by subway. Tactically smart, and no other choice, probably. She wouldn't have worn her winter coat in the car. Too hot. She probably had it on the back seat, or more likely in the trunk, with the bag and the gun, where the gun would be safe from prying eyes. Therefore she chose to park, and get out, and get herself battle-ready at a distance and in relative privacy.

But not at too much of a distance. Not too far from her ultimate destination. Because she had been delayed. She was seriously late. Therefore if she was headed way uptown, she would have parked in midtown. But she had parked downtown. In SoHo. Probably joined the train at Spring Street, one stop before I had. She was still sitting tight past 33rd Street. Then things had unravelled. If they hadn't, I figured she would have stayed on the train through Grand Central and gotten out at 51st Street. Maybe 59th. But no farther, surely. Sixty-eighth was a stop too far. Well into the Upper East Side. A whole new neighbourhood. If she was headed all the way up there, she would have used the Lincoln Tunnel, not the Holland, and she would have driven farther north before she parked. Because time was tight for her. So the 59th Street station was her upper limit. But having gotten wherever she was going, I felt she would have aimed to double back, even if just a little. Amateur psychology. Approach from the south, overshoot, come back from the north. And hope her opponents were facing the wrong way.

So I drew a box in my head, 42nd Street to 59th, and Fifth Avenue to Third. Sixty-eight square blocks. Containing what?

About eight million different things.

I stopped counting them well before we hit Philadelphia. By then I was distracted by the girl across the aisle. She was in her middle twenties, and completely spectacular. Maybe a model, maybe an actress, maybe just a great-looking lawyer or lobbyist. A total babe, as a USC jock might say. Which got me thinking about Peter Molina again, and the apparent contradiction in someone expert enough to use him for leverage against a source that was worthless.

* * *

Our principal brought a whole crew. New York City has six main public transportation gateways: Newark, LaGuardia, and JFK airports, plus Penn Station and Grand Central Terminal, plus the Port Authority bus depot. Newark has three terminals, LaGuardia has three plus the shuttle terminal, JFK has eight, Penn Station is big, Grand Central is huge, and the Port Authority is a warren. Total manpower required to make a sensible attempt at surveillance would run close to forty people. Eighty or more, to allow for round-the-clock coverage. And eighty people was an army, not a crew. So I got off the train with no more than normal caution.

Which, fortunately, was enough.

TWENTY-SEVEN

I saw the watcher immediately. He was leaning on a pillar in the centre of the Penn Station concourse, inert, with the kind of complete physical immobility that comes from being settled in for a long period of duty. He was stock-still, and the world was moving busily past him, like a river flows around a rock. He had a clamshell phone in his hand, open, held low down against his thigh. He was a tall guy, but reedy. Young, maybe thirty. At first sight, not impressive. He had pale skin with a shaved head and a dusting of ginger stubble. Not a great look. Scarier than an autograph hunter, maybe, but not by much. He was dressed in a shirt with a floral pattern and over it was a short tight leather jacket that was probably brown, but which looked lurid orange under the lights. He was staring at the oncoming crowd with eyes that had long ago grown tired, and then bored.

The concourse was full of people. I moved with the flow, slowly, hemmed in. I was carried along on the current. The watcher was about thirty feet away, ahead and on my left. His eyes were not moving. He was letting people walk through a fixed field of vision. I was about ten feet away from it. It was going to be like stepping through a metal detector hoop at the airport.

I slowed a little, and someone bumped into my back. I turned briefly, to check that they weren't tag-teaming me. They weren't. The person behind me was a woman with a stroller the size of an SUV, with two babies in it, maybe twins. There are a lot of twins in New York City. Plenty of older mothers, therefore plenty of laboratory fertilization. The twins in the stroller behind me were both crying, maybe because it was late and they were tired, or maybe they were just confused and bewildered by the forest of legs all around them. Their noise blended with the general hubbub. The concourse was tiled and full of echoes.

I drifted left, aiming to move six lateral feet in the next ten forward. I got near the edge of the stream and passed through the watcher's point of focus. His eyes were bright blue, but filmed with fatigue. He didn't react. Not at first. Then after a long second's delay his eyes opened wider and he raised his phone and flicked the lid to light the screen. He glanced at it. Glanced back at me. His mouth opened in surprise. By that point I was about four feet away from him.

Then he fainted. I lunged forward and caught him and lowered him gently to the ground. A Good Samaritan, helping out with a sudden medical emergency. That was what people saw, anyway. But only because people see what they want to see. If they had replayed the brief sequence in their heads and scrutinized it very carefully they might have noticed that I had lunged slightly before the guy had started to fall. They might have noticed that whereas my right hand was certainly moving to catch him by the collar, it was only moving a split second after my left hand had already stabbed him in the solar plexus, very hard, but close in to our bodies, hidden and surreptitious.

But people see what they want to see. They always have, and they always will. I crouched over the guy like the responsible member of the public I was pretending to be, and the woman with the stroller trundled on behind me. After that, a small crowd gathered, full of concern. New York's hostile reputation is undeserved. People are generally very helpful. A woman crouched down next to me. Other people stood close and looked down. I could see their legs and their shoes. The guy in the leather jacket was flat on the floor, twitching with chest spasms and gasping desperately for air. A hard blow to the solar plexus will do that to a person. But so will a heart attack and any number of other medical conditions.

The woman next to me asked, 'What happened?'

I said, 'I don't know. He just keeled over. His eyes rolled up.'

'We should call the ambulance.'

I said, 'I dropped my phone.'

The woman started to fumble in her purse. I said, 'Wait. He might have had an episode. We need to check if he's carrying a card.'

'An episode?'

'An attack. Like a seizure. Like epilepsy, or something.'

'What kind of a card?'

'People carry them. With instructions. We might have to stop him biting his tongue. And maybe he has medication with him. Check his pockets.'

The woman reached out and patted the guy's jacket pockets, on the outside. She had small hands, long fingers, lots of rings. The guy's outside pockets were empty. Nothing there. The woman folded the jacket back and checked inside. I watched, carefully. The shirt was unlike anything I had ever seen. Acrylic, floral, a riot of pastel colours. The jacket was cheap and stiff. Lined with nylon. There was an inside label, quite ornate, with Cyrillic writing on it.

The guy's inside pockets were empty, too.

'Try his pants,' I said. 'Quick.'

The woman said, 'I can't do that.'

So some take-charge executive dropped down next to us and stuck his fingers in the guy's front pants pockets. Nothing there. He used the pocket flaps to roll the guy first one way and then the other, to check the back pockets. Nothing there, either.

Nothing anywhere. No wallet, no ID, no nothing at all.

'OK, we better call the ambulance,' I said. 'Do you see my phone?'

The woman looked around and then burrowed under the guy's arm and came back with the clamshell cell. The lid got moved on the way and the screen lit up. My picture was right there on it, big and obvious. Better quality than I thought it would be. Better than the Radio Shack guy's attempt. The woman glanced at it. I knew people kept pictures on their phones. I've seen them.

Their partners, their dogs, their cats, their kids. Like a home page, or wallpaper. Maybe the woman thought I was a big-time egotist who used a picture of himself. But she handed me the phone anyway. By that time the take-charge executive was already dialling the emergency call. So I backed away and said, 'I'll go find a cop.'

I forced my way into the tide of people again and let it carry me onward, out the door, to the sidewalk, into the dark, and away.

TWENTY-EIGHT

Now I wasn't that guy any more. No longer the only man in the world without a cell phone. I stopped in the hot darkness three blocks away on Seventh Avenue and looked over my prize. It was made by Motorola. Grey plastic, somehow treated and polished to make it look like metal. I fiddled my way through the menus and found no pictures other than my own. It had come out quite well. The cross street west of Eighth, the bright morning sun, me frozen in the act of turning around in response to my shouted name. There was plenty of detail, from head to toe. Clearly huge numbers of megapixels had been involved. I could make out my features fairly well. And I thought I looked pretty good, considering I had hardly slept. There were cars and a dozen bystanders nearby, to give a sense of scale, like the ruler painted on the wall behind a police mug shot. My posture looked exactly like what I see in the mirror. Very characteristic.

I had been nailed but good, photographically.

That was for damn sure.

I went back to the call register menu and checked for calls dialled. There were none recorded. I checked calls received, and found only three, all within the last three hours, all from the same number. I guessed the watcher was supposed to delete information on a regular basis, maybe even after every call, but had gotten lazy about three hours ago, which was certainly consistent with his demeanour and his reaction time. I guessed the number the calls had come in from represented some kind of an organizer or dispatcher. Maybe even the big boss himself. If it had been a cell phone number, it would have been no good to me. No good at all. Cell phones can be anywhere. That's the point of cell phones.

But it wasn't a cell phone number. It was a 212 number.

A Manhattan land line.

Which would have a fixed location. That's the nature of land lines.

The best method of working backward from a phone number depends on how high up the food chain you are. Cops and private eyes have reverse telephone directories. Look up the number, get a name, get an address. The FBI has all kinds of sophisticated databases. The same kind of thing, but more expensive. The CIA probably owns the phone companies.

I don't have any of that stuff. So I take the low-tech approach.

I dial the number and see who answers.

I hit the green button and the phone brought up the number for me. I hit the green button again and the phone started dialling. There was ring tone. It cut off fairly fast and a woman's voice said, 'This is the Four Seasons, and how may I help you?'

I said, 'The hotel?'

'Yes, and how may I direct your call?'

I said, 'I'm sorry, I have the wrong number.'

I clicked off.

The Four Seasons Hotel. I had seen it. I had never been in it. It was a little above my current pay grade. It was on 57th Street between Madison Avenue and Park Avenue. Right there in my sixty-eight square-block box, a little west and a lot north of its geographic centre. But a short walk for someone getting off the 6 train at 59th Street. Hundreds of rooms, hundreds of telephone extensions, all routed out through the main switchboard, all carrying the main switchboard's caller ID.

Helpful, but not very.

I thought for a moment and looked around very carefully and then reversed direction and headed for the 14th Precinct.

* * *

I had no idea what time an NYPD detective would show up for a night watch, but I expected Theresa Lee to be there within about an hour. I expected to have to wait for her in the downstairs lobby. What I didn't expect was to find Jacob Mark already in there ahead of me. He was sitting on an upright chair against a wall and drumming his fingers on his knees. He looked up at me with no surprise at all and said, 'Peter didn't show up for practice.'

TWENTY-NINE

Right there in the precinct lobby Jacob Mark talked for about five straight minutes, with the kind of rambling fluency that is typical of the truly anxious. He said that the USC football people had waited four hours and then called Peter's father, who had called him. He said that for a star senior on a full scholarship to miss practice was completely unthinkable. In fact to make practice no matter what else was going on was a major part of the culture. Earthquakes, riots, wars, deaths in the family, mortal disease, everyone showed up. It emphasized to the world how important football was, and by implication how important the players were to the university. Because jocks were respected by most, but disrespected by some. And there was an unspoken mandate to live up to the majority's ideals and change the minority's minds. Then there were the straightforward machismo issues. To miss practice was like a firefighter declining a turn-out, like a hit-by-pitch batter rubbing his arm, like a gunslinger staying inside the saloon. Unthinkable. Unheard of. Doesn't happen. Hangovers, broken bones, torn muscles, bruises, it didn't matter. You showed up. Plus Peter was going to the NFL, and increasingly pro teams look for character. They've been burned too many times. So missing practice was the same thing as trashing his meal ticket. Inexplicable. Incomprehensible.

I listened without paying close attention. I was counting hours instead. Close to forty-eight since

Susan Mark had missed her deadline. Why hadn't Peter's body been found?

Then Theresa Lee showed up with news.

* * *

But first Lee had to deal with Jacob Mark's situation. She took us up to the second floor squad room and heard him out and asked, 'Has Peter been officially reported missing?'

Jake said, 'I want to do that right now.'

'You can't,' Lee said. 'At least, not to me. He's missing in LA, not in New York.'

'Susan was killed here.'

'She committed suicide here.'

'The USC people don't take missing persons reports. And the LAPD won't take it seriously. They don't understand.'

'Peter's twenty-two years old. It's not like he's a child.'

'He's been missing more than five days.'

'Duration isn't significant. He doesn't live at home. And who is to say he's missing? Who is to say what his normal pattern might be? Presumably he goes for long periods without contact with his family.'

'This is different.'

'What's your policy over there in Jersey?'

Jake didn't answer.

Lee said, 'He's an independent adult. It's like he got on a plane and went on vacation. It's like his friends were at the airport and watched him go. I can see where the LAPD is coming from on this.'

'But he missed football practice. That doesn't happen.'

'It just did, apparently.'

'Susan was being threatened,' Jake said.

'By who?'

Jake looked at me. 'Tell her, Reacher.'

I said, 'Something to do with her job. There was a lot of leverage. Had to be. I think a threat against her son would be consistent.'

'OK,' Lee said. She looked around the squad room and found her partner, Docherty. He was working at one of a pair of twinned desks at the far end of the space. She looked back at Jake and said, 'Go make a full report. Everything you know, and everything you think you know.'

Jake nodded gratefully and headed towards Docherty. I waited until he was gone and asked, 'Are you reopening the file now?'

Lee said, 'No. The file is closed and it's staying closed. Because as it happens there's nothing to worry about. But the guy's a cop and we have to be courteous. And I want him out of the way for an hour.'

'Why is there nothing to worry about?'

So she told me her news.

She said, 'We know why Susan Mark came up here.'

'How?'

'*We* got a missing persons report,' she said. 'Apparently Susan was helping someone with an inquiry, and when she didn't show, the individual concerned got worried and came in to report her missing.'

'What kind of inquiry?'

'Something personal, I think. I wasn't here. The day guys said it all sounded innocent enough. And it must have been, really, or why else come to the police station?'

'And Jacob Mark shouldn't know this why?'

'We need a lot more detail. And getting it will be easier without him there. He's too involved. He's a family member. He'll scream and yell. I've seen it before.'

'Who was the individual concerned?'

'A foreign national briefly here in town for the purpose of conducting the research that Susan was helping with.'

'Wait,' I said. 'Briefly here in town? Staying in a hotel?'

'Yes,' Lee said.

'The Four Seasons?'

'Yes,' Lee said.

'What's his name?'

'It's a her, not a him,' Lee said. 'Her name is Lila Hoth.'

THIRTY

It was very late in the evening but Lee called anyway and Lila Hoth agreed to meet with us at the Four Seasons, right away, no hesitation. We drove over in Lee's unmarked car and parked in the hotel's kerbside loading zone. The lobby was magnificent. All pale sandstone and brass and tan paint and golden marble, suspended halfway between dim intimacy and bright modernism. Lee showed her badge at the desk and the clerk called upstairs and then pointed us towards the elevators. We were headed for another high floor and the way the clerk had spoken made me feel that Lila

Hoth's room wasn't going to be the smallest or the cheapest in the place.

* * *

In fact Lila Hoth's room was another suite. It had a double door, like Sansom's in North Carolina, but no cop outside. Just a quiet empty corridor. There were used room service trays here and there, and some of the doorknobs had Do Not Disturb signs or breakfast orders on them. Theresa Lee paused and double-checked the number and knocked. Nothing happened for a minute. Then the right-hand panel opened and we saw a woman standing inside the doorway, with soft yellow light directly behind her. She was easily sixty, maybe more, short and thick and heavy, with steel-grey hair cut plain and blunt. Dark eyes, lined and hooded. A white slab of a face, meaty, immobile, and bleak. A guarded, unreadable expression. She was wearing an ugly brown house dress made of thick man-made material.

Lee asked, 'Ms Hoth?'

The woman ducked her head and blinked and moved her hands and made a kind of all-purpose apologetic sound. The universal dumb show for not understanding.

I said, 'She doesn't speak English.'

Lee said, 'She spoke English fifteen minutes ago.'

The light behind the woman was coming from a table lamp set deep inside the room. Its glow dimmed briefly as a second figure stepped in front of it and headed our way. Another woman. But much younger. Maybe twenty-five or twenty-six.

Very elegant. And very, very beautiful. Rare, and exotic. Like a model. She smiled a little shyly and said, 'It was me speaking English fifteen minutes ago. I'm Lila Hoth. This is my mother.'

She bent and spoke fast in a foreign language, Eastern European, quietly, more or less straight into the older woman's ear. Explanation, context, inclusion. The older woman brightened and smiled. We introduced ourselves by name. Lila Hoth spoke for her mother. She said her name was Svetlana Hoth. We all shook hands, back and forth, quite formally, crossing wrists, two people on our side and two on theirs. Lila Hoth was stunning. And very natural. She made the girl I had seen on the train look contrived in comparison. She was tall but not too tall, and she was slender but not too slender. She had dark skin, like a perfect beach tan. She had long dark hair. No make-up. Huge, hypnotic eyes, the brightest blue I had ever seen. As if they were lit from within. She moved with a kind of lithe economy. Half the time she looked young and leggy and *gamine*, and half the time she looked all grown up and self-possessed. Half the time she seemed unaware of how good she looked, and half the time she seemed a little bashful about it. She was wearing a simple black cocktail dress that probably came from Paris and cost more than a car. But she didn't need it. She could have been in something stitched together from old potato sacks without diminishing the effect.

We followed her inside and her mother followed us. The suite was made up of three rooms. A living room in the centre, and bedrooms either side. The living room had a full set of furniture, including a dining table. There were the remnants of a room-service supper on it. There were shopping bags in the corners of the room. Two from Bergdorf Goodman, and two from Tiffany. Theresa Lee pulled her badge and Lila Hoth stepped away to a credenza under a mirror and came back with two slim booklets which she handed to her. Their passports. She thought official visitors in New York needed to see papers. The passports were maroon and each had an eagle graphic printed in gold in the centre of the cover and words in Cyrillic above and below it that looked like *NACNOPT YKPAIHA* in English. Lee flipped through them and stepped away and put them back on the credenza.

Then we all sat down. Svetlana Hoth stared straight ahead, blank, excluded by language. Lila Hoth looked at the two of us, carefully, establishing our identities in her mind. A cop from the precinct, and the witness from the train. She ended up looking straight at me, maybe because she thought I had been the more seriously affected by events. I wasn't complaining. I couldn't take my eyes off her.

She said, 'I am so very sorry about what happened to Susan Mark.'

Her voice was low. Her diction was precise. She spoke English very well. A little accented, a little formal. As if she had learned the language from black and white movies, both American and British.

Theresa Lee didn't speak. I said, 'We don't know what happened to Susan Mark. Not really. Beyond the obvious facts, I mean.'

Lila Hoth nodded, courteously, delicately, and a

little contritely. She said, 'You want to understand my involvement.'

'Yes, we do.'

'It's a long story. But let me say at the very beginning that nothing in it could possibly explain the events on the subway train.'

Theresa Lee said, 'So let's hear the story.'

And so we heard it. The first part of it was background information. Purely biographical. Lila Hoth was twenty-six years old. She was Ukrainian. She had been married at the age of eighteen to a Russian. The Russian had been knee-deep in nineties-style Moscow entrepreneurship. He had grabbed oil leases and coal and uranium rights from the crumbling state. He had become a single-figure billionaire. Next step was to become a double-figure billionaire. He didn't make it. It was a tight bottleneck. Everyone wanted to squeeze through, and there wasn't room for everyone to succeed. A rival had shot the Russian in the head, one year ago, outside a nightclub. The body had lain in the snow on the sidewalk all the next day. A message, Moscow style. The newly widowed Lila Hoth had taken the hint and cashed out and moved to London with her mother. She liked London and planned on living there for ever, awash with money but with nothing much to do.

She said, 'There's a presumption that young people who get rich will do things for their parents. You see it all the time with pop stars and movie stars and athletes. And such a thing is a very Ukrainian sentiment. My father died before I was born. My mother is all I have left. So of course, I offered her anything she wanted. Houses, cars, holidays, cruises. She refused them all. All she wanted was a favour. She wanted me to help her track down a man from her past. It was like the dust had settled after a long and turbulent life, and at last she was free to concentrate on what meant most to her.'

I asked, 'Who was the man?'

'An American soldier named John. That was all we knew. At first my mother claimed him only as an acquaintance. But then it emerged that he had been very kind to her, at a particular time and place.'

'Where and when?'

'In Berlin, for a short period in the early eighties.'

'That's vague.'

'It was before I was born. It was in 1983. Privately I thought trying to find the man was a hopeless task. I thought my mother was becoming a silly old woman. But I was happy to go through the motions. And don't worry, she doesn't understand what we're saying.'

Svetlana Hoth smiled and nodded at nothing in particular.

I asked, 'Why was your mother in Berlin?'

'She was with the Red Army,' her daughter said.

'Doing what?'

'She was with an infantry regiment.'

'As what?'

'She was a political commissar. All regiments had one. In fact, all regiments had several.'

I asked, 'So what did you do about tracing the American?'

'My mother was clear that her friend John had been in the army, not the Marines. That was my starting point. So I telephoned from London to your Department of Defense and asked what I should do. After many explanations I was transferred to the Human Resources Command. They have a press office. The man I spoke to was quite touched. He thought it was a sweet story. Possibly he saw a public relations aspect, I don't know. Some good news at last, perhaps, instead of all the bad. He said he would make inquiries. Personally I thought he was wasting his time. John is a very common name. And as I understand it, most American soldiers rotate through Germany, and most visit Berlin. So I thought the pool of possibilities would grow enormous. Which apparently it did. The next thing I knew was weeks later when a clerk called Susan Mark telephoned me. I wasn't home. She left a message. She said she had been assigned the task. She told me that some names that sound like John are actually contractions of Jonathan, spelled without the letter H. She wanted to know if my mother had ever seen the name written down, perhaps on a note. I asked my mother and called Susan Mark back and told her we were sure it was John with the letter H. The conversation with Susan turned out to be very pleasant, and we had many more. We almost became friends, I think, the way you sometimes can on the phone. Like pen-pals, but talking instead of writing. She told me a lot about herself. She was a very lonely woman, and I think our conversations brightened her days.'

Lee asked, 'And then what?'

'Eventually I received news from Susan. She said she had arrived at some preliminary conclusions. I suggested we meet here in New York, almost as a way to consummate our friendship. You know, dinner and maybe a show. As a way of saying thank you for her efforts, certainly. But she never arrived.'

I asked, 'What time were you expecting her?'

'About ten o'clock. She said she would leave after work.'

'Too late for dinner and a show.'

'She planned to stay over. I booked a room for her.'

'When did you get here?'

'Three days ago.'

'How?'

'British Airways from London.'

I said, 'You hired a local crew.'

Lila Hoth nodded.

I asked, 'When?'

'Just before we got here.'

'Why?'

'It's expected,' she said. 'And sometimes useful.'

'Where did you find them?'

'They advertise. In the Moscow papers, and in the expatriate papers in London. It's good business for them, and it's a kind of status check for us. If you go overseas unassisted, you look weak. And it's better not to do that.'

'They told me you brought a crew of your own.'

She looked surprised.

'I don't have a crew of my own,' she said. 'Why on earth would they say that? I don't understand it.'

'They said you brought a bunch of scary types.'

For a second she looked mystified and a little annoyed. Then some kind of comprehension dawned in her face. She seemed to be a fast analyst. She said, 'Perhaps they were inventive, strategically. When Susan didn't arrive, I sent them out looking. I thought, I'm paying them, they might as well do some work. And my mother has a lot of hope invested in this business. So I didn't want to come all this way, and then fail at the last minute. So I offered them a bonus. We grow up believing that money talks loudest, in America. So perhaps those men were making up a story for you. Perhaps they were inventing a scary alternative. To make sure they got their extra money. So that you would be tempted to talk to them.'

I said nothing.

Then something else dawned in her face. Some new realization. She said, 'I have no crew, as you call it. Just one man. Leonid, one of my husband's old team. He couldn't get a new job. He's a bit of a lame duck, I'm afraid. So I kept him on. Right now he's at Penn Station. He's waiting for you. The police told me that the witness had gone to Washington. I assumed you would take the train, and come back the same way. Did you not?'

I said, 'Yes, I came back on the train.'

'Then Leonid must have missed you. He had your picture. He was supposed to ask you to telephone me. Poor man, he must still be there.'

She stood up and headed for the credenza. For the room phone. Which gave me a temporary tactical problem. Because Leonid's cell was in my pocket.

THIRTY-ONE

In principle I know how to turn off a cell phone. I have seen it done, and I have done it myself on more than one occasion. On most models you hold down the red button for two long seconds. But the phone was in my pocket. No room to open it, and no chance of finding the red button by feel alone. Too suspicious to take it out and turn it off in full view of everyone.

Lila Hoth hit nine for a line and dialled.

I put my hand in my pocket and used my thumbnail and found the catch and unlatched the battery. Separated it from the phone and turned it sideways to avoid any chance of accidental electrical contact.

Lila Hoth waited, and then she sighed and hung up.

'He's hopeless,' she said. 'But very loyal.'

I tried to track Leonid's likely progress in my head. Cops, paramedics, probably an obligatory trip to the St Vincent's emergency room, no ID, possibly no English, maybe worries and questions and detention. Then the trip back uptown.

How long of a detention, I didn't know.

How fast of a trip, I couldn't predict.

I said, 'The local crew mentioned John Sansom's name.'

Lila Hoth sighed again and shook her head in a tiny display of exasperation. She said, 'I briefed them when we arrived, obviously. I told them the story. And we all got along quite well. I think all of us felt that we were wasting our time, humouring my mother. We shared jokes about it, frankly. One of the men was reading the newspaper about Sansom. He said, here's an American soldier called John, of roughly the right vintage. He said, maybe Sansom is the guy you're looking for. For a day or two it became a kind of catchphrase. An in-joke, I suppose. We would say, let's just call John Sansom and have done with it. I was really only joking, of course, because what are the chances? A million to one, perhaps. And they were joking too, really, but later they became somehow quite earnest about it. Perhaps because of the impact it would have, because he is such a famous politician.'

'What impact? What did your mother do with this guy called John?'

Svetlana Hoth stared on into space, uncomprehending. Lila Hoth sat down again. She said, 'My mother has never spoken in detail about it. Certainly it can't have been espionage. My mother was not a traitor. I say that not as a loyal daughter, but as a realist. She is still alive. Therefore she was never suspected. And her American friend was not a traitor, either. Liaising with foreign traitors was a KGB function, not army. And personally I doubt that her interest was romantic. It was more likely aid of some sort, personal help, either financial or political. Possibly covert. Those were bad times for the Soviet Union. But possibly it was romantic. All she has ever said is that the man was very kind to her. She plays her cards close to her chest.'

'Ask her again, now.'

'I have asked her many times, as you can imagine. She's reluctant to say.'

'But you think Sansom isn't actually involved?'

'No, not at all. That was a joke that got out of hand. That's all. Unless, of course, it really is a million to one thing. Which would be extraordinary, don't you think? To joke about something and have it turn out to be true?'

I said nothing.

Lila Hoth said, 'Now may I ask you a question? Did Susan Mark give you the information intended for my mother?'

Svetlana Hoth smiled and nodded again. I began to suspect she recognized the words *my mother*. Like a dog that wags its tail when it hears its name. I said, 'Why would you think Susan Mark gave me information?'

'Because the people I hired here told me you told them that she had. Computerized, on a USB memory stick. They gave me that message, and transmitted your photograph, and resigned their commission. I'm not sure why. I was paying them very well.'

I moved in my chair and stuck my hand in my pocket. Scrabbled down past the disassembled phone and found the Radio Shack stick. I felt the soft pink neoprene sleeve against my fingernails. I pulled it out and held it up and watched Lila Hoth's eyes very carefully.

She looked at the stick the way a cat looks at a bird.

She asked, 'Is that really it?'

Theresa Lee moved in her chair and looked at me. Like she was asking, *Are you going to say it, or am I?* Lila Hoth caught the glance and asked, 'What?'

I said, 'The whole thing looked very different to

me, I'm afraid. Susan Mark was terrified on the train. She was in big trouble. She didn't look like a person coming to town to meet a friend for dinner and a show.'

Lila Hoth said, 'I told you at the beginning, I can't explain that.'

I put the memory stick back in my pocket. Said, 'Susan didn't bring an overnight bag.'

'I can't explain it.'

'And she dumped her car and approached by subway. Which is weird. If you were prepared to book a room for her, I'm sure you would have sprung for valet parking.'

'Sprung?'

'Paid for.'

'Of course.'

'And she was carrying a loaded gun.'

'She lived in Virginia. I heard it's compulsory there.'

'It's legal there,' I said. 'Not compulsory.'

'I can't explain it. I'm sorry.'

'And her son is missing. Last seen leaving a bar, with a woman of your age and roughly your description.'

'Missing?'

'Disappeared.'

'A woman of my description?'

'A total babe.'

'What does that mean?'

'A good-looking young woman.'

'What bar?'

'Somewhere in LA.'

'Los Angeles?'

'In California.'

'I haven't been to Los Angeles. Never in my life.

I have only been in New York.'

I said nothing.

She said, 'Look around you. I have been here in New York three days on a tourist visa and I occupy three rooms in a commercial hotel. I have no crew, as you call it. I have never been to California.'

I said nothing.

She said, 'Looks are subjective. And I'm not the only woman my age. There are six billion people in the world. Trending young, for sure. Half of them are fifteen or younger. Which means there are still three billion people sixteen or older. Following the curve, perhaps twelve per cent of them are in their middle twenties. That's three hundred and sixty million people. About half are women. That's a hundred and eighty million. Even if only one in a hundred of them might be judged good-looking, in a bar in California, then it's still ten times more likely that John Sansom was my mother's friend than I had anything to do with Susan Mark's son.'

I nodded. Arithmetically, Lila Hoth was right on the money. She said, 'And it's probably true that Peter is away somewhere with a girl, anyway. Yes, I know his name. In fact I know all about him. Susan told me. On the phone. We talked about all our problems. She hated her son. She despised what he is. He is everything she disliked. He is just a shallow fraternity boy with immature attitudes. He rejected her in favour of his father. And do you know why? Because he was obsessed with his ancestry. And Susan was adopted. Did you even know that? Her son thought of her only as a person conceived out of wedlock. He hated her for it. I know more about Susan than anybody. I talked to her many times. I listened to her. She was a lonely, isolated woman. I was her friend. She was excited to come here and meet me.'

*   *   *

At that point I sensed that Theresa Lee needed to get going and I certainly wanted to be out of there before young Leonid showed up again. So I nodded and shrugged as if I had nothing more to say and no further issues to pursue. Lila Hoth asked if I would give her the stick that Susan Mark had given to me. I didn't say yes and I didn't say no. I didn't answer at all. We just shook hands all around once more, and then we made an exit. The door closed behind us and we walked through the silent corridor and the elevator chimed open. We stepped in and we looked at each other in the mirrored walls and Lee said, 'Well, what did you think?'

'I thought she was beautiful,' I said. 'One of the most beautiful women I have ever seen.'

'Apart from that.'

'Amazing eyes.'

'Apart from her eyes.'

'I thought she was lonely too. Lonely and isolated. She was talking about Susan, but she could have been talking about herself.'

'What about her story?'

'Do good-looking people automatically get more credibility?'

'Not from me, pal. And get over it, anyway. Thirty years from now she'll look just like her mother. Did you believe her?'

'Did you?'

Lee nodded. 'I believed her. Because a story

like that is ridiculously easy to check. Only a fool would give us so many chances to prove her wrong. Like, does the army really have press officers?'

'Hundreds of them.'

'So all we have to do is find the one she spoke to, and ask. We could even track the phone calls from London. I could liaise with Scotland Yard. I'd love to do that. Can you imagine? Docherty interrupts me, I say, butt out, pal, I'm on the phone with Scotland Yard here. It's every detective's dream.'

'NSA will have the calls,' I said. 'A foreign number into the DoD? They're already part of an intelligence analysis somewhere.'

'And we could track Susan Mark's calls out of the Pentagon. If they talked as often as Lila claimed, we'd see them easily. International to the UK, they're probably flagged up separately.'

'So go for it. Check.'

'I guess I will,' she said. 'And she must know I could. She struck me as an intelligent woman. She knows British Airways and Homeland Security can track her in and out of the country. She knows we can tell if she ever flew to LA. She knows we can just go ahead and ask Jacob Mark whether his sister was adopted. It's all so easy to confirm. It would be crazy to lie about stuff like that. Plus she came in to the precinct house and involved herself voluntarily. And she just showed me her passport. Which is the exact opposite of suspicious behaviour. Those are big points in her favour.'

I took the cell phone from my pocket and reassembled the battery. I hit the on switch and the screen lit up. It was showing a missed call. Lila Hoth, presumably, from her room, ten minutes ago. I saw Lee looking at the phone and I said, 'It's Leonid's. I took it from him.'

'He actually found you?'

'I found him. Which is why I had gotten as far as this hotel.'

'Where is he now?'

'Walking home from St Vincent's Hospital, probably.'

'Is this something you really want to be telling to an NYPD detective?'

'He fainted. I helped. That's all. Talk to the witnesses.'

'Whatever, it's going to put the cat among the pigeons with Lila.'

'She thinks gun ownership is compulsory in Virginia. She probably thinks mugging is compulsory in New York. She grew up with propaganda.'

We got out of the elevator in the lobby and headed for the street door. Lee asked, 'But if all of this is so innocent, why are there feds involved?'

'If the story is true, then an American soldier met with a Red Army political commissar back during the Cold War. The feds want to be absolutely sure it's innocent. That's why HRC's response was delayed by weeks. They were taking policy decisions and putting surveillance in place.'

We got into Lee's car. She said, 'You aren't agreeing with me all the way, are you?'

I said, 'If the Hoth family business is innocent, so be it. But something wasn't innocent. That's for damn sure. And we're saying that other something brought Susan Mark to the exact same place at the exact same time. Which is a hell of a coincidence.'

'And?'

'How many times have you known a million-to-one chance turn out a winner?'

'Never.'

'Me either. But I think it's happening here. John Sansom is a million to one against, but I think he's involved.'

'Why?'

'I spoke to him.'

'In Washington?'

'Actually I had to follow him to North Carolina.'

'You don't give up, do you?'

'That's what he said. Then I asked him if he had heard the name Lila Hoth. He said no. I was watching his face. I believed him, and I thought he was lying, too. Both at the same time. And maybe he was.'

'How?'

'Maybe he had heard the name Hoth, but not Lila. So technically, no, he hadn't heard the name Lila Hoth. But maybe he had heard the name Svetlana Hoth. Maybe he was very familiar with it.'

'What would that mean?'

'Maybe more than we think. Because if Lila Hoth is telling the truth, then there's a kind of weird logic working here. Why would Susan Mark bust a gut on a case like this?'

'She had sympathy.'

'Why would she in particular?'

'I don't know.'

'Because she was adopted. Born out of wedlock, presumably wondering about her real folks from time to time. Sympathetic to other people in the same situation. Like Lila Hoth, maybe. Some guy was very kind to her mother before she was born? There are a lot of ways to interpret a phrase like that.'

'For example?'

'Best case, he gave her a warm coat in winter.'

'And worst case?'

'Maybe John Sansom is Lila Hoth's father.'

THIRTY-TWO

Lee and I went straight back to the precinct. Jacob Mark had finished his business with Docherty. That was clear. And something had changed. That was clear too. They were sitting opposite each other across Docherty's desk. Not talking any more. Jake looked happier. Docherty had a patient expression on his face, like he had just wasted an hour. He didn't look resentful about it. Cops are accustomed to wasting time. Statistically most of what they do leads nowhere. Lee and I walked over to them and Jake said, 'Peter called his coach.'

I asked, 'When?'

'Two hours ago. The coach called Molina and Molina called me.'

'So where is he?'

'He didn't say. He had to leave a message. His coach never answers his phone over dinner. Family time.'

'But Peter's OK?'

'He said he won't be back anytime soon. Maybe ever. He's thinking about quitting football. There was a girl giggling in the background.'

Docherty said, 'She must be some girl.'

I asked Jake, 'You OK with that?'

Jake said, 'Hell no. But it's his life. And he'll change his mind, anyway. The only question is how fast.'

'I meant, are you happy that the message was for real?'

'The coach knows his voice. Better than I do, probably.'

'Anyone try calling him back?'

'All of us. But his phone is off again.'

Theresa Lee said, 'So we're satisfied?'

'I guess.'

'Feeling better?'

'Relieved.'

'May I ask you a question about another subject?'

'Shoot.'

'Was your sister adopted?'

Jake paused. Switched gears. Nodded. 'We both were. As babies. Separately, three years apart. Susan first.' Then he asked, 'Why?'

Lee said, 'I'm corroborating some new information received.'

'What new information?'

'It seems that Susan came up here to meet a friend.'

'What friend?'

'A Ukrainian woman called Lila Hoth.'

Jake glanced at me. 'We've been through this. I never heard that name from Susan.'

Lee asked him, 'Would you expect to? How close were you? It seems to be a fairly recent friendship.'

'We weren't very close.'

'When was the last time you talked?'

'A few months, I guess.'

'So you're not completely up to date with her social life.'

Jake said, 'I guess not.'

Lee asked, 'How many people knew that Susan was adopted?'

'I guess she didn't advertise it. But it wasn't a secret.'

'How fast would a new friend find out?'

'Fast enough, probably. Friends talk about stuff like that.'

'How would you describe Susan's relationship with her son?'

'What kind of question is that?'

'An important one.'

Jake hesitated. He clammed up and turned away, physically, like he was literally dodging the issue. Like he was flinching from a blow. Maybe because he was reluctant to wash dirty linen in public, in which case his body language was really all the answer we needed. But Theresa Lee wanted chapter and verse. She said, 'Talk to me, Jake. Cop to cop. This is something I need to know about.'

Jake was quiet for a spell. Then he shrugged and said, 'I guess you could call it a love-hate relationship.'

'In what way exactly?'

'Susan loved Peter, Peter hated her.'

'Why?'

More hesitation. Another shrug. 'It's complicated.'

'How?'

'Peter went through a phase, like most kids do. Like girls want to be long-lost princesses, or boys want their grandfathers to have been admirals or generals or famous explorers. For a spell everyone wants to be something they're not. Peter wanted to live in a Ralph Lauren advertisement, basically. He wanted to be Peter Molina the Fourth, or at least the Third. He wanted his father to have an estate in Kennebunkport, and his mother to have the remnants of an old fortune. Susan didn't handle it well. She was the daughter of a drug-addicted teenage whore from Baltimore, and she made no secret of it. She thought honesty was the best policy. Peter handled it badly. They never really got past it, and then the divorce came, and Peter chose up sides, and they never got over it.'

'How did you feel about it?'

'I could see both points of view. I never inquired about my real mother. I didn't want to know. But I went through a spell where I wished she was a grand old lady with diamonds. I got over it. But Peter didn't, which is stupid, I know, but understandable.'

'Did Susan like Peter as a person, as opposed to loving him as a son?'

Jake shook his head. 'No. Which made things even worse. Susan had no sympathy for jocks and letter jackets and all that stuff. I guess in school and college she had bad experiences with people like that. She didn't like that her son was turning into one of them. But that stuff was important to Peter, in its own right at first, and then later as a weapon against her. It was a dysfunctional family, no question.'

'Who knows this story?'

'You mean, would a friend know?'

Lee nodded.

Jake said, 'A close friend might.'

'A close friend she met quite recently?'

'There's no timetable. It's about trust, isn't it?'

I said, 'You told me Susan wasn't an unhappy person.'

Jake said, 'And she wasn't. I know that sounds weird. But adopted people have a different view of family. They have different expectations. Believe me, I know. Susan was at peace with it. It was a fact of life, that's all.'

'Was she lonely?'

'I'm sure she was.'

'Did she feel isolated?'

'I'm sure she did.'

'Did she like to talk on the phone?'

'Most women do.'

Lee asked him, 'Have you got kids?'

Jake shook his head again.

'No,' he said. 'I don't have kids. I'm not even married. I tried to learn from my big sister's experience.'

Lee stayed quiet for a spell and then she said, 'Thanks, Jake. I'm happy that Peter's OK. And I'm sorry I had to bring all that bad stuff up.' Then she walked away and I followed her and she said, 'I'll check the other things too, but it will take time, because those channels are always slow, but right now my guess is that Lila Hoth will pan out just fine. She's two for two so far, on the adoption thing and the mother-son thing. She knows stuff only a genuine friend would know.'

I nodded agreement. 'You interested in the other thing? Whatever it was that got Susan so scared?'

'Not until I see actual evidence of a crime committed in New York City, somewhere between Ninth Avenue and Park, and 30th Street and 45th.'

'That's this precinct?'

She nodded. 'Anything else would be volunteer work.'

'You interested in Sansom?'

'Not even a little bit. Are you?'

'I feel like I should warn him, maybe.'

'About what? A million-to-one possibility?'

'It's actually much shorter odds than a million to one. There are five million men called John in America. Second only to James, for popularity. That's one in thirty guys. Which means that in 1983 there could have been about thirty-three thousand Johns in the U.S. Army. Discount it maybe ten per cent for military demographics, the chances are about one in thirty thousand.'

'Those are still very big odds.'

'I think Sansom should know, that's all.'

'Why?'

'Call it a brother officer thing. Maybe I'll head back to D.C.'

'No need. Save yourself the trip. He's coming here. Tomorrow midday, for a fundraiser lunch at the Sheraton. With all the heavy hitters from Wall Street. Seventh Avenue and 52nd Street. We got a memo.'

'Why? He wasn't getting much protection in Greensboro.'

'He isn't getting much protection here either. In fact he isn't getting any. But we get memos about everything. That's how it is now. That's the new NYPD.' Then she walked away, leaving me all alone in the middle of the empty squad room. And leaving me feeling a little uneasy. Maybe Lila Hoth really was as pure as the driven snow, but I couldn't shake the sensation that Sansom was walking into a trap, just by coming to the city.

THIRTY-THREE

It has been a long time since you could sleep well in New York for five dollars a night, but you can still do it for fifty, if you know how. The key is starting late. I walked down to a hotel I had used before, near Madison Square Garden. It was a big place, once grand, now just a faded old pile, perpetually close to renovation or demolition but never actually getting there. After midnight the front-of-house staff shrinks down to a lone night porter responsible for everything including the desk. I walked up to him and asked if he had a room available. He made a show of tapping on a keyboard and looking at a screen and then he said yes, he did have a room available. He quoted a price of a hundred and eighty-five dollars, plus tax. I asked if I could see the room before I committed. It was the kind of hotel where that kind of request seemed reasonable. And sensible. Mandatory, even. The guy came out from behind the desk and took me up in the elevator and along a corridor. He opened a door with a pass card attached to his belt by a curly plastic cord and stood back to let me enter.

The room was OK. It had a bed in it, and a bathroom. Everything I needed, and nothing I didn't. I took two twenties out of my pocket and said, 'Suppose we don't worry about that whole registration process downstairs?'

The guy said nothing. They never do, at that

point. I took out another ten and said, 'For the maid, tomorrow.'

The guy shuffled a little like I was putting him on the spot, but then his hand came out and he took the money. He said, 'Be out by eight,' and he walked away. The door closed behind him. Maybe a central computer would show that his pass card had unlocked the room, and when, but he would claim that he had shown me the accommodations, and that I had been unmoved by their attractions, and that I had left again immediately. It was probably a claim he made on a regular basis. I was probably the fourth guy he had stowed away that week. Maybe the fifth, or the sixth. All kinds of things happen in city hotels, after the day staff has quit.

* * *

I slept well and woke up feeling good and I was out five minutes before eight. I forced my way through the crowds heading in and out of Penn Station and got breakfast in the back booth of a place on 33rd. Coffee, eggs, bacon, pancakes, and more coffee, all for six bucks, plus tax, plus tip. More expensive than North Carolina, but only slightly. The battery on Leonid's cell was still about half charged. An icon was showing some bars blank and some bars lit. I figured I had enough juice for a few calls. I dialled 600 and then aimed to dial 82219 but before I got halfway through the sequence the earpiece started up with a fast little triplet trill pitched somewhere between a siren and a xylophone. A voice came on and told me my call could not be completed as dialled. It asked me to check and try again. I tried 1-600 and got exactly the same result. I tried 011 for an international line, and then 1 for North America, and then 600. A circuitous route, but the outcome was no better. I tried 001 as the international code in case the phone thought it was still in London. No result. I tried 8**101, which was the Eastern European international code for America, in case the phone had been hauled all the way from Moscow a year ago. No result. I looked at the phone's keypad and thought about using a 3 in place of the D, but the system was already beeping at me well before I got there.

So, 600-82219-D was not a phone number, Canadian or otherwise. Which the FBI must have known. Maybe they had considered the possibility for about a minute, and then dismissed it out of hand. The FBI is a lot of things, but dumb isn't one of them. So back on 35th Street they had buried their real questions for me behind a smokescreen.

What else had they asked me?

They had gauged my level of interest, they had asked yet again if Susan had given me anything, and they had confirmed that I was leaving town. They had wanted me incurious, and empty-handed, and gone.

Why?

I had no idea.

And what exactly was 600-82219-D, if it wasn't a phone number?

I sat another ten minutes with a final cup of coffee, sipping slowly, eyes open but not seeing much, trying to sneak up on the answer from below. Like Susan Mark had planned to sneak up out of the subway. I visualized the numbers in my mind, strung out, separately, together, different combinations, spaces, hyphens, groups.

The 600 part rang a faint bell.

Susan Mark.

600.

But I couldn't get it.

I finished my coffee and put Leonid's cell back in my pocket and headed north towards the Sheraton.

* * *

The hotel was a huge glass pillar with a plasma screen in the lobby that listed all the day's events. The main ballroom was booked for lunch by a group calling itself FT. Fair Tax, or Free Trade, or maybe even the *Financial Times* itself. Plausible cover for a bunch of Wall Street fat cats looking to buy yet more influence. Their affair was due to start at noon. I figured Sansom would try to arrive by eleven. He would want some time and space and calm beforehand, to prepare. This was a big meeting for him. These were his people, and they had deep pockets. He would need sixty minutes, minimum. Which gave me two more hours to kill. I walked over to Broadway and found a clothing store two blocks north. I wanted another new shirt. I didn't like the one I was in. It was a symbol of defeat. *Don't come dressed like that, or you won't get in*. If I was going to see Elspeth Sansom again I didn't want to be wearing a badge of my failure and her success.

I chose an insubstantial thing made from thin khaki poplin and paid eleven bucks for it. Cheap, and it should have been. It had no pockets and the sleeves ended halfway down my forearms. With the cuffs folded back they hit my elbows. But I liked it well enough. It was a satisfactory garment. And it was purchased voluntarily, at least.

By ten thirty I was back in the Sheraton's lobby. I sat in a chair with people all around me. They had suitcases. Half of them were heading out, waiting for cars. Half of them were heading in, waiting for rooms.

By ten forty I had figured out what 600-82219-D meant.

THIRTY-FOUR

I got up out of my chair and followed engraved brass signs to the Sheraton's business centre. I couldn't get in. You needed a room key. I hung around at the door for three minutes and then another guy showed up. He was in a suit and he looked impatient. I put on a big display of hunting through my pants pockets and then I stepped aside with an apology. The other guy pushed ahead of me and used his key and opened the door and I stepped in after him.

There were four identical work stations in the room. Each had a desk, a chair, a computer, and a printer. I sat down far from the other guy and killed the computer's screen saver by tapping on the keyboard's space bar. So far, so good. I checked the screen icons and couldn't make much sense of them. But I found that if I held the mouse pointer over them, as if hesitating or ruminating, then a label popped up next to them. I identified the Internet Explorer application that way and clicked on it twice. The hard drive chattered and the browser opened up. Much faster than the last time I had used a computer. Maybe technology really was moving on. Right there on the home page was a shortcut to Google. I clicked on it, and Google's search page appeared. Again, very fast. I typed *Army Regulations* in the dialogue box and hit enter. The screen redrew in an instant and gave me whole pages of options.

For the next five minutes I clicked and scrolled and read.

*   *   *

I got back to the lobby ten minutes before eleven. My chair had been taken. I went out to the sidewalk and stood in the sun. I figured Sansom would arrive by Town Car and come in through the front door. He wasn't a rock star. He wasn't the President. He wouldn't come in through the kitchen or the loading dock. The whole point was for him to be seen. The need to enter places undercover was a prize he had not yet won.

The day was hot. But the street was clean. It didn't smell. There was a pair of cops on the corner south of me, and another pair on the corner to the north. Standard NYPD deployment, in midtown. Proactive, and reassuring. But not necessarily useful, given the range of potential threats. Alongside me departing hotel guests climbed into taxis. The city's rhythm ground on relentlessly. Traffic on Seventh Avenue flowed, and stopped at the light, and flowed again. Traffic from the cross streets flowed, and stopped, and started. Pedestrians bunched on the corners and struck out for the opposite sidewalks. Horns honked, trucks roared, the sun bounced off high glass and beat down hard.

* * *

Sansom arrived in a Town Car at five past eleven. Local plates, which meant he had ridden up most of the way on the train. Less convenient for him, but a smaller carbon footprint than driving all the way, or flying. Every detail mattered, in a campaign. *Politics is a minefield.* Springfield climbed out of the front passenger seat even before the car had stopped, and then Sansom and his wife climbed out of the back. They stood for a second on the sidewalk, ready to be gracious if there were people to greet them, ready not to be disappointed if there weren't. They scanned faces and saw mine and Sansom looked a little quizzical and his wife looked a little worried. Springfield headed in my direction but Elspeth waved him off with a small gesture. I guessed she had appointed herself damage control officer as far as I was concerned. She shook my hand like I was an old friend. She didn't comment on my shirt. Instead she leaned in close and asked, 'Do you need to talk to us?'

It was a perfect politician's-wife inquiry. She freighted the word *need* with all kinds of meanings. Her emphasis cast me both as an opponent and a collaborator. She was saying, *We know you have information that might hurt us, and we hate you for it, but we would be truly grateful if you would be kind enough to discuss it with us first, before you make it public*.

Practically a whole essay, all in one short syllable.

I said, 'Yes, we need to talk.'

Springfield scowled but Elspeth smiled like I had just promised her a hundred thousand votes and took my arm and led me inside. The hotel staff didn't know or care who Sansom was, except that he was the speaker for the group that was paying a hefty fee for the ballroom, so they summoned up a whole lot of artificial enthusiasm and showed us to a private lounge and bustled about with bottles of lukewarm sparkling water and pots of weak coffee. Elspeth played host. Springfield didn't speak. Sansom took a call on his cell from his chief of staff back in D.C. They talked for four minutes about economic policy, and then for a further two about their afternoon agenda. It was clear from the context that Sansom was heading back to the office directly after lunch, for a long afternoon's work. The New York event was a fast hit-and-run, nothing more. Like a drive-by robbery.

The hotel people finished up and left and Sansom clicked off and the room went quiet. Canned air hissed in through vents and kept the temperature lower than I would have liked. For a moment we sipped water and coffee in silence. Then Elspeth Sansom opened the bidding. She asked, 'Is there any news on the missing boy?'

I said, 'A little. He skipped football practice, which apparently is rare.'

'At USC?' Sansom said. He had a good memory. I had mentioned USC only once, and in passing.

'Yes, that's rare.'

'But then he called his coach and left a message.'

'When?'

'Last night. Dinner time on the Coast.'

'And?'

'Apparently he's with a woman.'

Elspeth said, 'That's OK, then.'

'I would have preferred a live real-time conversation. Or a face to face meeting.'

'A message isn't good enough for you?'

'I'm a suspicious person.'

'So what do you need to talk about?'

I turned to Sansom and asked him, 'Where were you in 1983?'

He paused, just a fraction of a beat, and something flickered behind his eyes. Not shock, I thought. Not surprise. Resignation, possibly. He said, 'I was a captain in 1983.'

'That's not what I asked you. I asked where you were.'

'I can't tell you that.'

'Were you in Berlin?'

'I can't tell you that.'

'You told me you were spotless. You still stand by that?'

'Completely.'

'Is there anything your wife doesn't know about you?'

'Plenty of things. But nothing personal.'

'Are you sure?'

'Positive.'

'You ever heard the name Lila Hoth?'

'I already told you I haven't.'

'You ever heard the name Svetlana Hoth?'

'Never,' Sansom said. I was watching his face. It was very composed. He looked a little uncomfortable, but apart from that he was communicating nothing.

I asked him, 'Did you know about Susan Mark before this week?'

'I already told you I didn't.'

'Did you win a medal in 1983?'

He didn't answer. The room went quiet again. Then Leonid's cell rang in my pocket. I felt a vibration and heard a loud electronic tune. I fumbled the phone out and looked at the small window on the front. A 212 number. The same number that was already in the call register. The Four Seasons hotel. Lila Hoth, presumably. I wondered whether Leonid was still missing, or whether he had gotten back and told his story and now Lila was calling me specifically.

I pressed random buttons until the ringing stopped and I put the phone back in my pocket. I looked at Sansom and said, 'I'm sorry about that.'

He shrugged, as if apologies were unnecessary.

I asked, 'Did you win a medal in 1983?'

He said, 'Why is that important?'

'You know what 600-8-22 is?'

'An army regulation, probably. I don't know all of them verbatim.'

I said, 'We figured all along that only a dumb person would expect HRC to have meaningful information about Delta operations. And I think we were largely right. But a little bit wrong, too. I think a really smart person might legitimately expect it, with a little lateral thinking.'

'In what way?'

'Suppose someone knew for sure that a Delta

operation had taken place. Suppose they knew for sure it had succeeded.'

'Then they wouldn't need information, because they've already got it.'

'Suppose they wanted to confirm the identity of the officer who led the operation?'

'They couldn't get that from HRC. Just not possible. Orders and deployment records and after-action reports are classified and retained at Fort Bragg under lock and key.'

'But what happens to officers who lead successful missions?'

'You tell me.'

'They get medals,' I said. 'The bigger the mission, the bigger the medal. And army regulation 600-8-22, section one, paragraph nine, subsection D, requires the Human Resources Command to maintain an accurate historical record of each and every award recommendation, and the resulting decision.'

'Maybe so,' Sansom said. 'But if it was a Delta mission, all the details would be omitted. The citation would be redacted, the location would be redacted, and the meritorious conduct would not be described.'

I nodded. 'All the record would show is a name, a date, and an award. Nothing else.'

'Exactly.'

'Which is all a smart person thinking laterally really needs, right? An award proves a mission succeeded, the lack of a citation proves it was a covert mission. Pick any random month, say early in 1983. How many medals were awarded?'

'Thousands. Hundreds and hundreds of Good Conduct Medals alone.'

'How many Silver Stars?'

'Not so many.'

'If any,' I said. 'Not much was happening early in 1983. How many DSMs were handed out? How many DSCs? I bet they were as rare as hens' teeth early in 1983.'

Elspeth Sansom moved in her chair and looked at me and said, 'I don't understand.'

I turned towards her but Sansom raised a hand and cut me off. He answered for me. There were no secrets between them. No wariness. He said, 'It's a kind of back door. Direct information is completely unavailable, but indirect information is out there. If someone knew that a Delta mission had taken place and succeeded, and when, then whoever got the biggest unexplained medal that month probably led it. Wouldn't work in wartime, because big medals would be too common. But in peacetime, when nothing else is going on, a big award would stick out like a sore thumb.'

'We invaded Grenada in 1983,' Elspeth said. 'Delta was there.'

'October,' Sansom said. 'Which would add some background noise later in the year. But the first nine months were pretty quiet.'

Elspeth Sansom looked away. She didn't know what her husband had been doing during the first nine months of 1983. Perhaps she never would. She said, 'So who is asking?'

I said, 'An old battleaxe called Svetlana Hoth, who claims to have been a Red Army political commissar. No real details, but she says she knew an American soldier named John in Berlin in 1983. She says he was very kind to her. And the only way that inquiring about it through Susan Mark makes any sense is if there was a mission involved and the guy named John led it and got a medal for it. The FBI found a note in Susan's car. Someone had fed her the regulation and the section and the paragraph to tell her exactly where to look.'

Elspeth glanced at Sansom, involuntarily, with a question in her face that she knew would never be answered: *Did you get a medal for something you did in Berlin in 1983?* Sansom didn't respond. So I tried. I asked him straight out, 'Were you on a mission in Berlin in 1983?'

Sansom said, 'You know I can't tell you that.' Then he seemed to lose patience with me, and he said, 'You seem like a smart guy. Think about it. What possible kind of operation could Delta have been running in Berlin in 1983, for God's sake?'

I said, 'I don't know. As I recall you guys worked very hard to stop people like me knowing what you were doing. And I don't really care, anyway. I'm trying to do you a favour here. That's all. One brother officer to another. Because my guess is something is going to come back and bite you in the ass and I thought you might appreciate a warning.'

Sansom calmed down pretty fast. He breathed in and out a couple of times and said, 'I do appreciate the warning. And I'm sure you understand that I'm not really allowed to deny anything. Because logically, denying something is the same as confirming something else. If I deny Berlin and every other place I wasn't, then eventually by a process of elimination you could work out where I was. But I'll go out on a limb just a little, because I think we're all on the same side here. So listen up, soldier. I was not in Berlin at any point in 1983. I never met any Russian women in 1983. I don't think I was very kind to anyone, the whole year long. There were a lot of guys in the army called John. Berlin was a popular destination for sightseeing. This person you have been talking to is looking for someone else. It's as simple as that.'

* * *

Sansom's little speech hung in the air for a moment. We all sipped our drinks and sat quiet. Then Elspeth Sansom checked her watch and her husband saw her do it and said, 'You'll have to excuse us now. Today we have some really serious begging to do. Springfield will be happy to see you out.' Which I thought was an odd proposal. It was a public hotel. It was my space as much as Sansom's. I could find my own way out, and I was entitled to. I wasn't going to steal the spoons, and even if I did, they weren't Sansom's spoons. But then I figured he wanted to set up a little quiet time for Springfield and me, in a lonely corridor somewhere. For further discussion, perhaps, or for a message. So I stood up and headed for the door. Didn't shake hands or say goodbye. It didn't seem to be that kind of a parting.

Springfield followed me to the lobby. He didn't speak. He seemed to be rehearsing something. I stopped and waited and he caught up to me and said, 'You really need to leave this whole thing alone.'

I asked, 'Why, if he wasn't even there?'

'Because to prove that he wasn't there you'll start asking where he was instead. Better that you never know.'

I nodded. 'This is personal to you too, isn't it? Because you were right there with him. You went wherever he went.'

He nodded back. 'Just let it go. You really can't afford to turn over the wrong rock.'

'Why not?'

'Because you'll be erased, if you do. You won't exist any more. You'll just disappear, physically and bureaucratically. That can happen now, you know. This is a whole new world. I'd like to say I would help with the process, but I wouldn't get the chance. Not even close. Because a whole bunch of other people would come for you first. I would be so far back in line that even your birth certificate would be blank before I got anywhere near you.'

'What other people?'

He didn't answer.

'Government?'

He didn't answer.

'Those federal guys?'

He didn't answer. Just turned back and headed for the elevators. I stepped out to the Seventh Avenue sidewalk and Leonid's phone started ringing in my pocket again.

THIRTY-FIVE

I stood on Seventh Avenue with my back to the traffic and answered Leonid's phone. I heard Lila Hoth's voice, soft in my ear. Precise diction, quaint phrasing. She said, 'Reacher?'

I said, 'Yes.'

She said, 'I need to see you, quite urgently.'

'About what?'

'I think my mother might be in danger. Myself also, possibly.'

'From what?'

'Three men were downstairs, asking questions at the desk. While we were out. I think our rooms have been searched, too.'

'What three men?'

'I don't know who they were. Apparently they wouldn't say.'

'Why talk to me about it?'

'Because they were asking about you too. Please come and see us.'

I asked, 'You're not upset about Leonid?'

She said, 'Under the circumstances, no. I think that was just an unfortunate misunderstanding. Please come.'

I didn't answer.

She said, 'I would very much appreciate your help.' She spoke politely, appealingly, a little submissively, even diffidently, like a supplicant. But notwithstanding all of that something extra in her voice made me fully aware that she was so beautiful that the last time any guy had said no to her was probably a decade in the past. She sounded vaguely commanding, like everything was already a done deal, like to ask was to get. *Just let it go*, Springfield had said, and of course I should have listened to him. But instead I told Lila Hoth, 'I'll meet you in your hotel lobby, fifteen minutes from now.' I thought that avoiding her suite would be enough of a safeguard, against whatever complications might ensue. Then I closed the phone and headed straight for the Sheraton's taxi line.

* * *

The Four Seasons' lobby was divided into a number of separate areas on two separate levels. I found Lila Hoth and her mother at a corner table in a dim panelled space that seemed to be a tea room during the day and might have been a bar by night. They were alone. Leonid wasn't there. I checked carefully all around and saw no one else worth worrying about. No unexplained men in mid-priced suits, nobody lingering over the morning newspaper. No apparent surveillance at all. So I slid into a seat, next to Lila, across from her mother. Lila was wearing a black skirt and a white shirt. Like a cocktail waitress, except that the fabrics and the cut and the fit were like nothing a cocktail waitress could afford. Her eyes were twin points of light in the gloom, as blue as a tropical sea. Svetlana was in another shapeless house dress, this time muddy maroon. Her eyes were dull. She nodded uncomprehendingly as I sat down. Lila extended her hand and shook mine quite formally. The contrast between the two women was enormous, in every way. In terms of age and looks, obviously, but also in terms of energy, vivacity, manners, and disposition.

I settled in and Lila got straight to the point. She asked, 'Did you bring the memory stick?'

I said, 'No,' although I had. It was in my pocket, with my toothbrush and Leonid's phone.

'Where is it?'

'Somewhere else.'

'Somewhere safe?'

'Completely.'

She asked, 'Why did those men come here?'

I said, 'Because you're poking around in something that's still a secret.'

'But the press officer at the Human Resources Command was enthusiastic about it.'

'That's because you lied to him.'

'I'm sorry?'

'You told him it was about Berlin. But it wasn't. Berlin in 1983 was no kind of fun, but it was stable. It was a Cold War tableau, frozen in time. Maybe there was a little back and forth between the CIA and the KGB and the Brits and the Stasi, but there was no real U.S. Army involvement. For our guys it was just a tourist destination. Take the train, see the Wall. Great bars, and great hookers. Probably ten thousand guys called John passed through, but they didn't do anything except spend money and catch the clap. Certainly they didn't fight and they didn't win medals. So tracking one of them down would be next to impossible. Maybe HRC was prepared to waste a little time, just in case something good came of it. But from the beginning it was a ridiculous task. So you can't have gotten a positive outcome from Susan Mark. She can't have told you anything about Berlin that made it worth coming over here. Just not possible.'

'So why did we come?'

'Because during those first few phone calls you softened her up and you made her your friend and then when you judged the time was right you told her what you really wanted. And exactly how to find it. For her ears only. Not Berlin. Something else entirely.'

An unguarded person with nothing to hide

would have responded instantly and openly. Probably with outrage, possibly with hurt feelings. An amateur bluffer would have faked it, with bluster and noise. Lila Hoth just sat quiet for a beat. Her eyes showed the same kind of fast response as John Sansom's had, back in his room in the O. Henry Hotel. Rethink, redeploy, reorganize, all in a brief couple of seconds.

She said, 'It's very complicated.'

I didn't answer.

She said, 'But it's entirely innocent.'

I said,'Tell that to Susan Mark.'

She inclined her head. The same gesture I had seen before. Courteous, delicate, and a little contrite. She said, 'I asked Susan for help. She agreed, quite willingly. Clearly her actions created difficulties for her with other parties. So yes, I suppose I was the indirect cause of her troubles. But not the direct cause. And I regret what happened, very, very much. Please believe me, if I had known beforehand, I would have said no to my mother.'

Svetlana Hoth nodded and smiled.

I said, 'What other parties?'

Lila Hoth said, 'Her own government, I think. Your government.'

'Why? What did your mother really want?'

Lila said she needed to explain the background first.

THIRTY-SIX

Lila Hoth had been just seven years old when the Soviet Union had fallen apart, so she spoke with a kind of historical detachment. She had the same kind of distance from former realities that I had from the Jim Crow years in America. She told me that the Red Army had deployed political commissars very widely. Every infantry company had one. She said that command and discipline were shared uneasily between the commissar and a field officer. She said that rivalry was common and bitter, not necessarily between the two as individuals, but between tactical common sense and ideological purity. She made sure I understood the general background, and then she moved on to specifics.

Svetlana Hoth had been a political commissar assigned to an infantry company. Her company had gone to Afghanistan soon after the Soviet invasion of 1979. Initial combat operations had been satisfactory for the infantry. Then they had turned disastrous. Attritional losses had become heavy and constant. At first there had been denial. Then Moscow had reacted, belatedly. The order of battle had been reorganized. Companies had been merged. Tactical common sense had suggested retrenchment. Ideology had required renewed offensives. Morale had required unity of ethnicity and geographical origin. Companies had been reconstituted to include sniper teams. Expert marksmen were brought in, with their companion spotters. Thus pairs of ragged men used to living off the land had arrived.

Svetlana's sniper was her husband.

His spotter was Svetlana's younger brother.

The situation had improved, both in military and in personal terms. Svetlana's and other family and regional groupings had spent down time together very happily. Companies had dug in and settled down and achieved acceptable safety and security. Offensive requirements were satisfied by regular night-time sniper operations. The results were excellent. Soviet snipers had long been the best in the world. The Afghan mujahideen had no answer to them. Late in 1981 Moscow had reinforced a winning hand by shipping new weapons. A new-model rifle had been issued. It was recently developed and still top secret. It was called the VAL Silent Sniper.

I nodded. Said, 'I saw one once.'

Lila Hoth smiled, briefly, with a hint of shyness. And with a hint of national pride, perhaps, for a country that no longer existed. Probably just a shadow of the pride her mother had felt, way back when. Because the VAL was a great weapon. It was a very accurate silenced semi-automatic rifle. It fired a heavy nine-millimetre bullet at a subsonic velocity, and could defeat all types of contemporary body armour and thin-skinned military vehicles at ranges out to about four hundred yards. It came with a choice of powerful day telescopes or electronic night scopes. It was a nightmare, from an opponent's point of view. You could be killed with no warning at all, silently, suddenly and randomly, asleep in bed in a tent, in the latrines, eating, dressing, walking around, in the light, in the dark.

I said, 'It was a fine piece.'

Lila Hoth smiled again. But then the smile faded. The bad news started. The stable situation lasted a year, and then it ended. The Soviet infantry's inevitable military reward for good performance was to be handed ever more dangerous tasks. The same the world over, the same throughout history. You don't get a pat on the back and a ride home. You get a map instead. Svetlana's company was one of many ordered to push north and east up the Korengal Valley. The valley was six miles long. It was the only navigable route out of Pakistan. The Hindu Kush mountains reared up on the far left, impossibly barren and high, and the Abas Ghar range blocked the right flank. The six-mile trail in between was a major mujahideen supply line out of the North West Frontier, and it had to be cut.

Lila said, 'The British wrote the book over a hundred years ago, about operations in Afghanistan. Because of their empire. They said, when contemplating an offensive, the very first thing you must plan is your inevitable retreat. And they said, you must save the last bullet for yourself, because you do not want to be taken alive, especially by the women. The company commanders had read that book. The political commissars had been told not to. They had been told that the British had failed only because of their political unsoundness. Soviet ideology was pure, and therefore success was guaranteed. With that delusion our very own Vietnam began.'

The push up the Korengal Valley had been backed by air and artillery power and had succeeded for the first three miles. A fourth had been won yard by yard against opposition that had seemed ferocious to the grunts but strangely muted to the officers.

The officers were right.

It was a trap.

The mujahideen waited until Soviet supply lines were stretched four miles long and then they dropped the hammer. Helicopter resupply was largely interdicted by a constant barrage of US-supplied shoulder-launched ground-to-air missiles. Coordinated attacks pinched off the salient at its origin. Late in 1982 thousands of Red Army troops were essentially abandoned in a long thin chain of inadequate and improvised encampments. The winter weather was awful. Freezing blasts of wind howled constantly along the pass between the mountain ranges. And there were evergreen holly bushes everywhere. Pretty and picturesque in the right context, but not for soldiers forced to work among them. They were gratingly noisy in the wind and they limited mobility and they tore skin and shredded uniforms.

Then harassment raids had started.

Prisoners had been taken, in ones and twos.

Their fate was appalling.

Lila quoted lines that the old British writer Rudyard Kipling had put in a doom-laden poem about failed offensives and groaning abandoned battlefield casualties and cruel Afghan tribeswomen with knives: *When you're wounded and left on Afghanistan's plains, and the women come out to cut up what remains, just roll to your rifle and blow out your brains, and go to your God like a soldier*. Then she said that what had been true even at the zenith of the British Empire's power was still true, and worse. Soviet infantrymen would go missing and hours later in the dark the winter wind would carry the sound of their screaming, from unseen enemy camps close by. The screaming would start at a desperate pitch and move slowly and surely upward into insane banshee wailing. Sometimes it would last ten or twelve hours. Most corpses were never recovered. But sometimes bodies would be returned, missing hands and feet, or whole limbs, or heads, or ears, or eyes, or noses, or penises.

Or skin.

'Some were flayed alive,' Lila said. 'Their eyelids would be cut away, and their heads forced down in a frame so they would have no choice but to watch their skin being peeled back, first from their faces, and then from their bodies. The cold anaesthetized their wounds to some extent and stopped them dying of shock too soon. Sometimes the process lasted a very long time. Or sometimes they would be roasted alive on fires. Parcels of cooked meat would show up near our emplacements. At first the men thought they were gifts of food, perhaps from sympathetic locals. But then they realized.'

Svetlana Hoth stared on into the room, not seeing anything, looking even bleaker than before. Maybe the tone of her daughter's voice was prompting memories. Certainly it was very compelling. Lila had not lived through or witnessed the events she was describing, but it sounded like she had. It sounded like she had witnessed them yesterday. She had moved on from historical detachment. It struck me that she would make a fine storyteller. She had the gift of narrative.

She said, 'They liked to capture our snipers best of all. They hated our snipers. I think snipers are always hated, perhaps because of the way they kill. My mother was very worried about my father, obviously. And her baby brother. They went out most nights, into the low hills, with the electronic scope. Not too far. Maybe a thousand yards, to find an angle. Maybe a little more. Far enough to be effective, but close enough to feel safe. But nowhere was really safe. Everywhere was vulnerable. And they had to go. Their orders were to shoot the enemy. Their intention was to shoot the prisoners. They thought it would be a mercy. It was an awful time. And my mother was pregnant by then. With me. I was conceived in a rock trench hacked out of the Korengal floor, under a greatcoat that dated back to the end of World War Two, and on top of two others that were possibly even older. My mother said they had old bullet holes in them, maybe from Stalingrad.'

I said nothing. Svetlana stared on. Lila put her hands on the table and tangled her fingers loosely together. She said, 'For the first month or so my father and my uncle came back every morning, safe. They were a good team. Perhaps the best.'

Svetlana stared on. Lila took her hands off the table and paused a beat. Then she sat up straight and squared her shoulders. A change of pace. A change of subject. She said, 'There were Americans in Afghanistan at that time.'

I said, 'Were there?'

She nodded.

I said, 'What Americans?'

'Soldiers. Not many, but some. Not always, but

sometimes.'

'You think?'

She nodded again. 'The US Army was definitely there. The Soviet Union was their enemy, and the mujahideen were their allies. It was the Cold War by proxy. It suited President Reagan very well to have the Red Army worn down. It was a part of his anti-communist strategy. And he enjoyed the chance to capture some of our new weapons for intelligence purposes. So teams were sent. Special Forces. They were in and out on a regular basis. And one night in March of 1983, one of those teams found my father and my uncle and stole their VAL rifle.'

I said nothing.

Lila said, 'The loss of the rifle was a defeat, of course. But what was worse was that the Americans gave my father and my uncle to the tribeswomen. There was no need for that. Obviously they had to be silenced, because the American presence was entirely covert and had to be concealed. But the Americans could have killed my father and my uncle themselves, quickly and quietly and easily. They chose not to. My mother heard their screams all the next day and far into the night. Her husband, and her brother. Sixteen, eighteen hours. She said even screaming that badly she could still tell them apart, by the sound of their voices.'

THIRTY-SEVEN

I glanced around the Four Seasons' dim tea room and moved in my chair and said, 'I'm sorry, but I don't believe you.'

Lila Hoth said, 'I'm telling you the truth.'

I shook my head. 'I was in the U.S. Army. I was a military cop. Broadly speaking I knew where people went, and where they didn't. And there were no U.S. boots on the ground in Afghanistan. Not back then. Not during that conflict. It was purely a local affair.'

'But you had a dog in the fight.'

'Of course we did. Like you did when we were in Vietnam. Was the Red Army in-country there?'

It was a rhetorical question, designed to make a point, but Lila Hoth took it seriously. She leaned forward across the table and spoke to her mother, low and fast, in a foreign language that I presumed was Ukrainian. Svetlana's eyes opened a little and she cocked her head to one side as if she was recalling some small matter of arcane historical detail. She spoke back to her daughter, low and fast, and long, and then Lila paused a second to marshal her translation and said, 'No, we sent no troops to Vietnam, because we had confidence that our socialist brothers from the People's Republic could complete their task unaided. Which, my mother says, apparently they did, quite splendidly. Little men in pyjamas defeated the big green machine.'

Svetlana Hoth smiled and nodded.

I said, 'Just like a bunch of goat herders kicked

her ass.'

'Undisputedly. But with a lot of help.'

'Didn't happen.'

'But you admit that material help was provided, surely. To the mujahideen. Money, and weapons. Especially surface-to-air missiles, and things of that nature.'

'Like in Vietnam, only the other way around.'

'And Vietnam is an excellent example. Because, to your certain knowledge, whenever did the United States provide military aid anywhere in the world without also sending what they called military advisers?'

I didn't answer.

She asked, 'For instance, how many countries have you served in?'

I said nothing.

She asked, 'When did you join the army?'

'In 1984,' I said.

'Then these events of 1982 and 1983 were all before your time.'

'Only just,' I said. 'And there is such a thing as institutional memory.'

'Wrong,' she said. 'Secrets were kept and institutional memories were conveniently erased. There's a long history of illegal American military involvements all around the world. Especially during Mr Reagan's presidency.'

'You learn that in high school?'

'Yes, I did. And remember, the communists were gone long before I was in high school. Thanks, in part, to Mr Reagan himself.'

I said, 'Even if you're right, why assume Americans were involved on that particular night? Presumably your mother didn't see it happen. Why not assume your father and your uncle were captured directly by the mujahideen?'

'Because their rifle was never found. And my mother's position was never fired on at night by a sniper. My father had twenty rounds in his magazine, and he was carrying twenty spare. If the mujahideen had captured him directly, then they would have used his rifle against us. They would have killed forty of our men, or tried to, and then they would have run out of ammunition and abandoned the gun. My mother's company would have found it eventually. There was a lot of back-and-forth skirmishing. Our side overran their positions, and vice versa. It was like a crazy circular chase. The mujahideen were intelligent. They had a habit of doubling back to positions we had previously written off as abandoned. But over a period of time our people saw all their places. They would have found the VAL, empty and rusting, maybe in use as a fence post. They accounted for all their other captured weapons that way. But not that VAL. The only logical conclusion is that it was carried straight to America, by Americans.'

I said nothing.

Lila Hoth said, 'I'm telling you the truth.'

I said, 'I once saw a VAL Silent Sniper.'

'You told me that already.'

'I saw it in 1994,' I said. 'We were told it had just been captured. Eleven whole years after you claim it was. There was a big urgent panic, because of its capabilities. The army wouldn't wait eleven years to get in a panic.'

'Yes, it would,' she said. 'To unveil the rifle immediately after its capture might have started

World War Three. It would have been a direct admission that your soldiers were in direct face to face contact with ours, without any declaration of hostilities. Illegal at the very least, and completely disastrous in geopolitical terms. America would have lost the moral high ground. Support inside the Soviet Union would have been strengthened. The fall of communism would have been delayed, perhaps for years.'

I said nothing.

She said, 'Tell me, what happened in your army, in 1994, after the big urgent panic?'

I paused, in the same way that Svetlana Hoth had. I recalled the historical details. They were surprising. I checked and rechecked. Then I said, 'Not very much happened, actually.'

'No new body armour? No new camouflage? No tactical reaction of any kind?'

'No.'

'Is that logical, even for an army?'

'Not especially.'

'When was the last equipment upgrade before that?'

I paused again. Sought more historical details. Recalled the PASGT, introduced to much excitement and fanfare and acclaim during my early years in uniform. The Personal Armor System, Ground Troops. A brand new Kevlar helmet, rated to withstand all manner of assault by small arms fire. A thick new body-armour vest, to be worn either over or under the battledress blouse, rated safe even against long guns. Specifically, as I recalled, rated safe against incoming nine-millimetre rounds. Plus new camouflage patterns, carefully designed to work better, and available in two flavours, woodland and desert. The Marines got a third option, blue and grey, for urban environments.

I said nothing.

Lila Hoth asked, 'When was the upgrade?'

I said, 'In the late eighties.'

'Even with a big urgent panic, how long does it take to design and manufacture an upgrade like that?'

I said, 'A few years.'

'So let's review what we know. In the late eighties you received upgraded equipment, explicitly designed for better personal protection. Do you think it is possible that was the result of a direct stimulus derived from an unrevealed source in 1983?'

I didn't answer.

* * *

We all sat quiet for a moment. A silent and discreet waiter came by and offered us tea. He recited a long list of exotic blends. Lila asked for a flavour I had never heard of, and then she translated for her mother, who asked for the same thing. I asked for regular coffee, black. The waiter inclined his head about a quarter of an inch, as if the Four Seasons was willing to accommodate all and any requests, however appallingly proletarian they might be. I waited until the guy had retreated again and asked, 'How did you figure out who you are looking for?'

Lila said, 'My mother's generation expected to fight a land war with you in Europe, and they expected to win. Their ideology was pure, and yours wasn't. After a swift and certain victory, they expected to take many of you prisoner, possibly millions of you. In that phase, part of a political commissar's duties would have been to classify enemy combatants, to cull the ideologically irretrievable from the herd. To aid them in that task, they were made familiar with the structure of your military.'

'Made familiar by who?'

'By the KGB. It was an ongoing programme. There was a lot of information available. They knew who did what. In the case of elite units, they even knew names. Not just the officers, but the enlisted men too. Like a true soccer fan knows the personnel and the strengths and the weaknesses of all the other teams in the league, bench players included. For incursions into the Korengal Valley, my mother reasoned that there were only three realistic options. Either SEALs from the navy, or Recon Marines from the Corps, or Delta Force from the army. Contemporary intelligence argued against the SEALs or the Marines. There was no circumstantial evidence of their involvement. No specific information. The KGB had people throughout your organizations, and they reported nothing. But there was significant radio traffic out of Delta bases in Turkey, and out of staging posts in Oman. Our radar picked up unexplained flights. It was a logical conclusion that Delta was running the operations.'

The waiter came back with a tray. He was a tall dark guy, quite old, probably foreign. He had an air about him. The Four Seasons probably put him front and centre because of it. His bearing suggested he might once have been a tea expert in some dark-panelled place in Vienna or Salzburg. In reality he had probably been unemployed in Estonia. Maybe he had been drafted along with the rest of Svetlana's generation. Maybe he had endured the Korengal winters along with her, somewhere down the line in an ethnic grouping of his own. He made a big show of serving the tea and arranging the lemons on a plate. My coffee came in a nice cup. He put it down in front of me with elegantly disguised disapproval. When he was gone again Lila said, 'My mother estimated that the raid would have been led by a captain. A lieutenant would have been too junior and a major would have been too senior. The KGB had personnel lists. There were a lot of captains assigned to Delta at the time. But there had been some radio analysis. Someone had heard the name John. That narrowed the field.'

I nodded. Pictured a massive dish antenna somewhere, maybe in Armenia or Azerbaijan, a guy in a hut, headphones on, rubber cups clamped tight on his ears, sifting through the frequencies, hearing the whine and screech of scrambled channels, stumbling on a fragment of plain speech, writing the word *John* on a pad of coarse brown paper. A lot of stuff is snatched from the ether. Most of it is useless. A word that you understand is like a nugget of gold in a pan, or like a diamond in a rock. And a word that *they* understand is like a bullet in the back.

Lila said, 'My mother knew all about your army's medals. They were held to be important, as criteria for classifying prisoners. Badges of honour, that would become badges of dishonour immediately upon capture. She knew that the VAL rifle would be worth a major award. But which award? Remember, there had been no declaration of hostilities. And most of your major awards specify gallantry or heroism while in action against an armed enemy of the United States. Technically whoever stole the VAL from my father was not eligible for any of those awards, because technically the Soviet Union was not an enemy of the United States. Not in the military sense. Not in a formal political way. There had been no declaration of war.'

I nodded again. We had never been at war with the Soviet Union. On the contrary, for four long years we had been allies in a desperate struggle against a common foe. We had cooperated, extensively. The World War Two-era Red Army greatcoat that Lila Hoth claimed to have been conceived under had almost certainly been made in America, as part of the Lend-Lease programme. We had shipped a hundred million tons of woollen and cotton goods to the Russians. Plus fifteen million pairs of leather boots, four million rubber tyres, two thousand railroad locomotives and eleven thousand freight cars, as well as all the obvious heavy metal like fifteen thousand airplanes, seven thousand tanks, and 375,000 army trucks. All free, gratis, and for nothing. Winston Churchill had called the programme the least sordid in all of history. Legends had grown up around it. The Soviets were said to have asked for condoms, and in an attempt to impress and intimidate, they had specified that they should be eighteen inches long. The U.S. had duly shipped them, in cartons stamped *Size: Medium*.

So went the story.

Lila asked, 'Are you listening?'

I nodded. 'The Superior Service Medal would have fit the bill. Or the Legion of Merit, or the Soldier's Medal.'

'Not big enough.'

'Thanks. I won all three.'

'Capturing the VAL was a really big coup. A sensation. It was a completely unknown weapon. Its acquisition would have been rewarded with a really big medal.'

'But which one?'

'My mother concluded it would be the Distinguished Service Medal. That one is big, but different. The applicable standard is exceptionally meritorious service to the United States Government in a duty of great responsibility. It is completely independent of formal declared combat activities. It is normally awarded to politically pliable Brigadier Generals and above. My mother was under orders to execute all holders of the DSM immediately. Below the rank of Brigadier General it is awarded only very rarely. But it's the only significant medal a Delta captain could have won that night in the Korengal Valley.'

I nodded. I agreed. I figured Svetlana Hoth was a pretty good analyst. Clearly she had been well trained, and well informed. The KGB had done a decent job. I said, 'So you went looking for a guy called John who had been a Delta captain and won a DSM, both in March of 1983.'

Lila nodded. 'And to be certain, the DSM had to come without a citation.'

'And you made Susan Mark help.'

'I didn't *make* her. She was happy to help.'

'Why?'

'Because she was upset by my mother's story.'

Svetlana Hoth smiled and nodded.

Lila said, 'And she was a little upset by my story, too. I'm a fatherless child, the same as her.'

I asked, 'How did John Sansom's name come up even before Susan reported back? I don't believe that it was from a bunch of New York private eyes sitting around reading the newspaper and making jokes.'

'It's a very rare combination,' Lila said. 'John, Delta, DSM, but never a one-star general. We noticed it in the *Herald Tribune*, when his Senate ambitions were announced. We were in London. You can buy that paper all over the world. It's a version of the *New York Times*. John Sansom might well be the only man in your army's history who matches those criteria four for four. But we wanted to be absolutely sure. We needed final confirmation.'

'Before what? What do you want to do to the guy?'

Lila Hoth looked surprised.

'Do?' she said. 'We don't want to *do* anything. We just want to talk to him, that's all. We want to ask him, why? Why would he do that, to two other human beings?'

THIRTY-EIGHT

Lila Hoth finished her tea, and put her cup down on her saucer. Bone china clinked politely on bone china. She asked, 'Will you go get Susan's information for me?'

I didn't answer.

She said, 'My mother has waited a long time.'

I asked, 'Why has she?'

'Time, chance, means, opportunity. Money, mostly, I suppose. Her horizons have been very narrow, until recently.'

I asked, 'Why was your husband killed?'

'*My* husband?'

'Back in Moscow.'

Lila paused, and said, 'It was the times.'

'Same for your mother's husband.'

'No. I told you, if Sansom had shot him in the head, like what happened to my husband, or stabbed him in the brain, or broken his neck, or whatever else Delta soldiers were taught to do, it would have been different. But he didn't. He was cruel instead. Inhuman. My father couldn't even roll to his rifle, because they had stolen his rifle.'

I said nothing.

She said, 'You want a man like that in your Senate?'

'As opposed to what?'

'Will you give me Susan's confirmation?'

'No point,' I said.

'Why not?'

'Because you wouldn't get anywhere near John Sansom. If any of what you say actually happened, then it's a secret, and it's going to stay a secret for a very long time. And secrets are protected, especially now. There are already two federal agencies at work on this. You just had three guys asking questions. At best, you'll be deported. Your feet won't touch the ground, all the way back to the airport. They'll put you on the plane in handcuffs. In coach. The Brits will pull you off the plane at the other end and you'll spend the rest of your life under surveillance.'

Svetlana Hoth stared into space.

I said, 'And at worst, you'll just disappear. Right here. One minute you'll be on the street, and then you won't be. You'll be rotting in Guantanamo, or you'll be on your way to Syria or Egypt so they can kill you there.'

Lila Hoth didn't speak.

'My advice?' I said. 'Forget all about it. Your father and your uncle were killed in a war. They weren't the first, and they won't be the last. Shit happens.'

'We just want to ask him why.'

'You already know why. There had been no declaration of hostilities, therefore he couldn't kill your guys. It's about the rules of engagement. There's a heavy-duty briefing before every mission.'

'So he let someone else do it for him.'

'It was the times. Like you said, it might have started World War Three. It was in everyone's interest to avoid that.'

'Have you looked at the file? Did Susan really have the confirmation? Just tell me, yes or no. I won't do anything without actually seeing it. I can't.'

'You won't do anything, period.'

'It wasn't right.'

'Invading Afghanistan in the first place wasn't right. You should have stayed home.'

'Then so should you, from all the places you went.'

'No argument from me.'

'What about freedom of information?'

'What about it?'

'America is a country of laws.'

'True. But do you know what the laws actually say now? You should read the *Herald Tribune* more carefully.'

'Are you going to help us?'

'I'll ask the concierge to call you a cab to the airport.'

'Is that all?'

'That's the best help anyone could give you.'

'Is there anything I can do to change your mind?'

I didn't answer.

'Anything at all?'

'No,' I said.

We all went quiet after that. The tea expert brought the check. It was in a padded leather wallet. Lila Hoth signed it. She said, 'Sansom should be called to account.'

'If it was him,' I said. 'If it was anybody.' I took Leonid's phone out of my pocket and dumped it on the table. I pushed my chair back and got ready to leave.

Lila said, 'Please keep the phone.'

I said, 'Why?'

'Because my mother and I are staying. Just a few more days. And I would really like to be able to call you, if I wanted to.' She wasn't coy in the way she said it. Not coquettish. No lowered eyelids, no batted lashes. No hand on my arm, no attempt to seduce, no attempt to change my mind. It was just a plain statement, neutrally delivered.

Then she said, 'Even if you're not a friend,' and I heard the tiniest bat-squeak of a threat in her voice. Just a faint far-off chime of menace, a hint of danger, barely audible behind the words, accompanied by a perceptible chill in her amazing blue eyes. Like a warm summer sea changing to sunlit winter ice. Same colour, different temperature.

Or maybe she was just sad, or anxious, or determined.

I looked at her with a level gaze and put the phone back in my pocket and stood up and walked away. There were plenty of cabs on 57th Street, but none of them was empty. So I walked. The Sheraton was three blocks west and five blocks south. Twenty minutes, max. I figured I could get there before Sansom finished his lunch.

THIRTY-NINE

I didn't get to the Sheraton before Sansom finished his lunch, partly because the sidewalks were clogged with people moving slowly in the heat, and partly because it had been a short lunch. Which I guessed made sense. Sansom's Wall Street audience wanted to spend maximum time making money and minimum time giving it away. I didn't make it on to the same Amtrak as him, either. I missed a D.C. train by five minutes, which meant I trailed him back to the capital a whole hour and a half in arrears.

* * *

The same guard was on duty at the Cannon Building's door. He didn't recognize me. But he let me in anyway, mainly because of the Constitution. Because of the First Amendment in the Bill of Rights. *Congress shall make no law abridging the right of the people to petition the Government*. My pocket junk inched through an X-ray machine and I stepped through a metal detector and was patted down even though I knew the light had flashed green. There was a gaggle of House pages inside the lobby and one of them called ahead and then walked me to Sansom's quarters. The corridors were wide and generous and confusing. The individual offices seemed small but handsome. Maybe they had once been large and handsome, but now they were broken up into reception anterooms and multiple inner spaces, partly for senior staff to use, I guessed, and partly to make eventual labyrinthine access to the big guy seem more of a gift than it really was.

Sansom's place looked the same as all the others. A door off the corridor, lots of flags, lots of eagles, some oil paintings of old guys in wigs, a reception desk with a young woman behind it. Maybe a staffer, maybe an intern. Springfield was leaning on the corner of her desk. He saw me and nodded without a smile and pushed off the desk and came to the door to meet me and jerked his thumb farther along the corridor.

'Cafeteria,' he said.

We got there down a flight of stairs. It was a wide low room full of tables and chairs. Sansom was nowhere in it. Springfield grunted like he wasn't surprised and concluded that Sansom had returned to his office while we were out looking for him, by an alternative route, possibly via a colleague's billet. He said the place was a warren and that there were always conversations to be had and favours to be sought and deals to be struck and votes to be traded. We walked back the same way we had come and Springfield stuck his head around an inner door and then backed away and motioned me inside.

Sansom's inner office was a rectangular space larger than a closet and smaller than a thirty-dollar motel room. It had a window and panelled walls covered with framed photographs and framed newspaper headlines and souvenirs on shelves. Sansom himself was in a red leather chair behind a desk, with a fountain pen in his hand and a whole lot of papers spread out in front of him. He had his jacket off. He had the weary, airless look of a man who had been sitting still for a long time. He hadn't been out. The cafeteria detour had been a charade, presumably designed to allow someone to make an exit without me seeing him. Who, I didn't know. Why, I didn't know. But I sat down in the visitor chair and found it still warm from someone else's body. Behind Sansom's head was a large framed print of the same picture I had seen in his book. Donald Rumsfeld and Saddam Hussein, in Baghdad. *Sometimes our friends become our enemies, and sometimes our enemies become our friends*. Next to it was a cluster of smaller pictures, some of Sansom standing with groups of people, some of him alone and shaking hands and smiling with other individuals. Some of the group shots were formal, and some were of wide smiles and confetti-strewn stages after election victories. I saw Elspeth in most of them. Her hair had changed a lot over the years. I saw Springfield in some of the others, his small wary shape easily recognizable even though the images were tiny. The two-shots were what news photographers call grip-and-grins. Some of the individuals in them I recognized, and some I didn't. Some had autographed the pictures with extravagant dedications, and some hadn't.

Sansom said, 'So?'

I said, 'I know about the DSM in March of 1983.'

'How?'

'Because of the VAL Silent Sniper. The battleaxe I told you about is the widow of the guy you took it from. Which is why you reacted to the name. Maybe you never heard of Lila Hoth or Svetlana Hoth, but you met with some other guy called Hoth back in the day. That's for damn sure. It was obvious. You probably took his dog tags and had them translated. You've probably still got them, as souvenirs.'

There was no surprise. No denial. Sansom just said, 'No, actually those tags were locked up with the after-action reports, and everything else.'

I said nothing.

Sansom said, 'His name was Grigori Hoth. He was about my age at the time. He seemed competent. His spotter, not so much. He should have heard us coming.'

I didn't reply. There was a long silence. Then the situation seemed to hit home and Sansom's shoulders fell and he sighed and he said, 'What a way to get found out, right? Medals are supposed to be rewards, not penalties. They're not supposed to screw you up. They're not supposed to follow you around the rest of your life like a damn ball and chain.'

I said nothing.

He asked, 'What are you going to do?'

I said, 'Nothing.'

'Really?'

'I don't care what happened in 1983. And they lied to me. First about Berlin, and they're still lying to me now. They claim to be mother and daughter. But I don't believe them. The alleged daughter is the cutest thing you ever saw. The alleged mother fell out of the ugly tree and hit every branch. I first met them with a cop from the NYPD. She said thirty years from now the daughter will look just like the mother. But she was wrong. The younger one will never look like the older one. Not in a million years.'

'So who are they?'

'I'm prepared to accept that the older one is for real. She was a Red Army political commissar who lost her husband and her brother in Afghanistan.'

'Her brother?'

'The spotter.'

'But the younger woman is posing?'

I nodded. 'As a billionaire expatriate widow from London. She says her husband was an entrepreneur who didn't make the cut.'

'And she's not convincing?'

'She dresses the part. She acts it well. Maybe she lost a husband somewhere along the line.'

'But? What is she really?'

'I think she's a journalist.'

'Why?'

'She knows things. She's got the right kind of inquiring mind. She's analytical. She monitors the *Herald Tribune*. She's a hell of a storyteller. But she talks too much. She's in love with words and she embroiders details. She can't help herself.'

'For example?'

'She went for some extra pathos. She made out that the political commissars were in the trenches along with the grunts. She claims she was conceived on a rock floor under a Red Army greatcoat. Which is bullshit. Commissars were big-time rear-echelon pussies. They stayed well away from the action. They clustered together back at HQ, writing pamphlets. Occasionally they would visit up the line, but never if there was any danger involved.'

'And you know this how?'

'You know how I know it. We expected to fight a land war with them in Europe. We expected to win. We expected to take millions of them prisoner. MPs were trained to handle them all. The 110th was going to direct operations. Delusional, maybe, but the Pentagon took it very seriously. We were taught more about the Red Army than we were about the U.S. Army. Certainly we were told exactly where to find the commissars. We were under orders to execute them all immediately.'

'What kind of journalist?'

'Television, probably. The local crew she hired was tied to the television business. And have you ever seen Eastern European television? All the anchors are women, and they all look sensational.'

'What country?'

'Ukraine.'

'What angle?'

'Investigative, historical, with a little human interest mixed in. The younger one probably heard the older one's story and decided to run with it.'

'Like the History Channel in Russian?'

‘In Ukrainian,’ I said.

‘Why? What’s the message? They want to embarrass us now? After more than twenty-five years?’

‘No, I think they want to embarrass the Russians. There’s a lot of tension right now between Russia and the Ukraine. I think they’re taking America’s evil for granted, and saying that big bad Moscow shouldn’t have put poor helpless Ukrainians in harm’s way.’

‘So why haven’t we seen the story already?’

‘Because they’re way behind the times,’ I said. ‘They’re looking for confirmation. They still seem to have some kind of journalistic scruples over there.’

‘Are they going to get confirmation?’

‘Not from you, presumably. And no one else knows anything for sure. Susan Mark didn’t live long enough to say yea or nay. So the lid is back on. I advised them to forget all about it and head home.’

‘Why are they posing as mother and daughter?’

‘Because it’s a great con,’ I said. ‘It’s appealing. It’s like reality TV. Or those magazines they sell in the supermarket. Clearly they studied our culture.’

‘Why wait so long?’

‘It takes time to build a mature television industry. They probably wasted years on important stuff.’

Sansom nodded vaguely, and said, ‘It’s not true that no one knows anything for sure. You seem to know plenty.’

‘But I’m not going to say anything.’

‘Can I trust you on that?’

‘I served thirteen years. I know all kinds of

things. I don't talk about them.'

'I'm not happy about how easy it was for them to approach Susan Mark. And I'm not happy we didn't know about her from the get-go. We never even heard of her before the morning after. This whole thing was like an ambush. We were always behind the curve.'

I was looking at the photographs on the wall behind him. Looking at the tiny figures. Their shapes, their postures, their silhouettes. I said, 'Really?'

'We should have been told.'

I said, 'Have a word with the Pentagon. And with those guys from the Watergate.'

Sansom said, 'I will.' Then he went quiet, as if he was rethinking and reassessing, more calmly and at a slower pace than his usual fast field-officer style. *The lid is back on*. He seemed to examine that proposition for a spell, from all kinds of different angles. Then he shrugged, and got a slightly sheepish look on his face, and he asked, 'So what do you think of me now?'

'Is that important?'

'I'm a politician. It's a reflex inquiry.'

'I think you should have shot them in the head.'

He paused and said, 'We had no silenced weapons.'

'You did. You had just taken one from them.'

'Rules of engagement.'

'You should have ignored them. The Red Army didn't travel with forensics labs. They would have had no idea who shot who.'

'So what do you think of me?'

'I think you shouldn't have handed them over. That was uncalled for. That was going to be the point of the story, as a matter of fact, on Ukrainian TV. The idea was to get the old woman next to you and let her ask you why.'

Sansom shrugged again. 'I wish she could. Because the truth is, we didn't hand them over. We turned them loose instead. It was a calculated risk. A kind of double bluff. They'd lost their rifle. Everyone would have assumed that the mujahideen had taken it. Which was a sorry outcome and a major disgrace. It was clear to me that they were very scared of their officers and their political commissars. So they would have been falling over themselves to tell the truth, that it was Americans, not Afghans. It would have been a kind of exculpation. But their officers and their commissars knew how scared they were of them, so the truth would have sounded like a bullshit story. Like a pathetic excuse. It would have been discounted immediately, as a fantasy. So I felt it was safe enough to let them go. The truth would have been out there in plain sight, but unrecognized.'

I said, 'So what happened?'

Sansom said, 'I guess they were more scared than I thought. Too scared to go back at all. I guess they just wandered, until the tribespeople found them. Grigori Hoth was married to a political commissar. He was scared of her. That's what happened. And that's what killed him.'

I said nothing.

He said, 'Not that I expect anyone to believe me.'

I didn't reply.

He said, 'You're right about tension between Russia and the Ukraine. But there's tension between Russia and ourselves, too. Right now there's plenty of it. If the Korengal part of the story gets out, things could blow up big. It's like the Cold War all over again. Except different. At least the Soviets were sane, in their way. This bunch, not so much.'

* * *

After that we sat in silence for what felt like a long time, and then Sansom's desk phone rang. It was his receptionist on the line. I could hear her voice through the earpiece, and through the door. She rattled off a list of things that needed urgent attention. Sansom hung up and said, 'I have to go. I'll call a page to see you out.' He stood up and came around the desk and walked out of the room. Just like an innocent man with nothing to hide. He left me all alone, sitting in my chair, with the door open. Springfield had gone, too. I could see no one in the outer office except the woman at the desk. She smiled at me. I smiled at her. No page showed up.

We were always behind the curve, Sansom had said. I waited a long minute and then started squirming around like I was restless. Then after a plausible interval I got out of my chair. I stumped around with my hands clasped behind my back, like an innocent man with nothing to hide, just waiting around on turf that was not his own. I headed over to the wall behind the desk, like it was a completely random destination. I studied the pictures. I counted faces I knew. My initial total came to twenty-four. Four presidents, nine other politicians, five athletes, two actors, Donald

Rumsfeld, Saddam Hussein, Elspeth, and Springfield.

Plus someone else.

I knew a twenty-fifth face.

In all of the celebratory election-night victory pictures, right next to Sansom himself, was a guy smiling just as widely, as if he was basking in the glow of a job well done, as if he was not very modestly claiming his full share of the credit. A strategist. A tactician. A Svengali. A behind-the-scenes political fixer.

Sansom's chief of staff, presumably.

He was about my age. In all of the pictures he was dusted with confetti or tangled with streamers or knee-deep in balloons and he was grinning like an idiot, but his eyes were cold. They had a canny, calculating shrewdness in them.

They reminded me of a ballplayer's eyes.

I knew why the cafeteria charade had been staged.

I knew who had been sitting in Sansom's visitor chair before me.

We were always behind the curve.

Liar.

I knew Sansom's chief of staff.

I had seen him before.

I had seen him wearing chinos and a golf shirt, riding the 6 train late at night in New York City.

FORTY

I checked all the celebration pictures, very carefully. The guy from the subway was in all of them. Different angles, different years, different victories, but it was definitely the same guy, literally at Sansom's right hand. Then a page bustled into the office and two minutes later I was back on the Independence Avenue sidewalk. Fourteen minutes after that I was inside the railroad station, waiting for the next train back to New York. Fifty-eight minutes after that I was on it, sitting comfortably, leaving town, watching the dismal rail yards through the window. Far to my left a gang of men wearing hard hats and orange high-visibility vests was working on a section of track. Their vests glowed through the smog. The fabric must have had tiny beads of reflective glass mixed into the plastic weave. Safety, through chemistry. The vests were more than highly visible. They were attention-getting. They drew the eye. I watched the guys work until they were just tiny orange dots in the distance, and then until they were completely lost to sight, which was more than a mile later. And at that point I had everything I was ever going to get. I knew everything I was ever going to know. But I didn't know that I knew. Not then.

* * *

The train rolled into Penn and I got a late dinner in a place directly across the street from where I had gotten breakfast. Then I walked up to the 14th Precinct on West 35th. The night watch had started. Theresa Lee and her partner Docherty were already in place. The squad room was quiet, like all the air had been sucked out of it. Like there had been bad news. But no one was rushing around. Therefore the bad news had happened somewhere else.

The receptionist at the bullpen gate had seen me before. She turned on her swivel chair and glanced at Lee, who made a face like it wouldn't kill her one way or the other whether she ever spoke to me again, or not. So the receptionist turned back and made a face of her own, like the choice to stay or to go was entirely mine. I squeaked the hinge and threaded my way between desks to the back of the room. Docherty was on the phone, mostly listening. Lee was just sitting there, doing nothing. She looked up as I approached and she said, 'I'm not in the mood.'

'For what?'

'Susan Mark,' she said.

'Any news?'

'None at all.'

'Nothing more on the boy?'

'You sure are worried about that boy.'

'And you're not?'

'Not even a little bit.'

'Is the file still closed?'

'Tighter than a fish's asshole.'

'OK,' I said.

She paused a beat and sighed and said, 'What have you got?'

'I know who the fifth passenger was.'

'There were only four passengers.'

'And the earth is flat and the moon is made of cheese.'

'Did this alleged fifth passenger commit a crime somewhere between 30th Street and 45th?'

'No,' I said.

'Then the file stays closed.'

Docherty put his phone down and glanced at his partner with an eloquent look on his face. I knew what the look meant. I had been a cop of sorts for thirteen years and had seen that kind of look many times before. It meant that someone else had caught a big case, and that Docherty was basically glad that he wasn't involved, but a little wistful too, because even if being at the heart of the action was a pain in the neck bureaucratically, it was maybe a whole lot better than watching from the sidelines.

I asked, 'What happened?'

Lee said, 'Multiple homicide over in the 17th. A nasty one. Four guys under the FDR Drive, beaten and killed.'

'With hammers,' Docherty said.

I said, 'Hammers?'

'Carpentry tools. From the Home Depot on 23rd Street. Just purchased. They were found at the scene. The price tags are still on them, under the blood.'

I asked, 'Who were the four guys?'

'No one knows,' Docherty said. 'That seems to have been the point of the hammers. Their faces are pulped, their teeth are smashed out, and their fingertips are ruined.'

'Old, young, black, white?'

'White,' Docherty said. 'Not old. In suits. Nothing to go on, except they had phony business cards in their pockets, with some corporate name that isn't registered anywhere in New York State, and a phone number that is permanently disconnected because it belongs to a movie company.'

FORTY-ONE

Docherty's desk phone rang and he picked it up and started listening again. A friend in the 17th, presumably, with more details to share. I looked at Lee and said, 'Now you're going to have to reopen the file.'

She asked, 'Why?'

'Because those guys were the local crew that Lila Hoth hired.'

She looked at me and said, 'What are you? Telepathic?'

'I met with them twice.'

'You met some crew twice. Nothing says these are the same guys.'

'They gave me one of those phony business cards.'

'All those crews use phony business cards.'

'With the same kind of phone number?'

'Movies and TV are the only places to get those numbers.'

'They were ex-cops. Doesn't that matter to you?'

'I care about cops, not ex-cops.'

'They said Lila Hoth's name.'

'No, some crew said her name. Doesn't mean these dead guys did.'

'You think this is a coincidence?'

'They could be anybody's crew.'
'Like who else's?'
'Anybody in the whole wide world. This is New York. New York is full of private guys. They roam in packs. They all look the same and they all do the same stuff.'
'They said John Sansom's name, too.'
'No, some crew said his name.'
'In fact they were the first place I heard his name.'
'Then maybe they were his crew, not Lila's. Would he have been worried enough to have his own people up here?'
'He had his chief of staff on the train. That's who the fifth passenger was.'
'There you go, then.'
'You're not going to do anything?'
'I'll inform the 17th, for background.'
'You're not going to reopen your file?'
'Not until I hear about a crime my side of Park Avenue.'
I said, 'I'm going to the Four Seasons.'

* * *

It was late and I was pretty far west and I didn't find a cab until I hit Sixth Avenue. After that it was a fast trip to the hotel. The lobby was quiet. I walked in like I had a right to be there and rode the elevator to Lila Hoth's floor. Walked the silent corridor and paused outside her suite.
Her door was open an inch.
The tongue of the security deadbolt was out and the spring closer had trapped it against the jamb. I paused another second and knocked.

No response.

I pushed the door and felt the mechanism push back. I held it open forty-five degrees against my spread fingers and listened.

No sound inside.

I opened the door all the way and stepped in. Ahead of me the living room was dim. The lights were off but the drapes were open and there was enough of a glow from the city outside to show me that the room was empty. Empty, as in no people in it. Also empty as in checked-out-of and abandoned. No shopping bags in the corners, no personal items stowed either carefully or carelessly, no coats over chairs, no shoes on the floor. No signs of life at all.

The bedrooms were the same. The beds were still made, but they had suitcase-sized dents and rucks on them. The closets were empty. The bathrooms were strewn with used towels. The shower stalls were dry. I caught a faint trace of Lila Hoth's perfume in the air, but that was all.

I walked through all three rooms one more time and then stepped back to the corridor. The door closed behind me. I heard the spring inside the hinge doing its work and I heard the deadbolt tongue settle against the jamb, metal on wood. I walked away to the elevator and hit the down button and the door slid back immediately. The car had waited for me. A night-time protocol. No unnecessary elevator movement. No unnecessary noise. I rode back to the lobby and walked to the desk. There was a whole night staff on duty. Not as many people as during the day, but way too many for the fifty dollar trick to have worked. The Four Seasons wasn't that kind of a place. A guy looked up from a screen and asked how he could help me. I asked him when exactly the Hoths had checked out.

'The who, sir?' he asked back. He spoke in a quiet, measured, night-time voice, like he was worried about waking the guests stacked high above him.

'Lila Hoth and Svetlana Hoth,' I said.

The guy got a look on his face like he didn't know what I was talking about and refocused on his screen and hit a couple of keys on his keyboard. He scrolled up and down and hit a couple more keys and said, 'I'm sorry, sir, but I can't find a record of any guests under that name.'

I told him the suite number. He hit a couple more keys and his mouth turned down in puzzled surprise and he said, 'That suite hasn't been used at all this week. It's very expensive and quite hard to rent.'

I double-checked the number in my head and I said, 'I was in it last night. It was being used then. And I met the occupants again today, in the tea room. There's a signature on a check.'

The guy tried again. He called up tea room checks that had been charged to guest accounts. He half turned his screen so that I could see it too, in the sharing gesture that clerks use when they want to convince you of something. We had had tea for two plus a cup of coffee. There was no record of any such charge.

Then I heard small sounds behind me. The scuff of soles on carpet, the rattle of drawn breath, the sigh of fabric moving through the air. And the clink of metal. I turned around and found myself facing a perfect semicircle of seven men. Four of them were uniformed NYPD patrolmen. Three of them were the federal agents I had met before.

The cops had shotguns.

The feds had something else.

FORTY-TWO

Seven men. Seven weapons. The police shotguns were Franchi SPAS 12s. From Italy. Probably not standard NYPD issue. The SPAS 12 is a futuristic, fearsome-looking item, a semi-automatic 12-gauge smooth-bore weapon with a pistol grip and a folding stock. Advantages, many. Drawbacks, two. Cost was the first, but clearly some specialist division inside the police department had been happy to sign off on the purchase. Semi-automatic operation was the second drawback. It was held to be theoretically unreliable in a powerful shotgun. People who have to shoot or die worry about it. Mechanical failure happens. But I wasn't about to bet on four mechanical failures happening all at once, for the same reason I don't buy lottery tickets. Optimism is good. Blind faith is not.

Two of the feds had Glock 17s in their hands. Nine-millimetre automatic pistols from Austria, square, boxy, reliable, well proved through more than twenty years of useful service. I had retained a mild personal preference for the Beretta M9, like the Franchi also from Italy, but a million times out of a million and one the Glock would get the job done just as well as the Beretta.

Right then the job was to keep me standing still, ready for the main attraction.

The fed leader was in the exact centre of the semicircle. Three men on his left, three on his right. He was holding a weapon I had seen before only on television. I remembered it well. A cable channel, in a motel room in Florence, Texas. Not the Military Channel. The National Geographic Channel. A programme about Africa. Not civil wars and mayhem and disease and starvation. A wildlife documentary. Gorillas, not guerillas. A bunch of zoological researchers was tracking an adult male silverback. They wanted to put a radio tag in its ear. The creature weighed close to five hundred pounds. A quarter of a ton. They put it down with a dart gun loaded with primate tranquillizer.

That was what the fed leader was pointing at me.

A dart gun.

The National Geographic people had taken great pains to reassure their viewers that the procedure was humane. They had shown detailed diagrams and computer simulations. The dart was a tiny feathered cone, with a surgical steel shaft. The tip of the shaft was a sterile ceramic honeycomb laced with anaesthetic. The dart fired at high velocity and the shaft buried itself a half-inch into the gorilla. And stopped. The tip wanted to keep on going. Momentum. Newton's Law of Motion. The shock and the inertia exploded the ceramic matrix and the potion contained in the honeycomb flung itself onward, not quite droplets, not quite an aerosol. Like a heavy mist spreading under the skin, flooding tissue the way a paper towel soaks up a spilled drop of coffee. The gun itself was a one-shot deal. It had to be loaded with a single dart, and a single tiny bottle of compressed gas to power it. Nitrogen, as I recalled. Reloading was laborious. It was better to hit first time.

The researchers had hit first time in the documentary film. The gorilla had been groggy after eight seconds, and in a coma after twenty. Then it had woken up in perfect health ten hours later.

But it had weighed twice what I weigh.

Behind me was the hotel's reception counter. I could feel it against my back. It had a ledge about fourteen inches wide set probably forty-two inches off the floor. Bar height. Convenient for a customer to spread his papers on. Convenient to sign things on. Behind that was a drop to a regular desk-height counter for the clerks. It was maybe thirty inches deep. Or more. I wasn't sure. But the total obstacle was a high and wide hurdle impossible to clear from a standing start. Especially when facing the wrong way. And pointless, anyway. Clearing the counter would not put me in another room. I would still be right there, just behind the counter rather than in front of it. No net gain, and maybe a big net loss if I landed awkwardly on a rolling chair or got tangled up in a telephone wire.

I turned my head and glanced behind me. No one there. The desk people had filed out, left and right. They had been coached. Maybe even rehearsed. The seven men in front of me had a clear field of fire.

No way forward, no way back.

I stood still.

The fed leader was sighting down the barrel of

his dart gun and aiming directly at my left thigh. My left thigh made a moderately large target. No fat under the skin. Just hard flesh, full of capillaries and other aids to rapid and efficient blood circulation. Completely unprotected, except for my new blue pants, which were made of thin summer-weight cotton. *Don't come dressed like that, or you won't get in*. I tensed up, as if muscle tone would make the damn thing bounce off. Then I relaxed again. Muscle tone hadn't helped the gorilla, and it wouldn't help me. Way behind the seven men I could see a paramedic crew in a gloomy corner. Fire department uniforms. Three men, one woman. They were standing and waiting. They had a wheeled gurney ready.

When all else fails, start talking.

I said, 'If you guys have more questions, I'm quite happy to sit down for a conversation. We could get some coffee, keep things civilized. Decaf, if you prefer. Since it's late. They'll make fresh, I'm sure. This is the Four Seasons, after all.'

The fed leader didn't answer. He shot me instead. With the dart gun, from about eight feet, straight into the meat of my thigh. I heard a blast of compressed gas and felt pain in my leg. Not a sting. A dull, thumping blow, like a knife wound. Then a split second of nothing, like disbelief. Then a sharp, angry reaction. I thought if I was a gorilla I would want to tell the damn researchers to stay home and leave my ears alone.

The fed leader lowered the gun.

Nothing happened for a second. Then I felt my heart accelerate and my blood pressure spike and fall. I heard rushing in my temples, like Chinese food twenty years ago. I looked down. The dart's feathered butt was tight against my pants. I pulled it out. The shaft was smeared with blood. But the tip was gone. The ceramic material had fragmented to powder and the liquid it had held in suspension was already inside me, doing its work. A fat dot of blood welled out of the wound and soaked into the cotton fabric of my pants, following the warp and the weft like a map of an epidemic spreading through city streets. My heart was beating hard. I could feel blood rushing around inside me. I wanted to stop it. No practical way to do that. I leaned back against the counter. Just temporary, I figured. For relief. The seven men in front of me seemed to slide suddenly sideways. Like a wheel play in baseball. I wasn't sure if they had moved or if I had moved my head. Or perhaps the room had moved. Certainly there was a whole lot of fast rotation going on. Some kind of a spinning sensation. The edge of the counter hit me under the shoulder blades. Either it was rising up or I was sliding down. I put my hands back and flat on its surface. I tried to steady it. Or myself. No luck. The edge hit me in the back of the head. My internal clock wasn't working right. I was trying to count seconds. I wanted to get to nine. I wanted to outlast the silverback. Some last vestige of pride. I wasn't sure if I was succeeding.

My ass hit the ground. My vision went. It didn't go dim or dark. It brightened instead. It got full of mad whirling silver shapes, flashing horizontally right to left. Like a fairground ride running a thousand times too fast. Then I started a sequence of crazy dreams, urgent and breathless and vivid. Full of action and colour. Afterwards I realized that the start of the dreams marked the point where I officially lost consciousness, lying there on the Four Seasons' lobby floor.

FORTY-THREE

I don't know when exactly I woke up. The clock in my head still wasn't running right. But I surfaced eventually. I was on a cot. My wrists and my ankles were fastened to the rails with plastic handcuffs. I was still fully dressed. Apart from my shoes. Those were gone. In my fuddled state I heard my dead brother's voice in my head. A line he liked to use as a kid: *Before you criticize someone, you should walk a mile in his shoes. Then when you start criticizing him, you're a mile away and he's got to run after you in his socks*. I moved my toes. Then I moved my hips. I could feel that my pockets were empty. They had taken my stuff. Maybe they had listed it all on a form and bagged it up.

I ducked my head to my shoulder and scraped my chin across my shirt. Stubble, a little more than I remembered. Maybe eight hours' worth. The gorilla on the National Geographic Channel had slept for ten. Score one for Reacher, except they had probably used a lighter dose on me. At least I hoped they had. That huge primate had crashed down like a tree.

I raised my head again and looked around. I was inside a cell, and the cell was inside a room. No window. Bright electric light. New construction inside old construction. A row of three simple cages made of bright new spot-welded steel, sitting in a line inside a big old room made of brick. The cells were each about eight feet square and eight feet tall. They were roofed with bars, the same as their sides. They were floored with steel tread plate. The tread plate was folded up at the edges, to make a shallow inch-deep tray. To contain spilled liquids, I guessed. All kinds of liquids can get spilled in cells. The tray was spot-welded inside a horizontal rail that ran around the bottom of all the vertical bars. There were no bolts through the floors. The cells were not fixed down. They were just sitting there, three freestanding structures parked in a big old room.

The big old room itself had a high, barrelled ceiling. The brick was all painted fresh white, but it looked soft and worn. There are guys who can look at the dimensions of bricks and the bricklaying patterns they make and tell you exactly where a building is and exactly when it was constructed. I am not one of them. But even so the place looked like the East Coast to me. Nineteenth century, built by hand. Immigrant labour, working fast and dirty. I was probably still in New York. And I was probably underground. The place felt like a basement. Not damp, not cool, but somehow stabilized in terms of temperature and humidity by virtue of being buried.

I was in the centre cage of the three. I had the cot I was strapped to, and a toilet. That was all. Nothing else. The toilet was enclosed by a three-sided U-shaped privacy screen about three feet high. The toilet tank had a dished top that made a sink. I could see a faucet. Just one. Cold water only. The other two cages looked the same. Cots, toilets, nothing else. Leading away from each of the cells were recent excavations in the outer room's floor. Narrow trenches, three of them, exactly parallel, dug up and refilled and smoothed over with new concrete. Sewer lines to the toilets, I guessed, and water lines to the faucets.

The other two cages were empty. I was all alone.

In the far corner of the outer room where the walls met the ceiling there was a surveillance camera. A beady glass eye. A wide-angle lens, presumably, to see the whole room at once. To see into all three cells. I guessed there would be microphones, too. Many more than one, probably, some of them close by. Electronic eavesdropping is hard. Clarity is important. Room echo can ruin everything.

My left leg hurt a little. A puncture wound and a bruise, right where the dart had hit. The blood on my pants had dried. There wasn't much of it. I tested the strength of the cuffs around my wrists and my ankles. Unbreakable. I bucked and jerked against them for half a minute. Not trying to get free. Just checking whether I would pass out again from the effort, and aiming to attract attention from whoever was watching through the surveillance camera and listening through the microphones.

I didn't pass out again. My head ached a little as it cleared, and the exertion didn't make my leg throb any less. But apart from those minor symptoms I felt pretty good. The attention I attracted was delayed well over a minute and took the form of a guy I had never seen before walking in with a hypodermic syringe. Some kind of a medical technician. He had a wet cotton ball in his other hand, ready to swab my elbow. He stopped outside my cage and looked in at me through the bars.

I asked him, 'Is that a lethal dose?'

The guy said, 'No.'

'Are you authorized to give a lethal dose?'

'No.'

'Then you better back off. Because however many times you shoot me up, I'm always going to wake up later. And one of those times, I'm going to come and get you. Either I'll make you eat that thing, or I'll stick it up your ass and inject you from the inside.'

'It's a painkiller,' the guy said. 'An analgesic. For your leg.'

'My leg is fine.'

'Are you sure?'

'Just back off.'

So he did. He went out through a stout wooden door painted the same white as the walls. The door looked old. It was vaguely Gothic in shape. I had seen similar doors in old public buildings. City schools, and police stations.

I dropped my head back to the cot. I had no pillow. I stared up through the bars at the ceiling and prepared to settle in. But less than a minute later two of the men I knew came in through the wooden door. Two of the federal agents. The two sidekicks, not the leader. One of them had a Franchi 12 with him. It looked loaded and cocked and ready. The other guy had some kind of a tool in his hand and a bunch of thin chains looped over his arm. The guy with the shotgun stepped up close to my bars and poked the barrel through and jammed the muzzle into my throat and kept it there. The guy with the chains unlocked my gate. Not with a key, but by spinning a dial left and right. A combination lock. He opened the gate and came inside and stopped beside my cot. The tool in his hand was like a pair of pliers, but with blades instead of milled grips. Some kind of a cutter. He saw me looking at it and smiled. He leaned forward, above my waist. The shotgun muzzle pressed harder into my throat. A wise precaution. Even with my hands strapped down I could have folded forward from the waist and delivered a pretty good head butt. Not my best, maybe, but with plenty of snap from the neck I could have put the guy to sleep for longer than I had been out. Longer than the silverback, perhaps. I already had a headache. Another big impact wouldn't have made it much worse.

But the Franchi muzzle stayed firmly in place and I was reduced to the status of a spectator. The guy with the chains untangled them and laid them in place, like a trial run. One would cuff my wrists to my waist, one would chain my ankles, and the third would connect the first two together. Standard-issue prison restraints. I would be able to shuffle along a foot at a time and lift my hands as far as my hips, but that was all. The guy got the chains all locked and fastened and tested, and then he used the tool to cut off the plastic cuffs. He backed out of the cage and left the gate open and his partner pulled the Franchi away.

I guessed I was supposed to slide off the cot and stand up. So I stayed where I was. You have to ration your opponents' victories. You have to mete them out, slowly and meanly. You have to make your opponents subliminally grateful for every little bit of compliance. That way maybe you get away with giving up ten small losses a day, rather than ten big ones.

But the two feds had had the same training I had had. That was clear. They didn't stand there getting all beaten and frustrated. They just walked away, and the guy who had fitted the chains called back from the door and said, 'Coffee and muffins through here, any old time you want them.' Which put the onus right back on me, exactly like it was designed to. Not stylish to wait an hour and then hobble through and wolf stuff down like I was desperate. That would be getting beaten in public, by my own hunger and thirst. Not stylish at all. So I waited just a token interval and then I slid off the cot and shuffled out of the cage.

The wooden door led to a room about the same size and shape as the one the cages were in. Same construction, same colour paint. No window. There was a large wooden table in the centre of the floor. Three chairs on the far side, full of the three feds. One chair on my side, empty. Waiting for me. On the table, all lined up neatly, was the stuff from my pockets. My roll of cash, flattened out and trapped under a sprinkling of coins. My old passport. My ATM card. My folding toothbrush. The Metrocard I had bought for use on the subway. Theresa Lee's NYPD business card, which she had given to me in the white-tiled room under Grand Central Terminal. The phony business card that Lila Hoth's local crew had given to me on the corner of Eighth Avenue and 35th Street. The computer memory I had bought at Radio Shack, with its loud pink neoprene sleeve. Plus Leonid's clamshell cell phone. Nine separate items, each one of them stark and lonely under the bright bulbs on the ceiling.

To the left of the table was another door. Same Gothic shape, same wooden construction, same new paint. I guessed it led onward to another room, the third of three in an L-shaped chain. Or the first of three, depending on your point of view. Depending on whether you were a captive or a captor. To the right of the table was a low chest of drawers that looked like it belonged in a bedroom. On it were a pile of napkins and a tube of nested foam cups and a steel vacuum flask and a paper plate with two blueberry muffins. I shuffled over in my socks and poured a cup of coffee from the flask. The operation was easier than it might have been, because the chest was low. My chained hands didn't hamper me much. I carried the cup low and two-handed to the table. Sat down in the vacant chair. Dipped my head and sipped from the cup. The action made me look like I was yielding, like it was designed to. Or bowing, or deferring. The coffee was pretty bad too, and only lukewarm.

The fed leader cupped his hand and held it behind my stack of money, as if he was considering picking it up. Then he shook his head, as if money was too prosaic a subject for him. Too mundane. He moved his hand onward and stopped it behind my passport.

He asked, 'Why is it expired?'

I said, 'Because no one can make time stand still.'

'I meant, why haven't you renewed it?'

'No imminent need. Like you don't carry a condom in your wallet.'

The guy paused a beat and asked, 'When was the last time you left the country?'

I said, 'I would have sat down and talked to you,

you know. You didn't need to shoot me with a dart like I was something escaped from the zoo.'

'You had been warned many times. And you had been markedly uncooperative.'

'You could have put my eye out.'

'But I didn't. No harm, no foul.'

'I still haven't seen ID. I don't even know your name.'

The guy said nothing.

I said, 'No ID, no names, no Miranda, no charges, no lawyer. Brave new world, right?'

'You got it.'

'Well, good luck with that,' I said. I glanced at my passport, as if I had suddenly remembered something. I raised my hands as far as they would go and leaned forward. I shuffled my coffee cup well out of my way, which left it in the space between my passport and my ATM card. I picked up my passport and squinted down at it and leafed through the pages at the back. I shrugged, like my memory had been playing tricks on me. I went to put the passport back. But I was inexact with its placement. A little hampered by the chains. The stiff edge of the little booklet caught my coffee cup and tipped it over. Coffee spilled out and splashed on the table and flowed right over the far edge and into the fed leader's lap. He did the thing that everyone does. He jumped back, half stood, and batted at the air as if he could divert the liquid one molecule at a time.

'Sorry,' I said.

His pants were soaked. So now the onus was on him. Two choices: either disrupt the rhythm of the interrogation by taking a break to change, or continue with wet pants. I saw the guy debating.

He wasn't quite as inscrutable as he thought he was.

He chose to continue with wet pants. He detoured to the chest of drawers and dabbed at himself with napkins. Then he brought some back and dried the table. He made a big effort not to react, which was a reaction in itself.

He asked again, 'When was the last time you left the country?'

I said, 'I don't recall.'

'Where were you born?'

'I don't recall.'

'Everyone knows where they were born.'

'It was a long time ago.'

'We'll sit here all day, if necessary.'

'I was born in West Berlin,' I said.

'And your mother is French?'

'She was French.'

'What is she now?'

'Dead.'

'I'm sorry.'

'It wasn't your fault.'

'Are you sure you're an American citizen?'

'What kind of a question is that?'

'A straightforward one.'

'The State Department gave me a passport.'

'Was your application truthful?'

'Did I sign it?'

'I imagine you did.'

'Then I imagine it was truthful.'

'How? Were you naturalized? You were born overseas to a foreign parent.'

'I was born on a military base. That counts as U.S. sovereign territory. My parents were married. My father was an American citizen. He was a

Marine.'

'Can you prove all of that?'

'Do I have to?'

'It's important. Whether or not you're a citizen could affect what happens to you next.'

'No, how much patience I have will affect what happens to me next.'

The guy on the left stood up. He was the one who had held the Franchi's muzzle hard against my throat. He went directly left from behind the table and walked out, through the wooden door, into the third room. I glimpsed desks, computers, cabinets, and lockers. No other people. The door closed softly behind him and the room we were in went quiet.

The main guy asked, 'Was your mother Algerian?'

I said, 'I just got through telling you she was French.'

'Some French people are Algerian.'

'No, French people are French and Algerian people are Algerian. It's not rocket science.'

'OK, some French people were originally immigrants from Algeria. Or from Morocco, or Tunisia, or elsewhere in North Africa.'

'My mother wasn't.'

'Was she a Muslim?'

'Why do you want to know?'

'I'm making inquiries.'

I nodded. 'Safer to inquire about my mother than yours, probably.'

'What do you mean?'

'Susan Mark's mother was a teenage crack whore. Maybe yours worked with her. Maybe they turned tricks together.'

'Are you trying to make me mad?'

'No, I'm succeeding. You're all red in the face and you've got wet pants. And you're getting absolutely nowhere. All in all I don't think this particular session will be written up for the training manual.'

'This isn't a joke.'

'But it's heading that way.'

The guy paused and regrouped. He used his index finger to realign the nine items in front of him. He got them straight and then he pushed the computer memory an inch towards me. He said, 'You concealed this from us when we searched you. Susan Mark gave it to you on the train.'

I said, 'Did I? Did she?'

The guy nodded. 'But it's empty, and it's too small anyway. Where is the other one?'

'What other one?'

'This one is obviously a decoy. Where is the real one?'

'Susan Mark gave me nothing. I bought that thing at Radio Shack.'

'Why?'

'I liked the look of it.'

'With the pink sleeve? Bullshit.'

I said nothing.

He said, 'You like the colour pink?'

'In the right place.'

'What place would that be?'

'A place you haven't been in a long time.'

'Where did you conceal it?'

I didn't answer.

'Was it in a body cavity?'

'You better hope not. You just touched it.'

'Do you enjoy that kind of thing? Are you a

fairy?'

'That kind of question might work down at Guantanamo, but it won't work with me.'

The guy shrugged and used his fingertip and pulled the stick back into line, and then he moved the phony business card and Leonid's cell phone both forward an inch, like he was moving pawns on a chessboard. He said, 'You've been working for Lila Hoth. The card proves you were in communication with the crew she hired, and your phone proves she called you at least six times. The Four Seasons' number is in the memory.'

'It's not my phone.'

'We found it in your pocket.'

'Lila Hoth didn't stay at the Four Seasons, according to them.'

'Only because we told them to cooperate. We both know she was there. You met her there twice, and then she broke the third rendezvous.'

'Who is she, exactly?'

'That's a question you should have asked before you agreed to work for her.'

'I wasn't working for her.'

'Your phone proves that you were. It's not rocket science.'

I didn't answer.

He asked, 'Where is Lila Hoth now?'

'Don't you know?'

'How would I know?'

'I assumed you scooped her up when she checked out. Before you started shooting darts at me.'

The guy said nothing.

I said, 'You were there earlier in the day. You searched her room. I assumed you were watching her.'

The guy said nothing.

I said, 'You missed her, right? She walked right past you. That's terrific. You guys are an example to us all. A foreign national with some kind of weird Pentagon involvement, and you let her go?'

'It's a setback,' the guy said. He seemed a little embarrassed, but I figured he need not have been. Because leaving a hotel under surveillance is relatively easy to do. You do it by not doing it. By not leaving immediately. You send your bags down with the bellman in the service elevator, the agents cluster in the lobby, you leave the passenger elevator at a different floor and you hole up somewhere for two hours until the agents give up and leave. Then you walk out. It takes nerve, but it's easy to do, especially if you have booked another room under another name, which Lila Hoth certainly had, for Leonid, at least.

The guy asked, 'Where is she now?'

I asked, 'Who is she?'

'The most dangerous person you ever met.'

'She didn't look it.'

'That's why.'

I said, 'I have no idea where she is.'

There was a long pause and then the guy moved the phony business card and the cell phone back into line and advanced Theresa Lee's card in their place. He asked, 'How much does the detective know?'

'What does it matter?'

'We have a fairly simple sequence of tasks in front of us. We need to find the Hoths, we need to recover the real memory stick, but above all we need to contain the leak. So we need to know how far it has spread. So we need to know who knows what.'

'Nobody knows anything. Least of all me.'

'This is not a contest. You don't get points for resisting. We're all on the same side here.'

'Doesn't feel that way to me.'

'You need to take this seriously.'

'Believe me, I am.'

'Then tell us who knows what.'

'I'm not a mind reader. I don't know who knows what.'

I heard the door on my left open again. The leader looked across and nodded some kind of consent. I turned in my seat and saw the guy from the left-hand chair. He had a gun in his hand. Not the Franchi 12. The dart gun. He raised it and fired. I spun away, but far too late. The dart caught me high in the upper arm.

FORTY-FOUR

I woke up all over again, but I didn't open my eyes immediately. I felt like the clock in my head was back on track, and I wanted to let it calibrate and settle in undisturbed. Right then it was showing six o'clock in the evening. Which meant I had been out about another eight hours. I was very hungry and very thirsty. My arm hurt the same way my leg had. A hot little bruise, right up there at the top. I could feel that I still had no shoes. But my wrists and my ankles weren't fastened to the rails of the cot. Which was a relief. I stretched lazily and rubbed a palm across my face. More stubble. I was heading for a regular beard.

I opened my eyes. Looked around. Discovered two things. One: Theresa Lee was in the cage to my right. Two: Jacob Mark was in the cage to my left.

Both of them were cops.

Neither one of them had shoes on.

That was when I started to worry.

* * *

If I was right and it was six o'clock in the evening, then Theresa Lee had been hauled in from home. And Jacob Mark had been brought in from work. They were both looking at me. Lee was standing behind her bars, about five feet away. She was wearing blue jeans and a white shirt. She had bare feet. Jake was sitting on his cot. He was wearing a police officer's uniform, minus the belt and the gun and the radio and the shoes. I sat up on my cot and swung my feet to the floor and ran my hands through my hair. Then I stood up and stepped over to the sink and drank from the faucet. New York City, for sure. I recognized the taste of the water. I looked at Theresa Lee and asked her, 'Do you know exactly where we are?'

She said, 'Don't you?'

I shook my head.

She said, 'We have to assume this place is wired for sound.'

'I'm sure it is. But they already know where we are. So we won't be giving them anything they don't already have.'

'I don't think we should say anything.'

'We can discuss geographic facts. I don't think

the Patriot Act prohibits street addresses, at least not yet.'

Lee said nothing.

I said, 'What?'

She looked uneasy.

I said, 'You think I'm playing games with you?'

She didn't answer.

I said, 'You think I'm here to trap you into saying something on tape?'

'I don't know. I don't know anything about you.'

'What's on your mind?'

'Those clubs on Bleecker are nearer Sixth Avenue than Broadway. You had the A train right there. Or the B or the C or the D. So why were you on the 6 train at all?'

'Law of nature,' I said. 'We're hardwired. In our brains. Middle of the night, full dark, all mammals head east instinctively.'

'Really?'

'No, I just made that up. I had nowhere to go. I came out of a bar and turned left and walked. I can't explain it any better than that.'

Lee said nothing.

I said, 'What else?'

She said, 'You have no bags. I never saw a homeless person with nothing. Most of them haul more stuff around than I own. They use shopping carts.'

'I'm different,' I said. 'And I'm not a homeless person. Not like them.'

She said nothing.

I asked her, 'Were you blindfolded when they brought you here?'

She looked at me for a long moment and then she shook her head and sighed. She said, 'We're in a closed firehouse in Greenwich Village. On West 3rd. Street level and above is disused. We're in the basement.'

'Do you know exactly who these guys are?'

She didn't speak. Just glanced up at the camera. I said, 'Same principle. They know who they are. At least I hope they do. Doesn't hurt for them to know that we know, too.'

'You think?'

'That's the point. They can't stop us thinking. Do you know who they are?'

'They didn't show ID. Not today, and not that first night either, when they came to talk to you at the precinct.'

'But?'

'Not showing ID can be the same thing as showing it, if you're the only bunch that never does. We've heard some stories.'

'So who are they?'

'They work directly for the Secretary of Defense.'

'That figures,' I said. 'The Secretary of Defense is usually the dumbest guy in the government.'

Lee glanced up at the camera again, as if I had insulted it. As if she had caused it to be insulted. I said, 'Don't worry. These guys look ex-military to me, in which case they already know how dumb the Secretary of Defense is. But even so, Defense is a Cabinet position, which means ultimately these guys are working for the White House.'

Lee paused a beat and asked, 'Do you know what they want?'

'Some of it.'

'Don't tell us.'

'I won't,' I said.

'But is it big enough for the White House?'
'Potentially, I guess.'
'Shit.'
'When did they come for you?'
'This afternoon. Two o'clock. I was still asleep.'
'Did they have the NYPD with them?'
Lee nodded, and a little hurt showed in her eyes.
I asked, 'Did you know the patrolmen?'
She shook her head. 'Hotshot counterterrorism guys. They write their own rules and keep themselves separate. They ride around in special cars all day long. Fake taxis, sometimes. One in the front, two in the back. Did you know that? Big circles, up on Tenth, down on Second. Like the B-52s used to patrol the skies.'
'What time is it now? About six after six?'
She looked at her watch, and looked surprised.
'Dead on,' she said.
I turned the other way.
'Jake?' I said. 'What about you?'
'They came for me first. I've been here since noon. Watching you sleep.'
'Any word from Peter?'
'Nothing.'
'I'm sorry.'
'You snore, you know that?'
'I was full of gorilla tranquillizer. From a dart gun.'
'You're kidding.'
I showed him the bloodstain on my pants, and then the one on my shoulder.
'That's insane,' he said.
'Were you at work?'
He nodded. 'The dispatcher called my car back

to base, and they were waiting for me.'

'So your department knows where you are?'

'Not specifically,' he said. 'But they know who took me away.'

'That's something,' I said.

'Not really,' he said. 'The department won't do anything for me. Guys like these come for you, suddenly you're tainted. You're presumed guilty of something. People were already inching away from me.'

Lee said, 'Like when Internal Affairs comes calling.'

I asked her, 'Why isn't Docherty here?'

'He knows less than me. In fact he went out of his way to know less than me. Didn't you notice that? He's an old hand.'

'He's your partner.'

'Today he is. By next week he'll have forgotten he ever had a partner. You know how these things work.'

Jake said, 'There are only three cells here. Maybe Docherty is somewhere else.'

I asked, 'Have these guys talked to you yet?'

Both of them shook their heads.

I asked, 'Are you worried?'

Both of them nodded. Lee asked, 'Are you?'

'I'm sleeping well,' I said. 'But I think that's mostly because of the tranquillizers.'

* * *

At six thirty they brought us food. Deli sandwiches, in plastic clamshell packs that were turned sideways and pushed through the bars. Plus bottles of water. I drank my water first and refilled the bottle from the tap. My sandwich was salami and cheese. Finest meal I ever ate.

At seven o'clock they took Jacob Mark away for questioning. No restraints. No chains. Theresa Lee and I sat on our cots, about eight feet apart, separated by bars. We didn't talk much. Lee seemed depressed. At one point she said, 'I lost some good friends when the towers came down. Not just cops. Firefighters, too. People that I had worked with. People that I had known for years.' She said it as if she thought those truths should insulate her from the craziness that came afterwards. I didn't answer her. Mostly I sat quiet and re-ran conversations in my head. All kinds of people had been talking at me. For hours. John Sansom, Lila Hoth, the guys in the next room. I was running through what they had all said, the same way a cabinet maker runs his palm over a length of planed wood, looking for the rough spots. There were a few. There were strange half-comments, odd nuances, little off-key implications. I didn't know what any of them meant. Not then. But knowing that they were there was useful in itself.

* * *

At seven thirty they brought Jacob Mark back and took Theresa Lee away in his place. No restraints. No chains. Jake got on his cot and sat cross-legged with his back to the camera. I looked at him. An inquiry. He gave a millimetric shrug and rolled his eyes. Then he kept his hands in his lap, out of sight of the camera, and made a gun with his right thumb and forefinger. He tapped his thigh and looked at mine. I nodded. The dart gun. He put two fingers down between his knees and held a third in front and to the left. I nodded again. Two guys behind the table, and the third to the left with the gun. Probably in the doorway to the third room. On guard. Hence no restraints and no chains. I massaged my temples and while my hands were still up I mouthed, 'Where are our shoes?' Jake mouthed back, 'I don't know.'

After that we sat in silence. I didn't know what Jake was thinking about. His sister, probably. Or Peter. I was considering a binary choice. There are two ways to fight something. From the inside, or from the outside. I was an outside type of guy. Always had been.

At eight o'clock they brought Theresa Lee back and took me away again.

FORTY-FIVE

No restraints. No chains. Clearly they thought I was afraid of the dart gun. Which I was, to a degree. Not because I fear small puncture wounds. And not because I have anything against sleep, in and of itself. I like sleep as much as the next guy. But I didn't want to waste any more time. I felt like I couldn't afford another eight hours on my back.

The room was populated exactly as Jacob Mark had semaphored it. The main guy was already sitting in the centre chair. The guy who had fitted the chains that morning was the one who had brought me in, and he left me in the middle of the room and went to take his place at the table on the main guy's right. The guy who had wielded the Franchi was standing off to the left with the dart gun in his hands. My possessions were still on the table. Or, they were back on the table. I doubted that they had been there while Jake or Lee had been in the room. No point. No reason. No relevance. They had been laid out all over again, especially for me. Cash, passport, bank card, toothbrush, Metrocard, Lee's business card, the phony business card, the memory stick, and the cell phone. Nine items. All present and correct. Which was good, because I needed to take at least seven of them with me.

The guy in the centre chair said, 'Sit down, Mr Reacher.'

I moved towards my chair and I felt all three of them relax. They had been working all night and all day. Now they were into their third straight hour of interrogation. And interrogation is heavy work. It demands close attention and mental flexibility. It wears you out. So the three guys were tired. Tired enough to have lost their edge. As soon as I headed for my chair, they moved out of the present and into the future. They thought their troubles were over. They started thinking about their approach. Their first question. They assumed I would get to my chair and sit down and be ready to hear it. Be ready to answer it.

They were wrong.

Half a step short of my destination I raised my foot to the edge of the table and straightened my leg and shoved. Shoved, not kicked, because I had no shoes on. The table jerked back and the far edge hit the two seated guys in the stomach and pinned them against their chair backs. By that point I was already moving to my left. I came up from a crouch at the third guy and tore the dart gun up and out of his hands and while he was all straight and exposed I kneed him hard in the groin. He gave up on the gun and folded forward and I high-stepped and changed feet and kneed him in the face. Like a folk dance from Ireland. I spun away and levelled the gun and pulled the trigger and shot the main guy in the chest. Then I went over the table and battered the other guy in the head with the dart gun's butt, once, twice, three times, hard and vicious, until he went quiet and stopped moving.

Four noisy violent seconds, from beginning to end. Four discrete units of action and time, separately packaged, separately unleashed. The table, the dart gun, the main guy, the second guy. One, two, three, four. Smooth and easy. The two guys I had hit were unconscious and bleeding. The guy on the floor from a shattered nose, and the guy at the table from a gash to his scalp. Next to him the main guy was on his way under, chemically assisted, the same way I had been twice before. It was interesting to watch. There was some kind of muscle paralysis involved. The guy was sliding down in his chair, helpless, but his eyes were moving like he was still aware of things. I remembered the whirling shapes, and I wondered if he was seeing them too.

Then I turned and watched the door to the third room. There was still the medical technician unaccounted for. Maybe others. Maybe lots of others. But the door stayed closed. The third room stayed quiet. I knelt and checked under the third guy's jacket. No Glock. He had a shoulder holster but it was empty. Standard procedure, probably. No firearms in any closed room with a prisoner present. I checked the other two guys. Same result. Government-issue nylon shoulder rigs, both of them empty.

The third room stayed quiet.

I checked pockets. They were all empty. All sanitized. Nothing there at all, except neutral items like tissues and lonely dimes and pennies trapped down in the seams. No house keys, no car keys, no phones. Certainly no wallets, no badge holders, and no IDs.

I picked up the dart gun again and held it one-handed, out and ready. Moved to the third room's door. Swung it open and raised the gun and pretended to aim. A gun is a gun, even if it's empty and the wrong kind. It's all about first impressions and subliminal reactions.

The third room was unoccupied.

No medical technician, no back-up agents, no support staff. Nobody at all. Nothing there, except grey office furniture and fluorescent light. The room itself was the same as the first two, an old brick basement chamber painted flat white. Same size, same proportions. It had another door, which I guessed led onward, either to a fourth room or a stairwell. I crossed to it and eased it open.

A stairwell. No paint, beyond an ancient peeling layer of institutional green. I closed the door again and checked the office furniture. Three desks, five cabinets, four lockers, all grey, all plain and functional, all made of steel, all locked. With combination locks, like the cells, which made sense, because there had been no keys in the agents' pockets. The desks held no piles of paper.

Just three sleeping computers and three console telephones. I hit space bars and woke up each screen in turn. Each one asked for a password. I lifted receivers and hit redial buttons and got the operator every time. Extremely conscientious security. Painstaking, and consistent. Finish a call, dab the cradle, dial zero, hang up. The three guys weren't perfect, but they weren't idiots, either.

I stood still for a long moment. I was disappointed about the combination locks. I wanted to find their stores and reload the dart gun and shoot the other two agents with it. And I wanted my shoes.

I wasn't going to get either satisfaction.

I padded my way back to the cells. Jacob Mark and Theresa Lee looked up, looked away, looked back. Classic double takes, because I was alone and I had the dart gun in my hands. I guessed they had heard the noises and assumed I was getting smacked around. I guessed they hadn't expected me back so soon, or at all.

Lee asked, 'What happened?'

I said, 'They fell asleep.'

'How?'

'I guess my conversation bored them.'

'So now you're really in trouble.'

'As opposed to what?'

'You were innocent before.'

I said, 'Grow up, Theresa.'

She didn't answer. I checked the locks on the cell gates. They were fine items. They looked high quality and very precise. They had milled top-hat knobs graduated with neat engraving all around the edges, from the number one to the number thirty-six. The knobs turned both ways. I spun them and felt nothing at all in my fingers except the purr of slight and consistent mechanical resistance. The feel of great engineering. Certainly I didn't feel any tumblers falling.

I asked, 'Do you want me to get you out?'

Lee said, 'You can't.'

'If I could, would you want me to?'

'Why wouldn't I?'

'Because then you'd really be in trouble. If you stay, you're playing their game.'

She didn't answer.

I said, 'Jake? What about you?'

He asked, 'Did you find our shoes?'

I shook my head. 'But you could borrow theirs. They're about your size.'

'What about you?'

'There are shoe stores on Eighth Street.'

'You going to walk there barefoot?'

'This is Greenwich Village. If I can't walk around barefoot here, where can I?'

'How can you get us out?'

'Nineteenth-century problems and solutions, versus twenty-first-century expediency. But it will be difficult. So I need to know whether to start. And you need to make up your mind real fast. Because we don't have much time.'

'Before they wake up?'

'Before the Home Depot closes.'

Jake said, 'OK, I want out.'

I looked at Theresa Lee.

She said, 'I don't know. I didn't do anything.'

'Feel like sticking around and proving that? Because that's hard to do. Proving a negative always is.'

She didn't answer.

I said, 'I was telling Sansom about how we studied the Red Army. You know what they were most afraid of? Not us. They were most afraid of their own people. Their worst torment was spending their whole lives proving their own innocence, over and over again.'

Lee nodded.

'I want out,' she said.

'OK,' I said. I checked the things I needed to check. Estimated dimensions and weights by eye.

'Sit tight,' I said. 'I'll be back in less than an hour.'

* * *

First stop was the next room. The three federal agents were still out cold. The main guy would stay that way for eight solid hours. Or maybe much longer, because his body mass was less than two-thirds of mine. For a bad second it struck me that I might have killed him. A dose calibrated for a man of my size might have been dangerous for a smaller person. But the guy was breathing steadily right then. And he had started it, so the risk was his.

The other two would be waking up much earlier. Maybe fairly soon. Concussion was unpredictable. So I ducked through to the anteroom and tore all of the computer cords out of the walls and carried them back and used them to truss the two guys up like chickens. Wrists, elbows, ankles, necks, all tight and interconnected. Multistrand copper cores, tough plastic sheathing, unbreakable. I peeled my socks off and tied them together in line and used them for a gag on the guy with the head wound. Unpleasant for him, but I figured he was getting a hazardous duty supplement in his pay, and he might as well earn it. I left the other guy's mouth alone. His nose was smashed, and gagging him would have been the same thing as suffocating him. I hoped he would appreciate my benevolence in the fullness of time.

I checked my work and reloaded my pockets with my possessions from the table and then I left the building.

FORTY-SIX

The staircase led up to the first floor and came out at the back of what had once been the place where the fire trucks parked. There was a wide empty floor full of rat shit and the kind of mysterious random trash that accumulates in abandoned buildings. The big vehicle doors were locked shut with rusted iron bars and old padlocks. But there was a personnel door in the left hand wall. Getting to it wasn't easy. There was a half-cleared path. The trash on the floor had been mostly kicked to the side by the passage of feet, but there was still enough debris left around to make barefoot walking difficult. I ended up sweeping stuff out of the way with the side of my foot and stepping into the spaces I had made, one pace at a time. Slow progress. But I got there in the end.

The personnel door was fitted with a new lock, but it was designed to keep people out, not in. On the inside was just a simple lever. On the outside was a combination dial. I found a heavy brass hose coupler on the floor and used it to wedge the door open a crack. I left it that way for my return and stepped out to an alley and two careful paces later I was on the West 3rd Street sidewalk.

I headed straight for Sixth Avenue. Nobody looked at my feet. It was a hot night and there was plenty more attractive skin on display. I looked at some of it myself. Then I flagged down a cab and it took me twenty blocks north and half a block east to the Home Depot on 23rd Street. Docherty had mentioned the address. Hammers had been bought there, prior to the attack under the FDR Drive. The store was getting ready to close up, but they let me in anyway. I found a five-foot pry bar in the contractor section. Cold rolled steel, thick and strong. The trip back to the registers took me through the gardening section and I decided to kill two birds with one stone by picking up a pair of rubber gardening clogs. They were ugly, but better than literally nothing. I paid with my ATM card, which I knew would leave a computer trail, but there was no reason to conceal the fact that I was out buying tools. That purchase was about to become obvious in other ways.

Cabs cruised the street outside like vultures, looking for people with stuff too awkward to carry. Which made no sense economically. Save five bucks at the big-box store, spend eight hauling it home. But the arrangement suited me fine right then. Within a minute I was on my way back south. I got out on 3rd near but not right next to the firehouse.

Ten feet ahead of me I saw the medical tech step into the alley.

The guy looked clean and rested. He was

wearing chinos and a white T-shirt and basketball shoes. Staff rotation, I figured. The agents held the fort all day, and then the medical guy took over at night. To make sure the prisoners were still alive in the morning. Efficient, rather than humane. I imagined that the flow of information was considered more important than any individual's rights or welfare.

I put the pry bar in my left hand and hustled hard in my loose rubber shoes and made it to the personnel door before the guy was all the way through it. I didn't want him to kick the hose coupler away and let it close behind him. That would give me a problem I didn't need. The guy heard me and turned in the doorway and his hands came up defensively and I shoved him hard and tumbled him inside. He slid on the trash and went down on one knee. I picked him up by the neck and held him at arm's length and eased the brass coupler aside with my toe and let the door close until it clicked. Then I turned back and was about to explain the guy's options to him but I saw that he already understood them. Be good, or get hit. He chose to be good. He went into a crouch and raised his hands in a small abbreviated gesture of surrender. I hefted the pry bar in my left hand and straight-armed the guy onward towards the head of the stairs. He was meek all the way down to the basement. He gave me no trouble on the way through the office room. Then we got to the second room and he saw the three guys on the floor and sensed what was in store for him. He tensed up. Adrenalin kicked in. Fight or flight. Then he looked at me again, a huge determined man in ludicrous shoes, holding a big metal bar.

He went quiet.

I asked him, 'Do you know the combinations for the cells?'

He said, 'No.'

'So how do you give painkiller injections?'

'Through the bars.'

'What happens if someone has a seizure and you can't get in the cell?'

'I have to call.'

'Where is your equipment?'

'In my locker.'

'Show me,' I said. 'Open it.'

We went back to the anteroom and he led me to a locker and spun the combination dial. The door swung open. I asked him, 'Can you open any of the other cabinets?'

He said, 'No, just this one.'

His locker had a bunch of shelves inside, piled high with all kinds of medical stuff. Wrapped syringes, a stethoscope, small phials of colourless liquids, packs of cotton balls, pills, bandages, gauze, tape.

Plus a shallow box of tiny nitrogen capsules.

And a box of wrapped darts.

Which made some kind of bureaucratic sense. I imagined the management conference back when they were writing the operations manual. The Pentagon. Staff officers in charge. Some junior ranks present. An agenda. Some DoD counsel insisting that the dart gun's ammunition be held by a qualified medical officer. Because anaesthetic was a drug. And so on and so forth. Then some other active-duty type saying that compressed nitrogen wasn't medical. A third guy pointing out it made no sense at all to keep the propellant separate from the load. Around and around. I imagined exasperated agents eventually giving up and giving in. *OK, whatever, let's move on*.

I asked, 'What exactly is in the darts?'

The guy said, 'Local anaesthetic to help the wound site, plus a lot of barbiturate.'

'How much barbiturate?'

'Enough.'

'For a gorilla?'

The guy shook his head. 'Reduced dose. Calculated for a normal human.'

'Who did the calculation?'

'The manufacturer.'

'Knowing what it was for?'

'Of course.'

'With specifications and purchase orders and everything?'

'Yes.'

'And tests?'

'Down at Guantanamo.'

'Is this a great country, or what?'

The guy said nothing.

I asked him, 'Are there side effects?'

'None.'

'You sure? You know why I'm asking, right?'

The guy nodded. He knew why I was asking. I was fresh out of computer cords, so I had to keep half an eye on him while I found the gun and loaded it. Loading it was a jigsaw puzzle. I wasn't familiar with the technology. I had to proceed on common sense and logic alone. Clearly the trigger mechanism tripped the gas release. Clearly the gas propelled the dart. And guns are basically simple machines. They have fronts and backs. Cause and effect happens in a rational sequence. I got the thing charged up inside forty seconds.

I said, 'You want to lie down on the floor?'

The guy didn't answer.

I said, 'You know, to save bumping your head.'

The guy got down on the floor.

I asked him, 'Any preference as to where? Arm? Leg?'

He said, 'It works best into muscle mass.'

'So roll over.'

He rolled over and I shot him in the ass.

* * *

I reloaded the thing twice more and put darts into the two agents that were liable to wake up. Which gave me at least an eight-hour margin, unless there were other unanticipated arrivals on the horizon. Or unless the agents were supposed to call in with status checks every hour. Or unless there was a car already on its way to take us back to D.C. Which conflicting thoughts made me feel half relaxed and half urgent. I carried the pry bar through to the cell block. Jacob Mark looked at me and said nothing. Theresa Lee looked at me and said, 'They sell shoes like that on Eighth Street now?'

I didn't answer. Just stepped around to the back of her cell and jammed the flat end of the pry bar under the bottom of the structure. Then I leaned my weight on the bar and felt the whole thing move, just a little. Just a fraction of an inch. Not much more than the natural flex of the metal.

'That's stupid,' Lee said. 'This thing is a self-contained freestanding cube. You might be able to tip it over, but I'll still be inside.'

I said, 'Actually it's not freestanding.'

'It's not bolted to the floor.'

'But it's clamped down by the sewer connection. Under the toilet.'

'Will that help?'

'I hope so. If I tip it up and the sewer connection holds, then the floor will tear off, and you can crawl out.'

'Will it hold?'

'It's a gamble. It's a kind of competition.'

'Between what?'

'Nineteenth-century legislation and a sleazy twenty-first-century welding shop with a government contract. See how the floor isn't welded all the way around? Just in some places?'

'That's the nature of spot welding.'

'How strong is it?'

'Plenty strong. Stronger than the toilet pipe, probably.'

'Maybe not. There was cholera in New York in the nineteenth century. A big epidemic. It killed lots of people. Eventually the city fathers figured out what was causing it, which was cesspools mixing with the drinking water. So they built proper sewers. And they specified all kinds of standards for the pipes and the connectors. Those standards are still in the building code, all these years later. A pipe like this has a flange lapping over the floor. I'm betting it's fixed stronger than the spot welds. Those nineteenth-century public works guys erred on the side of caution. More so than some modern corporation wanting Homeland Security money.'

Lee paused a beat. Then she smiled, briefly. 'So either I get illegally busted out of a government jail cell, or the sewer pipe gets torn out of the floor. Either way I'm in the shit.'

'You got it.'

'Great choice.'

'Your call,' I said.

'Go for it.'

Two rooms away I heard a telephone start to ring.

I knelt down and eased the tip of the pry bar into the position it needed to be in, which was under the bottom horizontal rail of the cell, but not so far under that it also caught the edge of the floor tray. Then I kicked it sideways a little until it was directly below one of the upside-down T-welds, where the force would be carried upward through one of the vertical bars.

Two rooms away the telephone stopped ringing.

I looked at Lee and said, 'Stand on the toilet seat. Let's give it all the help we can.'

She climbed up and balanced. I took up all the slack in the pry bar and then leaned down hard and bounced, once, twice, three times. Two hundred and fifty pounds of moving mass, multiplied by sixty inches of leverage. Three things happened. First, the pry bar dug itself a shallow channel in the concrete under the cage, which was mechanically inefficient. Second, the whole assemblage of bars distorted out of shape a little, which was also inefficient. But third, a bright bead of metal pinged loose and skittered away.

'That was a spot,' Lee called. 'As in spot-weld.'

I moved the pry bar and found a similar position twelve inches to the left. Wedged the bar tight, took up the slack, and bounced. Same three results. The grind of powdered concrete, the screech of bending bars, and the ping of another metal bead torn loose.

Two rooms away a second phone started to ring. A different tone. More urgent.

I stood back and caught my breath. Moved the pry bar again, this time two feet to the right. Repeated the procedure, and was rewarded with another broken weld. Three down, many more to go. But now I had approximate hand-holds in the bottom rail, where the pry bar had forced shallow U-shaped bends into the metal. I put the pry bar down and squatted facing the cell and shoved my hands palms-up into the holds. Grasped hard and breathed hard and prepared to lift. When I quit watching the Olympics the weightlifters were moving more than five hundred pounds. I figured I was capable of much less than that. But I figured much less than that might do the trick.

Two rooms away the second telephone stopped ringing.

And a third started.

I heaved upward.

I got the side of the cell about a foot off the ground. The tread plate floor shrieked and bent like paper. But the welds held. The third telephone stopped ringing. I looked up at Lee and mouthed, 'Jump.' She got the message. She was a smart woman. She jumped high off the toilet and smashed her bare feet down together right where two welds were under pressure. I felt nothing through my hands. No impact. No shock. Because the welds broke immediately and the floor bent down into a radical V-shaped chute. Like a mouth. The opening was about a foot wide and a foot deep. Good, but not good enough. A kid might have gotten through it, but Lee wasn't going to.

But at least we had proved the principle. Score one for the nineteenth-century city fathers.

Two rooms away all three phones started to ring simultaneously. Competing tones, fast and urgent.

I caught my breath again and after that it was just a question of repeating the triple procedures over and over again, two welds at a time. The pry bar, the weightlifting, the jump. Lee wasn't a big woman, but even so we needed to tear free a line of welds nearly six feet long before the floor would bend down enough to let her out. It was a question of simple arithmetic. The straight edge of the floor became part of a curved circumference, in a ratio of one to three against us. It took us a long time to get the job done. Close to eight minutes. But we got it done eventually. Lee came out on her back, feet first, like a limbo dancer. Her shirt got caught and rode up to reveal a smooth tan stomach. Then she wriggled free and crabbed clear and stood up and hugged me hard. And longer than she needed to. Then she broke away and I rested for a minute and wiped my hands on my pants.

Then I repeated the whole procedure all over again, for Jacob Mark.

Two rooms away phones rang and stopped, rang and stopped.

FORTY-SEVEN

We got out fast. Theresa Lee took the lead agent's shoes. They were big on her, but not by much. Jacob Mark took the medical technician's whole outfit. He figured that an incomplete out-of-town cop's uniform would be conspicuous on the street, and he was probably right. The change was worth the delay. He looked much better in the chinos and the T-shirt and the basketball sneakers. They fit close to perfectly. There was a nickel-sized bloodstain on the back of the pants, but that was the only disadvantage. We left the medical guy sleeping in his underwear.

Then we headed out. Up the stairs, across the littered floor, through the alley, to the 3rd Street sidewalk. It was crowded. It was still hot. We turned left. No real reason. Just a random choice. But a lucky one. We got about five steps away and I heard the blare of a horn behind us and the yelp of tyres and I glanced back and saw a black car jamming to a stop ten feet the other side of the firehouse. A Crown Vic, new and shiny. Two guys spilled out. I had seen them before. And I knew for sure that Theresa Lee had seen them before. Blue suits, blue ties. The FBI. They had talked to Lee in the precinct house, and they had talked to me on 35th Street. They had asked me questions about Canadian phone numbers. Now twenty feet behind us they ran for the alley and ducked in. They didn't see us at all. But if we had turned right we would have collided head-on with them as they got out of their car. So we had been lucky. We celebrated by hustling hard, straight for Sixth Avenue. Jacob Mark got there first. He was the only one of us with decent shoes.

* * *

We crossed Sixth Avenue and followed Bleecker for a spell and then found refuge on Cornelia

Street, which was narrow and dark and relatively quiet, except for diners at sidewalk café tables. We stayed well away from them and they paid no attention to us. They were more interested in their food. I didn't blame them. It smelled good. I was still very hungry, even after the salami and cheese. We headed up to the quiet end of the street and took inventory there. Lee and Jake had nothing. All their stuff was locked away in the firehouse basement. I had what I had reclaimed from the table in the second room, the important components of which were my cash, my ATM card, my Metrocard, and Leonid's cell phone. The cash amounted to forty-three dollars and change. The Metrocard had four rides left on it. Leonid's cell was almost out of battery. We agreed it was beyond certain that my ATM number and Leonid's phone number were already flagged up in various computer systems. If we used either one, someone would know within seconds. But I wasn't too worried. Information has to be useful to be damaging. If we escaped from West 3rd and days later withdrew cash in Oklahoma City or New Orleans or San Francisco, then that data would be significant. If we withdrew cash immediately a couple of blocks from the firehouse, then that data was useless. It told them nothing they didn't already know. And there are so many cell antennas in New York that triangulation is difficult. A ballpark location is helpful out in the sticks. Not so much, in the city. A target area two blocks wide and two deep can contain fifty thousand people and take days to search.

So we moved on and found an ATM in a bright blue bank lobby and I withdrew all the cash I could, which was three hundred bucks. Apparently I had a daily limit. And the machine was slow. Probably on purpose. Banks cooperate with law enforcement. They sound the alarm and then slow down the transaction. The idea is to give the cops time to show up. Maybe possible, in some places. Not very likely, with city traffic to deal with. The machine waited and waited and waited and then it coughed up the bills. I took them and smiled at the machine. Most of them have surveillance cameras built in, connected to digital recorders.

We moved on again and Lee spent ten of my new dollars in a deli. She bought an emergency cell phone charger. It operated off a penlight battery. She plugged it into Leonid's phone and called Docherty, her partner. It was ten after ten, and he would be getting ready for work. He didn't pick up the call. Lee left a message and then switched off the phone. She said cell phones had GPS chips in them. I didn't know that. She said the chips bleeped away every fifteen seconds and could be pinned down within fifteen feet. She said GPS satellites were much more precise than antenna triangulation. She said the way to use a cell on the run was to keep it switched off except for brief moments just before leaving one location and moving on to the next. That way the GPS trackers were always one step behind.

So we moved on again. We were all aware of cop cars on the streets. We saw plenty of them. The NYPD is a big operation. The largest police department in America. Maybe the largest in the world. We found a noisy bistro in the heart of NYU territory after skirting north of Washington Square Park and then heading east. The place was dark and packed with undergraduate students. Some of the food it sold was recognizable. I was hungry and still dehydrated. I guessed my systems had been working overtime to flush out the double dose of barbiturate. I drank whole glasses of tap water and ordered a kind of shake made of yoghurt and fruit. Plus a burger, and coffee. Jake and Lee ordered nothing. They said they were too shaken to eat. Then Lee turned to me and said, 'You better tell us what exactly is going on.'

I said, 'I thought you didn't want to know.'

'We just crossed that line.'

'They didn't show ID. You were entitled to assume the detention was illegal. In which case busting out wasn't a crime. In fact it was probably your duty.'

She shook her head. 'I knew who they were, ID or no ID. And it's not the busting out that I'm worried about. It's the shoes. That's what's going to screw me. I stood over the guy and stole his footwear. I was looking right at him. That's premeditation. They'll say I had time to reflect and react appropriately.'

I looked at Jake, to see whether he wanted to be included, or whether he still figured that innocence was bliss. He shrugged, as if to say in for a penny, in for a pound. So I let the waitress finish up serving my order and then I told them what I knew. March of 1983, Sansom, the Korengal Valley. All the details, and all the implications.

Lee said, 'There are American troops in the Korengal Valley right now. I just read about it. In a magazine. I guess it never stops. I hope they're doing better than the Russians did.'

'They were Ukrainians,' I said.

'Is there a difference?'

'I'm sure the Ukrainians think so. The Russians put their minorities out front, and their minorities didn't like it.'

Jake said, 'I get it about World War Three. At the time, I mean. But this is a quarter-century later. The Soviet Union isn't even a country any more. How can a country be aggrieved about something, if it doesn't even exist today?'

'Geopolitics,' Lee said. 'It's about the future, not the past. Maybe we want to do similar stuff again, in Pakistan or Iran or wherever. It makes a difference if the world knows we did it before. It sets up preconceptions. You know that. You're a cop. You like it when we can't mention prior convictions in court?'

Jake said, 'So how big of a deal do you think this is?'

'Huge,' Lee said. 'As big as can be. For us, anyway. Because overall it's still small. Which is ironic, right? You see what I mean? If three thousand people knew, there's not much anyone could do about it. Or three hundred, even. Or thirty. It would be out there, end of story. But right now only the three of us know. And three is a small number. Small enough to be contained. They can make three people disappear without anyone noticing.'

'How?'

'It happens, believe me. Who's going to pay attention? You're not married. Me either.' She looked at me and asked, 'Reacher, are you married?'

I shook my head.

She paused a second. She said, 'No one left

behind to ask questions.'

Jake said, 'What about people where we work?'

'Police departments do what they're told.'

'This is insane.'

'This is the new world.'

'Are they serious?'

'It's a cost-benefit analysis. Three innocent people versus a big geopolitical deal? What would you do?'

'We have rights.'

'We used to.'

Jake said nothing in reply to that. I finished my coffee and washed it down with another glass of tap water. Lee called for the check and waited until it had arrived and I had paid it, and then she turned Leonid's phone back on. It came to life with a merry little tune and locked on to its network and ten seconds after that its network recognized it and told it there was a text message waiting. Lee hit the appropriate button and started scrolling.

'It's from Docherty,' she said. 'He hasn't dumped me yet.'

Then she read and scrolled, read and scrolled. I counted fifteen-second intervals in my head, and imagined the GPS chip sending out a little burst of data for every one of them, saying *Here we are! Here we are!* I got up to ten. A hundred and fifty seconds. Two and a half minutes. It was a long message. And it was full of bad news, according to Lee's face. Her lips compressed and her eyes narrowed. She checked back on a couple of paragraphs and then she shut the thing down again and handed it back to me. I put it in my pocket. She looked straight at me and said, 'You were right. The dead guys under the FDR Drive were Lila Hoth's crew. I guess the 17th called everyone in the phone book and checked out the only one that didn't answer. They broke into their offices and found billing records made out to Lila Hoth, in care of the Four Seasons Hotel.'

I didn't answer.

She said, 'But here's the thing. Those billing records go back three months, not three days. And the other data is in. Homeland Security has no record of two women called Hoth ever entering the country. Certainly not three days ago on British Airways. And Susan Mark never called London, either from work or from home.'

FORTY-EIGHT

Use the phone and move on immediately, was the rule. We took Broadway north. Taxis and police cruisers sped past us. Headlight beams washed over us. We hustled as far as Astor Place and then ducked underground and burned three of my four remaining Metrocard rides on the 6 train north. Where it all began. Another bright new R142A car. It was eleven in the evening and there were eighteen passengers in addition to ourselves. We got three spaces together on one of the eight-person benches. Lee sat in the middle. On her left Jake half turned and bent his head, ready for quiet talk. On her right I did the same thing. Jake asked, 'So which is it? Are the Hoths phony or is the government already covering its ass by erasing data?'

Lee said, 'Could be either.'

I said, 'The Hoths are phony.'

'You think or you know?'

'It was too easy at Penn station.'

'How?'

'They sucked me in. Leonid let me see him. He was wearing a jacket that looked bright orange under the lights. It was practically the same as the safety vests I saw some railroad workers wearing. It drew my eye. I was supposed to notice it. Then he let me hit him. Because I was supposed to take the phone from him and find out about the Four Seasons. They manipulated me. There are layers upon layers here. They needed to talk to me but they didn't want me to see everything. They didn't want to show their whole hand. So they set up a way in for me. They lured me to the hotel and tried a sweet, easy approach. Just one guy acting incompetent at the railroad station, and then the soft soap. They even had a back-up plan, which was coming to the precinct house and making the missing persons report. Either way I would have showed up eventually.'

'What do they want from you?'

'Susan's information.'

'Which was what?'

'I don't know.'

'Who are they?'

'Not journalists,' I said. 'I guess I was wrong about that. Lila was acting one thing, acting another thing. I don't know what she really is.'

'Is the old woman for real?'

'I don't know.'

'Where are they now? They bailed out of the hotel.'

'They always had somewhere else. They had two tracks running. Public consumption, and private business. So I don't know where they are now. Their alternative place, obviously. Some long-term secure location, I guess. Here in the city, probably. Maybe a town house. Because they have a crew with them. People of their own. Bad people. Those private guys were right. How bad, they just found out the hard way. With the hammers.'

Lee said, 'So the Hoths are covering their asses too.'

'Wrong tense,' I said. 'They already covered them. They're hunkered down someplace and anyone who might have known where is dead.'

* * *

The train stopped at 23rd Street. The doors opened. No one got on. No one got off. Theresa Lee stared at the floor. Jacob Mark looked across her at me and said, 'If Homeland Security can't even track Lila Hoth into the country, then they also can't tell if she went to California or not. Which means it could have been her, with Peter.'

'Yes,' I said. 'It could have been.'

The doors closed. The train moved on.

Theresa Lee looked up from the floor and turned to me and said, 'What happened to those four guys was our fault, you know. With the hammers. Your fault, specifically. You told Lila you knew about them. You turned them into a loose end.'

I said, 'Thanks for pointing that out.'

You tipped her over the edge.

Your fault, specifically.

The train rattled into the 28th Street station.

* * *

We got out at 33rd Street. None of us wanted to hit Grand Central. Too many cops, and in Jacob Mark's case at least, maybe too many negative associations. At street level Park Avenue was busy. Two cop cars came past in the first minute. To the west was the Empire State Building. Too many cops. We doubled back south and took a quiet cross street towards Madison. I was feeling pretty good by then. I had spent sixteen hours out of seventeen fast asleep, and I was full of food and fluids. But Lee and Jake looked beat. They had nowhere to go and weren't used to it. Obviously they couldn't go home. They couldn't go to friends, either. We had to assume all their known haunts were being watched.

Lee said, 'We need a plan.'

I liked the look of the block we were on. New York has hundreds of separate micro-neighbourhoods. Flavour and nuance vary street by street, sometimes building by building. Park and Madison in the high 20s are slightly seedy. The cross streets are a little down at heel. Maybe once they were high end, and maybe one day they will be again, but right then they were comfortable. We hid out under sidewalk scaffolding for a spell and watched drunks staggering home from bars, and people from nearby apartment houses walking their dogs before bed. We saw a guy with a Great Dane the size of a pony, and a girl with a rat terrier the size of the Great Dane's head. Overall I preferred the rat terrier. Small dog, big personality. The little guy thought he was boss of the world. We waited until the clock passed midnight and then we snaked back and forth west and east until we found the right kind of hotel. It was a narrow place with an out-of-date illuminated sign backed with low-wattage bulbs. It looked a little run down and grimy. Smaller than I would have liked. Bigger places work much better. Greater chance of empty rooms, more anonymity, less supervision. But all in all the place we were looking at was feasible.

It was a decent target for the fifty dollar trick.

Or maybe we could even get away with forty.

* * *

In the end we had to bid our way up to seventy-five, probably because the night porter suspected we had some kind of a sexual threesome in mind. Maybe because of the way Theresa Lee was looking at me. There was something going on in her eyes. I wasn't sure what. But clearly the night porter saw an opportunity to raise his rate. The room he gave us was small. It was at the back of the building and had twin beds and a narrow window on an air shaft. It was never going to show up in a tourist brochure, but it felt secure and clandestine and I could tell that Lee and Jake felt good about spending the night in it. But equally I could tell that neither one of them felt good about spending two nights in it, or five, or ten.

'We need help,' Lee said. 'We can't live like this indefinitely.'

'We can if we want to,' I said. 'I've lived like this for ten years.'

‘OK, a normal person can’t live like this indefinitely. We need help. This problem isn’t going to go away.’

‘It could,’ Jake said. ‘From how you were figuring it before. If three thousand people knew, it wouldn’t be a problem any more. So all we have to do is tell three thousand people.’

‘One at a time?’

‘No, we should call the newspapers.’

‘Would they believe us?’

‘If we were convincing.’

‘Would they print the story?’

‘Why wouldn’t they?’

‘Who knows what goes on with newspapers now? Maybe they would check with the government about a thing like this. Maybe the government would tell them to sit on it.’

‘What about freedom of the press?’

Lee said, ‘Yes, I remember that.’

‘So who the hell will help us?’

‘Sansom,’ I said. ‘Sansom will help us. He’s got the biggest investment here.’

‘Sansom *is* the government. He had his own guy trailing Susan.’

‘Because he has a lot to lose. We can use that.’ I took Leonid’s phone out of my pocket and dropped it on the bed next to Theresa Lee. ‘Text Docherty in the morning. Get the number for the Cannon House Office Building in D.C. Call Sansom’s office and demand to speak with him personally. Tell him you’re a police officer in New York and that you’re with me. Tell him we know his guy was on the train. Then tell him we know the DSM wasn’t for the VAL rifle. Tell him we know there’s more.’

FORTY-NINE

Theresa Lee picked up the phone and held it for a moment like it was a rare and precious jewel. Then she put it on the night stand and asked, 'What makes you think there's more?'

I said, 'Overall there has to be more. Sansom won four medals, not just one. He was a regular go-to guy. He must have done all kinds of things.'

'Like what?'

'Whatever needed doing. For whoever needed it done. Not just the army. Delta guys were loaned out, from time to time. To the CIA, on occasion.'

'To do what?'

'Covert interventions. Coups. Assassinations.'

'Marshal Tito died in 1980. In Yugoslavia. You think Sansom did that?'

'No, I think Tito got sick. But I wouldn't be surprised if there was a back-up plan, in case he stayed healthy.'

'Brezhnev died in 1982. In Russia. Then Andropov, pretty soon after that. Then Chernenko, real quick. It was like an epidemic.'

'What are you? A historian?'

'Amateur. But whatever, all that led to Gorbachev, and progress. You think that was us? You think that was Sansom?'

'Maybe,' I said. 'I don't know.'

'But whatever, none of that kind of stuff relates to March of 1983 in Afghanistan.'

'But think about it. Stumbling into a Soviet sniper team in the dark was a totally random chance. Would they have sent a go-to ace like

Sansom walking around in the hills, hoping for the best? A hundred times out of a hundred and one he would have come up empty. That's a massive risk for very little reward. That's no kind of mission planning. A mission needs an achievable objective.'

'A lot of them fail.'

'Of course they do. But they all start out with a realistic target. More realistic than blundering around in a thousand square miles of empty mountains hoping for a random face to face encounter. So there must have been something else going on.'

'That's pretty vague.'

'There's more,' I said. 'And it's not so vague. People have been talking to me for days. And I've been listening. Some of what I heard doesn't make much sense. Those federal guys snarled me up at the Watergate in D.C. I asked them what was going on. Their reaction was weird. It was like the sky was about to fall. It was way out of proportion for some technical trespass twenty-five years ago.'

'Geopolitics isn't simple.'

'I agree. And I'm the first to admit I'm no kind of an expert. But even so it seemed way over the top.'

'That's still vague.'

'I spoke to Sansom in D.C. At his office. He seemed sour about the whole thing. Gloomy, and kind of troubled.'

'It's election season.'

'But grabbing up the rifle was kind of cool, wasn't it? Nothing to be ashamed of. It was all about what the army used to call dash and daring. So his reaction was wrong.'

'Still vague.'

'He knew the sniper's name. Grigori Hoth. From his dog tags. I figured he had the tags as souvenirs. He said, no, those tags were locked up with the after-action reports and everything else. It was like a slip of the tongue. And everything else? What did that mean?'

Lee said nothing.

I said, 'We talked about the fate of the sniper and the spotter. Sansom said he had no silenced weapons. Which was like another slip of the tongue. Delta would never set up for clandestine night-time incursions without silenced weapons. They're particular about stuff like that. Which suggests to me that the whole VAL episode was an accidental byproduct of something else entirely. I thought the rifle *was* the story. But this thing is like an iceberg. Most of it is still hidden.'

Lee said nothing.

I said, 'Then we talked about the geopolitics. He saw a danger, for sure. He's worried about Russia, or the Russian Federation, or whatever it is they call themselves now. He thinks they're unstable. He said things could blow up big, if the Korengal part of the story gets out. You hear that? The Korengal *part of* the story? It was like a third slip of the tongue. It was effectively a direct admission that there's more. Direct from the horse's mouth.'

Lee didn't answer. Jacob Mark asked, 'What kind of more?'

'I don't know. But whatever it is, it's information-intensive. Right from the start Lila Hoth was looking for a USB memory. And the feds assume there's one out there somewhere.

They said their task is to recover the real memory stick. Real, because they took a look at the one I bought and assumed it was a decoy. They said, it's empty and it's too small anyway. Hear that? Too small? Which means there are some big files in play. Lots of information.'

'But Susan didn't have anything with her.'

'True. But everybody assumes she did.'

'What kind of information?'

'I have no idea. Except that Springfield talked to me here in New York. Sansom's security guy, at the Sheraton. In a quiet corridor. He was very uptight. He was warning me off. He chose a specific metaphor. He said, you can't afford to turn over the wrong rock.'

'So?'

'What happens when you turn over a rock?'

'Things crawl out.'

'Exactly. Present tense. Things crawl out. This is not about things just lying there, that died twenty-five years ago. This is about things that are squirming and wriggling right now. This is about things that are alive today.'

* * *

I saw Theresa Lee thinking it through. She glanced at the phone on the night table. Her eyes narrowed. I guessed she was rehearsing the morning call to Sansom. She said, 'He's kind of careless, isn't he? He made three slips of the tongue.'

I said, 'He was a Delta officer the best part of seventeen years.'

'And?'

'You don't last seventeen days if you're careless.'

'So?'

'He seems very engaged to me. He's aware of everything to do with his campaign. How he looks, what he says, how he travels. Every last little implication.'

'So?'

'So I don't think he's careless.'

'He made three slips of the tongue.'

'Did he? I'm not so sure. I wonder if he was setting a trap instead. He read my record. I was a good MP, and pretty close to his generation. I think maybe he was looking for help, any old place he could get it.'

'You think he was recruiting you?'

'Maybe,' I said. 'I think maybe he was dropping a couple of breadcrumbs, and waiting to see if I would follow them.'

'Because?'

'Because he wants the lid back on, and he's not sure who can do it for him.'

'He doesn't trust the DoD guys?'

'Would you?'

'That's not my world. Would you trust them?'

'About as far as I can spit.'

'Doesn't he trust Springfield?'

'With his life. But Springfield is just one guy. And Sansom has a big problem. So maybe he figures if some other guy is in, he might as well stay in. The more the merrier.'

'So he's bound to help us.'

'Not bound,' I said. 'His jurisdiction is strictly limited. But he might be inclined. Which is why I want you to call him.'

'Why don't you call him?'

'Because I'm not going to be here at start of business tomorrow.'

'You're not?'

'I'll meet you at ten, in Madison Square Park. A couple of blocks south of here. Be careful getting there.'

'Where are you going?'

'Out.'

'Where?'

'To look for Lila Hoth.'

'You won't find her.'

'Probably not. But she's got a crew. Maybe they'll find me. I'm sure they're out looking for me. And they've got my picture.'

'You're going to use yourself as bait?'

'Whatever works.'

'I'm sure the cops are out looking for you too. And the Defense Department, and the FBI. Maybe people we've never even heard of.'

'Busy night all around.'

'Take care, OK?'

'Always.'

'When are you leaving?'

'Now.'

FIFTY

New York City. One o'clock in the morning. The best place and the worst place in the world to be hunted. The streets were still warm. Traffic was light. Whole ten-second intervals went by with no cars on Madison. There were still people around.

Some of them were asleep, in doorways or on benches. Some of them were walking, either purposefully or aimlessly. I took the aimless route. I chose 30th Street and crossed to Park, and then Lex. I was never trained in the art of staying invisible. They picked smaller guys for that. The normal-sized people. They took one look at me and gave up on the whole proposition. They assumed that a guy my size would always be too easy to make. But I get by. I taught myself a few techniques. Some of them are counterintuitive. Night is better than day, because places are lonelier. When places are lonelier, I stand out less, not more. Because when people look for me, they look for a big guy. And size is easier to judge when there are handy comparisons all around. Put me in a crowd of fifty civilians, and I stand out, literally head and shoulders above the rest. On my own, people are less sure. No benchmarks. People are bad at judging height in isolation. We know that from experiments with eye-witness testimony. Stage an incident, ask for first impressions, and the same guy can be described as anywhere between five-eight and six-four. People see, but they don't look.

Except for people trained to look.

I paid a lot of attention to cars. No way to find an individual in New York City except by cruising the streets. The place is just too big for any alternative method. The NYPD's blue and white cruisers were easy to spot. Their light bars made a distinctive silhouette even far in the distance. Every time I saw one coming I paused in the nearest doorway and laid myself down. Just another homeless guy. Unconvincing in winter, because I didn't have a mound of old blankets over me. But the weather was still hot. The real homeless people were still in T-shirts.

Unmarked cop cars were harder to make. Their front-end silhouettes were the same as everything else's, which was the point. But domestic politics and law enforcement budgets restrict choice to a specific handful of makes and models. And most individual vehicles are characteristically neglected. They're dirty, they sag, they wallow.

Except for unmarked federal cars. Same makes, same models, but often new and clean and waxed and polished. Easy enough to spot, but not easy to distinguish from certain car service rides. Limousine companies use some of the same makes and models. Crown Vics, and their Mercury equivalents. And livery drivers keep their cars clean. I spent some time horizontal in doorways only to see T&LC plates flash past. Taxi and Limousine Commission. Which frustrated me, until I remembered Theresa Lee's comment about the NYPD's counterterrorism squad cruising around in fake cabs. After that I erred on the side of caution.

I figured Lila Hoth's crew would have rentals. Hertz, Avis, Enterprise, or whoever else was new on the scene. Again, a fairly specific handful of makes and models, mostly domestic pieces-of-shit, but new and clean and well maintained. I saw plenty of vehicles that fit the bill, and plenty that didn't. I took all reasonable precautions to stay out of law enforcement's way, and I made all reasonable efforts to let Lila Hoth's people see me. The late hour helped. It simplified things. It categorized the population. Innocent bystanders were mostly home in bed.

I walked for half an hour, but nothing happened.

Until one thirty in the morning.

Until I looped around to 22nd and Broadway.

FIFTY-ONE

By chance I saw the girl with the rat terrier again. She was walking south on Broadway, heading for 22nd. The little guy was peeing on some posts and ignoring others. I passed them by and the dog noticed me and barked. I turned around to reassure it that I was no kind of a major danger and I saw in the corner of my eye a black Crown Vic come through the 23rd Street light. Clean, shiny, the spike of needle antennas on the trunk lid shown up by the headlights of a car thirty yards behind it.

It slowed to a walk.

Broadway is double-wide on that block. Six lanes, all headed south, divided after the light by a short pedestrian refuge in the middle. I was on the left-hand sidewalk. Next to me, an apartment house. Beyond that, retail stores. On my right, six lanes away, the Flatiron Building. Beyond that, retail stores.

Dead ahead, a subway entrance.

The girl with the dog turned left behind me and entered the apartment building. I saw a doorman behind a desk. The Crown Vic stopped in the second of the six lanes. The car behind it pulled past and the wash of its headlights showed me two guys silhouetted in the Crown Vic's front seats. They were sitting still. Maybe checking a photograph, maybe calling in for instructions, maybe calling for backup.

I sat down on a low brick wall that ran around a planted area in front of the apartment house. The subway entrance was ten feet away.

The Crown Vic stayed where it was.

Far south of me the Broadway sidewalk was wide. Adjacent to the retail operations it was cast from concrete. The half next to the kerb was a long subway grate. The subway entrance ten feet from me was a narrow staircase. The south end of the 23rd Street station. The N and the R and the W trains. The uptown platform.

I made a bet with myself that it was a HEET entrance. A high entry-exit turnstile. Not a money wager. Something far more important. Life, liberty, and the pursuit of happiness.

I waited.

The guys in the car sat still.

At one thirty in the morning the subway was well into its night-time hours. Twenty-minute gaps between trains. I heard no rumbling or roaring from below. There was no rush of air. The trash on the distant sidewalk grates lay still.

The Crown Vic turned its front wheels. I heard the hiss of its power steering pump and the squelch of its tyres on the road. It turned sharply across four lanes and straightened through a tight S and stopped on the kerb alongside me.

The two guys stayed inside.

I waited.

It was a federal car, for sure. A pool car. Standard LX specification, not the Police

Interceptor model. Black paint, plastic wheel covers. The sidewalk wasn't busy, but it wasn't deserted, either. People were hurrying home alone, or strolling more slowly in couples. There were clubs on the cross streets to the south. I could tell, because small random knots of dazed people appeared from time to time and craned out into the traffic lanes, looking for cruising cabs.

The guys in the car moved. One tilted right and one tilted left, the way two people do in a car when they are both groping for the interior door handles at the same time.

I watched the subway grates in the sidewalk, forty yards south of me.

Nothing doing. Still air. No moving trash.

The two guys got out of their car. They were both in dark suits. Their jackets were creased low down at the back, from driving. The passenger came around and stood with the driver in the gutter close to the Crown Vic's hood. They were level with me, maybe twenty feet away across the width of the sidewalk. They had their shields already clipped on their breast pockets. FBI, I guessed, although I wasn't close enough to be sure. All those civilian shields look the same to me. The passenger called, 'Federal agents.' As if he needed to.

I didn't respond.

They stayed in the gutter. Didn't step up on the kerb. A subliminal defence mechanism, I guessed. The kerb was like a tiny rampart. It offered no real protection, but once they breached it they would have to commit. They would have to act, and they weren't sure how that would go.

The subway grates stayed still and silent.

The passenger called, 'Jack Reacher?'

I didn't answer. When all else fails, play dumb.

The driver called, 'Stay right where you are.'

My shoes were made of rubber, and much less tight and firm than I am used to. But even so I felt the first faint pre-echo of subway rumble through them. A train, either starting downtown from 28th Street, or heading uptown from 14th. A fifty-fifty chance. A downtown train was no good to me. I was on the wrong side of Broadway. An uptown train was what I wanted.

I watched the distant sidewalk grates.

The trash lay still.

The passenger called, 'Keep your hands where I can see them.'

I put one hand in my pocket. Partly to locate my Metrocard, and partly to see what would happen next. I knew that Quantico training placed great emphasis on public safety. Agents are instructed to draw their weapons only in situations of dire emergency. Many never draw their weapons at all, all the way from graduation to retirement, not even once. There were innocent people all around. An apartment house lobby directly behind me. The field of fire was high and wide and handsome, and full of collateral tragedies just waiting to happen. Passers-by, traffic, babies asleep in low-floor bedrooms.

The two agents drew their weapons.

Two identical moves. Two identical weapons. Glock pistols, taken smooth and fast and easy from shoulder holsters. Both guys were right-handed.

The passenger called, 'Don't move.'

Far to my left the trash on the subway grates stirred. An uptown train, heading my way. The dam of air in front of it moving fast, building pressure, finding escape. I stood up and walked around the railing to the head of the stairs. Not fast, not slow. I went down one step at a time. Behind me I heard the agents coming after me. Hard soles on concrete. They had better shoes than me. I turned my Metrocard in my pocket and pulled it out facing the right way around.

The fare control was high. Floor-to-ceiling bars, like a jail cell. There were two turnstiles, one on the left, one on the right. Both were narrow and full-height. No supervision necessary. No need for a manned booth. I slid my card and the last credit on it lit up the go light green and I pushed on through. Behind me the agents came to a dead stop. A regular turnstile, they would have jumped right over and explained later. But the unmanned HEET entrance took away that option. And they weren't carrying Metrocards of their own. They probably lived out on Long Island and drove to work. Spent their days at desks or in cars. They stood helplessly behind the bars. No opportunity for shouted threats or negotiations, either. I had timed it just right. The dam of air was already there in the station, skittering dust and rolling empty cups around. The first three cars were already around the curve. The train yelped and groaned and stopped and I stepped right on without even breaking stride. The doors closed and the train bore me away and the last I saw of the agents was the two of them standing there on the wrong side of the turnstile with their guns down by their sides.

FIFTY-TWO

I was on an R train. The R train follows Broadway to Times Square and then straightens a little until 57th Street and Seventh Avenue, where it hangs a tight right and stops at 59th and Fifth and then 60th and Lex before heading on under the river and east to Queens. I didn't want to go to Queens. A fine borough, no question, but unexciting at night, and anyway I felt in my gut that the action lay elsewhere. In Manhattan, for sure. On the East Side, probably, and not far from 57th Street. Lila Hoth had used the Four Seasons as a decoy. Which put her real base somewhere close by, almost certainly. Not adjacent, but comfortably proximate.

And her real base was a town house, not an apartment or another hotel. Because she had a crew with her, and they had to be able to come and go undetected.

There are a lot of town houses on the east side of Manhattan.

I stayed on the train through Times Square. A bunch of people got on there. For the minute it took to get up to 49th Street we had twenty-seven passengers on board. Then five people got out at 49th and the population started to decline. I got out at 59th and Fifth. Didn't leave the station. I just stood on the platform and watched the train go onward without me. Then I sat on a bench and waited. I figured the agents at 22nd Street would have gotten on their radio. I figured cops might be heading for the R train stations in a long sequential cascade. I pictured them sitting in their cars or standing on the sidewalks, timing the train's underground progress, tensing up, then relaxing again as they assumed I had passed by beneath them and was headed farther up the line. I pictured them staying around for five minutes or so, and then giving it up. So I waited. Ten whole minutes. Then I left. I came up from under the ground and found no one looking for me. I was alone on a deserted corner with the famous old Plaza Hotel directly in front of me, all lit up, and the park behind me, all dark.

I was two blocks north and a block and a half west of the Four Seasons.

I was exactly three blocks west of where Susan Mark would have come up out of the 6 train, right back at the beginning.

And right then I understood that Susan Mark had never been headed to the Four Seasons Hotel. Not dressed in black and ready for combat. No combat was possible in a hotel lobby or corridor or suite. No advantage was won by wearing black where there were lights. So Susan had been headed somewhere else. Directly to the secret location, presumably, which had to be on a dark, discreet cross street. But which still had to be in the original sixty-eight-block box, between 42nd Street and 59th, between Fifth Avenue and Third. Most likely in one of the upper quadrants, given the nature of the area. Either the upper left, or the upper right. One of two sixteen-block sub-boxes, maybe.

Which would contain what?

About two million different things.

Which was four times better than eight million

different things, but not so much better that I started jumping for joy. Instead I headed east across Fifth Avenue and resumed my aimless walking, watching for cars, staying in the shadows. There were many fewer homeless people than down in the 20s, and I figured that lying in doorways would be more provocative than not. So I watched the traffic and prepared either to run or to fight, depending on who found me first.

* * *

I crossed Madison Avenue and headed for Park. Now I was directly behind the Four Seasons, which was two blocks due south. The street was quiet. Mostly flagship retail and boutique commercial, all closed up. I turned south on Park and then east again on 58th. Didn't see much. Some town houses, but each one looked the same as all the others. Blank five- and six-storey brownstone façades, barred windows low down, shuttered windows above, no lights. Some of them were consulates belonging to small nations. Some of them were trophy offices for charitable foundations and small corporations. Some of them were residential, but broken up into multiple apartments. Some of them were definitely single-family homes, but all the single families appeared to be fast asleep behind locked doors.

I crossed Park and headed for Lex. Sutton Place was up ahead. Quiet, and very residential. Mostly apartments, but some houses. Historically the neighbourhood was centred more to the south and the east, but optimistic brokers had pushed its borders north and especially west, all the way to

Third Avenue. The new fringes were fairly anonymous.

Ideal territory, for a hideout.

I strolled on, west and east, north and south, 58th, 57th, 56th, Lexington, Third, Second. I quartered a lot of blocks. Nothing jumped out at me. And no one jumped out at me. I saw plenty of cars, but all of them were barrelling happily from A to B. None of them was showing the characteristic hesitant half-pace of a car whose driver is also making visual sweeps of the sidewalks. I saw plenty of people, but most of them were far in the distance and entirely innocent. Insomniac dog walkers, medical personnel heading home from the East Side hospitals, garbage workers, apartment house doormen out taking the air. One of the dog walkers came close enough to speak. The dog was an elderly grey mutt and the walker was an elderly white woman of about eighty. Her hair was done and she was fully made up. She was wearing an old-fashioned summer dress that really needed long white gloves to be complete. The dog paused and looked at me mournfully and the woman took that to be a sufficient social introduction. She said, 'Good evening.'

It was close to three o'clock, and therefore technically morning. But I didn't want to appear quarrelsome. So I just said, 'Hello.'

She said, 'Did you know that word is a recent invention?'

I said, 'What word?'

'Hello,' she said. 'It was developed as a greeting only after the invention of the telephone. People felt they needed something to say when they picked up the receiver. It was a corruption of the old word *halloo*. Which was really an expression of temporary shock or surprise. You would come upon something unexpected, and you would go, *halloo!* Perhaps people were startled by the shrillness of the telephone bell.'

'Yes,' I said. 'Perhaps they were.'

'Do you have a telephone?'

'I've used them,' I said. 'Certainly I've heard them ring.'

'Do you find the sound to be disturbing?'

'I always assumed that was the point.'

'Well, goodbye,' the woman said. 'It has been most pleasant chatting with you.'

Only in New York, I thought. The woman moved on, with her old dog by her side. I watched her go. She headed east and then south on Second Avenue and was lost to sight. I turned around and got set to head west again. But twenty feet ahead of me a gold Chevy Impala jammed to a stop in the gutter and Leonid climbed out of the back.

FIFTY-THREE

Leonid stood on the kerb and the car took off again and then stopped again twenty feet behind me. The driver got out. Good moves. I was boxed on the sidewalk, one guy in front of me, another guy behind. Leonid looked the same but different. Still tall, still thin, still bald apart from the ginger stubble, but now he was in sensible clothes and he had shed his sleepy demeanour. He was in black shoes, black knit pants, and a black hooded sweatshirt. He looked alive and alert and very dangerous. He looked like more than a gangster. More than a brawler or a hoodlum. He looked like a professional. Trained, and experienced.

He looked like an ex-soldier.

I backed up against the wall of the building next to me so that I could watch both guys at once. Leonid on my left, and the other guy on my right. The other guy was a squat man somewhere in his thirties. He looked more Middle Eastern than East European. Dark hair, no neck. Not huge. Like Leonid, but compressed vertically and therefore expanded laterally. He was dressed the same, in cheap black sweats. I looked at the knit pants and a word lodged in my mind.

The word was: *disposable*.

The guy took a step towards me.

Leonid did the same.

Two choices, as always: fight or flight. We were on 56th Street's southern sidewalk. I could have run straight across the road and tried to get away. But Leonid and his pal were probably faster than me. The law of averages. Most humans are faster than me. The old lady in the summer dress was probably faster than me. Her old grey mutt was probably faster than me.

And running away was bad enough. Running away and then getting caught immediately was totally undignified.

So I stayed where I was.

On my left, Leonid took another step closer.

On my right, the short guy did the same thing.

Whatever the army had failed to teach me about staying out of sight, they had made up for by teaching me a lot about fighting. They had taken one look at me and sent me straight to the gym. I was like a lot of military children. We had weird backgrounds. We had lived all over the world. Part of our culture was to learn from the locals. Not history or language or political concerns. We learned fighting from them. Their favoured techniques. Martial arts from the Far East, full-on brawling from the seamier parts of Europe, blades and rocks and bottles from the seamier parts of the States. By the age of twelve we had it all boiled down to a kind of composite uninhibited ferocity. Especially uninhibited. We had learned that inhibitions will hurt you faster than anything else. *Just do it* was our motto, well before Nike started making shoes. Those of us who signed up for military careers of our own were recognized and mentored and offered further tuition, where we were taken apart and put back together again. We thought we were tough when we were twelve. At eighteen, we thought we were unbeatable. We weren't. But we were very close to it, by the age of twenty-five.

Leonid took another step.

The other guy did the same.

I looked back at Leonid and saw brass knuckles on his hand.

Same for the short guy.

They had slipped them on, fast and easy. Leonid side-stepped. So did the other guy. They were perfecting their angles. I was backed up against a building, which gave me a hundred and eighty degrees of empty space in front of me. Each one of them wanted forty-five degrees of that space on his right and forty-five on his left. That way, if I bolted, they had every exit direction equally covered. Like doubles players, in tennis. Long practice, mutual support, and instinctive understanding.

They were both right-handed.

First rule when you're fighting against brass knuckles: don't get hit. Especially not in the head. But even blows against arms or ribs can break bones and paralyse muscles.

The best way not to get hit is to pull out a gun and shoot your opponents from a distance of about ten feet. Close enough not to miss, far enough to remain untouched. Game over. But I didn't have that option. I was unarmed. The next best way is either to keep your opponents far away or crush them real close. Far away, they can swing all night and never connect. Real close, they can't swing at all. The way to keep them far away is to exploit superior reach, if you have it, or use your feet. My reach is spectacular. I have very long arms. The silverback on the television show looked stumpy in comparison to me. My instructors in the army were always making puns about my reach, based on my name. But I was facing two guys, and I wasn't sure if kicking was an option I could add in. For one thing, I had lousy shoes. Rubber gardening clogs. They were loose on my feet. They would come off. And kicking with bare feet leads to broken bones. Feet are even punier than hands. Except in karate school, where there are rules. There are no rules on the street. Second thing, as soon as one foot is off the ground, you're unbalanced and potentially vulnerable. Next thing you know, you're on the floor, and then you're dead. I had seen it happen. I had made it happen.

I braced my right heel against the wall behind

me.

I waited.

I figured they would pile on together. Simultaneous launches, ninety degrees apart. Arrowing inward, more or less in step. The good news was they wouldn't be trying to kill me. Lila Hoth would have forbidden that. She wanted things from me, and corpses have nothing to offer.

The bad news was that plenty of serious injuries fall short of fatal.

I waited.

Leonid said, 'You don't have to get hurt, you know. You can just come with us, if you like, and talk to Lila.' His English was less upmarket than hers. His accent was rough. But he knew all the words.

I said, 'Go with you where?'

'You know I can't tell you that. You would have to wear a blindfold.'

I said, 'I'll take a pass on the blindfold. But you don't have to get hurt either. You can just move on, and tell Lila you never saw me.'

'But that wouldn't be true.'

'Don't be a slave to the truth, Leonid. Sometimes the truth hurts. Sometimes it bites you right in the ass.'

The upside of a concerted attack by two opponents is that they have to communicate a start signal. Maybe it's just a glance or a nod, but it's always there. It's a split second of warning. I figured Leonid for the main man. The one who speaks first usually is. He would announce the attack. I watched his eyes, very carefully.

I said, 'Are you mad about what happened at the railroad station?'

Leonid shook his head. 'I let you hit me. It was necessary. Lila said so.'

I watched his eyes.

I said, 'Tell me about Lila.'

'What do you want to know?'

'I want to know who she is.'

'Come with us, and ask her.'

'I'm asking you.'

'She's a woman with a job to do.'

'What kind of a job?'

'Come with us, and ask her.'

'I'm asking you.'

'An important job. A necessary job.'

'Which involves what?'

'Come with us, and ask her.'

'I'm asking you.'

No answer. No further conversation. I sensed them tensing up. I watched Leonid's face. Saw his eyes widen and his head duck forward in a tiny nod. They came straight for me, together. I pushed off the wall behind me and put my fists against my chest and stuck my elbows out like airplane wings and charged them as hard as they were charging me. We met at a singular point like a collapsing triangle and my elbows caught both of them full in the face. On my right I felt the short guy's upper teeth punch out and on my left I felt Leonid's lower jaw give way. Impact equals mass times velocity squared. I had plenty of mass, but my shoes were spongy and my feet were slick inside them from the heat and so my velocity was slower than it might have been.

Which reduced the impact a little.

Which left them both on their feet.

Which gave me a little more work to do.

I spun back instantly and clubbed the short guy with an enormous roundhouse right to the ear. No style. No finesse. Just a big ugly punch. His ear flattened against his head and took some of the force away, but plenty more went straight on through the crushed gristle into his skull. His neck snapped sideways and he hit his other ear with his own far shoulder. By that point I was squelching back the other way in my lousy footwear and driving my elbow deep into Leonid's gut. Same place I had hit him in Penn Station, but ten times harder. I almost popped his spine out of his back. I used the bounce to jump in the other direction, to the short guy again. He was hunching away and ready for a standing eight count. I put a low right in his kidney. That straightened him up and spun him around towards me. I bent my knees and drove forward and butted him between the eyes. Explosive. Whatever bones my elbow hadn't broken gave way and he went down like a sack. Leonid tapped me on the shoulder with his knuckleduster. He thought it was a punch, but in his depleted state a tap was all he could manage. I took my time and wound up and aimed carefully and dropped him with an uppercut to the jaw. His jaw was already broken from my elbow. Now it got broken a little more. Bone and flesh spattered out in a lazy red arc and showed up quite clearly in the street lights. Teeth, I figured, and maybe part of his tongue.

* * *

I was a little shaken. As always. Excess adrenalin was burning me up. The adrenal gland is a slow son of a bitch. Then it overcompensates. Too much, too late. I took ten seconds to get my breath. Ten more to calm down. Then I hauled both guys across the sidewalk and into a sitting position against the wall where I had been standing. Their hooded sweatshirts stretched a yard long as I was hauling on them. Cheap clothes. Disposable, in case they had gotten soaked with my blood. I got the two guys positioned so they wouldn't fall over and choke and then I dislocated their right elbows. They were both right-handed, and the odds were that I would be seeing them again. In which case I wanted them out of action. No permanent damage. Three weeks in a light cast would fix them up, good as new.

They had cell phones in their pockets. I took both of them. Both had my picture. Both call registers were blank. There was nothing else. No money. No keys. No material evidence. No clue as to where they had come from. No likelihood that they would be in a position to tell me anytime soon, either. I had hit them too hard. They were out for the count. And even when they woke up there was no guarantee they would remember anything anyway. Maybe not even their names. Concussion has unpredictable effects. Paramedics aren't kidding around when they ask concussion victims what day it is and who the President is.

No regrets on my part. Better to err on the side of safety. Guys in fights who think ahead to the aftermath usually don't get that far. They become the aftermath. So no regrets. But no net gain, either. Which was frustrating. Not even the brass knuckles fit my hand. I tried both sets on, and they were way too small. I dropped them down a storm drain twenty feet away.

Their car was still idling on the kerb. It had New York plates. No navigation system. Therefore no digital memory with a base location. I found a rental agreement in the door pocket made out to a name I had never heard and a London address that I assumed was fake. In the glove box I found instruction manuals for the car and a small spiral notebook and a ballpoint pen. The notebook had nothing written in it. I took the pen and walked back to the two guys and held Leonid's head steady with my left palm clamped down hard. Then I wrote on his forehead with the ballpoint, digging deep in his skin and tracing big letters over and over again for clarity.

I wrote: *Lila, call me*.

Then I stole their car and drove away.

FIFTY-FOUR

I drove south on Second Avenue and took 50th Street all the way east to the end and dumped the car on a hydrant half a block from the FDR Drive. I hoped the guys from the 17th Precinct would find it and get suspicious and run some tests. Clothes are disposable. Cars, not so much. If Lila's people had used that Impala to drive away from the hammer attack, then there would be some trace evidence inside. I couldn't see any with the naked eye, but CSI units don't rely on human vision alone.

I wiped the wheel and the shifter and the door handles with the tail of my shirt. Then I dropped the keys down a grate and walked back to Second and stood in a shadow and looked for a cab. There was a decent river of traffic flowing downtown and each car was lit up by the headlights behind it. I could see how many people were inside each vehicle. I was mindful of Theresa Lee's information: fake taxis, circling uptown on Tenth, down on Second, one guy in the front, two in the back. I waited for a cab that was definitively empty apart from its driver and I stepped out and flagged it down. The driver was a Sikh from India with a turban and a full beard and very little English. Not a cop. He took me south to Union Square. I got out there and sat on a bench in the dark and watched the rats. Union Square is the best place in the city to see them. By day the Parks Department dumps blood-and-bone fertilizer on the flower beds. By night the rats come out and feast on it.

At four o'clock I fell asleep.

At five o'clock one of the captured phones vibrated in my pocket.

* * *

I woke up and spent a second checking left and right and behind, and then I fumbled the phone out of my pants. It wasn't ringing. Just buzzing away to itself. Silent mode. The small monochrome window on the front said: *Restricted Call*. I opened it up and the big colour screen on the inside said the same thing. I put the phone to my ear and said, 'Hello.' A new word, recently invented. Lila Hoth answered me. Her voice, her accent, her diction. She said, 'So, you decided to declare war. Clearly there are no rules of engagement for you.'

I said, 'Who are you exactly?'

'You'll find out.'

'I need to know now.'

'I'm your worst nightmare. As of about two hours ago. And you still have something that belongs to me.'

'So come and get it. Better still, send some more of your guys. Give me some more light exercise.'

'You got lucky tonight, that's all.'

I said, 'I'm always lucky.'

She asked, 'Where are you?'

'Right outside your house.'

There was a pause. 'No, you're not.'

'Correct,' I said. 'But you just confirmed that you're living in a house. And that right now you're at a window. Thank you for that information.'

'Where are you really?'

'Federal Plaza,' I said. 'With the FBI.'

'I don't believe you.'

'Your call.'

'Tell me where you are.'

'Close to you,' I said. 'Third Avenue and 56th Street.'

She started to reply, and then she stopped herself immediately. She got no further than an inchoate little *th* sound. A voiced dental fricative. The start of a sentence that was going to be impatient and querulous and a little smug. Like, *That's not close to me*.

She wasn't anywhere near Third and 56th.

'Last chance,' she said. 'I want my property.' Her voice softened. 'We can make arrangements, if you like. Just leave it somewhere safe, and tell me where. I'll have it picked up. We don't need to meet. You could even get paid.'

'I'm not looking for work.'

'Are you looking to stay alive?'

'I'm not afraid of you, Lila.'

'That's what Peter Molina said.'

'Where is he?'

'Right here with us.'

'Alive?'

'Come over and find out.'

'He left a message with his coach.'

'Or maybe I played a tape he made before he died. Maybe he told me his coach never answers the phone at dinner time. Maybe he told me a lot of things. Maybe I forced him to.'

I asked, 'Where are you, Lila?'

'I can't tell you that,' she said. 'But I could have you picked up.'

A hundred feet away I saw a police car cruising 14th Street. Moving slow. Pink flashes at the window as the driver moved his head right and left.

I asked, 'How long have you known Peter Molina?'

'Since I picked him up in the bar.'

'Is he still alive?'

'Come over and find out.'

I said, 'You're on borrowed time, Lila. You killed four Americans in New York. No one is going to ignore that.'

'I killed nobody.'

'Your people did.'

'People that have already left the country. We're fireproof.'

'We?'

'You ask too many questions.'

'If your people acted on your orders, then

you're not fireproof. That's a conspiracy.'

'This is a nation of laws and trials. There's no evidence.'

'Car?'

'No longer exists.'

'You'll never be fireproof from me. I'll find you.'

'I hope you do.'

A hundred feet away the police car slowed to a crawl.

I said, 'Come out and meet with me, Lila. Or go home. One or the other. But either way you're beaten here.'

She said, 'We're never beaten.'

'Who is we?'

But there was no answer. The phone went dead. Nothing there, except the dumb silence of an empty line.

A hundred feet away the police car stopped.

I closed the phone and put it back in my pocket.

Two cops climbed out of the car and headed into the square.

I stayed where I was. Too suspicious to get up and run. Better to sit tight. I wasn't alone in the park. There were maybe forty people in there with me. Some of them seemed to be a permanent population. Others were temporary strays. New York is a big city. Five boroughs. Journeys home are long. Often easier to rest along the way.

The cops shone a flashlight beam in a sleeping guy's face.

They moved on. Lit up the next guy.

And the next.

Not good.

Not good at all.

But I was not the only person to reach that

conclusion. Here and there around the square I saw shapes rising up from benches and shuffling away in different directions. Maybe people with outstanding warrants, dealers with stuff in their backpacks, surly loners who didn't want contact, helpless paranoids wary of the system.

Two cops, an acre of ground, maybe thirty people still on benches, maybe ten newly mobile.

I watched.

The cops kept on coming. Their flashlight beams jerked through the night-time haze. Long shadows were thrown. They checked a fourth guy, and then a fifth. Then a sixth. More people stood up. Some left altogether, and others simply moved from bench to bench. The square was full of shapes, some inert, some moving. Everything was in slow motion. A tired, lazy dance.

I watched.

New indecision in the cops' body language. Like herding cats. They approached the people still on benches. They turned away and jerked their beams on the people moving out. They kept on walking, bending, turning. No pattern. Just random movement. They kept on coming. They got within ten yards of me.

Then they quit.

They played their flashlight beams one last time around a token circle and then they headed back to their car. I watched it drive away. I stayed on my bench and breathed out and started thinking about the GPS chips in the captured cell phones in my pockets. Part of me said it was impossible that Lila Hoth would have access to tracking satellites. But another part of me focused on her saying *We're never beaten*. And *we* is a big word. Only two letters, but a large implication. Maybe the bad guys from the Eastern bloc had grabbed more than oil and gas leases. Maybe they had taken over other kinds of infrastructure. The old Soviet intelligence machine had to have gone somewhere. I thought about laptop computers and broadband connections and all kinds of technology I didn't fully understand.

I kept the phones in my pockets, but I got up off the bench and headed for the subway.

Which was a bad mistake to make.

FIFTY-FIVE

The Union Square subway station is a major hub. It has an entrance hall as big as an underground plaza. Multiple entrances, multiple exits, multiple lines, multiple tracks. Stairs, booths, long rows of turnstiles. Plus long banks of machines for refreshing Metrocards, or buying new ones. I used cash and bought a new card. I fed two twenty dollar bills edge-first into the slot and was rewarded with twenty rides plus three free as a bonus. I collected my card and turned around and moved away. It was close to six o'clock in the morning. The station was filling up with people. The work day was starting. I passed a newsstand. It had a thousand different magazines. And squat bales of fresh tabloids ready for sale. Thick papers, piled high. Two separate titles. Both headlines were huge. One had three words, big letters, plenty of powdery black ink: FEDS SEEK TRIO. The other had three words too: FEDS HUNT TRIO.

Practically a consensus. On balance I preferred *seek* to *hunt*. More passive, less committed. Almost benign. I figured anyone would prefer to be sought than hunted.

I turned away.

And saw two cops watching me carefully.

Two mistakes in one. First theirs, which was then compounded by mine. Their mistake was conventional. The federal agents at 22nd and Broadway had put the word out that I had escaped by subway. Whereupon law enforcement generally had assumed that I would escape by subway again. Because given the choice, law enforcement always fights the last battle one more time.

My mistake was to walk straight into their lazy trap.

Because there were booths, there were supervisors. Because there were supervisors, there were no high entry-exit turnstiles. Just regular thigh-high bars. I swiped my new card and pushed on through. The plaza changed shape to a long wide walkway. Arrows pointed left and right and up and down, for different lines and different directions. I passed by a guy playing a violin. He had positioned himself where the echoes would help him. He was pretty good. His instrument had a solid, gutty tone. He was playing a mournful old piece I recognized from a movie about the Vietnam war. Perhaps not an inspired choice for early commuters. His violin case was open at his feet and not very full of contributions. I turned casually as if I was checking him out and saw the two cops step over the turnstile behind me.

I turned a random corner and followed a narrower passageway and found myself on an uptown platform. It was crowded with people. And it was part of a symmetrical pair. Ahead of me was the platform edge, and then the line, and then a row of iron pillars holding up the street above, and then the downtown line, and then the downtown platform. Two sets of everything, including two sets of commuters. Tired people, facing each other numbly, waiting to head out in opposite directions.

The live rails were back to back either side of the central iron pillars. They were shrouded, like live rails are in stations. The shrouds were three-sided box sections, open on the sides that faced the trains.

Behind me and far to my left, the cops pushed their way on to the platform. I checked the other way. To my right. Two more cops pushed into the crowd. They were wide and bulky with equipment. They moved people gently out of their way, palms against shoulders, short backhand moves, rhythmic, like swimming.

I moved to the middle of the platform. I edged forward until my feet were on the yellow warning stripe. I moved laterally until I had a pillar directly behind me. I looked left. Looked right. No trains were coming.

The cops kept moving. Behind them four more showed up. Two on one side of me, two on the other, threading through the crowd slowly and surely.

I craned forward.

No headlights in the tunnels.

The crowd moved and bunched beside me, pushed on by new arrivals, disturbed by the ripples of the cops' relentless progress, pulled forward by the subliminal certainty any subway rider feels that the train must be coming soon.

I checked again, over my shoulders, left and right.

Cops on my platform.

Eight of them.

No cops at all on the platform opposite.

FIFTY-SIX

People are scared of the third rail. No reason to be, unless you plan on touching it. Hundreds of volts, but they don't jump out at you. You have to go looking for them, to get in trouble.

Easy enough to step over, even in lousy shoes. I figured whatever my rubber footwear would subtract in terms of precision control, it would add in terms of electrical insulation. But even so, I planned my moves very carefully, like stage choreography. Jump down, land two-footed in the centre of the uptown line, right foot on the second rail, left foot beyond the third rail, squeeze through the gap between two pillars, right foot over the next third rail, left foot on the downtown track, small careful mincing steps, then a sigh of relief and a scramble up on to the downtown platform and away.

Easy enough to do.

Easy enough for the cops to do right behind me.

They had probably done it before.

I hadn't.

I waited. Checked behind me, left and right. The cops were close. Close enough to be slowing down and forming up and deciding exactly how they were going to do what would need to be done next. I didn't know what their approach would be. But whatever, they were going to take it slow. They didn't want a big stampede. The platform was crowded and any kind of sudden activity would put people over the edge. Which would lead to lawsuits.

I checked left. Checked right. No trains were coming. I wondered if the cops had stopped them. Presumably there was a well-rehearsed procedure. I took a half-step forward. People slipped in behind me, between me and the pillar. They started pressing against my back. I braced the other way against them. The warning strip at the edge of the platform was yellow paint over raised circular bumps. No danger of slipping or sliding.

The cops had formed up into a shallow semicircle. They were about eight feet from me. They were moving inward, shovelling people outward, collapsing their perimeter, slow and cautious. People were watching from the downtown platform opposite. They were nudging each other and pointing at me and going up on tiptoe.

I waited.

I heard a train. On my left. A moving glow in the tunnel. It was coming on fast. Our train. Uptown. Behind me the crowd stirred. I heard the rush of air and the squeal of iron rims. Saw the lighted cab sway and jerk through the curve. I figured it was doing about thirty miles an hour. About forty-four feet per second. I wanted two seconds. I figured that would be enough. So I would have to go when the train was eighty-eight feet away. The cops wouldn't follow. Their reaction time would rob them of the margin they needed. And they were eight feet back from the platform edge to start with. And they had different priorities from me. They had wives and families and ambitions and pensions. They had houses and yards and lawns to mow and bulbs to plant.

I took another tiny step forward.

The headlight was coming straight at me. Head on. Rocking and jerking. It made it hard to judge distance.

Then: I heard a train on my right.

A downtown train, approaching fast from the other direction. Symmetrical, but not perfectly synchronized. Like a pair of drapes closing, with the left-hand drape leading the right.

By how much?

I needed a three-second lag, for a total gap of five, because climbing up the downtown platform was going to take me a whole lot longer than jumping off the uptown.

I paused a whole second, guessing, estimating, feeling it, trying to judge.

The trains howled inward, one from the left, then one from the right.

Five hundred tons, and five hundred tons.

Closing speed, maybe sixty miles an hour.

The cops edged closer.

Decision time.

I went.

I jumped down, with the uptown train a hundred feet away. I landed two-footed between the rails and got steady and minced through the steps I had planned. Like a dance diagram in a book. Right foot, left foot high over the live rail, hands on the pillars. I paused a split second and checked right. The downtown train was very close. Behind me the uptown train slammed past. Its brakes were shrieking and grinding. A furious wind tore at my shirt. Lighted windows strobed by in the corner of my eye.

I stared right.

The downtown train looked huge.

Decision time.

I went.

Right foot high over the live rail, left foot down in the rail bed. The downtown train was almost on me. Just yards away. It was rocking and jerking. Its brakes were clamping hard. I could see the driver. His mouth was wide open. I could feel the air damming ahead of his cab.

I abandoned the choreography. Just flung myself towards the far platform. It was less than five feet away, but it felt infinitely distant. Like the plains horizon. But I got there. I stared right and saw every rivet and bolt on the front of the downtown train. It was coming right at me. I got my palms flat on the platform edge and vaulted up. I thought the dense press of people was going to knock me right back down. But hands grabbed at me and pulled me up. The train slammed past my shoulder and the wash of air spun me around. Windows flashed past. Oblivious passengers read books and papers or stood and swayed. Hands hauled on me and dragged me into the crowd. People all around me were screaming. I saw their mouths open in panic but I couldn't hear them. The yelp of the train's brakes was drowning them out. I put my head down and barged on through the crowd. People stepped left and right to let me pass. Some of them slapped me on the back as I went by. A ragged cheer followed me out.

Only in New York.

I pushed through an exit turnstile and headed for the street.

FIFTY-SEVEN

Madison Square Park was seven blocks north. I had the best part of four hours to kill. I spent the time shopping and eating on Park Avenue South. Not because I had things to buy. Not because I was especially hungry. But because it's always best to give pursuers what they don't expect. Fugitives are supposed to run far and fast. They're not supposed to dawdle through the immediate neighbourhood, in and out of stores and cafés.

It was just after six in the morning. Delis and supermarkets and diners and coffee shops were all that was open. I started in a Food Emporium that had an entrance on 14th Street and an exit on 15th. I spent forty-five minutes in there. I took a basket and wandered the aisles and pretended to choose stuff. Less conspicuous than just hanging out. Less conspicuous than wandering the aisles without a basket. I didn't want an alert manager to call anything in. I developed a fantasy where I had an apartment nearby. I stocked its imaginary kitchen with enough stuff to last two whole days. Coffee, of course. Plus pancake mix, eggs, bacon, a loaf of bread, butter, some jam, a pack of salami, a quarter-pound of cheese. When I got bored and the basket got heavy I left it in a deserted aisle and slipped out the back of the store.

Next stop was a diner four blocks north. I walked on the right-hand sidewalk with my back to the traffic. In the diner I ate pancakes and bacon that someone else had shopped and cooked. More my style. I spent another forty minutes in there. Then I moved on half a block to a French brasserie. More coffee, and a croissant. Someone had left a *New York Times* on the chair across from me. I read it from end to end. No mention of a manhunt in the city. No mention of Sansom's Senate race in the national section.

I split the final two hours four separate ways. I moved from a supermarket on the corner of Park and 22nd to a Duane Reade drugstore opposite and then to a CVS pharmacy on Park and 23rd. Visible evidence suggested that the nation spent more on hair care than food. Then at twenty-five minutes to ten I stopped shopping and stepped out to the bright new morning and looped around and took a good long careful look at my destination from the mouth of 24th Street, which was a shadowed anonymous canyon between two huge buildings. I saw nothing that worried me. No unexplained cars, no parked vans, no pairs or trios of dressed-down people with wires in their ears.

So at ten o'clock exactly I stepped into Madison Square Park.

* * *

I found Theresa Lee and Jacob Mark side by side on a bench near a dog run. They looked rested but nervous, and stressed, each in their own way. Each for their own reasons, presumably. They were two of maybe a hundred people sitting peacefully in the sun. The park was a rectangle of trees and lawns and paths. It was a small oasis, one block wide and three tall, fenced, surrounded by four busy sidewalks. Parks are reasonably good places for a clandestine rendezvous. Most hunters are attracted by moving targets. Most believe that fugitives stay in motion. Three of a hundred people sitting still while the city swirls around them attract less attention than three of a hundred hustling hard down the street.

Not perfect, but an acceptable risk.

I checked all around one last time and sat down next to Lee. She handed me a newspaper. One of the tabloids I had already seen. The HUNT headline. She said, 'It claims we shot three federal agents.'

'We shot four,' I said. 'Don't forget the medical guy.'

'But they make it sound like we used real guns. They make it sound like the guys died.'

'They want to sell papers.'

'We're in trouble.'

'We knew that already. We didn't need a journalist to tell us.'

She said, 'Docherty came through again. He was texting messages to me all night long, while the phone was off.'

She lifted up off the bench and took a sheaf of paper out of her back pocket. Three sheets of yellowed hotel stationery, folded four ways.

I said, 'You took notes?'

She said, 'They were long messages. I didn't want to keep the phone on, if there were things I needed to review.'

'So what do we know?'

'The 17th Precinct checked transportation gateways. Standard procedure, after a major crime. Four men left the country three hours after the likely time of death. Through JFK. The 17th is calling them potential suspects. It's a plausible scenario.'

I nodded.

'The 17th Precinct is right,' I said. 'Lila Hoth told me so.'

'You met with her?'

'She called me.'

'On what?'

'Another phone I took from Leonid. He and a pal found me. It didn't work out exactly how I wanted, but I made some limited contact.'

'She confessed?'

'More or less.'

'So where is she now?'

'I don't know exactly. I'm guessing somewhere east of Fifth, south of 59th.'

'Why?'

'She used the Four Seasons as a front. Why travel?'

Lee said, 'There was a burned-out rental car in Queens. The 17th thinks the four guys used it to get out of Manhattan. Then they ditched it and used that elevated train thing to get to the airport.'

I nodded again. 'Lila said the car they used no longer exists.'

'But here's the thing,' Lee said. 'The four guys didn't head back to London or Ukraine or Russia. They were routed through to Tajikistan.'

'Which is where?'

'Don't you know?'

'Those new places confuse me.'

'Tajikistan is right next to Afghanistan. They share a border. Also with Pakistan.'

'You can fly direct to Pakistan.'

'Correct. Therefore either those guys were from Tajikistan, or from Afghanistan itself. Tajikistan is where you go to get into Afghanistan without being too obvious about it. You cross the border in a pick-up truck. Roads are bad, but Kabul is not too far away.'

'OK.'

'And here's the other thing. Homeland Security has a protocol. Some kind of computer algorithm. They can trace groups of people through similar itineraries and linked bookings. Turns out those four guys entered the country three months ago from Tajikistan, along with some other folks, including two women with passports from Turkmenistan. One was sixty, and the other was twenty-six. They came through immigration together and claimed to be mother and daughter. And Homeland Security is prepared to swear their passports were genuine.'

'OK.'

'So the Hoths were not Ukrainian. Everything they told us was a lie.'

*　　*　　*

We all chewed on that for twenty long seconds, in silence. I went through all the stuff Lila had told us and deleted it, item by item. Like pulling files from a drawer, and leafing through them, and then pitching them in the trash.

I said, 'We saw their passports at the Four Seasons. They looked Ukrainian to me.'

Lee said, 'They were phony. Or they would have used them at immigration.'

I said, 'Lila had blue eyes.'

Lee said, 'I noticed.'

'Where exactly is Turkmenistan?'

'Also next to Afghanistan. A longer border. Afghanistan is surrounded by Iran, Turkmenistan, Uzbekistan, Tajikistan, and Pakistan, clockwise from the Gulf.'

'Easier when it was all the Soviet Union.'

'Unless you lived there.'

'Are Turkmenistan and Afghanistan ethnically similar?'

'Probably. All those borders are completely arbitrary. They're accidents of history. What matters are the tribal divisions. Lines on a map have got nothing to do with it.'

'Are you an expert?'

'The NYPD knows more about that region than the CIA. We have to. We've got people over there. We've got better intelligence than anyone.'

'Could a person from Afghanistan get a passport from Turkmenistan?'

'By relocating?'

'By asking for help and getting it.'

'From an ethnic sympathizer?'

I nodded. 'Maybe under the counter.'

'Why do you ask?'

'Some Afghan people have bright blue eyes. Especially the women. Some weird genetic strand in the population.'

'You think the Hoths are from Afghanistan?'

'They knew a hell of a lot about the conflict with the Soviets. A little dressed up, but they got most of the details right.'

'Maybe they read books.'

'No, they got the feelings right. And the atmosphere. Like the ancient greatcoats. Details like that were not widely available. That's insider information. In public the Red Army made out it was superbly equipped, for obvious reasons. Our propaganda said the same thing about them, for equally obvious reasons. But it wasn't true. The Red Army was falling apart. A lot of what the Hoths said sounded like first-hand information to me.'

'So?'

'Maybe Svetlana really did fight there. But on the other side.'

Lee paused a beat. 'You think the Hoths are Afghan tribeswomen?'

'If Svetlana fought there, but not for the Soviets, then they must be.'

Lee paused again. 'In which case Svetlana was telling the whole story from the other side. Everything was inverted. Including the atrocities.'

'Yes,' I said. 'She didn't suffer them. She committed them.'

* * *

We all went quiet again, another twenty seconds. I kept my eyes moving all around the park. *Look, don't see, listen, don't hear. The more you engage, the longer you survive*. But nothing jumped out at me. Nothing untoward was happening. People were coming and going, people were taking dogs to the run, a line was forming at a hamburger stand. Early, but every hour of the day or night is lunch time for someone. It depends on when the day starts. Lee was going through her notes. Jacob Mark was staring at the ground, but his gaze was focused somewhere far below the surface. Finally he leaned forward and turned his head and looked at me. I thought: *Here it comes*. The big question. The bump in the road.

He asked, 'When Lila Hoth called you, did she mention Peter?'

I nodded. 'She picked him up in the bar.'

'Why spend four hours doing that?'

'Tradecraft. And for fun and finesse. Because she could.'

'Where is he now?'

'She said he's here in the city.'

'Is he OK?'

'She wouldn't tell me.'

'Do you think he's OK?'

I didn't answer.

He said, 'Talk to me, Reacher.'

I said, 'No.'

'No you won't talk to me?'

'No, I don't think he's OK.'

'But he might be.'

'I could be wrong.'

'What did she tell you?'

'I said I wasn't scared of her, and she said that's what Peter Molina had said, too. I asked if he was OK, and she said I should come over and find out for myself.'

'So he could be OK.'

'It's possible. But I think you should be realistic.'

'About what? Why would two Afghan tribeswomen want to mess with Peter?'

'To get to Susan, of course.'

'For what? The Pentagon is supposed to be helping Afghanistan.'

I said, 'If Svetlana was a fighting tribeswoman, then she was one of the mujahideen. And when the Russians went home, the mujahideen did not go back to tending their goats. They moved right along. Some of them became the Taliban, and the rest of them became al-Qaeda.'

FIFTY-EIGHT

Jacob Mark said, 'I have to go to the cops about Peter.' He got halfway off the bench before I leaned across Theresa Lee and put my hand on his arm.

'Think hard,' I said.

'What's to think about? My nephew is a kidnapping victim. He's a hostage. The woman confessed.'

'Think about what the cops will do. They'll call the feds immediately. The feds will lock you up again and put Peter on the back burner, because they've got bigger fish to fry.'

'I have to try.'

'Peter's dead, Jake. I'm sorry, but you've got to face it.'

'There's still a chance.'

'Then the fastest way to find him is to find Lila. And we can do that better than those feds.'

'You think?'

'Look at their track record. They missed her once, and they let us break out of jail. I wouldn't send them to look for a book in a library.'

‘How the hell do we find her on our own?’

I looked at Theresa Lee. ‘Did you speak to Sansom?’

She shrugged, like she had good news and bad. She said, ‘I spoke to him briefly. He said he might want to come up here personally. He said he would call me back to coordinate the where and the when. I said he couldn’t do that, because I was keeping the phone switched off. So he said he would call Docherty’s cell instead, and I should call Docherty and pick up the message. So I did, and Docherty didn’t answer. So I tried the precinct switchboard. The dispatcher said Docherty was unavailable.’

‘What does that mean?’

‘I think it means he just got arrested.’

* * *

Which changed everything. I understood that even before Lee got around to spelling it out. She handed me her folded notes. I took them, like receiving the baton in a relay race. I was to go onward, as fast as I could. She was spilling off the track, her race finished. She said, ‘You understand, right? I have to turn myself in now. He’s my partner. I can’t let him face this madness alone.’

I said, ‘You thought he would ditch you in a heartbeat.’

‘But he didn’t. And I have my own standards, anyway.’

‘It won’t do any good.’

‘Maybe not. But I won’t turn my back on my partner.’

‘You’re just taking yourself off the board. You

can't help anyone from a jail cell. Outside is always better than inside.'

'It's different for you. You can be gone tomorrow. I can't. I live here.'

'What about Sansom? I need a time and a place.'

'I don't have that information. And you should take care with Sansom, anyway. He sounded weird on the phone. I couldn't tell whether he was real mad or real worried. It's hard to say whose side he's going to be on, when and if he gets here.'

Then she gave me Leonid's first cell phone, and the emergency charger. She put her hand on my arm and squeezed, just briefly, just a little. An all-purpose substitute for a hug and a good-luck gesture. And right after that our temporary three-way partnership fell apart completely. Jacob Mark was on his feet even before Lee had started to get up. He said, 'I owe it to Peter. OK, they might put me back in a cell, but at least they'll be out looking for him.'

'We could look for him,' I said.

'We have no resources.'

I looked at them both and asked, 'Are you sure about this?'

They were sure about it. They walked away from me, out of the park, to the Fifth Avenue sidewalk, where they stood and craned their necks, looking for a police car, the same way people stand when they are trying to hail a cab. I sat alone for a minute, and then I got up and walked the other way.

Next stop, somewhere east of Fifth and south of 59th.

FIFTY-NINE

Madison Square Park nestles against the south end of Madison Avenue, right where it starts at 23rd Street. Madison Avenue runs straight for 115 blocks, to the Madison Avenue Bridge, which leads to the Bronx. You can get to Yankee Stadium that way, although other routes are better. I planned on covering maybe a third of its length, to 59th Street, which was a little north and west of where Lila Hoth had said she wasn't, on Third and 56th.

It was as good a place to start as any.

I took the bus, which was a slow, lumbering vehicle, which made it a counterintuitive choice for a wild-eyed fugitive, which made it perfect cover for me. Traffic was heavy and we passed plenty of cops, some on foot, some in cars. I looked out the window at them. None of them looked back in at me. A man on a bus is close to invisible.

I stopped being invisible when I got out at 59th Street. Prime retail territory, therefore prime tourist territory, therefore reassuring pairs of policemen on every corner. I took a cross street over to Fifth and found a line of vendors at the base of Central Park and bought a black T-shirt with *New York City* written on it, and a pair of counterfeit sunglasses, and a black baseball cap with a red apple on it. I changed shirts in a restroom in a hotel lobby and came back to Madison looking a little different. It was four hours since any on-duty cop had spoken to his watch commander. And people forget a lot in four hours. I figured that *tall* and *khaki shirt* would be all that anyone remembered. Nothing I could do about my height, but the new black upper body might let me slide by. Plus the writing on the shirt, and the shades, and the hat, all of which made me look like a regular out-of-town idiot.

Which I was, basically. I had no real clue as to what I was doing. Finding any concealed hideout is difficult. Finding one in a densely populated big city is close to impossible. I was just quartering random blocks, following a geographic hunch that could have been completely wrong to start with, trying to find reasons to narrow it further. *The Four Seasons Hotel. Not adjacent, but comfortably proximate*. Which meant what? A two-minute drive? A five-minute walk? In which direction? Not south, I thought. Not across 57th Street, which is a major cross-town thoroughfare. Two-way, six lanes. Always busy. In the micro-geography of Manhattan, 57th Street was like the Mississippi River. An obstacle. A boundary. Much more inviting to slip away to the north, to the quieter, darker blocks beyond.

I watched the traffic and thought: not a two-minute drive. Driving implied a lack of control, a lack of flexibility, and delays, and one-way streets and avenues, and parking difficulties, and potentially memorable vehicles waiting in loading zones, and licence plates that could be traced and checked.

Walking was better than driving, in the city, whoever you were.

I took 58th Street, and walked to the hotel's back entrance. It was just as splendid as the front entrance. There was brass and stone and there were flags flying and porters in uniform and doormen in top hats. There was a long line of limousines waiting at the kerb. Lincolns, Mercedes, Maybachs, Rolls-Royces. Well over a million dollars' worth of automotive product, all crammed into about eighty feet. There was a loading dock, with a grey roll-up door, closed.

I stood next to a bell boy, with my back to the hotel door. Where would I go? Across the street was nothing but a solid line of high buildings. Mostly apartment houses, with the ground floors leased to prestige clients. Directly opposite was an art gallery. I squeezed between two chrome bumpers and crossed the street and glanced at some of the paintings in the window. Then I turned and looked back from the far sidewalk.

To the left of the hotel, on the side nearer Park Avenue, there was nothing very interesting.

Then I looked to the right, along the block as it approached Madison, and I got a new idea.

The hotel itself was recent construction on an insane budget. Neighbouring buildings were all quiet and prosperous and solid, some of them old, some of them new. But at the western end of the block there were three old piles in a row. Narrow, single-front, five-storey brick, weathered, peeling, spalling, stained, somewhat decrepit. Dirty windows, sagging lintels, flat roofs, weeds along the cornices, old iron fire escapes zigzagging down the top four floors. The three buildings looked like three rotten teeth in a bright smile. One had an old out-of-business restaurant for a ground-floor tenant. One had a hardware store. The third had an enterprise abandoned so long ago I couldn't tell what it had been. Each had a narrow door set unobtrusively alongside its commercial operation. Two of the doors had multiple bell pushes, signifying apartments. The door next to the old restaurant had a single bell push, signifying a sole occupier for the upper four floors.

Lila Hoth was not a Ukrainian billionaire from London. That had been a lie. So whoever she really was, she had a budget. A generous budget, certainly, to allow for suites in the Four Seasons as and when necessary. But presumably not an infinite budget. And town houses in Manhattan run to twenty or more million dollars to buy, minimum. And multiple tens of thousands of dollars a month to rent.

Privacy could be achieved much more cheaply in tumbledown mixed-use buildings like the three I was looking at. And maybe there would be other advantages, too. No doormen nearby, fewer prying eyes. Plus maybe a presumption that an operation like a restaurant or a hardware store would get deliveries at all hours of the night and day. Maybe all kinds of random comings and goings could happen without attracting much notice at all.

I moved down the street and stood on the kerb opposite the three old piles and stared up at them. People pushed past me in a continuous stream on the sidewalk. I stepped into the gutter, to get out of the way. There were two cops on the far corner of Madison and 57th. Fifty yards away, on a diagonal. They were not looking my way. I looked back at the buildings and reviewed my assumptions in my head. The 6 train at 59th and Lexington was close by. The Four Seasons was close by. Third Avenue and 56th Street was not close by. *That's not close to me*. Anonymity was guaranteed. Cost was limited. Five for five. Perfect. So I figured maybe I was looking for a place just like one of the three right in front of me, located somewhere within a fan-shaped five-minute radius east or west of the hotel's back door. Not north, or Susan Mark would have parked in midtown and aimed to get out of the subway at 68th Street. Not south, because of 57th Street's psychological barrier. Not somewhere else entirely, because they had used the Four Seasons as a front. Somewhere else entirely, they would have used a different hotel. New York City does not lack for impressive establishments.

Impeccable logic. Maybe too impeccable. Confining, certainly. Because if I stuck with the assumption that Susan Mark would have gotten out at 59th Street and aimed to approach from the north, and that 57th Street was a conceptual barrier to the south, then 58th Street was the whole ballgame, right there. And crosstown blocks in Manhattan take about five minutes to walk. Therefore a five-minute radius left or right out of the hotel's back door would end on either the exact block I was currently loitering on, or the next one to the east, between Park and Lex. And tumbledown mixed-use properties are rare on blocks like those. Big money chased them away long ago. It was entirely possible I was looking at the only three left standing in the whole of the zip code.

Therefore it was entirely possible I was looking at Lila Hoth's hideout.

Entirely possible, but most unlikely. I believe in luck as much as the next guy, but I'm not insane.

But I believe in logic too, probably more so than

the next guy, and logic had led me to the spot. I went over it all again, and ended up believing myself.

Because of one extra factor.

Which was that the same logic led someone else there, too.

Springfield stepped down into the gutter next to me and said, 'You think?'

SIXTY

Springfield was wearing the same suit I had seen him in before. Grey summer-weight wool, with a silky weave and a slight sheen. It was creased and crumpled, like he slept in it. Which maybe he did.

He said, 'You think this is the place?'

I didn't answer. I was too busy checking all around me. I looked at hundreds of people and dozens of cars. But I saw nothing to worry about. Springfield was alone.

I turned back.

Springfield asked the question again. 'You think this is it?'

I asked, 'Where's Sansom?'

'He stayed home.'

'Why?'

'Because this kind of thing is difficult, and I'm better than he is.'

I nodded. It was an article of faith with NCOs that they were better than their officers. And they were usually right. Certainly I had been happy with mine. They had done plenty of good work for me.

I asked, 'So what's the deal?'

'What deal?'

'Between you and me.'

'We don't have a deal,' he said. 'Yet.'

'Are we going to have a deal?'

'We should talk, maybe.'

'Where?'

'Your call,' he said. Which was a good sign. It meant that if there was going to be a trap or an ambush in my immediate future, it was going to be improvised, and therefore not optimally efficient. Maybe even to the point of being survivable.

I asked him, 'How well do you know the city?'

'I get by.'

'Make two lefts and go to 57 East 57th. I'll be ten minutes behind you. I'll meet you inside.'

'What kind of a place is that?'

'We can get coffee there.'

'OK,' he said. He took one more look at the building with the old restaurant at its base and then he crossed the street diagonally through the traffic and turned left on to Madison Avenue. I went the other way, just as far as the Four Seasons' back door. The Four Seasons' back door was right there on 58th Street. It was a block-through building. Which meant its front door was on 57th Street. At 57 East 57th, to be precise. I would be inside about four minutes ahead of Springfield. I would know if he had brought a crew. I would see whether anyone came in before him, or with him, or after him. I walked through to the lobby from the rear and took off my hat and my glasses and stood in a quiet corner and waited.

* * *

Springfield came in alone, right on time, which was four minutes later. No time for hurried deployment out on the street. No time for conversation. Probably no time even for a cell phone call. Most people slow their walk a little, dialling and talking.

There was a guy in formal morning dress near the door. A black tail coat, and a silver tie. Not a concierge, not a bell captain. Some kind of a greeter, although his title was probably much grander. He started towards Springfield and Springfield glanced at him once and the guy ducked away like he had been slapped. Springfield had that kind of a face.

He paused a moment and got his bearings and headed for the tea room, where I had once met the Hoths. I stayed in my corner and watched the street door. There was no back-up. No plain sedans stopped outside. I gave it ten minutes, and then added two more, just in case. Nothing happened. Just the regular ebb and flow of a high-end city hotel. Rich people came, rich people went. Poor people scurried around and did things for them.

I walked into the tea room and found Springfield in the same chair that Lila Hoth had used. The same dignified old waiter was on duty. He came over. Springfield asked for mineral water. I asked for coffee. The waiter nodded imperceptibly and went away again.

Springfield said, 'You met the Hoths here, twice.'

I said, 'Once at this exact table.'

'Which is technically a problem. Associating with them in any way at all could be classed as a felony.'

'Because?'

'Because of the Patriot Act.'

'Who are the Hoths, exactly?'

'And running across the subway tracks was also a felony. You could get up to five years in the state pen for that, technically. So they tell me.'

'I also shot four federal agents with darts.'

'No one cares about them.'

'Who are the Hoths?'

'I can't volunteer information.'

'So why are we here?'

'You help us, we'll help you.'

'How can you help me?'

'We can make all your felonies disappear.'

'And how can I help you?'

'You can help us find what we lost.'

'The memory stick?'

Springfield nodded. The waiter came back with his tray. Mineral water, and coffee. He arranged things carefully on the table and backed away.

I said, 'I don't know where the memory stick is.'

'I'm sure you don't. But you got as close to Susan Mark as anyone. And she left the Pentagon with it, and it isn't in her house or her car or anywhere else she ever went. So we're hoping you saw something. Maybe it didn't mean anything to you, but it might to us.'

'I saw her shoot herself. That was about all.'

'There must have been more.'

'You had your chief of staff on the train. What did he see?'

'Nothing.'

'What was on the memory stick?'

'I can't volunteer information.'

'Then I can't help you.'

'Why do you need to know?'

I said, 'I like to know at least the basic shape of the trouble I'm about to get myself into.'

'Then you should ask yourself a question.'

'What question?'

'The one you haven't asked yet, and the one you should have, right at the start. The key question, you dumbass.'

'What is this? A contest? NCOs against officers?'

'That battle was over long ago.'

So I spooled backward to the beginning, looking for the question I had never asked. The beginning was the 6 train, and passenger number four, on the right side of the car, alone on her eight-person bench, white, in her forties, plain, black hair, black clothes, black bag. Susan Mark, citizen, ex-wife, mother, sister, adoptee, resident of Annandale, Virginia.

Susan Mark, civilian worker at the Pentagon.

I asked, 'What exactly was her job?'

SIXTY-ONE

Springfield took a long drink of water and then smiled briefly and said, 'Slow, but you got there in the end.'

'So what was her job?'

'She was a systems administrator with responsibility for a certain amount of information technology.'

'I don't know what that means.'

'It means she knew a bunch of master passwords for the computers.'

'Which computers?'

'Not the important ones. She couldn't launch missiles or anything. But obviously she was authorized for HRC records. And some of the archives.'

'But not the Delta archives, right? They're in North Carolina. At Fort Bragg. Not the Pentagon.'

'Computers are networked. Everything is everywhere and nowhere now.'

'And she had access?'

'Human error.'

'What?'

'There was a measure of human error.'

'A measure?'

'There are a lot of systems administrators. They share common problems. They help each other. They have their own chat room, and their own message board. Apparently there was a defective line of code which made individual passwords less opaque than they should have been. So there was some leakage. We think they knew all about it, actually, but they liked it that way. One person could get in and help another person with minimum fuss. Even if the code had been correct, they would probably have deleted it.'

I remembered Jacob Mark saying: *She was good with computers*.

I said, 'So she had access to Delta's archives?'

Springfield just nodded.

I said, 'But you and Sansom quit five years before I did. Nothing was computerized back then. Certainly not the archives.'

'Times change,' Springfield said. 'The U.S.

Army as we know it is about ninety years old. We've got ninety years' worth of crap all built up. Rusty old weapons that somebody's grandfather brought back as souvenirs, captured flags and uniforms all mouldering away, you name it. Plus literally thousands and thousands of tons of paper. Maybe millions of tons. It's a practical problem. Fire risk, mice, real estate.'

'So?'

'So they've been cleaning house for the last ten years. The artefacts are either sent to museums or trashed, and the documents are scanned and preserved on computers.'

I nodded. 'And Susan Mark got in and copied one.'

'More than copied one,' Springfield said. 'She extracted one. Transferred it to an external drive, and then deleted the original.'

'The external drive being the memory stick?'

Springfield nodded. 'And we don't know where it is.'

'Why her?'

'Because she fit the bill. The relevant part of the archive was traced through the medal award. HRC people keep the medal records. Like you said. She was the systems administrator. And she was vulnerable through her son.'

'Why did she delete the original?'

'I don't know.'

'It must have increased the risk.'

'Significantly.'

'What was the document?'

'I can't volunteer information.'

'When was it dug out of the box room and scanned?'

'A little over three months ago. It's a slow process. Ten years into the programme and they're only up to the early 1980s.'

'Who does the work?'

'There's a specialist staff.'

'With a leak. The Hoths were over here more or less immediately.'

'Evidently.'

'Do you know who it was?'

'Steps are being taken.'

'What was the document?'

'I can't volunteer information.'

'But it was a big file.'

'Big enough.'

'And the Hoths want it.'

'I think that's clear.'

'Why do they want it?'

'I can't volunteer information.'

'You say that a lot.'

'I mean it a lot.'

'Who are the Hoths?'

He just smiled and made a circular *once again* gesture with his hand. *I can't volunteer information*. A great NCO's answer. Four words, the third of which was perhaps the most significant.

I said, 'You could ask me questions. I could volunteer guesses. You could comment on them.'

He said, 'Who do you think the Hoths are?'

'I think they're native Afghans.'

He said, 'Go on.'

'That's not much of a comment.'

'Go on.'

'Probably Taliban or al-Qaeda sympathizers, or operatives, or flunkies.'

No reaction.

‘Al-Qaeda,’ I said. ‘The Taliban mostly stay home.’

‘Go on.’

‘Operatives,’ I said.

No reaction.

‘Leaders?’

‘Go on.’

‘Al-Qaeda is using women leaders?’

‘They’re using whatever works.’

‘Doesn’t seem plausible.’

‘That’s what they want us to think. They want us searching for men that don’t exist.’

I said nothing.

‘Go on,’ he said.

‘OK, the one who calls herself Svetlana fought with the mujahideen and knew you captured the VAL rifle from Grigori Hoth. They used Hoth’s name and his story to get sympathy over here.’

‘Because?’

‘Because now al-Qaeda wants documentary proof of whatever else it was that you guys were doing that night.’

‘Go on.’

‘Which Sansom got a big medal for. So it must have looked pretty good, once upon a time, way back when. But now you’re worried about exposure. So I’m assuming it wouldn’t look so good any more.’

‘Go on.’

‘Sansom is miserable, but the government has got its panties in a wad, too. So it’s both personal and political.’

‘Go on.’

‘Did you get a medal that night?’

‘The Superior Service Medal.’

'Which comes directly from the Secretary of Defense.'

Springfield nodded. 'A nice little bauble, for a lowly sergeant.'

'So the trip was more political than military.'

'Obviously. We weren't officially at war with anyone at the time.'

'You know the Hoths killed four people, and probably Susan Mark's son too, right?'

'We don't know it. But we suspect it.'

'So why haven't you busted them?'

'I work security for a congressman. I can't bust anyone.'

'Those feds could.'

'Those feds work in mysterious ways. Apparently they consider the Hoths to be A-grade enemy combatants, and a very significant target, and extremely dangerous, but not currently operational.'

'Which means what?'

'Which means that right now there's more to be gained by leaving them in place.'

'Which actually means they can't find them.'

'Of course.'

'You happy about that?'

'The Hoths don't have the memory stick, or they wouldn't still be looking for it. So I don't really care either way.'

'I think you should,' I said.

'You think that's their place? Where you were?'

'This block or the next.'

'I think this one,' he said. 'Those feds searched their hotel suite. While they were out.'

'Lila told me.'

'They had shopping bags. Like window dressing.

To make the place look right.'

'I saw them.'

'Two from Bergdorf Goodman, and two from Tiffany. Those stores are close together, about a block from those old buildings. If their base was on the block east of Park, they'd have gone to Bloomingdales instead. Because they weren't really shopping. They just wanted accessories in their suite, to fool people.'

'Good point,' I said.

'Don't go looking for the Hoths,' Springfield said.

'You worried about me now?'

'You could lose two ways around. They're going to think the same as us, that even if you don't have the stick, then somehow you know where it went. And they might be even more vicious and persuasive than we are.'

'And?'

'They might actually tell you what's on it. In which case from our point of view you would become a loose end.'

'How bad is it?'

'I'm not ashamed. But Major Sansom would be embarrassed.'

'And the United States.'

'That, too.'

The waiter came back and inquired as to whether we needed anything else. Springfield said yes. He reordered for both of us. Which meant he had more to talk about. He said, 'Run down exactly what happened on the train.'

'Why weren't you there, instead of the chief of staff? It was more like your line of work than his.'

'It came on us fast. I was in Texas, with Sansom.

Raising money. We didn't have time for proper deployment.'

'Why didn't the feds have someone on the train?'

'They did. They had two people on the train. Two women. Undercover, borrowed from the FBI. Special Agents Rodriguez and Mbele. You blundered into the wrong car and rode with them all the way.'

'They were good,' I said. And they were. The Hispanic woman, small, hot, tired, her supermarket bag wrapped around her wrist. The West African woman in the batik dress. 'They were very good. But how did you all know she was going to take that train?'

'We didn't,' Springfield said. 'It was a huge operation. A big scramble. We knew she was in a car. So we had people waiting at the tunnels. The idea was to follow her from there, to wherever she was going.'

'Why wasn't she arrested on the Pentagon steps?'

'There was a short debate. Those feds won it. They wanted to roll up the whole chain in one go. And they might have.'

'If I hadn't screwed it up.'

'You said it.'

'She didn't have the memory stick. So nothing was going to get rolled up anyway.'

'She left the Pentagon with it, and it isn't in her house or her car.'

'You sure about that?'

'Her house has been torn down to the slab and I could eat the largest remaining part of her car.'

'How well did they search the subway train?'

'Car number 7622 is still in the yards at 207th Street. They say it might take a month or more to rebuild.'

'What the hell was on that memory stick?'

Springfield didn't answer.

One of the captured phones in my pocket started to vibrate.

SIXTY-TWO

I pulled all three phones out of my pocket and laid them on the table. One of them was skittering around, an eighth of an inch at a time. Vigorous vibration. Its window said *Restricted Call*. I opened it up and put it to my ear and said, 'Hello?'

Lila Hoth asked, 'Are you still in New York?'

I said, 'Yes.'

'Are you near the Four Seasons?'

I said, 'Not very.'

'Go there now. I left a package for you at the desk.'

I asked, 'When?'

But the line went dead.

I glanced at Springfield and said, 'Wait here.' Then I hustled out to the lobby. Saw no retreating back heading for the door. The scene was tranquil. The greeter in the tail coat was standing idle. I walked to the desk and gave my name and asked if they were holding anything for me. A minute later I had an envelope in my hands. It had my name handwritten across the front in thick black letters. It had Lila Hoth's name up in the top left corner, where the return address would be. I asked the desk clerk when it had been delivered. He said more than an hour ago.

I asked, 'Did you see who dropped it off?'

'A foreign gentleman.'

'Did you recognize him?'

'No, sir.'

The envelope was padded, about six inches by nine. It was light. It had something stiff in it. Round, and maybe five inches in diameter. I carried it back to the tea room and sat down again with Springfield. He said, 'From the Hoths?'

I nodded.

He said, 'It could be full of anthrax spores.'

'Feels more like a CD,' I said.

'Of what?'

'Afghan folk music, maybe.'

'I hope not,' he said. 'I've heard Afghan folk music. At length and up close.'

'You want me to wait to open it?'

'Until when?'

'Until you're out of range.'

'I'll take the risk.'

So I tore open the envelope and shook it. A single disc spilled out and made a plastic sound against the wood of the table.

'A CD,' I said.

'A DVD, actually,' Springfield said.

It was home made. It was a blank disc manufactured by Memorex. The words *Watch This* had been written across the label side with a black permanent marker. Same handwriting as the envelope. Same pen. Lila Hoth's handwriting and Lila Hoth's pen, presumably.

I said, 'I don't have a DVD player.'

'So don't watch it.'

'I think I have to.'

'What happened on the train?'

'I don't know.'

'You can play DVDs on a computer. Like people watch movies on their laptops on airplanes.'

'I don't have a computer.'

'Hotels have computers.'

'I don't want to stay here.'

'There are other hotels in the city.'

'Where are you staying?'

'The Sheraton. Where we were before.'

* * *

So Springfield paid our tea-room bill with a platinum credit card and we walked from the Four Seasons to the Sheraton. The second time I had made that trip. It took just as long. Crowded sidewalks, people moving slowly in the heat. It was one o'clock in the afternoon, and very warm. I was watching for cops the whole way, which didn't aid our progress. But we got there in the end. The plasma screen in the lobby listed a whole bunch of events. The ballroom was booked by a trade association. Something to do with cable television. Which made me think of the National Geographic Channel, and the silverback gorilla.

Springfield opened the door to the business centre with his key card. He didn't come in with me. He told me he would wait in the lobby, and then he walked away. Three of the four work stations were occupied. Two women, one man, all of them in dark suits, all of them with leather briefcases propped open and spilling paper. I took the empty chair and set about trying to figure out how to play a DVD on a computer. I found a slot on the tower unit that looked fit for the purpose. I pushed the disc in and met with some temporary resistance and then a motor whirred and the unit sucked at the disc and pulled it from my grasp.

Nothing much happened for five seconds. Just a lot of stopping and starting and whirring. Then a big window opened on the screen. It was blank. But it had a graphic in the bottom corner. Like a picture of a DVD player's buttons. Play, pause, fast forward, rewind, skip. I moved the mouse and the pointer arrow changed to a chubby little hand as it passed over the buttons.

The phone in my pocket started to vibrate.

SIXTY-THREE

I took the phone out of my pocket and opened it up. Glanced around the room. My three temporary colleagues were all hard at work. One had a bar chart on her screen. Columns of bold bright colours, some of them high, some of them low. The man was reading e-mail. The other woman was typing fast.

I put the phone to my ear and said, 'Hello.'

Lila Hoth asked, 'Have you got it yet?'

I said, 'Yes.'

'Have you watched it yet?'

'No.'

'I think you should.'

'Why?'

'You'll find it educational.'

I glanced again at the occupants of the room and asked, 'Is there sound on it?'

'No, it's a silent movie. Unfortunately. It would be better with sound.'

I didn't answer.

She asked, 'Where are you?'

'In a hotel business centre.'

'The Four Seasons?'

'No.'

'Are there computers in the business centre?'

'Yes.'

'You can play a DVD on a computer, you know.'

'So I was told.'

'Can anyone else see the screen?'

I didn't answer.

'Play it,' she said. 'I'll stay on the line. I'll do a commentary. Like a special edition.'

I didn't answer.

She said, 'Like a director's cut,' and laughed a little.

I moved the mouse and put the chubby little hand over the play button. It waited there, patiently.

I clicked the mouse.

The tower unit made more whirring sounds and the blank window on the screen lit up and showed two distorted horizontal lines. They flashed twice and then the picture settled to a wide-angle view of an open outdoor space. It was night. The camera was steady. Mounted high on a tripod, I guessed. The scene was brightly lit by harsh halogen lights just out of shot. The colour was raw. The space looked foreign. Beaten earth, a dark khaki tone. Small stones and one large rock. The rock was flat, bigger than a king-size bed. It had been drilled and fitted with four iron rings. One at each corner.

There was a naked man tied to the rings. He was short and thin and wiry. He had olive skin and a black beard. He was maybe thirty years old. He was on his back, stretched into a wide X shape. The camera was positioned maybe a yard from his feet. At the top of the picture his head was jerking from side to side. His eyes were closed. His mouth was open. Tendons in his neck stood out like ropes.

He was screaming, but I couldn't hear him.

It was a silent movie.

Lila Hoth spoke in my ear.

She asked, 'What are you seeing?'

I said, 'A guy on a slab.'

'Keep watching.'

'Who is he?'

'He *was* a taxi driver who ran an errand for an American journalist.'

The camera angle was about forty-five degrees, I guessed. It made the taxi driver's feet look large and his head look small. He thrashed and bucked for a whole minute. He was raising his head and banging it down on the rock. Trying to knock himself out. Or trying to kill himself, maybe. No luck. A slender figure ducked into shot at the top of the frame and slipped a folded square of cloth under the guy's head. The figure was Lila Hoth. No question about it. The video definition was not great, but there was no mistaking her. The hair, the eyes, the way she moved.

The square of cloth was probably a towel.

I said, 'I just saw you.'

'With the pad? It's necessary, to avoid self-inflicted injury. And it puts their heads at an angle.

It tempts them to look.'

'At what?'

'Keep watching.'

I glanced around the room. My three temporary colleagues were all still working. They were all focused hard on their own business.

On my screen nothing happened for close to twenty seconds. The taxi driver wailed away, silently. Then Svetlana Hoth stepped into the frame from the side. She was unmistakable, too. The fire-plug body, the blunt steel-grey hair.

She had a knife in her hand.

She crawled up on the rock and squatted beside the guy. She stared up at the camera for a long second. Not vanity. She was judging its angle, trying not to block its view. She adjusted her position until she was crouching unobtrusively in the angle made by the guy's left arm and the side of his chest.

The guy was staring at the knife.

Svetlana leaned forward and to her right and placed the tip of the blade on a spot about halfway between the guy's groin and his navel. She pressed down. The guy jerked uncontrollably. A fat worm of blood welled out of the cut. The blood looked black under the lights. The guy screamed on and on. I could see that his mouth was forming words. *No!* and *Please!* are clear in any language.

'Where was this?' I asked.

Lila Hoth said, 'Not far from Kabul.'

Svetlana moved the blade up towards the guy's navel. Blood chased it all the way. She kept it moving. Like a surgeon or a wholesale butcher, casual and practised and expert. She had made similar cuts many times before. The blade kept on moving. It stopped above the guy's sternum.

Svetlana put the knife down.

She used her index finger and traced the line of the cut. Blood lubricated its progress. She pressed down and put her finger right in the cut, to the first knuckle. She slid it up and down. She paused occasionally.

Lila Hoth said, 'She's checking that she's all the way through the muscle wall.'

I said, 'How do you know? You can't see these pictures.'

'I can hear your breathing.'

Svetlana picked up the knife again and returned to the places where her finger had paused. She used the tip of the blade quite delicately and nicked through what seemed to be minor obstructions.

Then she sat back.

The taxi driver's belly was open, like a zipper had been pulled. The long straight cut gaped a little. The wall of muscle was ruptured. It was no longer able to hold back the pressure from inside.

Svetlana rocked forward again. She used both hands. She worked them into the cut and parted the skin quite carefully and rooted around inside. She was in there up to her wrists. She tensed and squared her shoulders.

She lifted out the guy's intestines.

They made a shining, glistening pink mass about the size of a soft soccer ball. Coiled, sloppy, moving, wet and steaming.

She laid the mass on the guy's chest, quite gently.

Then she slid off the rock and stepped out of the frame.

The camera's unblinking eye stared on.

The taxi driver looked down in horror.

Lila Hoth said, 'Now it's just a matter of time. The cut doesn't kill them. We don't sever any important vessels. The bleeding stops quite fast. It's about pain and shock and infection. The strong ones resist all three. They die of hypothermia, we think. Their core temperature is compromised, obviously. It depends on the weather. Our record is eighteen hours. People say they've seen two full days, but I don't believe them.'

'You're crazy, you know that?'

'That's what Peter Molina said.'

'He saw this?'

'He's on it. Keep watching. Fast forward, if you like. Without the sound it's not so much fun anyway.'

I checked all around the room again. Three people, working hard. I put the fat hand on the fast forward button and clicked. The picture leapt into fast motion. The taxi driver's head moved back and forth through a tiny jerky arc.

Lila Hoth said, 'Normally we don't do this one at a time. It's better to have a sequence. The second guy waits until the first guy dies, and so on. It builds up the dread. You should see them, just willing the previous guy to live a minute longer. But eventually they die, and the spotlight moves on. That's when they have heart attacks. You know, if they're going to. If they're susceptible. But we can't always arrange a live sequence. That's why we use the video now, for an approximation.'

I wanted to tell her she was crazy again, but I didn't, because she would have told me about Peter Molina again.

'Keep watching,' she said.

The picture spooled onward. The taxi driver's arms and legs twitched. Strange brittle movements, at double speed. His head rolled left and right.

Lila Hoth said, 'Peter Molina saw all of this. He was willing the guy to hold on. Which was strange, because of course the guy died months ago. But that's the effect. Like I told you, the video is a fair equivalent.'

'You're sick,' I said. 'You're also dead. You know that? Like you just stepped out in the road. The truck hasn't hit you yet, but it's going to.'

'Are you the truck?'

'You bet your ass.'

'I'm glad. Keep watching.'

I clicked the fast forward button again and again, and the picture sped up to four times normal speed, then eight, then sixteen, then thirty-two. Time rushed by. An hour. Ninety minutes. Then the image went perfectly still. The taxi driver stopped moving. He lay completely inert for a long time and then Lila Hoth rushed into the frame. I hit the play button to get back to normal speed. Lila bent near the guy's head and felt for a pulse. Then she raised her head and smiled a happy smile.

Straight at the camera.

Straight at me.

On the phone she asked, 'Is it over yet?'

I said, 'Yes.'

'A disappointment. He didn't last long. He was sick. He had parasites. Worms. We could see them writhing in his guts the whole time. It was disgusting. I guess they died too. Parasites die if their host dies.'

'Like you're going to die.'

'We're all going to die, Reacher. The only questions are when and how.'

Behind me one of the business executives got up and headed for the door. I turned in my chair and tried to keep my body between him and the screen. I don't think I succeeded. He looked at me strangely and left the room.

Or maybe he had heard my end of the phone conversation.

'Keep watching,' Lila said, in my ear.

I hit fast forward again. The taxi driver lay dead near Kabul for a spell and then the picture shut down and was replaced by a flurry of video noise. Then it opened up on a new scene. I hit play. Normal speed. An interior. Same kind of harsh light. Impossible to say whether it was night or day. Impossible to say where it was. A basement, maybe. Floor and walls seemed to be painted white. There was a broad stone slab, like a table. Smaller than the Afghan rock. Rectangular, manufactured for a purpose. Part of an old kitchen, possibly.

A huge young man was tied to the slab.

He was maybe half my age and twenty per cent bigger all around.

He's three hundred pounds of muscle, Jacob Mark had said. *He's going to the NFL*.

Lila Hoth asked, 'Do you see him yet?'

'I see him.'

He was naked. Very white under the lights. Different in every way from the Kabul taxi driver. Pale skin, tousled fair hair. No beard. But he was moving just the same. His head was jerking back and forth and he was screaming words. *No!* and

Please! are recognizable in any language. And this was English. I could lip-read quite easily. I could even sense the tone. Disbelief, mainly. The kind of tone a person uses when what was assumed to be an empty threat or even a cruel joke turns out to have been deadly serious.

I said, 'I'm not going to watch this.'

Lila Hoth said, 'You should. Or you'll never be sure. Maybe we let him go.'

'When was this?'

'We set a deadline and we kept it.'

I didn't reply.

'Watch it.'

'No.'

She said, 'But I want you to watch it. I need you to watch it. It's a question of maintaining the sequence. Because I think you're going to be next.'

'Think again.'

'Watch it.'

I watched it. *Maybe we let him go. You'll never be sure.*

They didn't let him go.

SIXTY-FOUR

Afterwards I hung up the phone and put the DVD in my pocket and made it to the lobby restroom and threw up in a stall. Not really because of the pictures. I have seen worse. But because of anger and fury and frustration. All those corrosive emotions boiled up inside me and had to find some release. I rinsed my mouth and washed my face and drank some water from the tap and stood for a moment in front of the mirror.

Then I emptied my pockets. I kept my cash, and my passport, and my ATM card, and my subway card, and Theresa Lee's NYPD business card. I kept my toothbrush. I kept the phone that had rung. I dumped the other two phones in the trash, with the emergency charger, and the business card from the four dead guys, and the notes Theresa Lee had made from her partner's messages.

I dumped the DVD, too.

And the Radio Shack memory stick, pink sleeve and all.

I didn't need a decoy any more.

Then, cleansed, I headed out to see if Springfield was still around.

He was. He was in the lobby bar, in a chair, with his back to a right-angle corner. He had a glass of water on the table in front of him. He was relaxed, but he was watching everything. You can take the man out of Special Forces, and so on and so forth. He saw me coming. I sat down next to him. He asked, 'Was it folk music?'

'Yes,' I said. 'It was folk music.'

'On a DVD?'

'There was some dancing, too.'

'I don't believe you. You've gone all pale. Afghan folk dancing is pretty bad, I know, but it ain't that bad.'

'It was two guys,' I said. 'They had their bellies slit open and their guts lifted out.'

'Live on camera?'

'And then dead on camera.'

'Soundtrack?'

'Silent.'

'Who were the guys?'

‘One was a taxi driver from Kabul and the other was Susan Mark’s son.’

‘I don’t take taxis in Kabul. I prefer my own transportation. But it sucks for USC. They’re down a defensive tackle. Hard to find. I checked him out. Great feet, they say.’

‘Not any more.’

‘Are the Hoths on the tape?’

I nodded. ‘Like a confession.’

‘Doesn’t matter. They know we’re going to kill them anyway. Doesn’t really matter what we kill them for.’

‘It matters to me.’

‘Wise up, Reacher. That was the whole point of sending you the package. They want to make you mad and suck you in. They can’t find you. So they want you to come find them.’

‘Which I will.’

‘Your future plans are your business. But you need to take care. You need to understand. Because this has been their tactic for two hundred years. That’s why their abuse was always within earshot of the front lines. They wanted to bring out the rescue parties. Or provoke revenge attacks. They wanted a never-ending supply of prisoners. Ask the British. Or the Russians.’

‘I’ll take plenty of care.’

‘I’m sure you’ll try. But you’re not going anywhere until we’ve finished with you, about the train.’

‘Your guy saw what I saw.’

‘It’s in your interests to help us.’

‘Not so far. All I have is promises.’

‘All charges will be dropped when we have the memory stick in our possession.’

'Not good enough.'

'You want it in writing?'

'No, I want the charges dropped now. I need some freedom of action here. I can't be looking out for cops the whole time.'

'Freedom of action for what?'

'You know what.'

'OK, I'll do what I can.'

'Not good enough.'

'I can't give you guarantees. All I can do is try.'

'What are the chances you can succeed?'

'None at all. But Sansom can.'

'Are you authorized to speak for him?'

'I'll have to call him.'

'Tell him no more bullshit, OK? We're past that stage now.'

'OK.'

'And talk to him about Theresa Lee and Jacob Mark, too. And Docherty. I want a clean slate for all of them.'

'OK.'

'And Jacob Mark is going to need counselling. Especially if he sees a copy of that DVD.'

'He won't.'

'But I want him looked after. The ex-husband, as well. Molina.'

'OK.'

'Two more things,' I said.

'You drive a hard bargain, for a guy with nothing to offer.'

'Homeland Security traced the Hoths coming in from Tajikistan with their crew. Three months ago. Some kind of a computer algorithm. I want to know how many people were in the party.'

'To estimate the size of the opposing force?'

'Exactly.'

'And?'

'I want to meet with Sansom again.'

'Why?'

'I want him to tell me what is on that memory stick.'

'Not going to happen.'

'Then he doesn't get it back. I'll keep it and take a look for myself.'

'What?'

'You heard me.'

'You've actually got the stick?'

'No,' I said. 'But I know where it is.'

SIXTY-FIVE

Springfield asked, 'Where is it?'

I said, 'I can't volunteer information.'

'You're full of shit.'

I shook my head. 'Not this time.'

'You sure? You can take us there?'

'I can get you within fifteen feet. The rest is up to you.'

'Why? Is it buried? In a bank vault? In a house?'

'None of the above.'

'So where is it?'

'Call Sansom,' I said. 'Set up a meeting.'

* * *

Springfield finished what was left of his water and a waiter came by with the check. Springfield paid with his platinum card, the same way he had for both of us at the Four Seasons. Which I had taken to be a good sign. It had indicated a positive dynamic. So I chose to push my luck a little farther.

'Want to get me a room?' I asked.

'Why?'

'Because it's going to take time for Sansom to get me off the most-wanted list. And I'm tired. I was up all night. I want to take a nap.'

Ten minutes later we were on a high floor, in a room with a queen-size bed. A nice space, but tactically unsatisfactory. Like all high-floor hotel rooms it had a window that was no good to me and therefore only one way out. I could see that Springfield was thinking the same thing. He was thinking I was a lunatic to put myself in there.

I asked him, 'Can I trust you?'

He said, 'Yes.'

'Prove it.'

'How?'

'Give me your gun.'

'I'm not armed.'

'Answers like that don't help with the trust thing.'

'Why do you want it?'

'You know why. So if you bring the wrong people to my door I can defend myself.'

'I won't.'

'Reassure me.'

He stood still for a long moment. I knew he would rather stick a needle in his eye than give up his weapon. But he ran some calculations in his head and reached around under his suit coat to the small of his back and came out with a nine-millimetre Steyr GB pistol. The Steyr GB had been the sidearm of choice for 1980s-era U.S. Special Forces. He reversed it and handed it to me butt first. It was a fine old piece, well worn but well maintained. It had eighteen rounds in the magazine and one in the chamber.

'Thank you,' I said.

He didn't reply. Just walked out of the room. I double-locked the door after him, and put the chain on, and propped a chair under the handle. I emptied my pockets on the night stand. I put my clothes under the mattress to press. I took a long hot shower.

Then I lay down and went to sleep, with Springfield's gun under the pillow.

* * *

I was woken up four hours later by a knock at the door. I don't like to look through spy holes in hotel doors. Too vulnerable. All an assailant in the corridor has to do is wait until the lens darkens and then fire a gun straight through it. Even a silenced .22 would be completely lethal. There is nothing very substantial between the cornea and the brain stem. But there was a full-length mirror on the wall inside the door. For last-minute clothing checks, I guessed, before going out. I took a towel from the bathroom and wrapped it around my waist and collected the gun from under the pillow. I moved the chair and opened the door against the chain. Stood back on the hinge side and checked the view in the mirror.

Springfield, and Sansom.

It was a narrow crack and the image was reversed by the mirror and the corridor lighting was dim, but I recognized them easily enough. They were alone, as far as I could tell. And they were going to stay alone, unless they had brought more than nineteen people with them. No safety catch on the Steyr. Just a hefty double-action pull for the first shot, and then eighteen more. I took the slack out of the trigger and the chain off the door.

They were alone.

They came in, Sansom first, and then Springfield. Sansom looked the same as the morning I first saw him. Tanned, rich, powerful, full of energy and charisma. He was in a navy suit with a white shirt and a red tie and he looked as fresh as a daisy. He took the chair I had been using under the door handle and carried it back to the table near the window and sat down. Springfield closed the door and put the chain back on. I kept hold of the gun. I nudged the mattress off the box spring with my knee and pulled my clothes out one-handed.

'Two minutes,' I said. 'Talk among yourselves.'

I dressed in the bathroom and came back out and Sansom asked, 'Do you really know where that memory stick is?'

'Yes,' I said. 'I really do.'

'Why do you want to know what's on it?'

'Because I want to know how embarrassing it is.'

'You don't want me in the Senate?'

'I don't care how you spend your time. I'm curious, that's all.'

He asked, 'Why won't you tell me where it is right now?'

'Because I have something else to do first. And I need you to keep the cops out of my hair while I'm doing it. So I need a way of keeping your mind on the job.'

'You could be conning me.'

'I could be, but I'm not.'

He said nothing back.

I asked, 'Why do you want to be in the Senate anyway?'

'Why wouldn't I?'

'You were a good soldier and now you're richer than God. Why not go live on the beach?'

'These things are a way of keeping score. I'm sure you have your own way of keeping score.'

I nodded. 'I compare the number of answers I get to the number of questions I ask.'

'And how are you doing with that?'

'Lifetime average close to a hundred per cent.'

'Why ask at all? If you know where the stick is, just go get it.'

'I can't.'

'Why not?'

'It's going to take more resources than I could mobilize.'

'Where is it?'

I didn't answer.

'Is it here in New York?'

I didn't answer.

He asked, 'Is it secure?'

I said, 'It's safe enough.'

'Can I trust you?'

'Plenty of people have.'

'And?'

'I think most of them would be willing to give me a character reference.'

'And the others?'

'There's no pleasing some folks.'

He said, 'I saw your service record.'

I said, 'You told me that.'

'It was mixed.'

'I tried my best. But I had a mind of my own.'

'Why did you quit?'

'I got bored. You?'

'I got old.'

'What is on that stick?'

He didn't answer. Springfield was standing mute, in the lee of the TV cabinet, closer to the door than the window. Pure habit, I guessed. Simple reflex. He was invisible to a potential external sniper and close enough to the corridor to be all over an intruder the second the door swung open. Training stays with a person. Especially Delta training. I stepped over and gave him his gun back. He took it without a word and put it in his waistband.

Sansom said, 'Tell me what you know so far.'

I said, 'You were airlifted from Bragg to Turkey, and then Oman. Then India, probably. Then Pakistan, and the North West Frontier.'

He nodded and said nothing. He had a faraway look in his eyes. I guessed he was reliving the journey in his mind. Transport planes, helicopters, trucks, long miles on foot.

All long ago.

'Then Afghanistan,' I said.

'Go on,' he said.

'Probably you stayed on the flank of the Abas Ghar and headed south and west, following the line of the Korengal Valley, maybe a thousand feet from the floor.'

'Go on.'

'You stumbled over Grigori Hoth and took his

rifle and let him wander away.'

'Go on.'

'Then you kept on walking, to wherever it was you had been ordered to go.'

He nodded.

I said, 'That's all I know so far.'

He asked, 'Where were you in March of 1983?'

'West Point.'

'What was the big news?'

'The Red Army was trying to stop the bleeding.'

He nodded again. 'It was an insane campaign. No one has ever beaten the tribesmen in the North West Frontier. Not in the whole of history. And they had our own experience in Vietnam to study. Some things just can't be done. It was a slow-motion meat grinder. Like getting pecked to death by birds. We were very happy about it, obviously.'

'We helped,' I said.

'We sure did. We gave the mujahideen everything they wanted. For free.'

'Like Lend-Lease.'

'Worse,' Sansom said. 'Lend-Lease was about helping friends that happened to be bankrupt at the time. The mujahideen were not bankrupt. Quite the reverse. There were all kinds of weird tribal alliances that stretched all the way to Saudi. The mujahideen had more money than we did, practically.'

'And?'

'When you're in the habit of giving people everything they want, it's very hard to stop.'

'What more did they want?'

'Recognition,' he said. 'Tribute. Acknowledgement. Courtesy. Face time. It's hard to know exactly how to characterize it.'

'So what was the mission?'

'Can we trust you?'

'You want to get the file back?'

'Yes.'

'So what was the mission?'

'We went to see the mujahideen's top boy. Bearing gifts. All kinds of gaudy trinkets, from Ronald Reagan himself. We were his personal envoys. We had a White House briefing. We were told to pucker up and kiss ass at every possible opportunity.'

'And did you?'

'You bet.'

'It was twenty-five years ago.'

'So?'

'So who cares any more? It's a detail of history. And it worked, anyway. It was the end of communism.'

'But it wasn't the end of the mujahideen. They stayed in business.'

'I know,' I said. 'They became the Taliban and al-Qaeda. But that's a detail, too. Voters in North Carolina aren't going to remember the history. Most voters can't remember what they had for breakfast.'

'Depends,' Sansom said.

'On what?'

'Name recognition.'

'What name?'

'The Korengal was where the action was. Just a small salient, but that was where the Red Army met its end. The mujahideen there were doing a really fine job. Therefore the local mujahideen leader there was a really big deal. He was a rising star. He was the one we were sent to meet. And we did. We met with him.'

'And you kissed his ass?'

'Every which way we could.'

'Who was he?'

'He was a fairly impressive guy, initially. Young, tall, good-looking, very intelligent, very committed. And very rich, by the way. Very connected. He came from a billionaire family in Saudi. His father was a friend of Reagan's Vice President. But the guy himself was a revolutionary. He quit the easy life for the cause.'

'Who was he?'

'Osama bin Laden.'

SIXTY-SIX

The room stayed quiet for a long moment. Just muted city sounds from the window, and the hiss of air from a vent above the bathroom. Springfield moved away from his position by the TV cabinet and sat down on the bed.

I said, 'Name recognition.'

Sansom said, 'It's a bitch.'

'You got that right.'

'Tell me about it.'

'But it's a big file,' I said.

'So?'

'So it's a long report. And we've all read army reports.'

'And?'

'They're very dry.' Which they were. Take Springfield's Steyr GB, for instance. The army had tested it. It was a miracle of modern engineering.

Not only did it work exactly like it should, it also worked exactly like it shouldn't. It had a complex gas-delayed blowback system that meant it could be loaded with substandard or elderly or badly assembled rounds and still fire. Most guns have problems with variable gas pressures. Either they blow up with too much or fail to cycle with too little. But the Steyr could handle anything. Which was why Special Forces loved it. They were often far from home with no logistics, forced to rely on whatever they could scrounge up locally. The Steyr GB was a metal marvel.

The army report called it *technically acceptable*.

I said, 'Maybe they didn't mention you by name. Maybe they didn't mention *him* by name. Maybe it was all acronyms, for Delta leader and local commander, all buried in three hundred pages of map references.'

Sansom said nothing.

Springfield looked away.

I asked, 'What was he like?'

Sansom said, 'See? This is exactly what I'm talking about. My whole life counts for nothing now, except I'm the guy who kissed Osama bin Laden's ass. That's all anyone will ever remember.'

'But what was he like?'

'He was a creep. He was clearly committed to killing Russians, which we were happy about at first, but pretty soon we realized he was committed to killing everyone who wasn't exactly the same as him. He was weird. He was a psychopath. He smelled bad. It was a very uncomfortable weekend. My skin was crawling the whole time.'

'You were there a whole weekend?'

'Honoured guests. Except not really. He was an

arrogant son of a bitch. He lorded it over us the whole time. He lectured us on tactics and strategy. Told us how he would have won in Vietnam. We had to pretend to be impressed.'

'What gifts did you give him?'

'I don't know what they were. They were wrapped. He didn't open them. Just tossed them in a corner. He didn't care. Like they say at weddings, our presence was present enough. He thought he was proving something to the world. The Great Satan was bending its knee before him. I nearly puked a dozen times. And not just because of the food.'

'You ate with him?'

'We were staying in his tent.'

'Which will be called their HQ in the report. The language will be very neutral. The ass-kissing won't be mentioned. It will be three hundred tedious pages about a rendezvous attempted and a rendezvous kept. People will die of boredom before you're halfway over the Atlantic. Why are you so worried?'

'The politics is awful. The Lend-Lease thing. In as much as bin Laden wasn't dipping into his own personal fortune, it's like we were subsidizing him. Paying him, almost.'

'Not your fault. That's White House stuff. Did any sea captain get it in the neck for delivering Lend-Lease stuff to the Soviets during World War Two? They didn't stay our friends either.'

Sansom said nothing.

I said, 'It's just words on a page. They won't resonate. People don't read.'

Sansom said, 'It's a big file.'

'The bigger the better. The bigger it is, the more

buried the bad parts will be. And it will be very dated. I think we used to spell his name differently back then. With a U. It was Usama. Or UBL. Maybe people won't even notice. Or you could say it was someone else entirely.'

'You sure you know where that stick is?'

'Certain.'

'Because you sound like you don't. You sound like you're trying to console me, because you know it's staying out there for the world to see.'

'I know where it is. I'm just trying to get a handle on why you're so uptight. People have survived worse.'

'You ever used a computer?'

'I used one today.'

'What makes for the biggest files?'

'I don't know.'

'Take a guess.'

'Long documents?'

'Wrong. Large numbers of pixels make for the biggest files.'

'Pixels?' I said.

He didn't answer.

'OK,' I said. 'I see. It's not a report. It's a photograph.'

SIXTY-SEVEN

The room went quiet again. The city sounds, the forced air. Sansom got up and used the bathroom. Springfield moved back to his former position by the TV cabinet. There were bottles of water on the cabinet, with paper collars that said if you drank the water you would be charged eight dollars.

Sansom came out of the bathroom.

'Reagan wanted the photograph,' he said. 'Partly because he was a sentimental old geezer, and partly because he was a suspicious old man. He wanted to check we had followed his orders. The way I remember it, I'm standing next to bin Laden with the mother of all shit-eating grins on my face.'

Springfield said, 'With me on the other side.'

Sansom said, 'Bin Laden knocked down the Twin Towers. He attacked the Pentagon. He's the world's worst terrorist. He's a very, very recognizable figure. He's completely unmistakable. That photograph will kill me in politics. Stone dead. For ever.'

I asked, 'Is that why the Hoths want it?'

He nodded. 'So that al-Qaeda can humiliate me, and the United States along with me. Or vice-versa.'

I stepped over to the TV cabinet and took a bottle of water. Unscrewed the cap and took a long drink. The room was on Springfield's card, which meant that Sansom was paying. And Sansom could afford eight bucks.

Then I smiled, briefly.

'Hence the photograph in your book,' I said. 'And on your office wall. Donald Rumsfeld with Saddam Hussein, in Baghdad.'

'Yes,' Sansom said.

'Just in case. To show that someone else had done the very same thing. Like a trump card, just lying there in the weeds. No one knew it was a trump. No one even knew it was a card.'

'It's not a trump,' Sansom said. 'It's not even

close. It's like a lousy four of clubs. Because bin Laden is way worse than Saddam ever was. And Rumsfeld wasn't looking to get elected to anything afterwards. He was appointed to everything he did after that, by his friends. He had to be. No sane person would have voted for him.'

'You got friends?'

'Not many.'

'No one ever said much about Rumsfeld's photograph.'

'Because he wasn't running for office. If he had ever gotten into an election campaign, that would have been the most famous photograph in the world.'

'You're a better man than Rumsfeld.'

'You don't know me.'

'Educated guess.'

'OK, maybe. But bin Laden is worse than Saddam. And that image is poison. It doesn't even need a caption. There I am, grinning up at the world's most evil man like a puppy dog. People fake pictures like that for attack ads. And this one is real.'

'You'll get it back.'

'When?'

'How are we doing with the felony charges?'

'Slow.'

'But sure?'

'Not very. There's good news and bad news.'

'Give me the bad news first.'

'It's very unlikely that the FBI will want to play ball. And it's certain the Department of Defense won't.'

'Those three guys?'

'They're off the case. Apparently they're

injured. One has a broken nose and one has a cut head. But they've been replaced. The DoD is still hot to trot.'

'They should be grateful. They need all the help they can get.'

'Doesn't work like that. There are turf wars to be won.'

'So what's the good news?'

'We think the NYPD is prepared to be relaxed about the subway.'

'Terrific,' I said. 'That's like cancelling a parking ticket for Charles Manson.'

Sansom didn't reply.

I asked him, 'What about Theresa Lee and Jacob Mark? And Docherty?'

'They're back at work. With federal paper on file commending them for helping Homeland Security with a sensitive investigation.'

'So they're OK and I'm not?'

'They didn't hit anybody. They didn't bruise any egos.'

'What are you going to do with the memory stick when you get it back?'

'I'm going to check it's right, then I'm going to smash it up, and burn the pieces, and grind the ash to dust, and flush it down about eight separate toilets.'

'Suppose I asked you not to do that?'

'Why would you?'

'I'll tell you later.'

* * *

Depending on your point of view it was either late in the afternoon or early in the evening. But I had just woken up, so I figured it was time for breakfast. I called down to room service and ordered a big tray. About fifty bucks' worth, at Sheraton New York prices, with taxes and tips and charges and fees. Sansom didn't bat an eye. He was sitting forward in his chair, seething with frustration and impatience. Springfield was much more relaxed. He had shared that mountain journey a quarter of a century earlier, and he had shared the ignominy. *Sometimes our friends become our enemies, and sometimes our enemies become our friends*. But Springfield had nothing riding on it. No aims, no plans, no ambitions. And it showed. He was still exactly what he had been back then, just a guy doing his job.

I asked, 'Could you have killed him?'

'He had bodyguards,' Sansom said. 'Like an inner circle. Loyalties over there are fanatical. Think of the Marines, or the Teamsters, and multiply by a thousand. We were disarmed a hundred yards from the camp. We were never alone with him. There were always people milling about. Plus kids and animals. They lived like the Stone Age.'

'He was a long lanky streak of piss,' Springfield said. 'I could have reached up and snapped his scrawny neck any old time I wanted to.'

'Did you want to?'

'You bet I did. Because I knew. Right from the start. Maybe I should have done it right when the flashbulb went off. Like a breadstick in an Italian restaurant. That would have made a better picture.'

I said, 'Suicide mission.'

'But it would have saved a lot of lives later.'

I nodded. 'Just like if Rumsfeld had stuck a shiv in Saddam.'

*　　*　　*

The room service guy brought my meal and I moved Sansom out of his chair and ate at the table. Sansom took a cell phone call and confirmed that as of that moment I was off the hook for the subway transgression. I was no longer a person of interest as far as the NYPD was concerned. But then he made a second call and told me the jury was still out at the FBI, and the signs did not look good at all. Then he made a third call and confirmed that the DoD brass definitely would not let go. They were like dogs with a bone. I was in all kinds of trouble at the federal level. Obstruction of justice, assault and battery, wounding with a deadly weapon.

'End of story,' Sansom said. 'I would have to go to the Secretary direct.'

'Or the President,' I said.

'I can't do either. On the face of it the DoD is currently in hot pursuit of an active al-Qaeda cell. Can't argue against that, in today's climate.'

Politics is a minefield. Damned if you do, damned if you don't.

'OK,' I said. 'Just as long as I know the shape of the battlefield.'

'It's not your battle, strictly speaking.'

'Jacob Mark will feel better with a little closure.'

'You're doing this for Jacob Mark? The feds can give him all the closure he needs.'

'You think? The feds are nowhere. How long do you want to drag this out?'

'So are you doing it for Jacob Mark or for me?'

'I'm doing it for myself.'

'You're not involved.'

'I like a challenge.'

'There are lots of other challenges in the world.'

'They made it personal. They sent me that DVD.'

'Which was tactical. If you react, they win.'

'No, if I react, they lose.'

'This isn't the Wild West.'

'You got that right. This is the timid West. We need to roll the clock back.'

'Do you even know where they are?'

Springfield glanced at me.

I said, 'I'm working on a couple of ideas.'

'Do you still have an open channel of communication?'

'She hasn't called me since the DVD.'

'Since she set you up, you mean.'

'But I think she's going to call again.'

'Why?'

'Because she wants to.'

'She might win. One false step, and you're her prisoner. You'll end up telling her what she wants to know.'

I asked him, 'How many times have you flown commercial since September eleventh?'

He said, 'Hundreds.'

'And I bet every single time some small corner of your mind was hoping there were hijackers on board. So you could see them marching up the aisle, so you could jump up and beat the shit out of them. Or die trying.'

Sansom inclined his head and his mouth turned down in a rueful little smile. The first I had seen from him for a long time.

'You're right,' he said. 'Every single time.'

'Why?'

'I would want to protect the airplane.'

'And you would want to unload your frustrations. And burn off your hate. I know I would. I liked the Twin Towers. I liked the way the world used to be. You know, before. I have no political skills. I'm not a diplomat or a strategist. I know my weaknesses, and I know my strengths. So all in all for a guy like me the chance to meet an active al-Qaeda cell seems pretty much like all my birthdays and Christmases rolled into one.'

'You're crazy. This is not a thing to be done alone.'

'What's the alternative?'

'Homeland Security will find them eventually. Then they'll put something together. NYPD, FBI, SWAT teams, equipment, hundreds of guys.'

'A huge operation with lots of disparate components.'

'But carefully planned.'

'You been on operations like that before?'

'Couple of times.'

'How did they work out for you?'

Sansom didn't answer.

I said, 'Alone is always better.'

'Maybe not,' Springfield said. 'We checked on Homeland Security's computer algorithm. The Hoths brought a large party with them.'

'How many?'

'Nineteen men.'

SIXTY-EIGHT

I finished my breakfast. The coffee pot was empty. So I finished my eight-dollar bottle of water and lobbed it end over end towards the trash can. It struck the rim with a hollow plastic sound and bounced out and rolled away across the carpet. Not a good sign, if I were superstitious. But I'm not.

'Total of nineteen men,' I said. 'Four left the country already and two are walking wounded with broken jaws and elbows. That leaves thirteen on active service.'

Sansom said, 'Broken jaws and elbows? How did that happen?'

'They were out looking for me. They might be hot shit in the hills with grenade launchers, but scuffling on the street seems not to be their main strength.'

'Did you write on their foreheads?'

'One of them. Why?'

'The FBI got a call from the Bellevue emergency room. Two unidentified foreigners were dumped there after a beating. One of them had writing on his forehead.'

'Punishment,' I said. 'The Hoths must have been displeased with their performance. So they gave them up, to encourage the others.'

'Ruthless people.'

'Where are they now?'

'Secure rooms in the hospital. Because one of them was there before. Some previous emergency at Penn Station. He's not saying anything. The FBI is trying to work out who the hell he is.'

'What's taking them so long? I wrote Lila's name on his head. I wrote Lila, call me. How many people named Lila is the Bureau interested in right now?'

Sansom shook his head. 'Give them some credit. The part with the name had been skinned off with a knife.'

* * *

I stepped over and opened the second bottle of eight-dollar water. Took a sip. It tasted good. But no better than two-dollar water. Or free water, from the tap.

'Thirteen people,' I said.

'Plus the Hoths themselves,' Springfield said.

'OK, fifteen.'

'Suicide mission.'

'We're all going to die,' I said. 'The only questions are how and when.'

'We can't actively help you,' Sansom said. 'You understand that, right? This is going to end with a minimum of one and a maximum of fifteen homicides on the streets of New York City. We can't be a part of that. We can't be within a million miles of it.'

'Because of politics?'

'Because of a lot of reasons.'

'I'm not asking for help.'

'You're a maniac.'

'They're going to think so.'

'You got a schedule in mind?'

'Soon. No sense in waiting.'

'The minimum one homicide would be you, of

course. In which case I wouldn't know where to look for my photograph.'

'So keep your fingers crossed for me.'

'The responsible thing would be for you to tell me now.'

'No, the responsible thing would be for me to get a job as a school bus driver.'

'Can I trust you?'

'To survive?'

'To keep your word.'

'What did you learn in Officer Candidate School?'

'That brother officers are to be trusted. Especially brother officers of equal rank.'

'There you go, then.'

'But we weren't really brothers. We were in very different branches of the service.'

'You got that right. I was working hard while you were flying all over the world kissing terrorist ass. You didn't even get a Purple Heart.'

He didn't answer.

'Just kidding,' I said. 'But you better hope I'm not the first homicide, or you might be hearing that kind of thing all the time.'

'So tell me now.'

'I need you watching my back.'

He said, 'I read your record.'

'You told me that.'

'You got your Purple Heart for being blown up by that truck bomb in Beirut. The Marine barracks.'

'I remember it well.'

'You got a disfiguring scar.'

'Want to see it?'

'No. But you need to remember, that wasn't the

Hoths.'

'What are you, my therapist?'

'No. But that doesn't make my statement any the less true.'

'I don't know who it was in Beirut. Nobody does, for sure. But whoever, they were the Hoths' brother officers.'

'You're motivated by revenge. And you still feel guilty about Susan Mark.'

'So?'

'So you might not be operating at peak efficiency.'

'Worried about me?'

'About myself, mainly. I want my photograph back.'

'You'll get it.'

'At least give me a clue where it is.'

'You know what I know. I figured it out. So you'll figure it out.'

'You were a cop. Different skill set.'

'So you'll be slower. But it ain't rocket science.'

'So what kind of science is it?'

'Think like a regular person for once. Not like a soldier or a politician.'

He tried. He failed. He said, 'At least tell me why I shouldn't destroy it.'

'You know what I know.'

'What does that mean?'

'Or maybe you don't know what I know. Because you're too close to yourself. Me, I'm just a member of the public.'

'So?'

'I'm sure you're a hell of a guy, Sansom. I'm sure you'd be a great senator. But at the end of the day any senator is just one out of a hundred.

They're all fairly interchangeable. Can you give me a name? Of one individual senator who truly made a difference to anything?'

Sansom didn't answer.

'Can you tell me how you personally are going to screw al-Qaeda?'

He started to talk about the Armed Services Committee, and Foreign Relations, and Intelligence, and budgets, and oversight. Like a boilerplate speech. Like he was out on the stump. I asked him, 'What part of all that wouldn't be done by whoever else might get the job, assuming you don't?'

He didn't answer. I asked him, 'Imagine a cave in the northwest of Pakistan. Imagine the al-Qaeda brass sitting there, right now. Are they tearing their hair out and saying, holy shit, we better not let John Sansom make it to the U.S. Senate? Are you top of their agenda?'

He said, 'Probably not.'

'So why do they want the photograph?'

'Small victories,' he said. 'Better than nothing.'

'It's a lot of work for a small victory, don't you think? Two agents plus nineteen men plus three months?'

'The United States would be embarrassed.'

'But not very. Look at the Rumsfeld photograph. Nobody cared. Times change, things move on. People understand that, if they even notice at all. Americans are either very mature and sensible, or very oblivious. I'm never quite sure which. But either way, that picture would be a damp squib. It might destroy you personally, but destroying one American at a time isn't how al-Qaeda operates.'

'It would hurt Reagan's memory.'

'Who cares? Most Americans don't even remember him. Most Americans think Reagan is an airport in Washington.'

'I think you're underestimating.'

'And I think you're overestimating. You're too close to the process.'

'I think that photograph would hurt.'

'But who would it hurt? What does the government think?'

'You know that the Defense Department is trying like crazy to get it back.'

'Is it? Then why did they give the job to their B team?'

'You think those guys were their B team?'

'I sincerely hope so. If that was their A team, we should all move to Canada.'

Sansom didn't answer.

I said, 'The picture might do you some local damage in North Carolina. But apparently that's all. We're not seeing any kind of maximum effort from the DoD. Because there's no real national downside.'

'That's not an accurate read.'

'OK, it's bad for us. It's evidence of a strategic error. It's awkward, it's embarrassing, and it's going to put egg on our face. But that's all. It's not the end of the world. We're not going to fall apart.'

'So al-Qaeda's expectations are too high? You're saying they're wrong too? They don't understand the American people the way you do?'

'No, I'm saying this whole thing is a little lopsided. It's slightly asymmetric. Al-Qaeda fielded an A team and we fielded a B team. Therefore their desire to grab that photograph is just a little bit stronger than our desire to hold on to it.'

Sansom said nothing.

'And we have to ask, why wasn't Susan Mark just told to copy it? If their aim was to embarrass us, then copying it would have been a better idea. Because when it came to light, and sceptics claimed it had been faked, which they would, then the original would still be on file, and we couldn't have denied it with a straight face.'

'OK.'

'But Susan Mark wasn't told to copy it. She was told to steal it, effectively. To take it away from us. With no trace left behind. Which added considerable risk and visibility.'

'Which means what?'

'Which means they want to have it, and equally they want us *not* to have it.'

'I don't understand.'

'You need to cast your mind back. You need to figure out exactly what that camera saw. Because al-Qaeda doesn't want to publicize that photograph. They stole it because they want to suppress it.'

'Why would they?'

'Because however bad it is for you, there's something in it that's even worse for Osama bin Laden.'

SIXTY-NINE

Sansom and Springfield went quiet, like I knew they would. They were casting their minds back a quarter of a century, to a dim tent above the Korengal Valley floor. They were stiffening and straightening, subconsciously repeating their formal poses. One on the left, one on the right, with their host between them. The camera lens, trained on them, aimed, zoomed, adjusted, focused. The strobe, charging, then popping, bathing the scene with light.

What exactly did the camera see?

Sansom said, 'I don't remember.'

'Maybe it was us,' Springfield said. 'Simple as that. Maybe meeting with Americans looks like bad karma now.'

'No,' I said. 'That's good PR. It makes bin Laden look powerful and triumphant, and it makes us look like patsies. It has to be something else.'

'It was a zoo in there. Chaos and mayhem.'

'It has to be something fatally inappropriate. Little boys, little girls, animals.'

Sansom said, 'I don't know what they would regard as inappropriate. They have a thousand rules over there. Could be something he was eating, even.'

'Or smoking.'

'Or drinking.'

'There was no alcohol there,' Springfield said. 'I remember that.'

'Women?' I asked.

'No women, either.'

'Has to be something. Were there other visitors there?'

'Only tribal.'

'No foreigners?'

'Only us.'

'It has to be something that makes him look compromised, or weak, or deviant. Was he healthy?'

'He seemed to be.'

'So what else?'

'Deviant from their laws or deviant like we mean it?'

'Al-Qaeda HQ,' I said. 'Where the men are men and the goats are scared.'

'I don't remember. It was a long time ago. We were tired. We had just walked a hundred miles through the front lines.'

Sansom had gone quiet. Like I knew he would. Eventually he said, 'This is a real bitch.'

I said, 'I know it is.'

'I'm going to have to make a big decision.'

'I know you are.'

'If that picture hurts him more than it hurts me, I'm going to have to release it.'

'No, if it hurts him at all, even a little bit, you're going to have to release it. And then you're going to have to suck it up and face the consequences.'

'Where is it?'

I didn't answer.

'OK,' he said. 'I have to watch your back. But I know what you know. And you figured it out. Which means I can figure it out. But slower. Because it ain't rocket science. Which means the Hoths can figure it out too. Are they going to be slower? Maybe not. Maybe they're picking it up right now.'

'Yes,' I said. 'Maybe they are.'

'And if they're going to suppress it, maybe I should just go ahead and let them.'

'If they're going to suppress it, that means it's a valuable weapon that could be used against them.'

Sansom said nothing.

I said, 'Remember Officer Candidate School? Something about all enemies, foreign and domestic?'

'We take the same oath in Congress.'

'So should you let the Hoths suppress the picture?'

He was quiet for a very long time.

Then he spoke.

'Go,' he said. 'Go get the Hoths before they get the picture.'

* * *

I didn't go. Not right then. Not immediately. I had things to think about, and plans to make. And deficiencies to overcome. I wasn't equipped. I was wearing rubber gardening clogs and blue pants. I was unarmed. None of those things was good. I wanted to go in the dead of night, properly dressed in black. With proper shoes. And weapons. The more the merrier.

The outfit would be easy.

The weapons, not so much. New York City is not the best place on the planet to get hold of a private arsenal at the drop of a hat. There were probably places in the outer boroughs selling overpriced junk under the counter, but there were places in the outer boroughs selling used cars, too, and fastidious drivers were well advised to stay away from them.

Problem.

I looked at Sansom and said, 'You can't actively help me, right?'

He said, 'No.'

I looked at Springfield and said, 'I'm heading out to a clothing store now. I figure on getting black pants and a black T-shirt and black shoes. With a black windbreaker, maybe triple-XL, kind of baggy. What do you think?'

Springfield said, 'We don't care. We'll be gone when you get back.'

* * *

I went to the store on Broadway where I bought the khaki shirt prior to the Sansoms' fundraiser lunch. It was doing a little business and had plenty of items in stock. I found everything I needed there apart from socks and shoes. Black jeans, plain black T-shirt, and a black cotton zip-up windbreaker made for a guy with a much bigger gut than mine. I tried it on and as expected it fit OK in the arms and the shoulders and ballooned way out in front like a maternity smock.

Perfect, if Springfield had taken the hint.

I dressed in the changing cubicle and trashed my old stuff and paid the clerk fifty-nine dollars. Then I took her recommendation and moved on three blocks to a shoe store. I bought a pair of sturdy black lace-ups and a pair of black socks. Close to a hundred bucks. I heard my mother's voice in my head, from long ago: *At a price like that, you better make them last. Don't scuff them up.*

I stepped out of the store and stamped down on the sidewalk a couple of times to settle the fit. I stopped in at a drugstore and bought a pair of generic white boxers. I figured that since everything else was new I should complete the ensemble.

Then I started back to the hotel.

Three paces later the phone in my pocket started to vibrate.

SEVENTY

I backed up against a building on the corner of 55th Street and pulled the phone out of my pocket. *Restricted Call*. I opened the phone and raised it to my ear.

Lila Hoth said, 'Reacher?'

I said, 'Yes?'

'I'm still standing out in the road. I'm still waiting for the truck to hit me.'

'It's coming.'

'But when will it arrive?'

'You can sweat a spell. I'll be with you inside a couple of days.'

'I can't wait.'

'I know where you are.'

'Good. That will simplify things.'

'And I know where the memory stick is, too.'

'Again, good. We'll keep you alive long enough for you to tell us. And then maybe a few more hours, just for the fun of it.'

'You're a babe in the woods, Lila. You should have stayed home and tended your goats. You're going to die and that photograph is going all around the world.'

'We have a fresh blank DVD,' she said. 'The camera is charged up and ready for your starring role.'

'You talk too much, Lila.'

She didn't answer.

I closed the phone and headed back through the gathering evening darkness to the hotel. I went up in the elevator and unlocked my room and sat down on the bed to wait. I waited for a long time. Close to four hours. I thought I was waiting for Springfield. But in the end it was Theresa Lee who showed up.

* * *

She knocked on the door eight minutes before midnight. I did the thing with the chain and the mirror again and let her in. She was dressed in a version of the first outfit I had ever seen her in. Pants, and a silk short-sleeved shirt. Untucked. Dark grey, not mid-grey. Less silvery. More serious.

She was carrying a black gymnasium bag. Ballistic nylon. The way it hung from her hand I guessed it held heavy items. The way the heavy items moved and clinked I guessed they were made of metal. She put the bag on the floor near the bathroom and asked, 'Are you OK?'

'Are you?'

She nodded. 'It's like nothing ever happened. We're all back on the job.'

'What's in the bag?'

'I have no idea. A man I never saw before

delivered it to the precinct.'

'Springfield?'

'No, the name he gave was Browning. He gave me the bag and said in the interests of crime prevention I should make sure you never got your hands on it.'

'But you brought it anyway?'

'I'm guarding it personally. Safer than leaving it around.'

'OK.'

'You would have to overpower me. And assaulting police officers is against the law.'

'True.'

She sat down on the bed. A yard from me. Maybe less.

She said, 'We raided those three old buildings on 58th Street.'

'Springfield told you about them?'

'He said his name was Browning. Our counterterrorism people went in two hours ago. The Hoths aren't there.'

'I know.'

'They were, but they aren't any more.'

'I know.'

'How do you know?'

'They turned in Leonid and his buddy. Therefore they've moved somewhere Leonid and his buddy don't know. Layers upon layers.'

'Why did they turn in Leonid and his buddy?'

'To encourage the other thirteen. And to feed the machine. We'll rough them up a little, the Arab media will call it torture, they'll get ten new recruits. Net gain of eight. And Leonid and his pal are no big loss, anyway. They were hopeless.'

'Will the other thirteen be better?'

'Law of averages says yes.'
'Thirteen is an insane number.'
'Fifteen, including the Hoths themselves.'
'You shouldn't do it.'
'Especially unarmed.'
She glanced at the bag. Then she looked back at me. 'Can you find them?'
'What are they doing for money?'
'We can't trace them that way. They stopped using credit cards and ATMs six days ago.'
'Which makes sense.'
'Which makes them hard to find.'
I asked, 'Is Jacob Mark safely back in Jersey?'
'You think he shouldn't be involved?'
'No.'
'But I should?'
'You are,' I said. 'You brought me the bag.'
'I'm guarding it.'
'What else are your counterterrorism people doing?'
'Searching,' she said. 'With the FBI and the Department of Defense. There are six hundred people on the street right now.'
'Where are they looking?'
'Anywhere bought or rented inside the last three months. The city is cooperating. Plus they're inspecting hotel registers and business apartment leases and warehouse operations, across all five boroughs.'
'OK.'
'Word on the street is it's all about a Pentagon file on a USB memory stick.'
'Close enough.'
'Do you know where it is?'
'Close enough.'

'Where is it?'

'Nowhere between Ninth Avenue and Park and 30th Street and 45th.'

'I suppose I deserve that.'

'You'll figure it out.'

'Do you really know? Docherty figures you don't. He figures you're trying to bluff your way out of trouble.'

'Docherty is clearly a very cynical man.'

'Cynical or right?'

'I know where it is.'

'So go get it. Leave the Hoths for someone else.'

I didn't answer that. Instead I said, 'Do you spend time in the gym?'

'Not much,' she said. 'Why?'

'I'm wondering how hard it would be to overpower you.'

'Not very,' she said.

I didn't answer.

She asked, 'When are you planning on setting out?'

'Two hours,' I said. 'Then another two hours to find them, and attack at four in the morning. My favourite time. Something we learned from the Soviets. They had doctors working on it. People hit a low at four in the morning. It's a universal truth.'

'You're making that up.'

'I'm not.'

'You won't find them in two hours.'

'I think I will.'

'The missing file is about Sansom, right?'

'Partially.'

'Does he know you've got it?'

'I haven't got it. But I know where it is.'

'Does he know that?'

I nodded.

Lee said, 'So you made a bargain with him. Get me and Docherty and Jacob Mark out of trouble, and you'll lead him to it.'

'The bargain was designed to get myself out of trouble, first and foremost.'

'Didn't work for you. You're still on the hook with the feds.'

'It worked for me as far as the NYPD is concerned.'

'And it worked for the rest of us all around. For which I thank you.'

'You're welcome.'

She asked, 'How are the Hoths planning to get out of the country?'

'I don't think they are. I think that option disappeared a few days ago. I think they expected things to go more smoothly than they have. Now it's about finishing the job, do or die.'

'Like a suicide mission?'

'That's what they're good at.'

'Which makes it worse for you.'

'If they like suicide, I'm happy to help.'

Lee moved on the bed and the tail of her shirt got trapped underneath her and the silk pulled tight over the shape of the gun on her hip. A Glock 17, I figured, in a pancake holster.

I asked her, 'Who knows you're here?'

'Docherty,' she said.

'When is he expecting you back?'

'Tomorrow,' she said.

I said nothing.

She said, 'What do you want to do right now?'

'Honest answer?'

'Please.'

'I want to unbutton your shirt.'

'You say that to a lot of police officers?'

'I used to. Police officers were all the people I knew.'

'Danger makes you horny?'

'Women make me horny.'

'All women?'

'No,' I said. 'Not all women.'

She was quiet for a long moment and then she said, 'Not a good idea.'

I said, 'OK.'

'You're taking no for an answer?'

'Aren't I supposed to?'

She was quiet for another long moment and then she said, 'I've changed my mind.'

'About what?'

'About it not being a good idea.'

'Excellent.'

'But I worked Vice for a year. Entrapment stings. We needed proof that the guy had a reasonable expectation of what he thought he was going to get. So we made him take his shirt off first. As proof of intent.'

'I could do that,' I said.

'I think you should.'

'You going to arrest me?'

'No.'

I peeled my new T-shirt off. Tossed it across the room. It landed on the table. Lee spent a moment staring at my scar, the same way Susan Mark had on the train. The awful raised tracery of stitches from the shrapnel from the truck bomb at the Beirut barracks. I let her look for a minute and then I said, 'Your turn. With the shirt.'

She said, 'I'm a traditional kind of girl.'

'What does that mean?'

'You would have to kiss me first.'

'I could do that,' I said. And I did. Slowly and gently and a little tentatively at first, in a way that felt exploratory, and in a way that gave me time to savour the new mouth, the new taste, the new teeth, the new tongue. It was all good. Then we passed some kind of a threshold and got into it harder. A short minute later we were completely out of control.

* * *

Afterwards she showered, and then I showered. She dressed, and I dressed. She kissed me one more time, and told me to call her if I needed her, and wished me luck, and walked out through the door. She left the black bag on the floor near the bathroom.

SEVENTY-ONE

I hefted the bag over to the bed. About eight pounds, I figured. It hit the rucked sheet and made a satisfying metallic sound. I unzipped it and parted the flaps like a mouth and looked inside.

First thing I saw was a file folder.

It was legal sized, and khaki in colour, and made of thick paper or thin card, depending on your point of view. It held twenty-one printed-out sheets. Immigration records, for twenty-one separate people. Two women, nineteen men. Citizens of Turkmenistan. They had entered the

United States from Tajikistan three months ago. Linked itineraries. There were digital photographs and digital fingerprints, from the immigration booths at JFK. The photographs had a slight fish-eye distortion. They were in colour. I recognized Lila and Svetlana easily. And Leonid and his buddy. I didn't know the other seventeen. Four of them already had exit notations. They were the four that had left. I dropped their sheets in the trash and laid out the unknown thirteen on the bed for a better look.

All thirteen faces looked bored and tired. Local flights, connections, a long transatlantic flight, jet lag, a long wait in JFK's immigration hall. Sullen glances at the camera, faces held level, eyes swivelling up towards the lens. Which told me all thirteen were somewhat short in stature. I cross-checked with Leonid's sheet. His gaze was just as bored and tired as the others, but it was level. He was the tallest of the party. I checked Svetlana Hoth's sheet. She was the shortest. The others were all somewhere in between, small wiry Middle Eastern men worn down to bone and muscle and sinew by climate and diet and culture. I looked hard at them, one through thirteen, over and over again, until I had their expressions fixed firmly in my mind.

Then I turned back to the bag.

At the minimum I was hoping for a decent handgun. At best I was hoping for a short sub-machine gun. My point to Springfield about the baggy jacket was to make him see that I would have room to carry something under it, slung high on my chest on a shortened strap and then concealed by the excess fabric zipped over it. I had hoped he would get the message.

He had. He had gotten the message. He had come through in fine style.

Better than the minimum.

Better even than the best case.

He had given me a *silenced* short sub-machine gun. A Heckler & Koch MP5SD. The suppressed version of the classic MP5. No butt or stock. Just a pistol grip, a trigger, a housing for a curved 30-round magazine, and then a six-inch barrel radically fattened by a double-layered silencer casing. Nine-millimetre, fast, accurate, and quiet. A fine weapon. It was fitted with a black nylon strap. The strap had already been tightened up and reduced in length to its practical minimum. As if Springfield was saying: *I heard you, pal*.

I laid the gun on the bed.

He had supplied ammunition, too. It was right there in the bag. A single curved magazine. Thirty rounds. Short and fat, shiny brass cases winking in the light, polished lead noses nearly as bright. Nine-millimetre Parabellums. From the Latin motto *Si vis pacem para bellum*. *If you wish for peace, prepare for war*. A wise saying. But thirty rounds was not a lot. Not against fifteen people. But New York City is not easy. Not for me, not for Springfield.

I lined up the magazine next to the gun.

Checked the bag again, in case there was more.

There wasn't.

But there was a bonus of a kind.

A knife.

A Benchmade 3300. A black machined handle. An auto-opening mechanism. Illegal in all fifty states unless you were active-service military or law enforcement, which I wasn't. I thumbed the release and the blade snicked out, fast and hard. A double-edged dagger with a spear point. Four inches long. I am no kind of a knife fetishist. I don't have favourites. I don't really like any of them. But if you asked me to rely on one for combat, I would pick something close to what Springfield had supplied. The automatic mechanism, the point, the two-edged blade. Ambidextrous, good for stabbing, good for slashing either coming or going.

I closed it up and put it on the bed next to the H&K.

There were two final items in the bag. A single leather glove, black, sized and shaped for a large man's left hand. And a roll of black duct tape. I put them on the bed, in line with the gun and the magazine and the knife.

Thirty minutes later I was all dressed up and locked and loaded and riding south on the R train.

SEVENTY-TWO

The R train uses older cars with some front- and rear-facing seats. But I was on a side bench, all alone. It was two o'clock in the morning. There were three other passengers. I had my elbows on my knees and I was staring at myself in the glass opposite.

I was counting bullet points.

Inappropriate clothing, check. The windbreaker was zipped to my chin and looked way too hot and way too big on me. Under it the MP5's strap was looped around my neck and the gun itself was resting diagonally grip-high and barrel-low across my body and it didn't show at all.

A robotic walk: not immediately applicable with a seated suspect on public transportation.

Points three through six: irritability, sweating, tics, and nervous behaviour. I was sweating, for sure, maybe a little more than the temperature and the jacket called for. I was feeling irritable, too, maybe even a little more than usual. But I looked at myself hard in the glass and saw no tics. My eyes were steady and my face was composed. I saw no nervous behaviour, either. But behaviour is about external display. I was a little nervous inside. That was for damn sure.

Point seven: breathing. I wasn't panting. But I was prepared to accept that I was breathing a little harder and steadier than normal. Most of the time I am not aware of breathing at all. It just happens, automatically. An involuntary reflex, deep in the brain. But now I could feel a relentless in-through-the-nose, out-through-the-mouth rhythm. In, out, in, out. Like a machine. Like a man using equipment, underwater. I couldn't slow it down. I wasn't feeling much oxygen in the air. It was going in and coming out like an inert gas. Like argon or xenon. It wasn't doing me any good at all.

Point eight: a rigid forward stare. Check, but I excused myself because I was using it to assess all the other points. Or because it was a symbol of pure focus. Or concentration. Normally I would be gazing around, and not rigidly.

Point nine: mumbled prayers. Not happening. I was still and silent. My mouth was closed and not moving at all. In fact my mouth was closed so hard my back teeth were hurting and the muscles in the corners of my jaw were standing out like golf balls.

Point ten: a large bag. Not present.

Point eleven: hands in the bag. Not relevant.

Point twelve: a fresh shave. Hadn't happened. I hadn't shaved for days.

So, six for twelve. I might or might not be a suicide bomber.

And I might or might not be a suicide. I stared at my reflection and thought back to my first sight of Susan Mark: *a woman heading for the end of her life, as surely and certainly as the train was heading for the end of the line*.

I took my elbows off my knees and sat back. I looked at my fellow passengers. Two men, one woman. Nothing special about any of them. The train rocked on south, with all its sounds. The rushing air, the clatter of expansion joints under the wheels, the scrape of the current collector, the whine of the motors, the squeals as the cars lurched one after the other through the long gentle curves. I looked back at myself in the dark window opposite and smiled.

Me against them.

Not the first time.

And not the last.

* * *

I got out at 34th Street and stayed in the station. Just sat in the heat on a wooden bench and walked myself through my theories one more time. I replayed Lila Hoth's history lesson from the days of the British Empire: *when contemplating an offensive, the very first thing you must plan is your inevitable retreat*. Had her superiors back home followed that excellent advice? I was betting not. For two reasons. First, fanaticism. Ideological organizations can't afford rational considerations. Start thinking rationally, and the whole thing falls apart. And ideological organizations like to force their foot soldiers into no-way-out operations. To encourage persistence. The same way explosive belts are sewn together behind, not zippered or snapped.

And second, a plan for retreat carried with it the seeds of its own destruction. Inevitably. A third or a fourth or a fifth bolt-hole bought or rented three months ago would show up in the city records. Just-in-case reservations at hotels would show up, too. Same-day reservations would show up. Six hundred agents were combing the streets. I guessed they would find nothing at all, because the planners back in the hills would have anticipated their moves. They would have known that all trails would be exhausted as soon as the scent was caught. They would have known that by definition the only safe destination is an unplanned destination.

So now the Hoths were out in the cold. With their whole crew. Two women, thirteen men. They had quit their place on 58th Street and they were scuffling, and improvising, and crawling below the radar.

Which was exactly where I lived. They were in my world.

It takes one to find one.

* * *

I came up from under the ground into Herald Square, which is where Sixth Avenue and Broadway and 34th Street all meet. By day it's a zoo. Macy's is there. At night it's not deserted, but it's quiet. I walked south on Sixth and west on 33rd and came up along the flank of the faded old pile where I had bought my only uninterrupted night of the week. The MP5 was hard and heavy against my chest. The Hoths had only two choices: sleep on the street, or pay off a night porter. Manhattan has hundreds of hotels, but they break down quite easily into separate categories. Most of them are mid-market or better, where staffs are large and scams don't work. Most of the down-market dumps are small. And the Hoths had fifteen people to accommodate. Five rooms, minimum. To find five empty unobtrusive rooms called for a big place. With a bent night porter working alone. I know New York reasonably well. I can make sense of the city, especially from the kind of angles most normal people don't consider. And I can count the number of big old Manhattan hotels with bent night porters working alone on my thumbs. One was way west on 23rd Street. Far from the action, which was an advantage, but also a disadvantage. More of a disadvantage than an advantage, overall.

Second choice, I figured.

I was standing right next to the only other option.

The clock in my head was ticking past two thirty in the morning. I stood in the shadows and waited. I wanted to be neither early nor late. I wanted to time it right. Left and right I could see traffic heading up on Sixth and down on Seventh. Taxis, trucks, some civilians, some cop cars, some dark sedans. The cross street itself was quiet.

At a quarter to three I pushed off the wall and turned the corner and walked to the hotel door.

SEVENTY-THREE

The same night porter was on duty. Alone. He was slumped on a chair behind the desk, staring morosely into space. There were fogged old mirrors in the lobby. My jacket was puffed out in front of me. I felt I could see the shape of the MP5's pistol grip and the curve of its magazine and the tip of its muzzle. But I knew what I was looking at. I assumed the night porter didn't.

I walked up to him and said, 'Remember me?'

He didn't say yes. Didn't say no. Just gave a kind of all-purpose shrug that I took to be an invitation to open negotiations.

'I don't need a room,' I said.

'So what do you need?'

I took five twenties out of my pocket. A hundred bucks. Most of what I had left. I fanned the bills so he could see all five double-digits and laid them on his counter.

I said, 'I need to know the room numbers where you put the people who came in around midnight.'

'What people?'

'Two women, thirteen men.'

'Nobody came in around midnight.'

'One of the women was a babe. Young. Bright blue eyes. Not easy to forget.'

'Nobody came in.'

'You sure?'

'Nobody came in.'

I pushed the five bills towards him. 'You totally sure?'

He pushed the bills right back.

He said, 'I'd like to take your money, believe me. But nobody came in tonight.'

*　　*　　*

I didn't take the subway. I walked instead. A calculated risk. It exposed me to however many of the six hundred federal agents happened to be in the vicinity, but I wanted my cell phone to work. I had concluded that cell phones don't work in the subway. I had never seen anyone using one down there. Presumably not because of etiquette. Presumably because of a lack of signal. So I walked. I used 32nd Street to get over to Broadway, and then I followed Broadway south, past luggage outlets and junk jewellery stores and counterfeit perfume wholesalers, all of them closed up and shuttered for the night. It was dark down there, and messy. A micro-neighbourhood. I could have been in Lagos, or Saigon.

I paused at the corner of 28th Street to let a taxi slide by.

The phone in my pocket started to vibrate.

*　　*　　*

I backed into 28th and sat down on a shadowed stoop and opened the phone.

Lila Hoth said, 'Well?'

I said, 'I can't find you.'

'I know.'
'So I'll deal.'
'You will?'
'How much cash have you got?'
'How much do you want?'
'All of it.'
'Have you got the stick?'
'I can tell you exactly where it is.'
'But you don't actually have it?'
'No.'
'So what was the thing you showed us in the hotel?'
'A decoy.'
'Fifty thousand dollars.'
'A hundred.'
'I don't have a hundred thousand dollars.'
I said, 'You can't get on a bus or a train or a plane. You can't get out. You're trapped, Lila. You're going to die here. Don't you want to die a success? Don't you want to be able to send that coded e-mail home? Mission accomplished?'
'Seventy-five thousand.'
'A hundred.'
'OK, but only half tonight.'
'I don't trust you.'
'You'll have to.'
I said, 'Seventy-five, all of it tonight.'
'Sixty.'
'Deal.'
'Where are you?'
'Way uptown,' I lied. 'But I'm on the move. I'll meet you in Union Square in forty minutes.'
'Where is that?'
'Broadway, between 14th Street and 17th.'
'Is it safe?'

'Safe enough.'
'I'll be there,' she said.
'Just you,' I said. 'Alone.'
She clicked off.

*   *   *

I moved on two blocks to the north end of Madison Square Park and sat on a bench a yard from a homeless woman who had a shopping cart piled high like a dump truck. I fished in my pocket for Theresa Lee's NYPD business card. I read it in the dim glow of a street light. I dialled her cell number. She answered after five rings.

'This is Reacher,' I said. 'You told me to call you if I needed you.'

'What can I do for you?'

'Am I still off the hook with the NYPD?'

'Absolutely.'

'So tell your counterterrorism people that forty minutes from now I'll be in Union Square and I'll be approached by a minimum of two and a maximum of maybe six of Lila Hoth's crew. Tell your guys they're theirs for the taking. But tell them to leave me alone.'

'Descriptions?'

'You looked in the bag, right? Before you delivered it?'

'Of course.'

'Then you've seen their pictures.'

'Where in the square?'

'I'll aim for the southwest corner.'

'So you found her?'

'First place I looked. She's in a hotel. She paid off the night porter. And put a scare in him. He denied everything and called her room from the desk the minute I was out of the lobby.'

'How do you know?'

'Because she called me less than a minute later. I like coincidences as much as the next guy, but that kind of timing is too good to be true.'

'Why are you meeting with her crew?'

'I set up a deal with her. I told her to come alone. But she'll double-cross me and send some of her people instead. It will help me if your guys grab them up. I don't want to have to shoot them all.'

'Got a conscience?'

'No, I've got thirty rounds of ammunition. Which isn't really enough. I need to parcel it out.'

* * *

Nine blocks later I entered Union Square. I walked all around it once and crossed it on both diagonals. Saw nothing that worried me. Just somnolent shapes on benches. One of New York City's zero-dollar hotels. I sat down near the statue of Gandhi and waited for the rats to come out.

SEVENTY-FOUR

Twenty minutes into my forty I saw the NYPD's counterterrorism squad begin to assemble. Good moves. They came in beat-up unmarked sedans and confiscated minivans full of dents and scrapes. I saw an off-duty taxicab park outside a coffee shop on 16th Street. I saw two guys climb out of the back and cross the road. Altogether I counted sixteen men, and I was prepared to accept that I had missed maybe four or five others. If I didn't know better I would have suspected that a long late session in a martial arts gym had just let out. All the guys were young and fit and bulky and moved like trained athletes. They were all carrying gym bags. They were all inappropriately dressed. They had on Yankees warm-up jackets, or dark windbreakers like mine, or thin fleece parkas, like it was already November. To hide their Kevlar vests, I guessed, and maybe their badges, which would be on chains around their necks.

None of them eyeballed me directly but I could tell they had spotted me and identified me. They formed up in ones and twos and threes all around me and then they stepped back in the dark and disappeared. They just melted into the scenery. Some sat on benches, some lay in nearby doorways, some went places I didn't see.

Good moves.

Thirty minutes into my forty I was feeling pretty optimistic.

Five minutes later, I wasn't.

Because the feds showed up.

Two more cars stopped, right on Union Square West. Black Crown Vics, waxed and bright and shiny. Eight men stepped out. I sensed the NYPD guys stirring. Sensed them staring through the dark, sensed them glancing at each other, sensed them asking: *Why the hell are those guys here?*

I was good with the NYPD. Not so, with the FBI and the Department of Defense.

I glanced at Gandhi. He told me nothing at all.

I pulled out the phone again and hit the green

button to bring up Theresa Lee's number. She was the last call I had made. I hit the green button again to dial. She answered immediately.

I said, 'The feds are here. How did that happen?'

'Shit,' she said. 'Either they're monitoring our dispatcher or one of our guys is looking for a better job.'

'Who takes precedence tonight?'

'They do. Always. You should get the hell out of there.'

I closed the phone and put it back in my pocket. The eight guys from the Crown Vics stepped into the shadows. The square went quiet. There was a faulty letter in a lit-up sign to my left. It sputtered on and off at random intervals. I heard rats in the mulch behind me.

I waited.

Two minutes. Three.

Then thirty-nine minutes into my forty I sensed human movement far to my right. Footfalls, disturbed air, holes in the darkness. I watched and saw figures moving through shadows and dim light.

Seven men.

Which was good news. The more now, the fewer later.

And which was flattering. Lila was risking more than half her force, because she thought I would be hard to take.

All seven men were small, and neat, and wary. They were all dressed like me, in dark clothes baggy enough to conceal weapons. But they weren't going to shoot me. Lila's need to know was like body armour. They saw me and paused thirty yards away.

I sat still.

In theory this should have been the easy part. They approach me, the NYPD guys move in, I walk away and go about my business.

But not with the feds on the scene. At best they would want all of us. At worst they would want me more than them. I knew where the memory stick was. Lila's people didn't.

I sat still.

Thirty yards away the seven men separated. Two stood still, anchored half-right of my position. Two scooted left and looped around and headed for my other flank. Three walked on, to get around behind me.

I stood up. The two men on my right started to move in. The two on my left were halfway through their flanking manoeuvre. The three behind me were out of sight. I guessed the NYPD guys were already on their feet. I guessed the feds were moving too.

A fluid situation.

I ran.

Straight ahead, to the subway gazebo twenty feet in front of me. Down the stairs. I heard feet clattering after me. Loud echoes. A big crowd. Probably close to forty people, all strung out in a crazy Pied Piper chase.

I made it into a tiled corridor and out again into the underground plaza. No violinist this time. Just stale air and trash and one old guy pushing a broom with a threadbare head a yard wide. I ran past him and stopped and skidded on my new soles and changed direction and headed for the uptown R train. I jumped the turnstile and ran on to the platform and all the way to the end.

And stopped.

And turned.

Behind me three separate groups followed one after the other. First came Lila Hoth's seven men. They raced towards me. They saw I had nowhere to go. They stopped. I saw looks of wolfish satisfaction on their faces. Then I saw their inevitable conclusion: too good to be true. Some thoughts are clear in any language. They turned suddenly and saw the NYPD counterterrorism squad hustling right behind them.

And right behind the NYPD guys were four of the eight federal agents.

No one else on the platform. No civilians. On the downtown platform opposite was a lone guy on a bench. Young. Maybe drunk. Maybe worse. He was staring across at the sudden commotion. It was twenty minutes to four in the morning. The guy looked dazed. Like he wasn't making much sense out of what he was seeing.

It looked like a gang war. But what he was actually seeing was a fast and efficient takedown by the NYPD. None of their guys stopped running. They all piled in yelling with weapons drawn and badges visible and they exploited their big physiques and their three-to-one numerical advantage and simply swamped the seven men. No contest. No contest at all. They clubbed all seven to the ground and threw them on their fronts and slammed cuffs on their wrists and hauled them away. No pauses. No delays. No Miranda warnings. Just maximum speed and brutality. Perfect tactics. Literally seconds later they were gone again. Echoes clattered and died. The station went quiet. The guy opposite was still staring but suddenly he was seeing nothing except a silent platform with me standing alone at one end and the four federal agents about thirty feet from me. Nothing between us. Nothing at all. Just harsh white light and empty space.

Nothing happened for the best part of a minute. Then across the tracks I saw the other four federal agents arrive on the downtown platform. They took up position directly opposite me and stood still. They all smiled a little, like they had made a smart move in a game of chess. Which they had. No point in more cross-track exploits. The four agents on my side were between me and the exit. At my back was a blank white wall and the mouth of the tunnel.

Checkmate.

I stood still. Breathed the tainted underground air and listened to the faint roar of ventilation and the rumble of distant trains elsewhere in the system.

The agent nearest me took a gun out from under his coat.

He took a step towards me.

He said, 'Raise your hands.'

SEVENTY-FIVE

Night-time schedules. Twenty-minute gaps between trains. We had been down there maybe four minutes. Therefore arithmetically the maximum delay before the next train would be sixteen minutes. The minimum would be no delay at all.

The minimum delay didn't happen. The tunnel stayed dark and quiet.

'Raise your hands,' the lead agent called again. He was a white man of about forty. Certainly ex-military. DoD, not FBI. Similar type to the three I had already met. But maybe a little older. Maybe a little wiser. Maybe a little better. Maybe this was an A team, not a B team.

'I'll shoot,' the lead agent called. But he wouldn't. Empty threat. They wanted the memory stick. I knew where it was. They didn't.

Median delay before the next train, eight minutes. As likely to be more as less. The guy with the gun took another step forward. His three colleagues followed. Across the tracks the other four stood still. The young guy on the bench was watching, vacantly.

The tunnel stayed dark and quiet.

The lead agent said, 'All this hassle could be over a minute from now. Just tell us where it is.'

I said, 'Where what is?'

'You know what.'

'What hassle?'

'We're running out of patience. And you're missing one important factor.'

'Which is?'

'Whatever intellectual gifts you have, they're hardly likely to be unique. In fact they're probably fairly ordinary. Which means that if you figured it out, we can figure it out too. Which means your continued existence would become surplus to requirements.'

'So go ahead,' I said. 'Figure it out.'

He raised his gun higher and straighter. It was a Glock 17. Maybe twenty-five ounces fully loaded.

By far the lightest service pistol on the market. Made partly from plastic. The guy had short thick arms. He could probably hold the pose indefinitely.

'Last chance,' he said.

Across the tracks the young guy got off his bench and walked away. Long inconsistent strides, not entirely in a straight line. He was prepared to waste a two-dollar Metrocard swipe in exchange for a quiet life. He made it to the exit and disappeared from sight.

No witnesses.

Median delay before the next train, maybe six minutes.

I said, 'I don't know who you are.'

The guy said, 'Federal agents.'

'Prove it.'

The guy kept his gun aimed at my centre mass but nodded over his shoulder at the agent behind him, who stepped out and moved forward into the no-man's-land between us. He paused there and put his hand in his inside jacket pocket and came back with a leather badge holder. He held it eye-height to me and let it fall open. There were two separate pieces of ID in it. I couldn't read either one of them. They were too far away, and both of them were behind scratched plastic windows.

I stepped forward.

He stepped forward.

I got within four feet of him and saw a standard Defense Intelligence Agency ID in the upper window of the wallet. It looked genuine and it was in date. In the lower window was some kind of a warrant or commission that stated the holder was to be afforded every assistance because he was acting directly for the President of the United States.

'Very nice,' I said. 'Beats working for a living.'

I stepped back.

He stepped back.

The lead agent said, 'No different than you were doing, back in the day.'

'Back in prehistory,' I said.

'What is this, an ego thing?'

Median delay before the next train, five minutes.

'It's a practical thing,' I said. 'If you want something done properly, you do it yourself.'

The guy dropped the angle of his arm below the horizontal. Now he was aiming at my knees.

'I'll shoot,' he said. 'You don't think or talk or remember with your legs.'

No witnesses.

If all else fails, start talking.

I asked, 'Why do you want it?'

'Want what?'

'You know what.'

'National security.'

'Offence or defence?'

'Defence, of course. It would ruin our credibility. It would set us back years.'

'You think?'

'We know.'

I said, 'Keep working on those intellectual gifts.'

He aimed his gun more precisely. At my left shin.

He said, 'I'll count to three.'

I said, 'Good luck with that. Tell me if you get stuck along the way.'

He said, 'One.'

Then: the rails hissed in the track bed next to me. Strange metallic harmonic sounds speeding ahead of a train way back in the tunnel. The harmonics were chased all the way by the push of hot air and a deeper rumbling. A curve in the tunnel wall was lit up by a headlight. Nothing happened for a long second. Then the train rushed into view, moving fast, canted over by the camber of the curve. It rocked and straightened and came on at speed and then the brakes bit down and moaned and shrieked and the train slowed and pulled in right alongside us, all bright shining stainless steel and hot light, hissing, grinding, and groaning.

An uptown R train.

Maybe fifteen cars, each one of them dotted with a small handful of passengers.

Witnesses.

I glanced back at the lead agent. His Glock was back under his coat.

We were at the north end of the platform. The R train uses older cars. Each car has four sets of doors. The lead car was halted right next to us. I was more or less in line with the first set of doors. The DoD guys were closer to sets three and four.

The doors opened, the whole length of the train.

Way down at the back end two people got out. They walked away and were gone.

The doors stayed open.

I turned to face the train.

The DoD guys turned to face the train.

I stepped forward.

They stepped forward.

I stopped.

They stopped.

Choices: I could get on through door one, whereupon they would get on through doors three and four. *Into the same car*. We could ride together all night long. Or I could let the train go without me and spend a minimum twenty more minutes trapped with them on the same platform as before.

The doors stayed open.

I stepped forward.

They stepped forward.

I stepped into the car.

They stepped into the car.

I paused a beat and backed right out again. Back to the platform.

They backed out.

We all stood still.

The doors closed in front of me. Like a final curtain. The rubber bumpers thumped together.

I felt the draw of electricity in the air. Volts and amps. Massive demand. The motors spun up and whined. Five hundred tons of steel started to roll.

The R train uses older cars. They have toe boards and rain gutters. I ducked forward and hooked my fingers into the gutter and jammed my right toes on to the board. Then my left. I flattened myself against the metal and the glass. I hugged the car's exterior curve like a starfish. The MP5 dug into my chest. I clung on, fingers and toes. The train moved. Breeze tugged at me. The hard edge of the tunnel came right at me. I held my breath and spread my hands and feet wider and ducked my head and laid my cheek against the glass. The train sucked me sideways into the tunnel with about six inches to spare. I glanced back past my locked elbow and saw the lead agent standing still on the platform, one hand in his hair, the other raising his Glock and then lowering it again.

SEVENTY-SIX

It was a nightmare ride. Incredible speed, howling blackness, battering noise, unseen obstructions hurtling straight at me, extreme physical violence. The whole train swayed and bounced and bucked and jerked and rocked under me. Every single expansion joint threatened to tear me loose. I dug all eight fingers hard into the shallow gutter and pressed upward with the balls of my thumbs and downward with my toes and held on desperately. Wind tore at my clothes. The door panels swayed and juddered. My head bounced against them like a jackhammer.

I rode nine blocks like that. Then we hit 23rd Street and the train braked hard. I was pitched forward against my left hand's grip and my right foot's resistance. I hung on tight and was carried sideways straight into the station's dazzling brightness at thirty miles an hour. The platform rushed past. I was clamped on the lead car like a limpet. It stopped right at the north end of the station. I arched my body and the doors slid open under me. I stepped inside and collapsed into the nearest seat.

Nine blocks. Maybe a minute. Enough to cure me of subway surfing for life.

There were three other passengers in my car. None of them even looked at me. The doors sucked shut. The train moved on.

* * *

I got out at Herald Square. Where 34th Street meets Broadway and Sixth. Ten to four in the morning. Still on schedule. I was twenty blocks and maybe four minutes north of where I got on the train in Union Square. Too far and too fast for organized DoD resistance. I came up from under the ground and walked east to west along Macy's imposing flank. Then I headed south on Seventh all the way to the door of Lila Hoth's chosen hotel.

The night porter was behind the counter. I didn't unzip my jacket for him. I didn't think it would be necessary. I just walked up to him and leaned over and slapped him on the ear. He fell off his stool. I vaulted over the counter and caught him by the throat and hauled him upright.

I said, 'Tell me the room numbers.'

And he did. Five separate rooms, not adjacent, all of them on the eighth floor. He told me which one the women were in. The men were spread out over the other four. Originally thirteen guys, and eight available beds. Five short straws.

Or five on sentry duty.

I took the roll of black duct tape out of my pocket and used about eight yards of it to bind the porter's arms and legs. A dollar and a half from any hardware store, but as much a part of standard-issue Special Forces equipment as the thousand-dollar rifles and the satellite radios and the navigation systems. I stuck a final six-inch length across his mouth. I stole his pass card. Just tore it right off its curly cord. Then I left him out of sight on the floor behind the counter and headed for the elevator bank. Got in and pressed the highest number available, which was eleven. The doors slid shut and the car bore me upward.

At that point I unzipped my jacket.

I settled the gun at a nice angle on its strap and I took the leather glove out of my other pocket and slipped it on my left hand. The MP5SD has no fore grip. Not like the stubby K variant, which has a fat little handle under the muzzle. With the SD you use your right hand on the pistol grip and your left hand supports the barrel casing. The inner barrel has thirty holes drilled in it. The powder in the round neither burns nor explodes. It does both. It deflagrates. It creates a bubble of superheated gas. Some of the gas escapes through the thirty holes, which quiets the noise and slows the bullet to a subsonic velocity. No point in silencing a gun if its bullet is going to create a supersonic snap all its own. A slow bullet is a quiet bullet. Just like the VAL Silent Sniper. The escaping gas comes through the thirty holes and expands and swirls around in the inner silencer chamber. Then it passes to the second chamber and expands some more and swirls some more. Expanding cools the gas. Basic physics. But not by much. Maybe it reduces from superheated to extremely hot. And the outer barrel casing is metal. Hence the glove. No one uses an MP5SD without one. Springfield was the kind of guy who thinks of everything.

On the left side of the gun was a combined safety and fire selector switch. The older versions of the SD that I remembered had a three-position lever. S, E, and F. S for safe, E for single shots, and F for automatic fire. German abbreviations, presumably. E for *ein*, and so on and so forth, even though Heckler & Koch had been owned by a British corporation for many years. I guessed they decided that tradition counts. But Springfield had given me a newer model. The SD4. It had a four-position selector switch. No abbreviations. Just pictograms. For foreign convenience, or illiterate users. A plain white dot for safe, one little white bullet shape for single shots, three bullet shapes for three-round bursts, and a long string of bullet shapes for continuous automatic fire.

I chose three-round bursts. My favourite. One pull of the trigger, three nine-millimetre rounds inside a quarter of a second. An inevitable degree of muzzle climb, minimized by careful control and the weight of the silencer, resulting in a neat little stitch of three fatal wounds climbing a vertical line maybe an inch and a half high.

Works for me.

Thirty rounds. Ten bursts. Eight targets. One burst each, plus two over for emergencies.

The elevator chimed open on the eleventh floor, and I heard Lila Hoth's voice in my head, talking about old campaigns long ago in the Korengal: *you must save the last bullet for yourself, because you do not want to be taken alive, especially by the women*.

I stepped out of the elevator into a silent corridor.

* * *

Standard tactical doctrine for any assault: attack from the high ground. The eighth floor was three below me. Two ways down: stairs or elevator. I preferred the stairs, especially with a silenced weapon. The smart defensive tactic would be to put a man in the stairwell. Early warning for them. Easy pickings for me. He could be dealt with quietly and at leisure.

The stairwell had a battered door set next to the elevator core. I eased it open and started down. The stairs were dusty concrete. Each floor was marked with a large number painted by hand in green paint. I was quiet all the way down to nine. Super-silent after that. I paused and peered over the metal rail.

No sentry in the stairwell.

The landing inside the eighth floor door was empty. Which was a disappointment. It made the job on the other side of the door twenty-five per cent harder. Five men in the corridor, not four. And the way the rooms were distributed meant that some of them would be on my left, and some on my right. Three and two, or two and three. A long second spent facing the wrong way, and then a crucial spin.

Not easy.

But it was four in the morning. The lowest ebb. A universal truth. The Soviets had studied it, with doctors.

I paused on the stairwell side of the door and took a deep breath. Then another. I put my gloved hand on the handle. I took the slack out of the MP5's trigger.

I pulled the door.

I held it at forty-five degrees with my foot. Cradled the MP5's barrel in my glove. Looked and listened. No sound. Nothing to see. I stepped into the corridor. Whipped one way. Whipped the other.

No one there.

No sentries, no guards, no nothing. Just a length of dirty matted carpet and dim yellow light and two rows of closed doors. Nothing to hear, except the subliminal hum and shudder of the city and muted faraway sirens.

I closed the stairwell door behind me.

I checked numbers and walked quickly to Lila's door. Put my ear on the crack and listened hard.

I heard nothing.

I waited. Five whole minutes. Ten. No sound. No one can stay still and silent longer than me.

I dipped the porter's pass card into the slot. A tiny light flashed red. Then green. There was a click. I smashed the handle down and was inside a split second later.

The room was empty.

The bathroom was empty.

There were signs of recent occupation. The toilet roll was loose and ragged. The sink was wet. A towel was used. The bed was rucked. The chairs were out of position.

I checked the other four rooms. All empty. All abandoned. Nothing left behind. No evidence pointing towards an imminent return.

Lila Hoth, one step ahead.

Jack Reacher, one step behind.

* * *

I took my glove off and zipped up again and rode down to the lobby. I hauled the night porter into a sitting position against the back of his counter and tore the tape off his mouth.

He said, 'Don't hit me again.'

I said, 'Why shouldn't I?'

'Not my fault,' he said. 'I told you the truth. You asked what rooms I put them in. Past tense.'

'When did they leave?'

'About ten minutes after you came the first time.'

'You called them?'

'I had to, man.'

'Where did they go?'

'I have no idea.'

'What did they pay you?'

'A thousand,' he said.

'Not bad.'

'Per room.'

'Insane,' I said. Which it was. For that kind of money they could have gone back to the Four Seasons. Except they couldn't. Which was the point.

*   *   *

I paused in the shadows on the Seventh Avenue sidewalk. *Where did they go?* But first, *how* did they go? Not in cars. On the way in they had fifteen people. They would have needed three cars, minimum. And faded old piles with night porters working alone don't have valet parking.

Taxis? Possible, on the way in, late in the evening from midtown. Going out again, at three in the morning on Seventh Avenue? Eight people would have required at least two simultaneous empty cabs.

Unlikely.

Subway? Possible. Probable, even. There were three lines within a block's walk. Night-time schedules, a maximum twenty-minute wait on the platform, but then escape either uptown or downtown. But to where? Nowhere that needed a long walk at the other end. A gaggle of eight people hustling hard on the sidewalk was very noticeable. There were six hundred agents on the streets. The only other hotel option I knew was way west of even the Eighth Avenue line. A fifteen-minute walk, maybe more. Too big a risk of exposure.

So, the subway, but to where?

New York City. Three hundred and twenty square miles. Two hundred and five thousand acres. Eight million separate addresses. I stood there and sorted possibilities like a machine.

I drew a blank.

Then I smiled.

You talk too much, Lila.

I heard her voice in my head again. From the tea room at the Four Seasons. She was talking about the old Afghan fighters. Complaining about them, from her pretended perspective. In reality she was boasting about her own people, and the Red Army's fruitless back-and-forth skirmishing against them. She had said: *The mujahideen were intelligent. They had a habit of doubling back to positions we had previously written off as abandoned*.

I set off back to Herald Square. To the R train. I could get out at Fifth and 59th. From there it was a short walk to the old buildings on 58th Street.

SEVENTY-SEVEN

The old buildings on 58th Street were all dark and quiet. Four thirty in the morning, in a neighbourhood that does little business before ten. I was watching from fifty yards away. From a shadowed doorway on the far sidewalk across Madison Avenue. There was crime scene tape across the door with the single bell push. The left-hand building of the three. The one with the abandoned restaurant on the ground floor.

No lights in the windows.

No signs of activity.

The crime scene tape looked unbroken. And inevitably it would have been accompanied by an official NYPD seal. A small rectangle of paper, glued across the gap between door and jamb, at keyhole height. It was probably still there, untorn.

Which meant there was a back door.

Which was likely, with a restaurant on the premises. Restaurants generate all kinds of unpleasant garbage. All day long. It smells, and it attracts rats. Not acceptable to pile it on the sidewalk. Better to dump it in sealed cans outside the kitchen door, and then wheel the cans to the kerb for the night-time pick-up.

I moved twenty yards south to widen my angle. Saw no open alleys. The buildings were all cheek-by-jowl, all along the block. Next to the door with the crime scene tape was the old restaurant's window. But next to that was another door. Architecturally it was part of the restaurant building's neighbour. It was set into the ground floor of the next building along. But it was plain, it was black, it was unlabelled, it was a little scarred, it had no step, and it was a lot wider than a normal door. It had no handle on the outside. Just a keyhole. Without a key it opened only from the inside. I made a bet with myself that it let out of a covered alley. I figured that the restaurant's neighbour was two rooms wide on the ground floor, and three rooms wide above. At the second-floor level the block was solid. But below that, at street level, there were passageways leading to rear entrances, all of them discreetly boxed in and built over. Air rights in Manhattan are worth a fortune. The city sells itself up and down, as well as side to side.

I moved back to my shadowed doorway. I was counting time in my head. Forty-four minutes from the time Lila's guys had been due to grab me up. Maybe thirty-four from the time Lila had expected their mission-accomplished call. Maybe twenty-four from the time she had finally accepted that things had not gone well. Maybe fourteen from the time she had first been tempted to call me.

Lila, you talk too much.

I pressed back in the darkness and waited. The scene in front of me was absolutely deserted. Occasional cars or taxicabs on Madison. No traffic at all on 58th. No pedestrians anywhere. No dog walkers, no partygoers staggering home. Garbage collection was over. Bagel deliveries hadn't started.

The dead of night.

The city that doesn't sleep was at least resting comfortably.

I waited.

Three minutes later the phone in my pocket

started to vibrate.

* * *

I kept my eyes on the restaurant building and opened the phone. Raised it to my ear and said, 'Yes?'

She asked, 'What happened?'

'You didn't show.'

'Did you expect me to?'

'I didn't give it much thought.'

'What happened to my people?'

'They're in the system.'

'We can still deal.'

'How? You can't afford to lose any more men.'

'We can work something out.'

'OK. But the price just went up.'

'How much?'

'Seventy-five.'

'Where are you now?'

'Right outside your house.'

There was a pause.

There was movement at a window. Fourth floor, the left-hand of two. A darkened room. Faint, ghostly, barely perceptible from fifty yards.

Maybe the shift of a drape.

Maybe a white shirt.

Maybe imaginary.

She said, 'No, you're not outside my house.'

But she didn't sound sure.

She said, 'Where do you want to meet?'

I said, 'What does it matter? You won't show.'

'I'll send someone.'

'You can't afford to. You're down to your last six guys.'

She started to say something, and stopped.

I said, 'Times Square.'

'OK.'

'Tomorrow morning at ten.'

'Why?'

'I want people around.'

'That's too late.'

'For what?'

'I want it now.'

'Tomorrow at ten. Take it or leave it.'

She said, 'Stay on the line.'

'Why?'

'I have to count my money. To check that I have seventy-five.'

I unzipped my jacket.

I put my glove on.

I heard Lila Hoth, breathing.

Fifty yards away the black door opened. The covered alley. A man stepped out. Small, dark, wiry. And wary. He checked the sidewalk, left and right. He peered across the street.

I put the phone in my pocket. Still open. Still live.

I raised the MP5.

Sub-machine guns were developed for close-quarters combat, but many of them are as accurate as rifles out to medium ranges. Certainly the H&K was reliable out to at least a hundred yards. Mine was fitted with iron sights. I moved the selector lever to single shot and put the front sight square on the guy's centre mass.

Fifty yards away he stepped to the kerb. Scanned right, scanned left, scanned ahead. He saw the same nothing I was seeing. Just cool air and a thin night mist.

He stepped back to the door.

A taxicab passed by in front of me.

Fifty yards away the guy pushed the door.

I waited until I judged his momentum was all set to move forward. Then I pulled the trigger and shot him in the back. Bull's-eye. A slow bullet. A perceptible delay. Fire, hit. The SD is advertised as silent. It isn't. It makes a sound. Louder than the polite little spit you would get in a movie. But not worse than the kind of thump you would get from dropping a phone book on a table from about a yard. Noticeable in any environment, but not remarkable in a city.

Fifty yards away the guy pitched forward and went down with his torso in the alley and his legs on the sidewalk. I put a second bullet into him for safety's sake and let the gun fall against its strap and took the phone back out of my pocket.

I said, 'You still there?'

She said, 'We're still counting.'

You're one short, I thought.

I zipped my jacket. Started walking. I hugged the far side of Madison and overshot 58th by a couple of yards. I crossed the avenue and came around the corner with my shoulder tight against the frontage of the buildings. I needed to keep below her line of sight. I passed the first old building. Passed the second.

I said from forty feet below her, 'I have to go now. I'm tired. Times Square, tomorrow morning at ten, OK?'

She answered from forty feet above me. She said, 'OK, I'll send someone.'

I clicked off and put the phone back in my pocket and dragged the dead guy all the way into the alley. I closed the door behind us, slowly and quietly.

SEVENTY-EIGHT

There was a light in the alley. A single dim bulb, in a dirty bulkhead fixture. I recognized the dead guy from the photographs in Springfield's Homeland Security folder. He had been number seven of the original nineteen. I didn't remember his name. I dragged him the length of the space. The floor was old concrete, worn to a shine. I searched him. Nothing in his pockets. No ID. No weapon. I left him by a small wheeled trash receptacle covered in baked-on grime so old it didn't smell any more.

Then I found the inner door to the building, and unzipped my jacket, and waited. I wondered how long it would take for them to get worried about the missing guy. Less than five minutes, I figured. I wondered how many there would be in the search party. Just one, probably, but I hoped for more.

* * *

They waited seven minutes and sent two men. The inner door opened and the first guy stepped out. Number fourteen on Springfield's list. He took a pace towards the alley door and the second guy stepped out after him. Number eight on Springfield's list.

Then three things happened.

First, the first guy stopped. He saw that the alley door was closed. Which did not compute. It could not be opened from the outside without the key. Therefore the original searcher would have left it standing open while he prowled the sidewalk. But it was closed. Therefore the original searcher was already back inside.

The first guy turned around.

Second thing, the second guy also turned around. To close the inner door quietly and precisely. I let him get it done.

Then he raised his eyes and saw me.

The first guy saw me.

Third thing, I shot them both. Two three-round bursts, brief muted purring explosions each a quarter of a second long. I aimed for the base of their throats and let the muzzle climb stitch upward towards their chins. They were small men. Their necks were narrow and mostly full of arteries and spinal cords. Ideal targets. The noise of the gun was much louder in the roofed alley than it had been out in the open. Loud enough for me to worry about it. But the inner door was closed. And it was a stout piece of wood. Once upon a time it had been an outer door, before some earlier owner had sold his air rights.

The two guys went down.

My spent shell cases rattled away across the concrete.

I waited.

No immediate reaction.

Eight rounds gone. Twenty-two remaining. Seven men captured, three more down, three still walking and talking.

Plus the Hoths themselves.

I searched the new dead guys. No ID. No weapons. No keys, which meant the inner door wasn't locked.

I left the two new bodies next to the first one, in the shadow of the trash can.

Then I waited. I didn't expect anyone else to come through the door. Presumably the old Brits on the North West Frontier had eventually gotten wise about sending out rescue parties. Presumably the Red Army had. Presumably the Hoths knew their history. They ought to have. Svetlana had written some of it.

I waited.

The phone vibrated in my pocket.

I pulled it out and checked the window on the front. *Restricted Call*. Lila. I ignored her. I was all done talking. I put the phone back in my pocket. It stopped vibrating.

I put my gloved fingers on the inner door's handle. I eased it down. I felt the latch let go. I was fairly relaxed. Three men had gone out. Conceivable that any one of them might return. Or all three of them. If anyone was inside, watching and waiting, there would be a fatal split second of delay for recognition and a decision, friend or foe. Like a major league batter sorting a fastball from a curveball. A fifth of a second, maybe more.

But no delay for me. Anyone I saw was my enemy.

Anyone at all.

I opened the door.

No one there.

I was looking at an empty room. The abandoned restaurant's kitchen. It was dark and dismantled. There were shells of old cabinets and gaps in the countertops where appliances had been hauled away to the secondhand stores on the Bowery. There were old pipes in the walls where once faucets had been attached. There were hooks in the ceiling, where once saucepans had hung. There was a large stone table in the centre of the room. Cool, smooth, slightly dished from years of wear. Maybe once pastry had been rolled on it.

More recently Peter Molina had been murdered on it.

There was no doubt in my mind that it was the table I had seen in the DVD. No doubt at all. I could see where the camera must have been positioned. I could see where the lights had been set. I could see knots of frayed rope on the table legs, where Peter's wrists and ankles had been tied.

The phone vibrated in my pocket.

I ignored it.

I moved on.

There were two swinging doors leading to the dining room. One in, one out. Standard restaurant practice. No collisions. The doors had porthole windows set eye-high to an average man of fifty years ago. I ducked down and peered through. An empty room, large and rectangular. Nothing in it except a lone orphan chair. Dust and rat shit on the floor. Yellow light coming in from the street through the big filthy window.

I pushed the out door with my foot. Its hinges yelped a little but it opened. I stepped into the dining room. Turned left and left again. Found a back hallway with restrooms. Two doors, labelled *Ladies* and *Gentlemen*. Brass signs, proper words. No pictograms. No stick figures in skirts or pants.

Plus two more doors, one in each of the side walls. Brass signs: *Private*. One would lead back to the kitchen. The other would lead to the stairwell, and the upper floors.

The phone vibrated in my pocket.

I ignored it.

Standard tactical doctrine for any assault: attack from the high ground. Couldn't do it. Not an available option. Around the time the Israeli list was being written the SAS in Britain had been developing a tactic of rappelling off roofs into upper-storey windows, or smashing through the roof tile itself, or blowing through directly from one adjacent attic to another. Fast, dramatic, and usually very successful. Nice work if you could get it. I couldn't. I was stuck with the pedestrian approach.

For the time being, at least.

I opened the stairwell door. It swept an arc through a tiny thirty-inch by thirty-inch ground-floor hallway. Directly across from me, close enough to touch, was the door that led out to the residential entrance. To the street door with the single bell push and the crime scene tape.

Directly out of the tiny hallway rose a single narrow staircase. It turned back on itself halfway up and rose the rest of the way to the second floor out of sight.

The phone vibrated in my pocket.

I pulled it out and checked it. *Restricted Call*. I put it back in my pocket. It stopped vibrating.

I started up the stairs.

SEVENTY-NINE

The safest way up the first half of a dog-legged staircase is to walk backwards, looking upward, with your feet spread wide. Backwards and looking upward, because if overhead resistance comes your way, you need to be facing it. Feet spread wide, because if stairs are going to creak, they're going to creak most in the middle and least at the edges.

I shuffled up like that to the halfway break and then sidled sideways and went up the second half forwards. I came out in a second-floor hallway that was twice the size of the first-floor version but still tiny. Thirty inches by sixty. One room to the left, one to the right, and two dead ahead. Doors all closed.

I stood still. If I was Lila I would have one guy in each of the two rooms dead ahead. I would have them listening hard with weapons drawn. I would have them ready to fling open their doors and start up two parallel fields of fire. They could get me going up or coming down. But I wasn't Lila and she wasn't me. I had no idea of her likely deployment. Except that as her numbers diminished I felt she would want to keep her remaining guys reasonably close. Which would put them on the third floor, not the second. Because the flutter I had seen had been at a fourth-floor window.

At the fourth-floor window on the left, to be precise, looking at the building from the outside. Which meant her room was the room on the right, looking at it from the inside. I doubted that there would be any significant difference in the floor plans as I went up. It was a cheap, utilitarian structure. No call for custom features. Therefore a walk through the second-floor room on the right would be the same thing as a walk through Lila's room two floors above. It would give me the lie of the land.

I squeezed the slack out of the MP5's trigger

and put my gloved fingers on the door handle. Pushed down. Felt the latch let go.

I opened the door.

An empty room.

In fact, an empty and part-demolished studio apartment. It was as deep as but half the width of the restaurant dining room below. A long, narrow space. A closet at the back, a bathroom, a kitchenette, and a living area. I could see the layout at a single glance because all the dividing walls had been torn back to the studs. The bathroom fitments were all still there, odd and naked behind a vertical array of old two-by-twos, like ribs, like the spaced bars of a cage. The kitchen equipment was intact. The floors were pine boards, except for ragged-edged old-fashioned mosaic in the bathroom and linoleum tile in the kitchen. The whole place smelled of vermin and rotten plaster. The window over the street was black with soot. It was bisected diagonally by the bottom of the fire escape.

I walked quietly to the window. The fire escape was a standard design. A narrow iron ladder came down from the floor above and gave on to a narrow iron walkway under the windows themselves. Beyond the walkway a counterbalanced section lay ready to fold down towards the sidewalk under the weight of a fleeing person.

The window was a sash design. The lower pane was designed to slide upward inside the upper pane. Where the panes met they were locked together with a simple brass tongue in a slot. The lower pane had brass handles, like the ones you see on old file cabinets. The handles had been painted over many times. So had the window frames.

I undid the lock and put three fingers into each of the handles and heaved. The frame moved an inch, and stuck. I increased the pressure. I got close to the force I had used on the barred cages in the firehouse basement. The frame shuddered upward, an inch at a time, sticking on the left, sticking on the right, fighting me all the way. I got my shoulder under the bottom rail and straightened my legs. The frame moved another eight inches and jammed solid. I stepped back. Night air came in at me. Total gap, about twenty inches.

More than enough.

I got one leg out, bent at the waist, ducked through, got the other leg out.

The phone vibrated in my pocket.

I ignored it.

I went up the iron ladder, one slow quiet step after another. Halfway up my head was at the level of the third-floor sills and I could see both front-room windows.

Both had closed drapes. Old soot-coloured cotton material behind soot-stained glass. No apparent light inside. No sounds. No evidence of activity. I turned and looked down at the street. No pedestrians. No passers-by. No traffic.

I moved on upward. To the fourth storey. Same result. Dirty glass, closed drapes. I paused a long time under the window where I had seen movement. Or imagined movement. I heard nothing and sensed nothing.

I moved up to the fifth floor. The fifth floor was different. No drapes. Empty rooms. The floors were stained and the ceilings sagged and bowed. Rainwater leaks.

The fifth-floor windows were locked. The same simple brass tongue-and-slot mechanisms I had seen below, but there was nothing I could do about them without busting the glass. Which would make noise. Which I was prepared to do, but not yet. I wanted to time it right.

I hauled the strap around until the MP5 hung down my back and I got a foot up on the window sill. I stepped up and grabbed the crumbling cornice high above my head. I heaved myself over it. Not an elegant process. I am no kind of a graceful gymnast. I finished up panting and sprawled face-down on the roof with a face full of weeds. I lay there for a second to get my breath and then I got to my knees and looked around for a trapdoor. I found one about forty feet back, right above where I judged the stairwell hallway would be. It was a simple shallow upside-down wooden box sheathed in lead and hinged on one side. Presumably locked from below, probably with a hasp and a padlock. The padlock would be strong, but the hasp would be screwed into the frame, and the frame would be weak from age and rot and water damage.

No contest.

Standard tactical doctrine for any assault: attack from the high ground.

EIGHTY

The lead sheath around the trapdoor lid had been beaten with felt hammers into gentle curves. No sharp corners. I got my gloved fingers under the edge opposite the hinge and yanked hard. No result. So I got serious. Two hands, eight fingers, bent legs, deep breath. I closed my eyes. I didn't want to think about Peter Molina. So instead I pictured Lila Hoth's insane smile at the camera right after she checked the Kabul taxi driver's departed pulse.

I jerked the lid.

And the night started to unravel, right there and then.

I had hoped that the hasp's screws would pull out of either the door or the frame. But they pulled out of both together. The padlock with the hasp still attached free-fell ten feet and thumped hard on the bare wooden floor below. A loud, emphatic, tympanic sound. Deep, resonant, and clear, followed immediately by the tinkle of the hasp itself and the patter of six separate screws.

Not good.

Not good at all.

I laid the trapdoor lid back and squatted on the roof and watched and listened.

Nothing happened for a second.

Then I heard a door open down on the fourth floor.

I aimed the MP5.

Nothing happened for another second. Then a head came into view up the stairs. Dark hair. A man. He had a gun in his hand. He saw the padlock on the floor. I saw the wheels turning in his head. *Padlock, floor, screws, vertical fall.* He peered upward. I saw his face. Number eleven on Springfield's list. He saw me. The cloud above me was all lit up by the city's glow. I guessed I was silhouetted quite clearly. He hesitated. I didn't. I shot him more or less vertically through the top of his head. A burst of three. A triple tap. A brief muted purr. He went down with a loud clatter of shoes and hands and limbs, with two final big thumps as first the remains of his head and then his gun hit the boards. I watched the stairs for another long second and then vaulted through the open trapdoor and fell through the air and landed feet first next to the guy, which made another loud noise.

We were all through with secrecy.

Eleven rounds gone, nineteen remaining, four men down, two still up.

Plus the Hoths.

The phone vibrated in my pocket.

Not now, Lila.

I picked up the guy's gun and opened the door to the front room on the left and backed into the shadow. Rested my shoulder on the wall and looked out at the stairs.

No one came up.

Stalemate.

The gun I had taken from the dead guy was a Sig-Sauer P220, with a fat silencer on it. Swiss manufacture. Nine-millimetre Parabellum, nine rounds in a detachable box magazine. The same ammunition I was using. I thumbed the rounds out and dropped them loose into my pocket. I put the empty gun on the floor. Then I stepped back to the hallway and ducked into the front room on the right. It was bare and empty. I paced out the studio layout as I remembered it from below. Closet, bathroom, kitchen, living room. I made it to what I guessed was the centre of the living room and stamped down hard. One man's ceiling is another man's floor. I figured Lila was directly below me, listening. I wanted to shake her up, way back in the lizard part of her brain. The scariest feeling of all. *There's something up there*.

I stamped again.

I got a response.

The response came in the form of a bullet smashing up through the boards three feet to my right. It tore a splintered hole and buried itself in the ceiling above me and left dust and traces of smoke in the air.

No gunshot. They all had silencers.

I fired back, a triple tap vertically downward, straight through the same hole. Then I stepped away to where I guessed their kitchen was.

Fourteen rounds gone. Sixteen remaining. Nine loose in my pocket.

Another shot came up through the floor. Seven feet from me. I fired back. They fired back. I fired back one more time and figured they were starting to understand the pattern, so I crept out to the hallway and the head of the stairs.

Where I found that they had been figuring exactly the same thing: that I was getting into the rhythm. A guy was sneaking up on me. Number two on Springfield's list. He had another Sig P220 in his hand. With a silencer. He saw me first. Fired once, and missed. I didn't. I put a triple tap into the bridge of his nose and it climbed to the middle of his forehead and blood and brain spattered on the wall behind him and he went back down where he had come from in a heap.

His gun went with him.

My spent brass tinkled away across the pine.

Twenty-three rounds gone. Seven left, plus nine loose.

One guy up, plus the Hoths themselves.

The phone vibrated in my pocket.

Too late for bargains, Lila.

I ignored her. I pictured her crouching one floor below. Svetlana at her side. One last guy between them and me. How would they use him? They weren't dumb. They were the heirs of a long and tough tradition. They had dodged and weaved and feinted through the hills for two hundred years. They knew what they were doing. They wouldn't send the guy up the stairs. Not again. That was fruitless. They would try to outflank me. They would send the guy up the fire escape. They would distract me with the phone and let the guy line up through the glass and shoot me in the back.

When?

Either immediately or much later. No middle ground. They would want me either surprised or bored.

They chose immediately.

The phone vibrated in my pocket.

I stepped back into the left-hand room and checked the view. The iron ladder rose right-to-left from my perspective. I would see the guy's head as he came up from below. Which was good. But my angle wasn't good. The street was narrow. Nine-millimetre Parabellums are handgun rounds.

They are considered suitable for urban environments. They are much more likely than a rifle round to stick in the target and go no farther. Subsonic Parabellums, more likely still. But nothing is guaranteed. And there were innocent non-combatants across the street. Bedroom windows, slumbering children. Through-and-through bull's-eyes could reach them. Wild deflections could reach them. And ricochets, or fragments. Certainly out-and-out misses could reach them.

Collateral damage, just waiting to happen.

I crept through the room and flattened myself against the window wall. Glanced out. Nothing there. I extended my arm and flipped the window latch. Tried the handles. The window was stuck. I glanced out again. Nothing there. I stepped in front of the glass and grabbed the handles and heaved. The window moved and stuck and moved again and then shot up in the frame and slammed open so hard the pane cracked end to end.

I backed up against the wall again.

Listened hard.

Heard the dull muted clang of rubber soles on iron. A steady little rhythm. He was coming up fast, but he wasn't running. I let him come. I let him get all the way up. I let him get his head and shoulders in the room. Dark hair, dark skin. He was number fifteen on Springfield's list. I lined up parallel with the front wall of the building. He glanced left. He glanced right. He saw me. I pulled the trigger. A triple tap. He moved his head.

I missed. Maybe the first or the last of the three bullets tore his ear off but he stayed alive and conscious and fired back wildly and then ducked back outside. I heard him fall against the narrow iron walkway.

Now or never.

I went out after him. He was scrambling head first down the stairs. He made it back to the fourth floor and rolled on his back and raised his gun like it was a hundred-pound weight. I came down the ladder after him and leaned away from the building and stitched a triple tap into the centre of his face. His gun spun and clanged end over end two floors down and lodged ten feet above the sidewalk.

I breathed in.

I breathed out.

Six men down. Seven arrested. Four back home. Two in a locked ward.

Nineteen for nineteen.

The fourth floor window was open. The drapes were drawn back. A studio apartment. Derelict, but not demolished. Lila and Svetlana Hoth were standing together behind the kitchenette counter.

Twenty-nine rounds gone.

One left.

I heard Lila's voice in my head again: *you must save the last bullet for yourself, because you do not want to be taken alive, especially by the women*.

I climbed over the sill and stepped into the room.

EIGHTY-ONE

The apartment was laid out the same as the ruined place on the second floor. Living room at the front, then the kitchenette, then the bathroom, then the closet at the back. The walls were still up. The plaster was all still in place. There were two lights burning. There was a folded-up bed against the wall in the living room. Plus two hard chairs. Nothing else. The kitchenette had two parallel counters and one wall cupboard. A tiny space. Lila and Svetlana were crammed hip to hip in it. Svetlana on the left, Lila on the right. Svetlana was in a brown house dress. Lila was in black cargo pants and a white T-shirt. The shirt was cotton. The pants were made of rip-stop nylon. I guessed they would rustle as she moved. She looked as beautiful as ever. Long dark hair, bright blue eyes, perfect skin. A quizzical half-smile. It was a bizarre scene. Like a radical fashion photographer had posed his best model in a gritty urban setting.

I aimed the MP5. Black and wicked. It was hot. It stank of gunpowder and oil and smoke. I could smell it quite clearly.

I said, 'Put your hands on the counter.'

They complied. Four hands appeared. Two brown and gnarled, two paler and slim. They spread them like starfish, two blunt and square, two longer and more delicate.

I said, 'Step back and lean on them.'

They complied. It made them more immobile. Safer.

I said, 'You're not mother and daughter.'

Lila said, 'No, we're not.'

'So what are you?'

'Teacher and pupil.'

'Good. I wouldn't want to shoot a daughter in front of her mother. Or a mother in front of her daughter.'

'But you would shoot a pupil in front of her teacher?'

'Maybe the teacher first.'

'So do it.'

I stood still.

Lila said, 'If you mean it, this is where you do it.'

I watched their hands. Watched for tension, or effort, or moving tendons, or increased pressure on their fingertips. For signs they were about to go somewhere.

There were no such signs.

The phone vibrated in my pocket.

In the silent room it made a tiny sound. A whir, a hum, a grind. A rhythmic little pulse. It jumped and buzzed against my thigh.

I stared at Lila's hands. Flat. Still. Empty. No phone.

She said, 'Perhaps you should answer that.'

I juggled the MP5's grip into my left hand and pulled out the phone. *Restricted Call*. I opened it and put it to my ear.

Theresa Lee said, 'Reacher?'

I said, 'What?'

'Where the hell have you been? I've been trying to call you for twenty minutes.'

'I've been busy.'

'Where are you?'

'How did you get this number?'

'You called my cell, remember? Your number is

in the call log.'

'Why is your number blocked?'

'Precinct switchboard. I'm on the landline now. Where the hell are you?'

'What's up?'

'Listen carefully. You have bad information. Homeland Security got back to us again. One of the Tajikistan party missed a connection in Istanbul. He came in through London and Washington instead. There are twenty men, not nineteen.'

Lila Hoth moved and the twentieth man stepped out of the bathroom.

EIGHTY-TWO

Scientists measure time all the way down to the picosecond. A trillionth of a regular second. They figure all kinds of things can happen in that small interval. Universes can be born, particles can accelerate, atoms can be split. What happened to me in the first few picoseconds was a whole bunch of different things. First, I dropped the phone, still open, still live. By the time it was down level with my shoulder whole lines of conversation with Lila were screaming in my head. On the same phone, minutes ago, from Madison Avenue. I had said, *You're down to your last six guys*. She had started to reply, and then she had stopped. She had been about to say, *No I've got seven*. Like earlier, when she had started to say, *That's not close to me*. The voiced dental fricative. But she had stopped herself. She had learned.

For once, she hadn't talked too much.

And I hadn't listened enough.

By the time the phone was down level with my waist I was focusing on the twentieth guy himself. He looked just like the previous four or five. He could have been their brother or their cousin, and probably was. Certainly he looked familiar. Small, sinewy, dark hair, lined skin, body language bridging wariness and aggression. He was dressed in a pair of dark knit sweatpants. A dark knit sweatshirt. He was right-handed. He was holding a silenced handgun. He was sweeping it through a long upward arc. He was aiming to bring it level. His finger was tightening on the trigger. He was going to shoot me in the chest.

I was holding the MP5 left-handed. The magazine was empty. The last round was already chambered. It had to count. I wanted to change hands. I didn't want to fire from my weaker side, under my weaker eye.

No choice. To change hands would take half a second. Five hundred billion picoseconds. Too long. The other guy's arm was nearly there. By the time the phone was down around my knees my right palm was slapping upward to meet the barrel. I was turning and straightening and tucking the grip back towards my chest. My right palm stopped and cradled the barrel and my left index finger squeezed the trigger with exaggerated calm. Lila was moving on my left. She was stepping out into the room. My finger completed its squeeze and the gun fired and my last round hit the twentieth guy in the face.

The phone hit the floor. It sounded like the padlock. A loud wooden thump.

My last spent shell case ejected and rattled away across the room.

The twentieth guy went down in a clatter of limbs and head and gun, dead before he hit the boards, shot through the base of the brain.

A head shot. A hit. Not bad for my left hand. Except that I had been aiming for his centre mass.

Lila kept on moving. Gliding, swooping, ducking down.

She came back up with the dead guy's gun. Another Sig P220, another silencer.

Swiss manufacture.

A nine-round detachable box magazine.

If Lila was scrambling for the gun, it was the only one in the apartment. In which case it had been fired at least three times, through the ceiling.

Maximum six rounds left.

Six versus zero.

Lila pointed the gun at me.

I pointed mine at her.

She said, 'I'm faster.'

I said, 'You think?'

Way off to my left Svetlana said, 'Your gun is empty.'

I glanced at her. 'You speak English?'

'Fairly well.'

'I reloaded upstairs.'

'Bullshit. I can see from here. You're set to three-round bursts. But you fired only once. Therefore that was your last bullet.'

* * *

We stood like that for what seemed like a long time. The P220 was as steady as a rock in Lila's hand. She was fifteen feet from me. Behind her the dead guy was leaking fluid all over the floor. Svetlana was in the kitchen. There were all kinds of smells in the air. There was a draught from the open window. Air was moving in and stirring through the room and funnelling up the staircase and out through the hole in the roof.

Svetlana said, 'Put your gun down.'

I said, 'You want the memory stick.'

'You don't have it.'

'But I know where it is.'

'So do we.'

I said nothing.

Svetlana said, 'You don't have it but you know where it is. Therefore you employed a deductive process. Do you think you are uniquely talented? Do you think that deductive processes are unavailable to others? We all share the same facts. We can all arrive at the same conclusions.'

I said nothing.

She said, 'As soon as you told us you knew where it was, we set about thinking. You spurred us on. You talk too much, Reacher. You made yourself disposable.'

Lila said, 'Put the gun down. Have a little dignity. Don't stand there like an idiot, holding an empty gun.'

I stood still.

Lila dropped her arm maybe ten degrees and fired into the floor between my feet. She hit a spot level with and exactly equidistant between the toecaps of my shoes. Not an easy shot. She was a great markswoman. The floorboard splintered. I flinched a little. The Sig's silencer was louder than the H&K's. Like a phone book smashed down, not dropped. A wisp of wood smoke drifted upward, where the friction of the bullet had burned the pine. The spent shell case ejected in a brassy arc and tinkled away.

Five rounds left.

Lila said, 'Put the gun down.'

I looped the strap up over my head. Held the gun by the grip down by my side. It was no longer any use to me, except as a seven-pound metal club. And I doubted that I would get near enough to either one of them for a club to be effective. And if I did, I would prefer bare-knuckle hand-to-hand combat. A seven-pound metal club is good. But a 250-pound human club is better.

Svetlana said, 'Throw it over here. But carefully. If you hit one of us, you die.'

I swung the gun slowly and let it go. It cartwheeled lazily through the air and bounced off its muzzle and clattered against the far wall.

Svetlana said, 'Now take off your jacket.'

Lila pointed her gun at my head.

I complied. I shrugged the jacket off and threw it across the room. It landed next to the MP5. Svetlana came out from behind the kitchen counter and rooted through the pockets. She found the nine loose Parabellum rounds and the part-used roll of duct tape. She stood the nine loose rounds upright on the counter, in a neat little line. She put the roll of tape next to it.

She said, 'Glove.'

I complied. I bit the glove off and tossed it after the jacket.

'Shoes and socks.'

I hopped from foot to foot and leaned back against the wall to steady myself and undid my laces and eased my shoes off and peeled my socks down. I threw them one after the other towards the pile.

Lila said, 'Take your shirt off.'

I said, 'I will if you will.'

She dropped her arm ten degrees and put another round into the floor between my feet. The bang of the silencer, the splintering wood, the smoke, the hard tinkle of the spent case.

Four left.

Lila said, 'Next time I'll shoot you in the leg.'

Svetlana said, 'Your shirt.'

So for the second time in five hours I peeled my T-shirt off at a woman's request. I kept my back against the wall and threw the shirt overhand into the pile. Lila and Svetlana spent a moment looking at my scars. They seemed to like them. Especially the shrapnel wound. The tip of Lila's tongue came out, pink and moist and pointed between her lips.

Svetlana said, 'Now your pants.'

I looked at Lila and said, 'I think your gun is empty.'

She said, 'It isn't. I have four left. Two legs and two arms.'

Svetlana said, 'Take your pants off.'

I unbuttoned. I unzipped. I pushed the stiff denim down. I stepped out. I kept my back against the wall and kicked the pants towards the pile. Svetlana picked them up. Went through the pockets. Made a mound of my possessions on the kitchen counter next to the nine loose rounds and the roll of tape. My cash, plus a few coins. My old expired passport. My ATM card. My subway card. Theresa Lee's NYPD business card. And my clip-together toothbrush.

'Not much,' Svetlana said.

'Everything I need,' I said. 'Nothing I don't.'

'You're a poor man.'

'No, I'm a rich man. To have everything you need is the definition of affluence.'

'The American dream, then. To die rich.'

'Opportunity for all.'

'We have more than you, where we come from.'

'I don't like goats.'

The room went quiet. It felt damp and cold. I stood there in nothing except my new white boxers. The P220 was rock steady in Lila's hand. Muscles like thin cords stood out in her arm. Next to the bathroom the dead guy continued to leak. Outside the window it was five o'clock in the morning and the city was starting to stir.

Svetlana bustled about and balled up my gun and my shoes and my clothes into a tidy bundle and threw it behind the kitchen counter. She followed it with the two hard chairs. She picked up my phone, and shut it off, and tossed it away. She was clearing the space. She was emptying it. The living room part of the studio was about twenty feet by twelve. I was backed up against the centre of one of the long walls. Lila tracked around in front of me, keeping her distance, pointing the gun. She stopped in the far corner, by the window. Now she was facing me at a shallow angle.

Svetlana went into the kitchen. I heard a drawer rattle open. Heard it close. Saw Svetlana come back.

With two knives.

They were long butcher's tools. For gutting or filleting or boning. They had black handles. Steel blades. Wicked wafer-thin cutting edges. Svetlana threw one of them to Lila. She caught it expertly by the handle with her free hand. Svetlana moved to the corner opposite her. They had me triangulated. Lila was forty-five degrees to my left, Svetlana was forty-five degrees to my right.

Lila twisted her upper body and jammed the P220's silencer hard into the angle where the front wall met the side. She found the catch at the heel of the butt with her thumb and dropped the magazine. It fell out and hit the floor in the corner of the room. Three rounds showed in the slot. Therefore one was still chambered. She threw the gun itself into the other corner, behind Svetlana. The gun and the magazine were now twenty feet apart, one behind one woman, and the other behind the other.

'Like a treasure hunt,' Lila said. 'The gun won't fire without the magazine in place. To prevent an accidental discharge if a round is mistakenly left in the chamber. The Swiss are very cautious people. So you need to pick up the gun, and then pick up the magazine. Or vice versa. But first, of course, you need to get past us.'

I said nothing.

She said, 'If you should succeed, in a mad wounded scramble, then I recommend you use the first round on yourself.'

And then she smiled, and stepped forward a pace. Svetlana did the same. They held their knives low, fingers below the handle, thumbs above. Like street fighters. Like experts.

The long blades winked in the light.

I stood still.

Lila said, 'We're going to enjoy this more than you could possibly imagine.'

I did nothing.

Lila said, 'A delay is good. It heightens the anticipation.'

I stood still.

Lila said, 'But if we get bored waiting, we'll come and get you.'

I said nothing. Stood still.

Then I reached behind me and came out with my Benchmade 3300, from where it had been duct-taped to the small of my back.

EIGHTY-THREE

I thumbed the release and the blade snapped out with a sound that was halfway between a click and a thump. A loud sound, in the silent room. And an unhappy sound. I don't like knives. I never have. I have no real talent with them.

But I have as much of an instinct for self-preservation as any guy.

Maybe more than most.

And by that point I had been scuffling since the age of five, and all of my defeats had been minor. And I'm the kind of guy who watches and learns. I had seen knife fights all over the world. The Far East, Europe, the hardscrabble scrublands outside army bases in the southern United States, in streets, in alleys, outside bars and pool halls.

First rule: don't get cut early. Nothing weakens you faster than blood loss.

Svetlana was more than a foot shorter than me and she was thick and wide and her arms were proportional. Lila was taller, more loose-limbed, more graceful. But all in all I figured that even against blades six inches longer than mine, I still had the advantage.

Plus I had just changed the game, and they were still dealing with the surprise.

Plus they were fighting for fun, and I was fighting for my life.

I wanted to get to the kitchen, so I danced towards Svetlana, who was between me and it. She was up on her toes, knife down at her knees, feinting left, feinting right. I kept my blade down low, to match hers. She swung. I arched back. Her blade hissed past my thigh. I jammed my ass back and my shoulders forward and clubbed her with an overarm left hook. It grazed her eyebrow and then caught her full on the side of the nose.

She looked astonished. Like most knife fighters she thought it was all about the steel. She forgot that people have two hands.

She rocked back on her heels and Lila came in from my left. Blade low. Darting, jabbing. Mouth open in an ugly grimace. Concentrating hard. She understood. This was no longer a game. No longer fun. She ducked in, she ducked out, feinting, backing off, always working. For a time we all danced like that. Frantic, breathless, abrupt abbreviated movements, dust and sweat and fear in the air, their eyes locked on my blade, mine switching constantly between theirs.

Svetlana stepped in. Stepped out. Lila came at me, balanced, up on her toes. I kept my hips back and my shoulders forward. I swung my blade hard for Lila's face. Huge. Convulsive. Like I was aiming to throw a ball four hundred feet. Lila ducked back. She knew the swing was going to miss, because she was going to make it miss. Svetlana knew it was going to miss, because she trusted Lila.

I knew it was going to miss, because I planned not to let it hit.

I stopped the violent manoeuvre halfway through and reversed direction and aimed a vicious surprise backhand straight at Svetlana. I sliced her forehead. A solid blow. I felt the blade hit bone. A lock of her hair hit her chest. The Benchmade worked exactly the way it should. D2 steel. You could have dropped a ten-dollar bill on it and gotten two fives in exchange. I put a six-inch horizontal gash halfway between Svetlana's hairline and her eyebrows. Open to the bone.

She rocked back and stood still.

No pain. Not yet.

Forehead cuts are never fatal. But they bleed a lot. Within seconds blood was sheeting down into her eyes. Blinding her. If I had been wearing shoes I could have killed her there and then. Bring her down with a blow to the knees, and then kick her head to pulp. But I wasn't about to risk the bones in my feet against her fire-plug body. Lack of mobility would have killed me just as fast.

I danced back.

Lila came straight after me.

I kept my hips back and dodged the hissing arc of her blade. Left, right. I hit the wall behind me. I timed it and waited until her arm was across her body and turned sideways and shoulder-charged her and bounced her away. I spun onward to where Svetlana was tottering around and trying to wipe the pouring blood from her eyes. I swatted her knife arm away and stepped in and nicked her neck above her collar bone and dodged back out.

Then Lila cut me.

She had figured out the reach issue. She was holding her knife in her fingertips way at the end of the handle. She lunged in. Her hair was flying. Her shoulders were hunched forward. She was looking for every half-inch of advantage she could get. She stopped on a stiff front leg and bent low and leaned in and slashed wildly at my stomach.

And hit it.

A bad cut. A wild swing, a strong arm, a razor-sharp blade. Very bad. It was a long diagonal slice below my navel and above the waistband of my boxers. No pain. Not yet. Just a brief strange signal from my skin, telling me it was no longer all connected together.

I paused a beat. Disbelief. Then I did what I always do when someone hurts me. I stepped in, not away. Her momentum had carried her knife beyond my hip. My blade was low. I slashed backhand at her thigh and cut her deep and then pushed off my back foot and hit her in the face with my left fist. Bull's-eye. A major, stunning blow. She spun away and I barged on towards Svetlana. Her face was a mask of blood. She swung her blade right. Then left. She opened up. I stepped in and slashed down on the inside of her right forearm. I cut her to the bone. Veins, tendons, ligaments. She howled. Not from pain. That would come later. Or not. She howled from fear, because she was done. Her arm was useless. I spun her around with a blow to the shoulder and stabbed her in the kidney. All four inches, with a savage sideways jerk. Safe to do. No ribs in that region. No chance of hitting bone and jamming the blade. Lots of blood flows through the kidneys. All kinds of arteries. Ask any dialysis patient. All of a person's blood passes through the kidneys many times a day. Pints of it. Gallons of it. Now in Svetlana's case it was going in and it wasn't coming back out.

She went down to her knees. Lila was trying to clear her head. Her nose was broken. Her flawless face was ruined. She charged me. I feinted left and moved right. We danced around Svetlana's kneeling form. A whole circle. I got back to where I had started and ducked away to the kitchenette. Stepped between the counters. Grabbed one of the hard chairs that Svetlana had piled there. I threw it left-handed at Lila. She ducked away and hunched and it smashed against her back.

I came out of the kitchen and stepped behind Svetlana and put a hand in her hair and hauled her head back. Leaned around and cut her throat. Ear to ear. Hard work, even with the Benchmade's great blade. I had to pull and tug and saw. Muscle, fat, hard flesh, ligaments. The steel scraped across bone. Weird tubercular sounds came up at me out of her severed windpipe. Wheezing and gasping. There were fountains of blood as her arteries went. It pulsed and sprayed way out in front of her. It hit the far wall. It soaked my hand and made it slippery. I let go of her hair and she pitched forward. Her face hit the boards with a thump.

I stepped away, panting.

Lila faced me, panting.

The room felt burning hot and it smelled of coppery blood.

I said, 'One down.'

She said, 'One still up.'

I nodded. 'Looks like the pupil was better than the teacher.'

She said, 'Who says I was the pupil?'

Her thigh was bleeding badly. There was a neat slice in the black nylon of her pants and blood was running down her leg. Her shoe was already soaked. My boxers were soaked. They had turned from white to red. I looked down and saw blood welling out of me. A lot of it. It was bad. But my old scar had saved me. My shrapnel wound, from Beirut, long ago. The ridged white skin from the clumsy MASH stitches was tough and gnarled and it had slowed Lila's blade and deflected it. Without it the tail of the cut would have been much longer and deeper. For years I had resented the hasty work by the emergency surgeons. Now I was grateful for it.

Lila's busted nose started to bleed. The blood ran down to her mouth and she coughed and spat. Looked down at the floor. Saw Svetlana's knife. It was mired in a spreading pool of blood. The blood was already thickening. It was soaking into the old boards. It was running into the cracks between them. Lila's left arm moved. Then it stopped. To bend down and pick up Svetlana's knife would make her vulnerable. Likewise for me. I was five feet from the P220. She was five feet from the magazine.

The pain started. My head spun and buzzed. My blood pressure was falling.

Lila said, 'If you ask nicely I'll let you walk away.'

'I'm not asking.'

'You can't win.'

'Dream on.'

'I'm prepared to fight to the death.'

'You don't have a choice in the matter. That decision has already been taken.'

'You could kill a woman?'

'I just did.'

'One like me?'

'Especially one like you.'

She spat again and breathed hard through her mouth. She coughed. She looked down at her leg. She nodded and said, 'OK.' She looked up at me with her amazing eyes.

I stood still.

She said, 'If you mean it, this is where you do it.'

I nodded. I meant it. So I did it. I was weak, but it was easy. Her leg was slowing her down. She was having trouble with her breathing. Her sinuses were smashed. Blood was pooling in the back of her throat. She was dazed and dizzy, from when I had hit her. I took the second chair from the kitchen and charged her with it. Now my reach was unbeatable. I backed her into the corner with it and hit her with it twice until she dropped her knife and fell. I sat down beside her and strangled her. Slowly, because I was fading fast. But I didn't want to use the blade. I don't like knives.

* * *

Afterwards I crawled back to the kitchen and rinsed the Benchmade under the tap. Then I used its dagger point to cut butterfly shapes out of the black duct tape. I pinched my wound together with my fingers and used the butterflies to hold it together. A dollar and a half. Any hardware store. Essential equipment. I struggled back into my clothes. I reloaded my pockets. I put my shoes back on.

Then I sat down on the floor. Just for a minute. But it turned out longer. A medical man would say I passed out. I prefer to think I just went to sleep.

EIGHTY-FOUR

I woke up in a hospital bed. I was wearing a paper gown. The clock in my head told me it was four in the afternoon. Ten hours. The taste in my mouth told me most of them had been chemically assisted. I had a clip on my finger. It had a wire. The wire must have been connected to a nurses' station. The clip must have detected some kind of an altered heartbeat pattern, because about a minute after I woke up a whole bunch of people came in. A doctor, a nurse, then Jacob Mark, then Theresa Lee, then Springfield, then Sansom. The doctor was a woman and the nurse was a man.

The doctor fussed around for a minute, checking charts and staring at monitors. Then she picked up my wrist and checked my pulse, which seemed a little superfluous with all the high technology at her disposal. Then in answer to questions I hadn't asked, she told me I was in Bellevue Hospital and that my condition was very satisfactory. Her ER people had cleaned the wound and sutured it and filled me full of antibiotics and tetanus injections and given me three units of blood. She told me to avoid heavy lifting for a month. Then she left. The nurse went with her.

I looked at Theresa Lee and asked, 'What happened to me?'

'You don't remember?'

'Of course I remember. But what's the official version?'

'You were found on the street in the east Village. Unexplained knife wound. Happens all the time. They ran a tox screen and found traces of barbiturate. They put you down as a dope deal gone bad.'

'Did they tell the cops?'

'I am the cops.'

'How did I get to the east Village?'

'You didn't. We brought you straight here.'

'We?'

'Me and Mr Springfield.'

'How did you find me?'

'We triangulated the cell phone. Which led us to the general area. The exact address was Mr Springfield's idea.'

Springfield said, 'A certain mujahideen leader told us all about doubling back to abandoned hideouts twenty-five years ago.'

I asked, 'Is there going to be any comeback?'

John Sansom said, 'No.'

Simple as that.

I said, 'Are you sure? There are nine corpses in that house.'

'The DoD guys are there right now. They'll issue a loud no comment. With a knowing smirk. Designed to make everyone give them the credit.'

'Suppose the wind changes direction? That happens from time to time. As you know.'

'As a crime scene, it's a mess.'

'I left blood there.'

'There's a lot of blood there. It's an old building. If anyone runs tests they'll come up with rat DNA, mostly.'

'There's blood on my clothes.'

Theresa Lee said, 'The hospital burned your clothes.'

'Why?'

'Biohazard.'

'They were brand new.'

'They were soaked with blood. No one takes a risk with blood any more.'

'Right-hand fingerprints,' I said. 'Inside the window handles and on the trapdoor.'

'Old building,' Sansom said. 'It will be torn down and redeveloped before the wind changes.'

'Shell cases,' I said.

Springfield said, 'Standard DoD issue. I'm sure they're delighted. They'll probably leak one to the media.'

'Are they still looking for me?'

'They can't. It would confuse the narrative.'

'Turf wars,' I said.

'Which they just won, apparently.'

I nodded.

Sansom asked, 'Where is the memory stick?'

I looked at Jacob Mark. 'You OK?'

He said, 'Not really.'

I said, 'You're going to have to hear some stuff.'

He said, 'OK.'

* * *

I hauled myself into a sitting position. Didn't hurt at all. I guessed I was full of painkiller. I pulled my knees up and tented the sheet and moved the hem of my paper gown and took a peek at the cut. Couldn't see it. I was wrapped with bandages from my hips to my rib cage.

Sansom said, 'You told us you could get us within fifteen feet.'

I shook my head. 'Not any more. Time has moved on. We're going to have to do it by dead reckoning.'

'Great. You were bullshitting all along. You don't know where it is.'

'We know the general shape of it,' I said. 'They planned for the best part of three months and then executed during the final week. They coerced Susan by using Peter as leverage. She drove up from Annandale, got stuck in a four-hour traffic jam, say from nine in the evening until one in the morning, and then she arrived in Manhattan just before two in the morning. I assume we know exactly when she came out of the Holland Tunnel. So what we have to do is work backwards and figure out exactly where her car was jammed up at midnight.'

'How does that help us?'

'Because at midnight she threw the memory stick out her car window.'

'How can you possibly know that?'

'Because when she arrived she didn't have a cell phone with her.'

Sansom glanced at Lee. Lee nodded. Said, 'Keys and a wallet. That was all. Not in her car, either. The FBI inventoried the contents.'

Sansom said, 'Not everyone uses a cell phone.'

'True,' I said. 'And I'm that guy. The only guy in the world without a cell phone. Certainly a person like Susan would have had one.'

Jacob Mark said, 'She had one.'

Sansom said, 'So?'

'The Hoths set a deadline. Almost certainly midnight. Susan didn't show, the Hoths went to work. They made a threat, and they carried it out. And they proved it. They phoned through a cell phone picture. Maybe a live video clip. Peter on the slab, that long first cut. Susan's life changed, effectively, on the stroke of midnight. She was helpless in a traffic jam. The phone in her hand was suddenly appalling and repugnant. She threw it out the window. Followed it with the memory stick, which was the symbol of all her troubles. They're both still there, in the trash on the side of I-95. No other explanation.'

Nobody spoke.

I said, 'The median, probably. Subconsciously Susan would have put herself in the overtaking lane, because she was in a hurry. We could have triangulated the cell phone, but I think it's too late now. The battery will be dead.'

Silence in the room. A whole minute. Just the hum and beep of medical equipment.

Sansom said, 'That's insane. The Hoths must have known they were losing control of the stick as soon as they phoned the picture through. They were giving up their leverage. Susan could have driven straight to the police.'

'Two answers,' I said. 'The Hoths *were* insane, in a way. They were fundamentalists. They could act the part in public, but underneath it was all black and white for them. No nuance. A threat was a threat. Midnight was midnight. But anyway, their risk was minimal. They had a guy tailing Susan all the way. He could have stopped her going off message.'

'Who?'

'The twentieth guy. I don't think going to Washington was a mistake. It wasn't a missed connection in Istanbul. It was a last-minute change of plan. They suddenly realized that for a thing like this they needed someone on the ground in D.C. Or across the river, more likely, in one of the Pentagon dormitories. So the twentieth guy went straight there. Then he followed Susan all the way up. Five or ten cars back, like you do. Which was fine, until the traffic jammed up. Five or ten cars back in a traffic jam is as bad as a mile. All boxed in, maybe a big SUV in front of you, blocking the view. He didn't see what happened. But he stayed with her. He was on the train, wearing an NBA shirt. I thought he looked familiar, when I saw him again. But I couldn't confirm it, because I shot him in the face a split second later. He got all messed up.'

More silence. Then Sansom asked, 'So where was Susan at midnight?'

I said, 'You figure it out. Time, distance, average speed. Get a map and a ruler and paper and pencil.'

Jacob Mark was from Jersey. He started talking about Troopers he knew. About how the Troopers could help. They patrolled I-95 night and day. They knew it like the backs of their hands. They had traffic cameras. Their recorded pictures could calibrate the paper calculations. The highway department would cooperate. Everyone got into a big conversation. They paid me no more attention. I lay back on my pillow and they all started edging out of the room. Last out was Springfield. He paused in the doorway and looked back and asked, 'How do you feel about Lila Hoth?'

I said, 'I feel fine.'

'Really? I wouldn't. You nearly got taken down by two girls. It was sloppy work. Things like that, you do them properly or not at all.'

'I didn't have much ammunition.'

'You had thirty rounds. You should have used single shots. Those triple taps were all about anger. You let emotion get in the way. I warned you about that.'

He looked at me for a long second with nothing in his face. Then he stepped out to the corridor and I never saw him again.

* * *

Theresa Lee came back two hours later. She had a shopping bag with her. She told me the hospital wanted its bed, so the NYPD was putting me in a hotel. She had bought clothes for me. She showed me. Shoes, socks, jeans, boxers, and a shirt, all sized the same as the items the ER staff had burned. The shoes and the socks and the jeans and the boxers were fine. The shirt was weird. It was made of soft, worn white cotton. It was almost furry, down at a microscopic level. It was long-sleeved and tight. It had three buttons at the neck. It was like an old-fashioned undershirt. I was going to look like my grandfather. Or like a gold miner in California, way back in 1849.

'Thank you,' I said.

She told me the others were working on the math problem. She told me they were arguing about the route Susan would have used from the

Turnpike to the Holland Tunnel. Locals used shortcuts through surface streets that looked wrong according to the road signs.

I said, 'Susan wasn't a local.'

She agreed. She felt that Susan would have used the obvious signposted route.

Then she said, 'They won't find the picture, you know.'

I said, 'You think?'

'Oh, they'll find the stick, for sure. But they'll say it was unreadable, or run over and damaged or broken, or there was nothing sinister on it after all.'

I didn't answer.

'Count on it,' she said. 'I know politicians, and I know the government.'

Then she asked, 'How do you feel about Lila Hoth?'

I said, 'All in all I'm regretting the approach on the train. With Susan. I wish I had given her a couple more stops.'

'I was wrong. She couldn't possibly have gotten over it.'

'The opposite,' I said. 'Was there a sock in her car?'

Lee thought back to the FBI inventory. Nodded.

'Clean?' I asked.

'Yes,' she said.

'So think about Susan setting out. She's living a nightmare. But she's not sure exactly how bad it is. She can't bring herself to believe it's as bad as she suspects. Maybe it's all a sick joke or an empty threat. Or a bluff. But she's not sure. She's dressed in what she wore for work. Black pants, white blouse. She's heading for an unknown situation in the big bad city. She's a woman on her own, she lives in Virginia, she's been around the military for years. So she takes her gun. It's probably still wrapped in a sock, like she stores it in her drawer. She puts it in her bag. She leaves. She gets stuck in the jam. She calls ahead. Maybe the Hoths call her. They won't listen. They're fanatics and they're foreign. They don't understand. They think a traffic jam is a dog-ate-my-homework kind of thing.'

'Then she gets the midnight message.'

'And she changes. The point is, she has *time* to change. She's stuck in traffic. She can't take off. She can't go to the cops. She can't drive into a telephone pole at ninety miles an hour. She's trapped. She has to sit there and think. No alternative. And she arrives at a decision. She's going to avenge her son. She makes a plan. She takes the gun out of the sock. Stares at it. She sees an old black jacket dumped on the back seat. Maybe it was there since the winter. She wants dark clothing. She puts it on. Eventually the traffic moves. She drives on to New York.'

'What about the list?'

'She was a normal person. Maybe working around to killing someone else produces the same feelings as working around to killing yourself. That's what she was doing. She was climbing up on the plateau. But she wasn't quite there yet. I disturbed her too early. So she quit. She took the other way out. Maybe by 59th Street she would have been ready.'

'Better that she was spared that fight.'

'Maybe she would have won. Lila would have been expecting her to take something out of her pocket or her bag. There would have been an element of surprise.'

'She had a six-shooter. There were twenty-two of them.'

I nodded. 'She'd have died, for sure. But maybe she would have died satisfied.'

* * *

A day later in the hotel Theresa Lee came back to visit. She told me that Sansom had scoped out a likely target area about half a mile long and the Jersey highway people had closed it off with orange barrels. Three hours into the search they found Susan's cell phone. A second later, four feet away, they found the memory stick.

It had been run over. It was crushed. It was unreadable.

* * *

I left New York the next day. I moved south. I spent a large part of the next two weeks obsessing over what might have been in that picture. I came up with all kinds of speculations, some involving technical breaches of Sharia law, some involving domesticated animals. Alternating with the lurid imagined scenarios from the Korengal tent were repeated flashback memories of hitting Lila Hoth in the face. The straight left, the crunch of bone and cartilage under my fist. The ruined appearance. The episode replayed constantly in my mind. I didn't know why. I had just cut her with a knife and later I strangled her, and I could barely remember those acts at all. Maybe hitting women ran counter to my subliminal values. Which was entirely illogical.

But eventually the images faded and I grew bored with imagining Osama bin Laden having his way with goats. By the time a month had passed I had forgotten all of it. My cut had healed very nicely. The scar was thin and white. The stitches were neat and tiny. My lower body was like a textbook illustration: this one is how it should be done, and that one is how it shouldn't. But I never forgot how those earlier, clumsier stitches had saved me. What goes around comes around. A benign legacy, from the truck bomb in Beirut, planned and paid for and driven there by persons unknown.